Trained as an actress, Barbara Nadel is now a public relations officer for the National Schizophrenia Fellowship's Good Companions Service. Her previous job was a mental health advocate in a psychiatric hospital. She has also worked with sexually abused teenagers and taught psychology in both schools and colleges. Born in the East End of London, she has been a regular visitor to Turkey for over twenty years.

Also by Barbara Nadel

Belshazzar's Daughter
A Chemical Prison
Arabesk

Deep Waters

Barbara Nadel

headline

First published in hardback in 2002
by HEADLINE BOOK PUBLISHING

First published in paperback in 2002
by HEADLINE BOOK PUBLISHING

10 9 8 7 6 5 4 3 2 1

ISBN 0 7472 6719 7

Typeset by Palimpsest Book Production Limited,
Polmont, Stirlingshire
Printed and bound in Great Britain by
Clays Ltd, St Ives plc

HEADLINE BOOK PUBLISHING
A division of Hodder Headline
338 Euston Road
London NW1 3BH

www.headline.co.uk
www.hodderheadline.com

This book is dedicated to the memory of my beloved father. His untimely death in August 2001 robbed the world of a generous, funny and magical soul. No words I can write will ever do him real justice.

Chapter 1

The woman's hooded eyes widened in alarm.

'You're not going out, are you?' she said to the young man's back as he squinted to see himself in the mirror fragment over the sink.

'We need money,' he replied simply.

The woman, who was only fourteen years older than her son, moved her bulk between man and mirror and faced him foursquare, her hands on her hips.

'If you're stealing cars—'

'No, I'm not stealing cars, Mother,' he said, his voice beginning to exhibit irritation.

'When you tried to take wallets from people's pockets you got caught.'

'But I got away, didn't I?' He looked up into his mother's prematurely aged face. 'And anyway, this isn't about that, is it?'

'No.'

For a few seconds, silence replaced words as the young man and his mother looked intensely into each other's eyes. On the floor various old baby toys plus several packets of disposable nappies moved gently in the draught that rocked the door of the family's washroom.

'If they see you they'll try to kill you. They must.' Her words were starkly factual, only the familiar ear could have detected the fierce emotion that lay behind them.

Her son sighed. 'What, Mehti? It's *only* Mehti, Mother. I see him every day! He's an idiot, he's retarded . . .'

The woman, her eyes now downcast, bit thoughtfully on her bottom lip. 'If we need money then I will get it,' she said. 'I can beg and I can steal . . . It's dark now, evil.'

'This is business, Mother.' He rubbed way too much cheap aftershave lotion into his chin and then wiped the residue off his hands onto his jeans. 'Big money.'

'But what—'

'Don't ask! Don't make me lie to my own blood!'

'Rifat—'

'No!'

Turning away from his mother, Rifat took a thin belt down from one of the hooks on the wall and threaded it round the waistband of his jeans. Though well-proportioned, he was a short man, beginning to exhibit signs of impending obesity. But still he was, so his mother thought now, a very handsome man, not unlike his father, or rather the man his father had once been.

Just the thought of it made her next words shake with emotion. 'If they kill you then the blood will never stop running. You know that, don't you, Rifat?'

Rifat opened the door to a quick and wicked wind from the central Asian steppes. As his hair moved slightly in the draught, he smoothed it down with one hand and with the other picked up a small, brightly wrapped parcel. Then, smiling, he said, 'If they kill me, I would expect the blood never to end. Not for a man like me.'

And then he was gone. As he pulled the door shut behind him, a small wisp of the dense night-time fog puffed muscularly into the room before expiring down on the floor.

When she was certain that he could no longer hear her, his mother muttered, 'Stupid, stupid, stupid boy!'

Only the walls were in a position to respond; the rest of her family were either asleep or dead.

There had been a time, Dr Zelfa Halman recalled, when to put a call through from İstanbul to anywhere outside Turkey had necessitated lengthy planning and patience. And although she was an educated woman who knew that progress was inevitable, she still never ceased to marvel at just how quickly she could now connect with her maternal family in the Irish Republic. Quickly, that is, provided one allowed for the slow progress of one Father Francis Collins from his favourite chair to the old dial telephone that always had and always would live in the hall. Uncle Frank, as he was to Zelfa, was nearly eighty years old now; just three years senior to her mother, had she lived.

A deep cough preceded Father Collins' recitation of his telephone number.

It made Zelfa smile. 'Still smoking then, Uncle?' she said, the lilt of her Irish voice increasing with each English word spoken.

'Now then, Bridget, is that any way to speak to a man of God?'

She laughed both at the irony in his tone and at the use of her Irish name. After twelve years in Turkey, 'Bridget' was somebody she could only sometimes, and selectively, relate to.

'So to what do I owe the pleasure of your call?' the old priest inquired. 'Are you coming home for a bit or what?'

'Well, I do hope to come home soon, yes, but . . .' she paused briefly to light a cigarette. 'What I actually wanted to do was ask for your advice.'

'I thought you lot had that sort of thing sewn up pretty much,' he replied, the irony still there in his voice.

'Even psychiatrists need help sometimes, Uncle Frank.'

'True. But since you and God parted company when you were about eighteen, I can't see what I can offer you in the way of advice that you won't find risible. Fags and booze aside, my own views about morality are informed by Our Lord as opposed to your man Freud.'

'Uncle Frank, a Turk has asked me to marry him.' There now, it was out. Briefly she looked into the mirror across the hall, seeing herself as a small, grey blob. Purposefully she addressed herself to the telephone again. 'Uncle Frank?'

'Er . . .' The old man cleared his throat of what sounded like several pounds of phlegm. 'Oh, well, that's, um . . . Your father must be pleased . . .'

'Dad doesn't know yet.'

'Well, shouldn't you be—'

'Uncle Frank, I'm forty-seven years old, for God's

sake! I can tell whoever I like in whatever order I choose!'

A brief moment of silence ensued, a moment during which the priest, at least, drew breath.

'Seeing as your father's a Turk,' he said, 'and you now live there yourself, I can't see what your problem might be, Bridget. I mean, were you even slightly interested in your faith—'

'This man, Mehmet he's called, is twelve years younger than I am, Uncle Frank.'

A sharp intake of breath on the part of the priest caused Zelfa to scale even higher reaches of verbal desperation.

'I look so old compared to him! He's about as fit as a man can be, Uncle Frank, and I just look like a fat, grey troll at his side! And I'm too old to have his children! I mean, what the hell can he see in me? I mean—'

'Well, if we discount the good living you people tend to make, which I am sure this man gives not a hoot for,' Father Frank said, 'then we're left only with your wit, intelligence, beauty and charm. And given that these qualities are all that you have, then I suppose this lad must be quite mad to want to marry you.'

In spite of herself, Zelfa smiled. OK, the old man was biased but she knew that when it came to the matter of her attractiveness, she was her own worst enemy and her hardest critic. Very deep down indeed, she knew that the truth lay somewhere between what her uncle had said about her and her own perception of herself. However . . .

'But when I'm sixty he'll only be forty-eight!'

'And when you're a hundred he'll be eighty-eight and you'll both look like shite! But if he still loves you and you still love him then what of it?' Although the old man was over two thousand miles away from her, Zelfa distinctly heard him take a cigarette out of his packet, stick it in his mouth and light up. 'What I'm saying, Bridget, I suppose, is that if he loves you, nothing much else matters. Does he love you?'

'He says he does, although I can't think why.'

Frank Collins sighed. So like her mother in so many ways – except the most important one. Bridget, although twice as clever and considerably prettier than her mother, had never matched Bernadette Halman's supreme self-confidence. Perhaps it had something to do with the fact that Bernadette had pursued and won so many lovers in her short life – several while she was still living with Bridget's father. Maybe that knowledge had undermined Bridget's confidence in the concept of marriage. Or maybe it was as she said, that this man was too young to be able to give her any sense of security. Only Bridget and this Mehmet character could know. But then his niece was asking for his advice and, for good or ill, he had to give it to her. After all, if a priest couldn't give advice (and do a little bit around saying Mass too!) then what could he do?

'Well, you either trust his word or you don't, Bridget,' he said at length, 'and only you can make that decision. Do you love him?'

'I'd happily die for him, Uncle Frank.' Such passionate words made her seem much younger than she was – they sounded almost like the protestations of a teenager.

But then as the Irish branch, at least, of Bridget's family had always been sadly aware, there had never been even the slightest whiff of marriage in her life before. She was really quite green when it came to affairs of the heart.

'So if you love him,' the priest began, 'and he—'

'How can he love me? I keep thinking he must be some kind of deviant or gold digger!' she cried mournfully, now very close to tears.

'Is he poor?'

'No. His family reckon they're impoverished but that's only in comparison to the shitloads of money they once had. They're aristocrats.'

'Are they so?'

'But he, Mehmet, he's just a policeman. They earn sweet fa here.' She put her cigarette out in the ashtray and then immediately lit another. 'Not, of course, that he's ever asked me for money. He's spent a lot of money on me, taken me out and . . .'

'Made you very happy, by the sound of it,' the priest added tartly.

Zelfa, now a little more subdued, especially in light of what her uncle had just said, bowed her blonde head. 'Yes. Yes, he has.'

'Well, that's something to cling on to and to use as a starting point for your thoughts on this too, isn't it?'

'What?' Perhaps it was because it was so late and she was tired, but Zelfa could not, for the moment, quite catch her uncle's drift.

'I mean,' he said, 'that maybe you shouldn't look at the money or the age difference or any of that just now. Maybe you should just concentrate on the love.'

'Yeah, but—'

'No, Bridget, no "buts".'

She could see him, in her mind, his right index finger raised, as she so clearly remembered it, to silence dissenters in her long ago Holy Communion classes. Zelfa, in spite of her current mood of confusion, smiled.

'If you love him and he loves you then that is, if my understanding of such things is correct, enough,' said Frank Collins with some vigour. 'And anyway,' he added, with a large helping of that rare cynicism Zelfa knew and loved him for, 'your father's property must be worth bugger all since that earthquake and so I wouldn't worry about gold digging.'

'If we have another one like that I'll be lucky to have a head to worry with,' she said with the type of graveyard humour those who have experienced great trauma frequently indulge in.

'Yes, a man can quickly meet with his maker.'

'I know. Mehmet's sister-in-law died and his best friend had to have his legs amputated during . . .' Suddenly she could not bring herself to use the word 'earthquake' for fear of losing control of her emotions. Everyone had lost someone during that cataclysmic event. Everyone. 'During the events of last year. He's still, at times, very sad.'

'Oh, well then,' the priest said briskly, 'you'd better go about cheering him up one way or the other. I'm not saying I wouldn't rather you marry a Padraig or a Declan, but . . .'

'But what if he's just marrying me in order to provide some measure of security in his world? I mean, there are problems with his mother and I have thought that perhaps I could be some sort of substitute figure.'

'Or you could just be analysing the ins and outs of a duck's arse,' the old man said with a smile in his voice. 'You people do tend to do that. But at the end of the day, Bridget, it's all down to strength of feeling and risk. If you love him then you'll take a risk with him and if you do not, you won't.'

Dr Zelfa Halman frowned. What her uncle had said was undoubtedly true and that she did love Mehmet Suleyman was undeniable. But whether she could ignore her professional training and just sink into this desire was another matter.

He knew that really he shouldn't be here. Even though martial law was now a thing of the past, any passing cop could, if the mood took him, question him, move him on or just generally give him a hard time. But only, Enver thought with a smile, if they could see him through the thick fog. And given that he wasn't moving, coupled with the fact that they, the police, didn't seem to be about at the present time, that eventuality appeared to be unlikely. More relaxed now that he'd explored the probability of police appearance in detail, Enver leaned on the rail and sighed. Usually at this time of the morning – it was now 4 a.m. – one could see the lights coming on over in Karaköy as people there either rose to go to work or, in some cases, expelled paying guests from their beds. But not this morning. This morning the close bulk of the Galata Bridge disappeared completely in the middle of the Golden Horn, obscured by both the darkness and the lung-wrenching fog. Not that the lack of Karaköy made Enver stop looking towards it. It was the only place he had ever been happy.

Both the Refah Party and the unruly earth itself could do what they liked, but certain parts of Karaköy would always cater to those twin obsessions of men: drink and sex. And in his younger days, Enver had known all about both. In fact, his now deceased wife had been helping her mother to run a certain 'establishment' when Enver first met her. His children, although to this day they still didn't know it, had frequently visited their grandmother at her brothel when they were small. But now that his eldest son, with whom Enver had lived for several years, ran a very respectable coffee shop just five minutes from where he was standing, there could be no allusion to anything even slightly 'unseemly'. Eminönü was, although so often thronged with tourists, the 'Old City', quite opposed to the louche 'European-ness' of naughty Karaköy. But Enver's heart was full of nostalgia. And it was this, combined with an increasing insomnia problem, that so often, like now, found him out of his bed either looking across at or going to Karaköy. Not that the latter option was very realistic at the present time. As well as concealing him, Enver knew that the fog could also conceal other more malignant individuals who might wish, for the price of a few cigarettes, to do him harm. There had always been an element like this, the truly desperate, in the old days, usually poor migrants from the country. Now, however, what with all the Russians, Albanians and other, Allah alone knew who, folk entering the city, it was rather more problematic working out just who had stolen your watch, your wallet or whatever.

So, on balance, best stay put. With Reşadiye Caddesi just behind him, Enver was within striking distance, even with his elderly gait, of Hasırcılar Caddesi and home. And if something were to go wrong between here and there, well, that was the will of Allah and therefore unavoidable. When a car pulled up somewhere behind Enver, just beyond the Eminönü tram stop, the old man did nevertheless briefly hold his breath. Who, apart from the police or the military, might be stopping beside an impenetrably foggy waterway at this time in the morning, he couldn't imagine. Indeed, the thought that it *must* be a police car was so hard to shift that he sought confirmation by peering in the direction of the sound of the vehicle's powerful engine. But whatever type of vehicle it was remained shrouded from him by the combined forces of the fog and his own failing eyesight.

When, after what seemed like a considerable number of minutes, one of the car's doors opened, Enver took evasive action and, with remarkable agility, skipped lightly into the underpass beneath the Galata Bridge. There, his breath now coming in short rasps, he waited for the sound of 'official' voices, his ears almost reaching out from the side of his head in order to catch them.

But they never came. Only a dull thud, like the sound of something heavy being flung to the ground, registered on Enver's straining ears. No voices, no guns, just a thick and, to him, quite muffled thump. Without voices, it signified nothing, and when he heard the car door shut once again and the engine roar off first towards him and then over the bridge, he assumed that whoever had been in the car had now done what they wanted to in Eminönü. He was just glad that whatever it was had not involved him.

Still, he did leave it quite some minutes before he dared to step out of the underpass and back onto the street. Rather than go back to his musings by the water, Enver decided to make his way home again. There was little to see in all this fog, which was now really spooking him. And so with half an eye out for policemen, soldiers or thieves, Enver made his way warily back across Reşadiye Caddesi. As he went, he observed that whatever had thumped out of that mysterious vehicle was no longer around. At least not in his immediate vicinity. For Enver, that was quite good enough.

For the last hundred metres of his journey, Enver closed his eyes and imagined the smell of his son's delicious coffee guiding him home.

Chapter 2

When Fatma İkmen woke to yet another bone-chilling dawn, she found her husband not beside her in their bed but over by the window. Already dressed and smoking heavily, Inspector Çetin İkmen turned to his wife as she sat up and levelled an accusatory cigarette in the direction of a small cage that sat on the floor beside the bed.

'I'm going to end up dying from lack of sleep because of that animal,' he said sternly. 'I want it gone.'

Fatma pushed her long black and grey hair back over her shoulders before calmly replying, 'Hamsters can tell when the earth is going to move before we can. My little friend is simply an early warning system, as I have told you many times before.'

'Yes, and as I have told you many times before,' Çetin said, his voice rising with his increasing anger, 'these buggers are nocturnal. They move around at night, Fatma! Earthquake or no earthquake, the bastards get up when the sun goes down and go to sleep when it rises!'

'I don't care. I would rather be awake for the rest of my life than have my children die underneath the ruins of this building. Wouldn't you?'

13

'Of course I would,' he said as he braced himself via one thin hand against the damp window frame. 'Correct me if I'm wrong, Fatma, but I thought that our early warning pet was supposed to be the cat, not that—'

'Oh, the cat that sleeps both day and night, much use he is!' Fatma said as she swung her short plump legs over the side of the bed and stood up.

Her husband rubbed the deepening lines in his face with his hands in an attempt to wake himself up. 'Marlboro can make enough noise when he wants to.'

'Oh, yes, when he's courting!' Fatma replied tartly. 'Out amongst the rubbish he's quite the hero, but in here? In here we need something we can rely on to wake us up, and that thing is my friend Squeaky and his little metal wheel.'

Gently, due to the rheumatism this damp weather encouraged into the bones in her back these days, Fatma bent down across the cage and whistled softly at the sleeping form of the hamster inside.

Seeing this made her husband rage yet again. 'Oh, for the love of Allah,' he said angrily. 'If we have this monstrous earthquake some seismologists are predicting could happen, the whole city will fall into a massive fault and we'll all be dead within seconds. And that will include little Squeaky and his fucking little wheel!'

'Oh?' His wife, rising slowly from her crouched position, put her hands on her hips and looked Çetin İkmen straight in the eye. 'If it's that bad, why won't you let us move to another city? Well?'

İkmen, his usually thin patience stretched to its limit,

exploded. 'We've discussed this! The whole country's on a fucking fault line, where in the—'

'Konya isn't. I've looked at where the faults are on a map. It's a very safe place. They need good policemen there. You could apply.'

'Oh, I could, Fatma, yes.' He moved his thin body forward to meet her more voluptuous form. 'But,' he suddenly and violently flung his arms high above his head, 'for an atheist drinker like me, life in our most religious city would be like a living death. I would far rather face the earthquake and die quickly than endure so much as a day in that place!'

'But the children, Çetin,' his wife pleaded, her hands held in what appeared to be a gesture of supplication against his chest. 'What of the children?'

Just for a moment, it seemed to Fatma that her husband was, unusually, lost for words. His breath came in gulps, his face visibly changed from white to grey before Fatma's eyes; a change that caused her to place a concerned hand upon his cheek. He'd been this colour the day after the big earthquake, the day when his friend Dr Arto Sarkissian had 'joked' that if all the cardiograph machines in the city had not been either destroyed or in use, he'd really like to hook Çetin up to one for a while. And that was before they'd received the news about one of Çetin's colleagues' horrific injuries. After that, Fatma clearly recalled, her husband had cried in his sleep.

'Çetin . . .' she began.

'I just don't think that the children will get what they need in a place like Konya,' he said, slightly mollified

15

by his wife's soothing touch. 'I haven't worked like a slave all these years to see my younger children waste themselves in the country. All the older ones want to stay here anyway and,' he sighed deeply and with tremendous weariness, 'oh, I just feel that I'd rather we were all together somehow. I mean, how would you feel if we left here with the little ones and then the quake came and Sınan, Orhan, Çiçek and Bülent all died? I mean—'

'Don't!' As if blocking out these hypothetical events, Fatma put her hand up to what was on the point of becoming a tear-stained face. 'Don't talk of such things, Çetin! Allah was so merciful to this family last time. It must have been written that we should all be spared.'

'And anyway, how we would afford to move to another city, I don't know.' Çetin placed a loving hand on Fatma's shoulder. 'My brother has paid for so much that this family has needed, I can't ask him for anything more.'

With tears still standing in her eyes, Fatma wrapped her arms round her husband's neck. She squeezed him as tightly as her plump stomach would allow, and received a comfortingly familiar kiss on the back of the neck.

'Oh, Çetin,' she whispered softly just in case one of the children might be passing the door of their room and hear what she was about to say. 'I'm so scared all the time! Every time one of the children bounces on the floor, my heart flies into my throat thinking it might be the earthquake again. Sometimes my heart can take hours to settle down and,' she pulled his head out of her hair so that she could see into his eyes, 'sometimes

I think I'm going to have a heart attack because of all this – that or go mad!'

Çetin smiled and then kissed her lightly on the cheek. 'You know, I think that for once I must advise you to take refuge in your religion, my darling. If you leave things like earthquakes in the hands of Allah, it means you can kind of hand the worry about that over to Him. I must confess, I thought that was what all you religious types did anyway.'

'The earthquake has tested us all, Çetin.' Breaking free from her husband's arms, Fatma sat down on the edge of the bed, her head bowed. 'Even Auntie Arın, who is the most pious person I know, slept out in the street for weeks after the soldiers told her she could go back into her house.' She looked up sharply into her husband's face. 'She said it wasn't that she didn't have faith in Allah, it was that the earth had let her down. And that is how I feel. I feel let down and scared and even when my mind is no longer panicking, my heart keeps on pounding. I want to be safe, Çetin! I want my children to be safe!'

With a sigh, he sat down next to his wife and took one of her hands in his. Although he could fully appreciate what she was saying, he could not, he knew, do anything real to lessen her anxiety. Moving was impractical, the older children were opposed to it anyway, and without the slightest clue as to when or even if the next big earthquake might occur, speculation was pointless. There was nothing he could even say beyond, 'Look, Fatma, keep the hamster if it makes you happy.' And although this did seem to cheer her, as evidenced by the thin smile that ghosted across her face, when a few silent minutes later he got up to leave for work, her eyes followed him with a troubling intensity.

It was, he thought later, as if she were trying to etch every inch of his features onto her memory.

Nobody knew how long it had been there. Haluk the taxi driver, who the others were rapidly concluding was the sort of person who liked people to think he knew everything, gave his opinion that it must have been there for some time.

'Just the bruising will tell you that,' he said as he pulled at the dead man's shirt. 'See?'

'Put that down!' cried Beyazıt, the now outraged bus driver. He attempted to snatch the taxi man's hand away from the body. 'The police might take fingerprints off that and if they find your marks—'

'Oh, like they're going to take prints off cloth?' Haluk said contemptuously. 'What kind of idiot do you take me for?'

One of the assorted Eminönü fishermen who had come over to what was now developing into quite a crowd on Reşadiye Caddesi rather volubly agreed with the bus driver. And seeing as the fisherman was considerably bigger than he was, Haluk for the moment kept his counsel.

Just ten minutes before, Haluk's car had hit what he had thought at the time was a particularly hard bundle of rubbish. He stopped to check his taxi for damage, intending to give the pile only a cursory glance, until he saw that it had a human face.

At first Haluk had thought that perhaps he had actually killed the man himself. After all, his car had made contact with him. Indeed, with this in mind, the taxi driver's first instinct had been to run away. But then as the knowledge began to sink in that when he had stopped, so had the bus behind him, not to mention the appearance of the bus driver and several passengers, Haluk changed his mind. After all, even if he had killed the man, he must have been lying in the gutter at the time, which was not the kind of behaviour a sane person would exhibit. And given the man's bundled appearance, it could surely not be his fault if he had hit him.

'Some of this blood is very dry,' said another, smaller fisherman as he bent over and peered at the body. 'He could've been here for some time. Probably got hit before the fog cleared. There was no way a man could see his path in that.'

Several people muttered in agreement. As they all knew only too well, the previous night had been filthy and impenetrable. It had been the sort of night when their ancestors would have said that witches, djinn and all sorts of other supernatural horrors walked abroad. Not that that made the death of what was, by the look of what was left of him, quite a young man any less horrific. And indeed the fact that silence reigned amongst the crowd from then until the arrival of the police suggested that this was a feeling shared by all those present.

The police, when they arrived, consisted of two young leather-clad 'Dolphins', motorbike-riding rapid-response officers, who immediately drew a large group of admiring young men around their bikes.

The shorter Dolphin was just removing his helmet when Haluk began.

'This man is dead,' he said, waving a hand in the direction of the corpse. 'He was dead before my vehicle even touched him.' Then looking up at the fishermen for support, he added, 'Is that no so, brothers?'

'Well, in truth . . .'

'Let's just see the body, shall we?' the slightly taller Dolphin, a man by the name of Rauf, replied firmly. As his partner attempted to push the crowd back, he bent down and looked at a face that appeared to be emerging from both the remnants of a shirt and large swathes of either a curtain or a bedcover. Like the fisherman before him, Rauf immediately noticed that although a lot of blood did appear to be in evidence, most of it had long since dried out. The man's face had sustained heavy bruising, but where so much blood had come from was not immediately apparent. Rauf gently moved the man's chin up from inside his heavily stained shirt, and all became very clear. Widening his eyes just a little in response to what he saw, Rauf called his partner over to his side.

'Look at this,' he said as he lifted the heavy chin once again.

His partner briefly raised his eyes up to heaven before unclipping his radio from his jacket and speaking into it. He and his colleague, he said, had been called to what could be an unlawful death.

As soon as he shut his office door behind him, Inspector Mehmet Suleyman took the packet of photographs out of his pocket and opened it onto his desk. Taking the first picture out as he sat down, Suleyman smiled as he saw the wicked little face of his friend Balthazar Cohen smile back at him. Wreathed as ever in curtains of cigarette smoke, Balthazar had his arm round the shoulders of a young, somewhat taller man whom Suleyman knew to be his friend's son, Berekiah. Home now after finishing his military service, the young man had walked unwittingly into what had been a large gathering of his family and friends. He had, Suleyman recalled, dealt with it very well. After all, it cannot have been easy, even with prior knowledge, to confront the image of your once active father as a cripple with no job.

Although his home had been untouched by the massive earthquake that struck İstanbul on 17 August 1999, Constable Cohen, as he had been then, had not been there at the time. He'd been staying with a recently divorced lady in one of the newer apartment blocks in Yeşilköy, out by the airport. When the earthquake came, the building collapsed like a set of badly stacked plates, and Balthazar Cohen had been trapped under the rubble, which was where he stayed for the next thirty-six hours – beside the body of his dead mistress. Suleyman, who had lodged with the Cohens in their crowded Karaköy apartment since his separation from his wife almost two years previously, noted with some admiration that not once had Balthazar's wife mentioned the circumstances surrounding her husband's present infirmities. But then perhaps Estelle Cohen believed, as some of her husband's old colleagues did, that Balthazar was now well and truly paying for his sins.

Suleyman flicked quickly through the rest of the pictures, smiling at the occasional sight of his own camera-shy face amongst their number, before putting them back into his pocket again. Estelle, he thought as he allowed himself a moment to look out of his fog-grimed window, would like them. Berekiah particularly looked well. Perhaps the young man would, in time, come round to his father's idea of joining the police. Suleyman hoped so, even though Cohen's little 'talks' on this subject to his son did sometimes smack of vicarious living. But that was understandable. Cohen, by losing his legs, had also lost his liberty and independence and had come, over the months since the disaster, to rely more and more upon reports from the 'outside world' from the likes of Suleyman, Estelle and Berekiah. Suleyman knew that when he did eventually leave the Cohens' apartment, Balthazar would take it badly. If, of course, he did leave. Moving on without the presence of the woman he now hoped would be his wife would be pretty pointless. But trying to convince Zelfa Halman that he really did love her was proving problematic. With no confidence in what he saw as her voluptuous looks and nursing numerous psychological theories regarding the sometimes impulsive behaviour of people who have lived through disasters, Zelfa was treating his proposal with some caution. If only he could convince her that nothing beyond having her in his life mattered to him. But then he observed with a visible scowl that he was, after all, dealing with a psychiatrist and everybody knew what they were like.

Now, however, he had to push such thoughts aside.

He switched on his computer terminal and watched as the machine started its laborious journey towards anything relevant to him. While he was waiting, Suleyman emptied his ashtray into the bin and then lit up his first cigarette of the day. He would, he knew, smoke many more before the day was out. With his sergeant, Çöktin, off with flu, he was going to be alone in this office probably for some days to come. Given the vast heap of paperwork he knew he needed to catch up on, that was no bad thing – even if his lungs were not particularly looking forward to the experience.

His finger was poised to press the series of buttons that would give him access to his files when he heard a knock on his door.

'Come in,' he said, just as the short, thin individual outside the door moved inside.

'I've been called to an incident in Eminönü,' Çetin İkmen said brightly. 'Couple of Dolphins reckon they've stumbled upon a gangland execution.'

Suleyman frowned. 'Really? What makes them think that?'

'Classic execution mode. The victim's had his throat slit, apparently. Ear to ear.' İkmen illustrated this by dragging one finger across his own throat. 'Are you busy?'

'I've got a lot of paperwork to catch up on.'

'Quite free to accompany me then,' İkmen said and unhooked his colleague's overcoat from behind the office door.

'I don't think our superiors would share your disdain for the bureaucratic niceties, Çetin,' Suleyman replied with a smile. 'However . . .' He started the sequence necessary to shut down the computer.

'Good man!' İkmen said with some passion. He handed Suleyman his coat. 'Now that the fog has gone, it's really not a bad day.'

'Good.'

'It's been a long time since you and I attended a crime scene together,' İkmen said.

'Yes,' Suleyman agreed, 'but then I'm only coming along as your guest, aren't I? I mean, Tepe is your sergeant now and—'

'Oh, yes,' İkmen said with a wave of his hand, 'but the trouble with him is that he just isn't you, my dear Mehmet.'

'Oh, Çetin, now . . .'

But İkmen had gone. And after he had put his coat on, a slightly amused, if somewhat exasperated, Suleyman followed.

Chapter 3

The late owner of the identity card that Orhan Tepe was now clutching between his latex-gloved fingers had been called Rifat Berisha. The name made Tepe frown. As far as he could tell, Berisha was not a common Turkish name, but then it didn't have any of the usual minority hallmarks either. It was obviously neither Armenian nor Greek and it was doubtful that it was Jewish. Not that this aspect was of particular importance. More to the point was that Mr Berisha was only twenty-five years old and that he had, in all probability, been murdered. Or at least that was what many members of the crowd Tepe had so recently helped push back from the scene thought. Now lurking beyond the barriers erected around the site by his fellow officers, these onlookers had, if anything, increased in number in the half-hour since the area had been cleared. This was not something that, by the look of the thunderous expression that now hung across his features, particularly pleased Tepe's superior, Inspector İkmen.

'Haven't these bastards got work to do?' he asked a bored-looking officer to Tepe's left.

The officer didn't really have an answer to what was anyway a rhetorical question and he grimaced in an embarrassed fashion. This would have irritated İkmen had not the man who used to be his sergeant prior to Tepe intervened.

'Unless this man killed himself,' Suleyman said as he peered down at the heavily stained corpse, 'somebody as yet unknown must have some very gory clothes to dispose of. Our friend here has been almost decapitated.'

'The doctor will confirm that or not,' İkmen said distractedly as he lit yet another cigarette. 'When he gets here.'

Then with a sigh he moved towards the Bosphorus side of the site. Perhaps he was thinking that a view of the water might make him feel better about the sudden depression he was experiencing. Tepe, the ID card clutched firmly between his fingers, followed his boss to the waterside rail.

'Sir?'

İkmen turned briefly towards his young deputy, smiled and then looked out across the water once again, towards the Asian side of the city.

'You know, Tepe,' he said just as the younger man was beginning to think that perhaps his boss had entered some sort of fugue state, 'my mother used to say that it was possible to see our house in Üsküdar from here. However, try as I might, I have never been able to spot it myself. Perhaps there are just too many buildings in the way now or maybe my mother was simply telling lies.' He turned again and once more he smiled at Tepe. 'It would have been in character for her, you know.'

Tepe, who was aware of the stories that were told about İkmen's late mother – her interest in witchcraft for instance – blushed slightly by way of reply. After all, it was not every day you heard a man brand his own mother a liar. Mothers were, usually, almost sacred beings to the average Turkish man. But then İkmen was about as far from average as it was possible to get.

A few seconds later, Tepe remembered what was in his hands and very obviously cleared his throat.

'Yes?' İkmen said, roused once again from his reverie.

'I did find this.' Tepe held up the stained card for İkmen's perusal. 'It was sticking out of the pocket of his jeans and so—'

'You should have waited for forensic,' İkmen said with a frown, but then as he moved closer to look at the item, he muttered, 'Mmm.'

'Anything interesting?' a younger, more cultured voice asked.

Tepe, looking up into Suleyman's gravely handsome features, said, 'Looks like the victim's ID card, sir.'

'Oh?'

'Yes,' İkmen said as he stared at it. 'An Albanian if I'm not mistaken.'

'Ah.'

'Berisha is an Albanian name,' İkmen said. 'One of their more recent despots was, I believe, called Berisha. It will be interesting to discover whether this man is one of his clan.'

'Could that have a bearing on his death?' Suleyman inquired.

'Oh, it could,' the older man said thoughtfully, 'it could. But whatever the reason for this man's death, his clan will get themselves involved, of that you can be sure.'

Tepe, who had up until that point been listening in silence, asked 'So, do you know a lot about Albanians then, sir?'

Both İkmen and Suleyman smiled. 'No more than what my Albanian mother told me,' İkmen replied, 'which was not a great deal.'

'Oh.'

'But then is it not in the nature of witches, djinn and other creatures of the night to be just a little vague?' said the plump, bespectacled man who had suddenly appeared at İkmen's side.

'Oh, yes, doctor,' İkmen replied with a smile, 'absolutely.'

'Good morning, Dr Sarkissian,' Suleyman said as he watched İkmen and his old friend embrace warmly. 'Have you seen the body yet?'

'Briefly,' the Armenian replied and silently shook hands with Sergeant Tepe.

'And?'

'And I think that whoever killed him was pretty serious about it.'

İkmen leaned against the waterside rail and pulled his thin raincoat hard round his small frame. The cold seemed to be eating into his bones. 'Why is that, Arto?'

'Because even after a cursory glance I can see that whoever did this almost took the poor fellow's head off.'

'Just as you thought, Inspector,' İkmen said, nodding in Suleyman's direction. 'Vicious.'

'I'll be able to tell you exactly how it was done when I've had a proper look,' the pathologist said brightly. 'Do we have a name for this unfortunate?'

'It's Rifat Berisha, sir,' Tepe offered. 'Or at least—'

'Oh, yes, that really is very Albanian, isn't it?' the doctor said. 'Do we know whether Mr Berisha is a Kosovan refugee or a more long-term resident?'

'His ID would seem to suggest the latter,' İkmen replied. 'Although being Albanian there is always, of course, the possibility that his papers and even his name are counterfeit.'

'That's a harsh judgement,' Suleyman observed with a frown.

İkmen smiled wryly. 'Albania is a harsh place,' he said, and began to walk back towards the crime scene. 'It engenders witches and demons, dictators, gangsters and liars.'

And then, briefly, he laughed.

Since coming to İstanbul nine years before, Aliya Berisha had three times put a man's bloodstained shirt in the window of wherever the family were living. The first time, when the shirt had been her father-in-law's, they had been staying in Balat, in a house belonging to an elderly Jew. And although it was said that the Jew had expressed 'opinions' on both the death of Aliya's father-in-law and the shirt, nothing had ever been mentioned to either her or the rest of the family. Besides, shortly afterwards, when her cousin Mimoza married the Turk, Dilek Özer, they all decamped to his apartments on Kutucular Caddesi, not five minutes away from where the İstanbul police were currently opening up a murder investigation.

The two further bloodied shirts that Aliya had displayed since moving into Mr Özer's extensive property had belonged to her husband's only brother, Muhammed, and the youngest of her sons, the then fifteen-year-old Egrem. Dilek Özer, who neither spoke nor understood the Albanian language, readily believed his wife's explanation for these strange exhibits of the dead. 'We expose their shirts to honour them,' Mimoza had said when she first caught sight of her husband looking doubtfully at the gruesome artefact. 'It is a signal to other Albanians that our men died bravely.'

And having absolutely no knowledge of his wife's culture, how could Dilek Özer with his hundred per cent İstanbuli heritage argue?

Had he ever pushed Mimoza on this point or indeed bothered to seek out literature on the matter, Dilek Özer's attitude to this 'custom', or rather to what followed on from it, might have been radically different. He might well have thrown the entire Berisha clan out onto the street, including Mimoza.

On this particular morning, however, there were no shirts at the windows of the Berishas' apartment, only the white face of Aliya's daughter, Engelushjia, her eyes nervously scanning the features of the people in the street below. Behind her, within the darkness of their spare living room, Aliya sat motionless save for the brief movement of her fingers as she puffed on a cigarette. Her other hand lay protectively across what had only in the last few days become an obvious pregnancy. And although the thick bouts of coughing that burst periodically from some unseen part of the property made the women stir from time to time, not even that seemed able to rouse them completely from their frozen poses.

Beyond speech, neither woman gave voice to what they were thinking. Engelushjia was seeking good news amongst the many faces of those in the street below; Aliya, more pragmatic than her daughter, simply kept track of the time. As it stretched still further into the blackness that encapsulated the future, the spirit that allows people to hope was slowly dying inside Aliya's mind. Were midday to come and go with nothing, then she would know. Even a man with hot, youthful appetites would be finished with a woman by then. And if trouble had come which involved the police, Aliya would surely know about that by then too. Not that she believed either of these scenarios was likely. Neither Rifat nor the police would come. Soon, she knew, she would have to send Engelushjia across to Tahtakale Caddesi in order to retrieve her brother's body. Unlike with Egrem, Aliya was not in a condition to do it herself. Just the thought of her own inadequacy made Aliya choke on what was a flood of rising tears.

'I do appreciate your coming with me, you know,' İkmen said as he slipped neatly into step beside his much taller colleague.

'I don't suppose Tepe feels quite so joyful about it,' Suleyman replied.

İkmen shrugged. 'Somebody needs to remain in

charge of the scene until the body has been moved. And I don't see the virtue in not informing these Berisha people as soon as possible. If we can get a positive ID on that body today perhaps we can start to ask questions which might tell us what young Rifat was involved in.'

'Your use of the word "we" does not, I hope, pertain to myself,' Suleyman said as he first lit up a cigarette and then pointedly ignored the man who had appeared at his elbow, pressing him to buy a battered packet of condoms.

İkmen gave no sign that he had heard Suleyman's comment. Closing his mind to what he did not want to address or felt incapable of dealing with was a well-practised trait of his. 'Don't your brother's in-laws have premises in the Mısır Çarşısı?' he asked as they skirted round the right-hand side of the ornate entrance to what was also known as the Spice Bazaar.

'Yes,' a tight-lipped Suleyman replied. 'A caviar specialist. My mother calls it a grocer's shop. Very lively. Very Greek.'

'So does your brother see much of them? I mean . . .' İkmen, aware that the death of Suleyman's sister-in-law was still a very raw and delicate issue, uncharacteristically stumbled over his words. 'I mean, er, since Elena . . .'

'Murad's in-laws have been very supportive. Mrs Papas looks after my niece every day, now that Murad works in Beşiktaş.' Then under his breath he added, 'Which is more than Edibe's Turkish family do.'

'Oh, I don't know,' İkmen said. 'The little one

spends quite a bit of time over at the Cohens' place with you.'

'When I talk of Edibe's Turkish family what I mean is my parents, actually, Çetin,' Suleyman said with some passion.

'Oh.'

Knowing from experience that further discussion of Suleyman's family, now that his archaic Ottoman parents had been mentioned, was impossible, İkmen lapsed into silence. Not for the first time, he felt pleased that he was just a peasant – if from, on one side, rather dubious Albanian stock. Ayşe İkmen, that crafty weaver of unintelligible Albanian spells, may have been dead for over forty years now, but on days like this she lived very strongly in the head of at least one of her sons.

Negotiating, the narrow, packed thoroughfare that was Hasırcılar Caddesi, İkmen wondered how much, if any, Turkish language skills the Berisha family would have. He hoped they were at least reasonably fluent. Between the twin facts of his mother's early death and his father's disdain for a language he said sounded like a madman's ravings, Çetin İkmen knew very little Albanian. And, apart from a few commonly held beliefs about the superstitious nature of Albanians, the only thing that he really grasped about them was their enthusiastic pursuit of what they called *gjakmaria* – the blood feud. Not that these thoughts occupied his mind for very long. Weaving through throngs of heavily muffled shoppers and avoiding handcarts stacked with coats, socks, vine tomatoes and anything else imaginable did tend to fully occupy one's senses. That and trying to keep up with the rapid progress of Suleyman was not easy for one as unfit as İkmen. Only when Hasırcılar Caddesi had eventually resolved into Kutucular Caddesi, the home of the Berisha family, did the younger man start to slow his steps somewhat.

Hemmed in by tiny shops selling electrical goods, cigarette lighters, buttons and underwear, the two men peered intently at the occasional doorways between the businesses in order to find what they were looking for. Such doorways, they knew, led up to both store-houses and apartments that occupied the crumbling seventeenth-century shells into which the shops had been inserted many years before. İkmen, at least, knew that a clean and bright electrical shop could very well exist underneath a damp hovel of almost indescribable sordidness.

It was Suleyman who first spotted the faded number lurking above the darkened entranceway. 'This is number thirty-two,' he said. He turned his nose up at the small gang of local toughs who stared hungrily at his elegant Italian suit and briskly made his way up the stairs.

Before İkmen followed, he happened to look up at the windows of the upper apartment. At one of them was a young, very white female face. When she saw him, the girl put her hand to her mouth before she disappeared into the depths of the building.

While Mehmet Suleyman was entering the Berishas' apartment, the man some people ruefully called 'Prince' Muhammed waited for the doctor to call him into her office. Tall and, like his son, gravely attractive,

Muhammed Suleyman tried hard to concentrate on his copy of *A la Recherche du Temps Perdu* without success. Not that this failure was, under the circumstances, surprising. There was a very strange man sitting opposite who, for some reason, kept on repeating the word 'two' over and over to a veiled woman, who Muhammed supposed was the man's mother. A thin young boy with ravenous eyes and a frightful toothless hag made up the rest of the waiting group. All, apart from Muhammed himself, perfectly mad of course. Had his elder son Murad not given his father to believe that young Mehmet might be serious about this female psychiatrist, he would never have come through the door.

But then sane people didn't often come to visit psychiatrists, did they? Not that this doctor, pleasingly blonde from what he'd seen of her so far, would appreciate his lack of bizarre symptoms. In fact she would probably be furious when she discovered the real reason for his visit. Sizing up those one's children intended to marry, the traditional function of the *görücü*, or marriage broker, was not something Muhammed would expect a foreigner to understand. This doctor would probably consider such a thing a waste of time and everyone knew that western foreigners in particular hated wasting time.

For quite different reasons, Muhammed's wife, Nur, would also be furious if she knew what her husband was doing now. For not only was the role of the *görücü* always held by a woman, Nur was in addition particularly at odds with the younger of her two sons at the moment. In fact, ever since Mehmet had left his wife, one of Nur's more forceful nieces, two years previously, he and his mother had barely spoken. Autocratic and unforgiving, Nur Suleyman's pursuit of what she felt her aristocratic sons should want had over the years poisoned her relations with both of them. Strange, really, considering that it was her husband who had the aristocratic background. Nur herself was actually from a rather ambitious peasant family. Muhammed smiled to himself. Of course he should have been firmer with her years ago but . . .

Dr Halman smiled as she ushered the toothless hag into her office. She did briefly glance towards Muhammed as she moved back into her room but not, he thought, with any sense of recognition. It wasn't a bad face. And although she was obviously middle-aged, Muhammed could see that Zelfa Halman was still an attractive prospect. Whether or not she was worthy of his son, though, he would not be able to deduce until he spoke to her. Although, of course, worthy or not, if Mehmet loved her then that would be that. His lovely little boy had, Muhammed mused rather sadly, grown into early middle age almost without his noticing. He was still handsome, but Mehmet's eyes had, on the few occasions Muhammed had seen them lately, shown signs of having looked upon more than was good for them. Working with death for all these years cannot have helped, and then when the earthquake came, well . . . Muhammed, like so many other inhabitants of the north-western corner of the country, turned away from what was an almost unbearable memory. But when the small blonde woman came out of her office again, this time to usher the strange man and his mother into her room, Muhammed considered that perhaps such a soft and curvy little thing was just what his son needed to keep the spiky ghosts of the past at bay. And when Dr Halman smiled at him, Muhammed found himself smiling back with some enthusiasm.

Just after the smile, though, he left. One always thinks that courage should be natural to princes. But in this case it was not so.

Chapter 4

'Do you have any ideas about who might have wanted to harm your son, Mrs Berisha?' İkmen asked when the ticking of the old clock in the corner of that darkened room threatened to damage his sanity.

'No.'

Like all the rest of the Berishas' responses so far, Aliya's was heavily accented and monosyllabic. Only the blood drawn by their fingernails raking down their cheeks gave any hint of the anguish İkmen knew the mother and her daughter were experiencing. Real, if strangely silent, peasant mourning, not unlike the dramas he'd seen when Fatma's father had died. A quick glance at a wide-eyed Suleyman told him that the younger man had not experienced as much of this sort of thing as he had.

İkmen looked at the dead man's father, a motionless study in elderly disaffection. Not that Rahman Berisha was necessarily old. A windswept, disappointed face like that could be anything from fifty to seventy years old. 'Anything you wish to add to what your wife has said, Mr Berisha?'

'No.'

Even if the family's answers had not been as suspiciously rapid and sure as they were, the look that fleetingly passed between Rahman and his daughter would have alerted İkmen to the possibility of something being amiss. It was a look, on the girl's part at least, of almost hysterical fear. Not that İkmen, at this stage in the proceedings, gave voice to his suspicions.

'So, what you're saying then, Mr Berisha,' he said, 'is that you know everything there is to know about your twenty-five-year-old son.'

'There are no secrets between blood,' the Albanian replied. His use of the word 'blood' where İkmen would have used 'family' was something the policeman was accustomed to hearing from some of his own relatives. It was yet another cue for mental sirens to sound in his head. If Rifat's murder was what it looked and sounded like, it was going to be very easy to solve. But then that was, İkmen knew from experience, all the more reason to act with extreme caution. Things were rarely, if ever, what they seemed.

After yet another pause that seemed to last several lifetimes, İkmen, now convinced that the traumatised Berishas had little more to offer on the subject of Rifat at this time, finally came to what victims' families dreaded most. Looking at Rahman, the only contender for the task, İkmen said, 'Of course the body will have to be formally identified.'

'Why?'

For just a moment, both officers thought that they might have misheard, and frowned doubtfully at each other. Only when an uncomfortable length of time had once again passed did Suleyman break the silence and answer the question.

'We must know that the victim is definitely Rifat,' he said. 'Even though his description and papers are consistent with those of your son, we have to be certain. People do sometimes plant false papers on dead bodies in order to confound us.'

'So, will you bring him here then? Rifat?' Aliya Berisha asked as she rubbed one bloodied hand across the swollen hump of her belly.

İkmen said, 'No, madam, you will have to come to the hospital.'

'No.'

'Pardon?'

'Go to the hospital, no,' the woman said. 'No.'

'Well,' İkmen said smoothly, thinking that he knew why Aliya Berisha was refusing – as a religious woman she might well object to being in the presence of a body of the opposite sex, even her own son's – 'I was actually thinking that your husband—'

'No.'

'But, madam,' Suleyman said and leaned towards the couple, the better to impress upon them the seriousness of the issue at hand, 'as I thought I explained to you—'

'Engelushjia will go,' the woman said, looking fiercely at the face of her daughter – a girl of sixteen at most.

'But—'

'No, I'll go.' Her words were firm even though both İkmen and Suleyman saw that her eyes moved uneasily as she spoke.

'Well, if you insist, Miss Berisha.'

'She does,' her father answered for her.

41

'Right. Good.' İkmen looked at the Berishas; smiling at them, he had quickly discovered, had little effect. The whole family, together with the wife of their landlord, also some sort of relative, had sunk back into stone-like silence once again. Only the girl, marble-white Engelushjia, seemed alert, if terrified. In some ways, thought İkmen, it was probably best if she identified her brother's body. He just hoped that she wouldn't find the process too distressing, though he knew that she almost certainly would. Dead bodies were not pretty at the best of times but Rifat Berisha's, with its head almost hanging off, was particularly unpleasant. Briefly İkmen experienced a wave of anger towards this family who were, seemingly without thought, sending such a young girl to look into the face of horror.

'Well,' İkmen said as he braced his hands on his knees and then stood up, 'if we are going to go through these processes and make a start on your son's case . . .'

'When will we be able to bury my son?' Rahman asked, not moving his gaze from the floor in front of him.

Knowing how important it was for Muslims to be able to bury their dead quickly, İkmen frowned as he started to tell the traumatised family why it would not be possible in this case. Murder, as both İkmen and Suleyman knew only too well, changed the rules governing people's lives in so many ways.

'I am afraid you will have to wait, Mr Berisha,' he said gravely, 'until our doctor has firstly determined cause of death and secondly gathered from your son's body as much evidence as he can. Victims' bodies can often provide us with enough clues to narrow the scope of an investigation down considerably. As you—'

'If my son is dead, what is it to you?'

İkmen and Suleyman turned to look at the source of this extraordinary comment – the now slightly more animated Aliya Berisha.

'We think that your son has been murdered, Mrs Berisha,' Suleyman began.

'And so?'

One of those deep, thick silences rolled into the room yet again – time during which İkmen briefly closed his eyes to gain some sort of respite from what he was increasingly viewing as an extreme case of the irrationality of grief.

'Murder is a crime,' he said slowly as if he were speaking to a group of children, 'and as policemen it is our job to investigate it and, if possible, arrest the person responsible.'

'Back home men resort only to the police if they are without family,' Rahman Berisha said with some passion. 'We make our own arrangements.'

From the little he had learned from his Albanian relatives, İkmen knew that even with the fall of Albania's corrupt communist regime in 1992, the country was still pretty much without coherent law enforcement. One of the few things he could recall his late father telling him about his mother was her amusement at even the idea of an Albanian legal system. Such a thing was, she had apparently said, a contradiction in terms.

'Well, sir,' İkmen said, 'that may be so in Albania, but this is Turkey. And in Turkey if a man dies in mysterious circumstances, policemen like Inspector Suleyman and myself are obliged to investigate.'

'If it is your will,' Rahman Berisha said with a shrug.

'Oh, it is,' İkmen replied as he moved towards Engelushjia Berisha. 'It is my will, Mr Berisha, of that you can be certain.' He put his hand out to the girl. With a quick glance at her father, she took it and left the apartment with the officers.

Not another sound was made until Engelushjia and the policemen had gone. Then, her mouth stretched wide with pain, Aliya Berisha let out the kind of scream that freezes blood.

The two orderlies had to use some vigour to get the stretcher up onto the table. This was not unusual. The orderlies knew that death tended to increase both the weight and the unwieldiness of bodies. Even small children could, on occasion, prove problematic – an unpleasant experience that all but one of those present in the room had been through several times.

The older of the two orderlies unzipped the bag and the younger one pulled the two sides apart to reveal what remained of the young man inside. Then Arto Sarkissian moved a metal gurney into position beside the table. Looking at the two orderlies, he said, 'Lift on three?'

'OK, doctor.'

'One . . .'

The two men slipped their hands underneath the body and braced themselves.

'Two . . . Three.'

With one smooth, breathless movement, the body almost seemed to float out of the bag and onto the gurney, the tatters of its once white shirt flapping briefly before the corpse came to rest on the metal trolley.

'Good,' Arto said. He moved into position beside the corpse.

'Do you want us to get ready, sir?' asked the older assistant, Ali Mertez.

'You can,' the doctor replied as he adjusted his spectacles to look closely at the corpse, 'although best keep out of the way until I call you. We can't start straight away. Inspector İkmen is bringing this boy's young sister in to do the formal identification. They should be here any time now.'

'Shouldn't we clean him up a bit for her then?' the younger man – who was Ali's nephew, İsmet – said.

'Don't be stupid,' his uncle began. 'You—'

'Sadly, Miss Berisha will have to see her brother in this state,' the doctor said, looking rather more kindly upon İsmet Mertez than his uncle was. 'This looks like a murder and so we must treat the corpse as a source of forensic evidence. All we can do is place a clean sheet across it. As long as Miss Berisha can see her brother's face . . .'

'I'll get you one, doctor,' Ali said and quickly left the room.

Now alone with the Armenian and his charge, Ali's nephew felt both awkward and stupid at his naïveté and said, 'I'm sorry, doctor, for being a bit slow about this being a murder and . . . well . . . I am new. I mean, I find the work interesting . . .'

'That's good,' his superior murmured as, with the aid of a pair of large tweezers, he lifted strands of shredded shirt out to one side.

'Do you—'

'If you would just be quiet for the moment please, İsmet,' the Armenian said, peering at what İsmet now knew they called the torso. 'Mmm.'

Several minutes passed, during which the doctor moved in close and then away from the torso, muttering as he went. Not that he touched the body at all. Apart from exposing the skin underneath the shirt he left it alone, presumably, so İsmet imagined, until the autopsy began later.

By the time Ali returned with a sheet, Arto Sarkissian had moved away from the trolley and was leaning against one of the large medical sinks. But his eyes were still fixed to the body, as were İsmet's – not that the latter knew why. As Ali Mertez covered the corpse with the sheet, Sarkissian said, 'I've a feeling this is going to be an interesting autopsy from a medical point of view.'

'Oh? Why's that then, doctor?' Ali asked.

'Because this man has had major surgery,' the doctor replied, 'of a kind one doesn't see too often.'

As Samsun Bajraktar pulled the blinds down across what she now dared to call *her* windows in *her* apartment, she thought again about just how happy she was. In nearly fifty-six years of breathing, nothing had even begun to get this close to her own personal paradise. And that it was all due to the kindness and the beauty of that great big man who was even now working for their future down in the leather shop below was just one more example of how totally and wonderfully her life had turned around.

Abdurrahman, seller of leather in every imaginable colour, ex-grease wrestler, ten years younger than she was – just his name made her heart flutter, not to mention his thick, dark muscles, his body like a glistening marble statue, his . . . No, she thought with what was really quite uncharacteristic modesty, best not think about what else she loved and desired about Abdurrahman. Later. She smiled. When the shop closed she would do what Abdurrahman most liked her to do. And in the darkness when her dress and her jewels hit the floor at the end of their bed, she and Abdurrahman would both receive and give pleasure, one to the other, as equals – as it should be, as Samsun had always dreamed.

When she had pulled the blinds, shutting out the frantic activity that always accompanied the shutting of the Kapalı Çarşı opposite, Samsun walked into the bedroom and lit the candelabra that stood on her dressing table. She then muttered, eyes closed, in a language few in this city could understand, communing with beings even fewer could imagine. Beings which, only if properly appeased, would ensure the continuance of her relationship with her lover. And although she could have been interrupted at any time during her spell weaving, as if by magic the knock at her door did not come until she had finished. When she opened the door, Samsun saw the figure of a small, rumpled individual who smiled when his eye found hers.

'Cousin!' Samsun exclaimed and reached down to embrace Çetin İkmen within the circle of her powerful arms. 'This is a nice surprise. Come in! Come in!'

With a smile the policeman stepped over the threshold into the apartment, removing his shoes as he went.

'You're looking very well,' he said, looking up at his relative with approval. 'Uncle Ahmet said that you had, er, found somebody, um . . .'

Samsun giggled and visibly reddened, just like a girl. 'Abdurrahman,' she said, raising her voice as she spoke her lover's name. 'He's working in his shop downstairs.'

İkmen, who had noticed a well-built man in the leather shop below, nodded. 'Yes, I think I saw him as I came up.'

'He's very big, Abdurrahman,' Samsun said as she led İkmen through into a room which, had it boasted a bed, would have qualified for the term tart's boudoir. Red and black frills dominated. İkmen sat down and swallowed hard before lighting up one of his ubiquitous Maltepe cigarettes. He didn't find being around Samsun easy, much as he liked her. For various reasons his mother's Albanian relatives had always been difficult and although Samsun, like Ayşe İkmen before her, was a renowned soothsayer and familiar to İkmen, she was something extra too. Until she had fallen in with a notorious group of like minds in her early twenties, Samsun had been known as Mustafa Bajraktar. Now, quite a lot of expensive Italian surgery later, Mustafa was Samsun who lived with Abdurrahman, a character İkmen felt had the look of a Spanish fighting bull about him.

'I can make sahlep to warm you,' Samsun said as she placed a clean ashtray on the coffee table in front of him.

'That's very kind,' İkmen said with a smile, 'but if I tell you I've just come from the mortuary would that qualify me for something a little stronger?'

Samsun smiled. 'Kanyak OK?'

'Old addictions still taste just as sweet,' İkmen replied and leaned back into the depths of a huge red sofa.

After a brief retreat into the kitchen, Samsun returned bearing a large golden-coloured bottle and two glasses. Her ability to hold all of these items in just one large hand made İkmen smile.

'So,' she began as she sat down and began pouring out the drinks, 'what brings this country's most celebrated murder detective to the door of an ex-working woman like me?'

Despite being family, Samsun had never entirely trusted her cousin. The fact that he was only half Albanian, together with his profession, meant she felt the need to stress her position as an *ex*-prostitute. Her assessment of him as one who cared about such details was entirely erroneous but it was an attitude İkmen had over the years come to accept as unchangeable. Rather like her opinion of him as some sort of investigative genius, it reflected Samsun's overblown view of the world and of everyone in it.

İkmen, as was his strangely un-Turkish wont, came

straight to the point. 'I want to know about *gjakmaria*, Samsun,' he said. 'I need to understand how it works.'

Samsun passed a large glass of brandy to İkmen and then took a long draught from her own glass.

'I'm involved in something to which it may be pertinent,' İkmen continued, trying without success to catch Samsun's down-turned eyes.

'If Albanians are involved in *gjakmaria* then there's no place for you, the police, in that,' Samsun said, reflecting the sentiments of Rahman Berisha. 'All the worse, of course, if they're Ghegs.'

'Ghegs?'

She turned on him what İkmen felt was a disdainful eye. 'You really know nothing, don't you?' She sighed. 'Ghegs are from the north, Ghegeria, real mountain people, very traditional. Lek Dukagjini, who put the rules governing *gjakmaria*, amongst other things, in the book we call the Kunan, was a Gheg. The southern Tosks are more outward looking.'

'And you are?' İkmen asked.

'Like your mother, I am a Gheg,' Samsun replied.

'But you're not currently involved in *gjakmaria*, I—'

'Your Turkish father must have told you that we do this sort of thing.'

'Well . . .'

'As far as our family are concerned, we settled all of our differences before we came to this country.' Just briefly she smiled. 'I have never seen a bloodied shirt at the window of any of our relatives, Çetin.'

'The bloodied shirt meaning . . . ?'

'That a dead man waits to be avenged. There are some villages back home where such things hang in every window.'

'No wonder Grandfather decided to leave,' İkmen said acidly.

Samsun sighed and leaned back in her chair. 'If you're dealing with a *fis* in blood, Çetin,' she said, 'the "something" with which you are involved will not be the end of the matter. If blood has been shed then that blood will have to be avenged. These are very deep waters, laced with a history and a tradition you barely understand. Your status as a police officer won't help you here. You can threaten the whole lot of them with the death penalty if you wish, but it will make no difference to the outcome.'

İkmen took a long drink from his glass and then placed it, empty, on the coffee table. 'So, assuming that I'm dealing with a *fis* in blood, in other words a clan involved in a blood feud, what happens now?'

'When the shirt is hung, the rival *fis* will know they mean business. All of the men will stay inside the house for the time being.'

This sounded familiar, and İkmen recalled Rahman Berisha's grave face. This in turn conjured up the look of horror on the face of Rahman's daughter when she saw her brother's all but severed head. A girl, little more than a child, made to follow the harsh dictates of her 'blood'.

'Whatever they tell you about it must be treated with caution,' Samsun went on. 'We have a saying that goes, "You are free to be faithful to your word; you are free to be faithless to it."' At this, Samsun laughed. It was, in spite of all the surgery she had had, a remarkably deep sound.

After a pause during which the full import of the saying Samsun had just quoted at him sank into his brain, İkmen said, 'Of course I'm trying not to jump to conclusions about this. The incident may be clan related, but then it may not be.'

'You are right to take that line,' Samsun said and poured what looked like about half the brandy bottle into İkmen's glass. 'The Berishas have been in blood with the Vlora *fis* for as long as anyone from Ghegeria can remember.'

Amazed that Samsun, even allowing for her well-known 'powers', not to mention her addiction to gossip, would know, and reveal, such intimate details about his case, İkmen exclaimed, 'Allah! But how do you . . .'

'We are Albanians, Çetin.' The transsexual smiled, 'We are accustomed to tragedy. News of it travels fast. The cousin, Mimoza Özer, is telling everyone that Rifat Berisha's head was almost severed from his body. That would point away from his death being blood related.'

'Why is that?' İkmen asked, after which he made a deliberate effort to close his mouth which was beginning to look fish-like.

'Because to sever a man's head is dishonourable,' Samsun explained and then added with a shrug, 'Not of course that this will stop the Berishas from avenging Rifat. In fact I expect that plans are well in hand to kill a Vlora even as we speak. I suggest that you enlist the services of a disinterested party immediately. That rather lovely Suleyman would do.' Then leaning forward right into İkmen's face she said, 'You might like to think you're all Turk, but if either the Berishas or the Vloras find out that you have "connections", you could be in for some very big trouble indeed, my little cousin.'

Chapter 5

Although the pressure of Zelfa's warm, naked body across his chest was comforting, it did not, sadly, manage to expunge completely the image of that horrified girl's face from Mehmet Suleyman's mind. When Engelushjia Berisha had seen what someone had done to her brother Rifat she had first vomited and then screamed so long and hard that Dr Sarkissian had been obliged to medicate her. Poor child. It made Mehmet mad to think that one so young had been forced to do that by apparently perfectly capable parents.

But when Zelfa started to stir from her post-coital stupor, he found his mind was, after all, ready to be fully occupied by her considerable figure.

'I need a cigarette,' Zelfa said and reared up suddenly from within a thick heap of hair and bedclothes.

'Oh, don't move yet!' Mehmet said as he grabbed her round the shoulders and pulled her back down onto his chest. 'I'll get cold if you go.'

As a sweetener, he moved her mouth down hard onto his. And all thoughts of cigarettes momentarily disappeared as Zelfa allowed herself to be tasted and explored.

When at last he loosened his grasp on her, Mehmet,

his eyes still full of lust for her, said, 'You're so soft and warm . . .'

'I think you'll find that's the menopause,' she replied, and with a laugh she rolled towards the edge of the bed and retrieved her cigarettes and lighter from the floor.

'I don't know why you bring that subject up so frequently,' her now annoyed lover retorted. 'It's not romantic. Why do you do that, Zelfa?'

After first lighting a cigarette for herself and then one for him, she answered, 'Well, firstly, because I'm a medic and I relate to the world in medical terms.'

'Yes? And?'

'And, also,' she said, moving in closer the better to see his face, 'I want to bring it to your attention, Mehmet. This process has already started in my body; I've put on weight, I get hot flushes, I didn't have a period last month . . . I'm a doctor, I know this stuff. You and I can screw like rabbits but the chances of our having children are slim, you know.'

'Yes.' He sat up a little straighter now, angry. His face, she thought, looked very sexy when it was haughtily jutting above a long cigarette. 'But I've told you that I want you more than children.'

'You need to be very, very sure, Mehmet.'

'Yes, I know and I am,' he said, his voice now rising in line with his increased anger, 'although you constantly asking me to think about my commitment to you infuriates me. You seem to think I'm incapable of knowing my own mind.'

'I know you're not incapable, Mehmet . . .'

'I am not one of your patients!' Sitting up straight

now, he turned the full force of his aristocratically handsome countenance on her. 'I come from a long line of men who have known exactly what they want – they used to rule both this country and its empire! Decision-making is second nature to us and so if I have decided that I want to marry you, Zelfa, you can be pretty certain that that is what I want for myself!' He turned aside in order, she thought, to flick ash from his cigarette into the ashtray, but when he turned back his hands were empty.

'Mehmet . . .'

With one quick movement, he hopped lightly across her body, pinning her to the bed with his tall, dark form.

'Do you know how many times a day I think about making love to you?' he said, his lips close to hers. 'Or how often I imagine your laugh or replay your funny remarks in my head?'

Noticing only that his eyes were fierce with passion, she said in conciliatory tones, 'Mehmet . . .'

'I love you,' he said. 'I love your kindness and your intelligence and your beauty and I know you hate the little pieces of fat underneath your skin, but—'

'But I must be certain you won't leave me, Mehmet!' she said with a desperation she had not meant to impart to him. 'Because if we married and then you left me for—'

'You don't leave things that you worship, you stupid woman!'

As if propelled by words that he, in his turn, had not wanted to confess to her, Mehmet threw himself

57

off Zelfa's body and landed heavily back on his side of the bed.

Several minutes of silence passed as both of them stared fixedly at the heavily cracked ceiling of Zelfa's bedroom, reminding them of the all too recent upheavals in the earth. The sombreness that this evoked brought them to rather more quiet places in their minds.

It was Zelfa who finally broke the silence. 'I do want to say yes, you know,' she said softly. 'I just need a few more days to explore all the implications.'

'Like what?'

'Like the fact that if I marry you I'll never live in Ireland again.' She turned to face him with a smile. 'I know that we can visit, but . . .'

'I can't help feeling that all this thinking you are doing means that you don't love me,' he said, his face now drawn and anxious.

Zelfa placed both her hands round his jaw and kissed him. 'Oh, but I do, Mehmet, but I have to consider all the options before I commit to anything.'

Slowly, if sadly, he smiled at her words. 'I know. I know.'

'If you knew just how much I love you, it would scare you to death,' she said and then, as if to underline her point, she began moving her hands down his chest, towards his lower abdomen.

He smiled.

It was exactly the same smile that the no-show patient with the surname Suleyman had given her earlier in the day. Mr Muhammed Suleyman's anxiety had obviously got the better of him before his appointment – either that or the old man had decided to bottle out of meeting his son's lover, if indeed Mehmet was his son. Oh, but with a smile like that he had to be, didn't he? Although how the old man, who according to Mehmet had little contact with him, knew about her she didn't know. But as she caressed her lover, Zelfa decided that perhaps now was not the time to mention such issues.

Orhan Tepe had had a long, tiring day. As soon as he had finished securing what they now knew was not the site of Rifat Berisha's murder but simply the place where his body had been dumped, he had followed Dr Sarkissian and the corpse over to the mortuary. Arriving just after the formal identification by the victim's sister, he had seen İkmen only briefly before the latter, plus Suleyman, returned the distressed young woman to her home. İkmen and Suleyman, he thought sadly, looked just as comfortable together as they had when Suleyman used to work for the old man. The two of them had been a team, a real partnership in ways he knew was not the case with himself and İkmen. Not that he and İkmen had been working together for that long – just a year. But it was a year during which, Tepe felt, his superior had been mourning, for want of a better word, the elevation of his closest ally. Add to that the post-earthquake anxiety they all seemed to suffer from now and it was easy, if galling, to see why İkmen was not, for a 'new boy' like him, easy to reach. But this train of thought, he knew, didn't ultimately help. İkmen would either come round to him or not, as Allah willed.

Orhan took a sip from the glass of tea Aysel had

given him before she'd gone off to try to get some sleep – before Cemal, no doubt, woke her for a feed in the early hours of the morning. Love that child as he did, Orhan couldn't help wondering how his wife would cope should they have another highly active baby – if, of course, they could afford to have one at all. Unfortunately, living in a recently active earthquake zone didn't mean that your rent went down or even stablised. Becoming not only a poorly paid policeman but also a policeman in the employ of the ruthlessly incorruptible İkmen had probably not been his smartest move. Not that he was known for his good decisions – the latest of which, a somewhat tawdry affair with a colleague, was causing him more than just mild anxiety. He turned his mind away from such insoluble issues.

Although he didn't usually attend autopsies, he had witnessed some of Rifat Berisha's. Dr Sarkissian had spoken only to his assistants during the course of the process, but he had disclosed some of his findings when İkmen had returned from the Berishas' home. As they already knew, Rifat Berisha had died from massive loss of blood following what the doctor said were multiple deep slashes to the throat. The weapon, which the doctor suggested could be either a hunting knife or some similar unserrated blade, had been wielded like a saw, until it almost decapitated the victim. He had suggested the assailant would have to be strong and possibly angry if not necessarily powerful. An interesting aside to this had been the small, but visible, shards of glass that were present both in the wound and in the victim's face. Although the death blow had undoubtedly been delivered by a knife, the glass fragments had damaged Berisha's facial skin and added to the mess that had once been his throat.

Paucity of blood at the scene indicated that Rifat had been killed elsewhere. In addition, the battering he had suffered, either on Reşadiye Caddesi or just before, had occurred, so Dr Sarkissian felt, post-mortem. İkmen was going to appeal for witnesses who may have seen something suspicious in the early hours of the morning, although given the heaviness of the fog at that time, it seemed unlikely that many people would have been around.

More interesting to Orhan than any of these details was the enormous scar, now also covered with bruises, the doctor had pointed out on the left-hand side of Rifat's torso. It was consistent with the type of scar one would expect to have after kidney removal, and the autopsy had confirmed that young Rifat Berisha did indeed possess only one kidney; his body, as the doctor had put it, had almost been cut in half. To Orhan's surprise, this was standard procedure; indeed Dr Sarkissian was full of praise for the work some unknown surgeon had performed upon Berisha. What was less clear, however, was why a seemingly healthy young man like Rifat had needed the organ removed in the first place. With no obvious sign of disease in the body, there was a possibility, the doctor had said, that Berisha had sold his healthy kidney. Orhan knew that the sale of healthy organs, usually to foreign buyers by poorer citizens of the Republic, was not unknown. Removal was usually performed abroad with the 'vendor' taking a short 'holiday' in London or Rome or somewhere else in western Europe. But such cases were difficult to prove. Police both in the Republic and abroad were faced with the fact that provided everybody in the transaction was happy, unscrupulous or simply unknowing, surgeons could carry on doing this without hindrance. And, the doctor had added, a poor Albanian like Rifat was a likely candidate for this sort of money-raising activity. For one whose mother had been, Orhan had learned just that day, an Albanian herself, İkmen's comment on the doctor's words had sounded rather callous. 'What do you expect,' he had said, 'of a people addictively at odds with themselves?'

Quite what this meant, Orhan didn't know, but if Rifat Berisha had sold one of his kidneys, he and his family had to have been in desperate straits. And people in desperate straits were very vulnerable, not just to the needs of rich foreigners but also to the whims and desires of any number of less than honest types. It would be interesting to know what, if anything, Rifat had in his system when he died. The toxicology tests, when completed, would indicate whether the nagging spectre of Albanian drug-running had any substance.

The tones of his mobile telephone broke into Tepe's thoughts.

'Hello?'

'Orhan, it's Inspector İkmen here,' a familiar voice said. 'I'm just ringing you to let you know that I'm mounting an observation on the Berisha house which I would like you to participate in. I'd like you in early.'

Tepe frowned. To mount an observation on a victim's

home at this early stage in the investigation was most irregular. But he knew of old that to question İkmen was usually a mistake. One would generally, even in the face of the old man's most bizarre ideas, end up feeling stupid oneself.

'Right.'

'I'll tell you all about it in the morning,' İkmen said and then added, a little stiffly Tepe felt, 'An interesting autopsy, I thought.'

'Yes, sir.'

'Mmm.' And then, or so Tepe thought, either running out of things to say or feeling awkward speaking to his inferior so late at night, İkmen concluded, 'Very well then, Orhan, I'll see you tomorrow.'

'Yes, sir.'

And with that İkmen put his phone down, leaving Tepe listening to the hum of a disconnected line. He had no way of knowing what the old man had in mind but there had to be some reason why he wanted the Berisha house watched. The toxicology reports couldn't possibly be complete yet, but perhaps the doctor or forensic had found something that maybe implicated the Berishas themselves or possible associates of the family in Rifat's death. After all, as Orhan knew even from his limited professional experience, the bosom of one's family is not always the safest place to be.

Although he thought about ringing Mehmet Suleyman as soon as he finished the call to Orhan Tepe, İkmen managed to resist the urge. The man was probably in bed by this time and besides, there was always the chance that a late call, even to Mehmet's mobile, might wake up poor old Cohen. Completely immobile since the amputation of both legs just below the knee, ex-constable Balthazar Cohen, despite a battery of pain-killing and tranquillising drugs, slept very little these days. Troubled by tortuous visions of both past and possible future earthquakes, not to mention the spectre of his lost virility, Cohen spent his days and much of his nights in a state of unsettled angst. Even so, thought İkmen, it would be too bad to telephone just as Cohen had finally dropped off.

Anyway, quite what he would say to Mehmet, should he speak to him, was unformed in his mind. Samsun's revelation that the Berishas were involved in a blood feud with the Vlora family troubled him. Did this have any bearing on Rifat's death? If it did, and if it became known that he himself was related to another Gheg *fis*, that could, as Samsun had said, cause problems. He would have to be careful to keep his Albanian origins a secret. İstanbul, he knew, could be a very small place at times.

Hopefully, observation of the Berisha household would help to establish whether or not they were moving against the Vlora family. Engelushjia Berisha had not asked for her brother's bloodied shirt. Perhaps this was a good sign – not that she would have been given it had she asked for it. If the Berishas didn't move against their 'enemies', then all well and good, but if they did, he should perhaps do as Samsun had suggested and give the case to a disinterested party like Suleyman. It was crazy stuff. Although he had grown up knowing that the practice of *gjakmaria* existed amongst his mother's people, İkmen had never considered that it might impact upon him personally. He knew that he had to beware of ascribing everything about this case to it, but the idea of blood revenge would not leave his mind. It was, he felt, another of those times when his late mother intruded on his mind.

Ayşe İkmen had died when Çetin, her youngest son, was ten years old. Despite numerous attempts to recall it, İkmen could not remember anything much about her last illness. All he could now recall was how he and his thirteen-year-old brother Halil had come home from school and found their mother dead in her bed. Not that Çetin had actually seen her. Halil's much taller form had deliberately blocked his view – the older boy protecting the younger by screaming and bullying him out of the room. Halil hadn't realised that Çetin had wanted to say goodbye. İkmen sometimes wished that he could tackle Halil about that time. He clearly remembered how, later that afternoon, Halil had allowed the policemen to look at her. Over forty years on from those events, there were still times when, feeling Ayşe close as he did now, İkmen fancied that some long-ago intoned spell might bring her back to life. Perhaps a visit to the Karaca Ahmet Cemetery was in order. Perhaps he needed to be with his parents again.

He lit a cigarette and looked out of his window as the gathering night-time fog started to swirl around and then obscure great hulking sections of the Sultan Ahmet Mosque.

Chapter 6

When Engelushjia Berisha woke up that morning, it wasn't only the coldness of the cheap linoleum beneath her feet that made her smart with pain as she jumped down from her bed. The memory of what they had done to Rifat hurt too. Where they'd cut his throat, it had looked like the necks of the still living sheep sacrificed in honour of the Prophet Abraham at Kurban Bayram, raw and outraged. Except that Rifat had not been a sheep, he had been a person and, like her other brother Egrem, he was dead – killed by a *fis* whose only purpose was to pursue all of her people until they no longer existed. And that point was not far away. Now there only remained her parents, possibly cousin Mimoza, although she was not related to the Berishas by blood, and of course herself.

As she started to pull on the first of the many jumpers she would wear on top of her thin cotton dress, Engelushjia began to cry. Her beloved brother Rifat's death made her something she could never have imagined being, an only child. Her parents were both fearful and vengeful, and with her mother now pregnant again Engelushjia was the only member of the family who could safely go out into the street. She alone was a true woman, her milk uncontaminated by the blood of a man's growing seed inside her. It made her wonder if, should a man ever love her, she might just kill herself after she had experienced her one taste of bliss. After all, there would be no one left to avenge her by that time. At least if she killed herself she would deprive the Vloras of the satisfaction. As soon as Rifat's shirt was in the window, her father's days would be numbered. There were any number of Vloras he could kill – and he would – but only one male Berisha – Rahman, her father. As soon as Mehmet, Aryan or Mehti Vlora had fallen victim to her father's knife, Engelushjia knew that he would be nothing more than a walking dead man.

Why it had all started up again so suddenly, she didn't know. Perhaps Rifat had done something that none of them knew about. Since Egrem's death he had spent a lot of time away from home, often teasing that poor fool Mehti Vlora. And then there had, of course, been his trip abroad with that woman. Engelushjia still had the number Rifat had given her – she would have to let the woman know of his death; after what Rifat had done for her, she would want to know. It had been the woman who had given Rifat his car – not that their parents knew about that. They assumed he must have stolen it. But the car was not of immediate concern now for, with Rifat's death, it had seemingly disappeared. Engelushjia knew better than to suggest that her parents report it missing to the police. Thinking it was stolen, they wouldn't dare, and for her to tell them the hurtful truth about all that now was pointless. The fact was the Vloras, maybe even that moron Mehti, had killed Rifat and proved themselves dishonourable scum by all but cutting his head off. And in time they would kill her father too.

Attempting to swim against a rising tide of misery and panic, Engelushjia dried her eyes roughly on the sleeve of her jumper. In the kitchen there would only be tea to drink and nothing to eat, a fact that would normally depress Engelushjia. But not today. Today her stomach was sore and as tight as a current, wanting nothing except to have the whole thing over and done with once and for ever.

As she entered the kitchen she was reminded by her parents' measured actions of the tortuous pace at which their tragedies would be played out. Rahman was patiently rolling a stack of cigarettes to get him through the day while Aliya, her belly big in contrast to her sunken, sleepless face, made tea like one in a dream. It had taken her father months to avenge Egrem's death – the Vloras had still not found the body. They must have seen Egrem's shirt disappear from the Berishas' window, but they still did not *know*. And while they did not know, it had been thought dangerous but acceptable for Rahman and Rifat to go outside – except at night when all sorts could occur under the cover of darkness. But night-time was when Rifat had liked to go out most, and night-time was when he had died.

'I don't want any tea,' Engelushjia said as her mother made to pour a glass for her.

'Oh.'

'I'm going out,' the young girl said, throwing a scarf round her head and tying it tightly under her chin.

Looking up briefly from his cigarette making, his eyes red with sleeplessness, Rahman asked, 'Where are you going? To do what?'

'I don't know,' Engelushjia said without, her father noted, the usual tone of respect in her voice. 'I feel restless, I—'

'All the more reason to stay inside then,' Aliya commented. 'You've had a shock and with the streets so unsafe . . .'

'Oh, the streets are safe enough for me, aren't they, Mother?' the girl retorted hotly. 'Even the Vloras won't touch a virgin girl, though I hate them all and wish them dead. Such is the stupidity of our customs!'

'You should not abuse the laws laid down by Lek Dukagjini,' her father said angrily. 'Good Gheg that he was, he set them down for a reason.'

'If a man's honour is tainted he has no choice but to take his revenge in blood,' Aliya added. 'Even though it kills my soul, we must accept what has happened to Rifat and do the best that we can for him, which is to avenge his blood.'

'So Father will kill a Vlora man and then those that remain will get to Father and kill him.'

'If that is what Allah wills,' Aliya said, lowering her eyes respectfully to the floor.

It was almost as if, in that moment, Engelushjia Berisha saw her parents with new eyes. What her father was saying was that he, the gentle Rahman Berisha she had always been able to take her troubles to, intended to kill a man for the second time. Her ancient-looking pregnant mother approved. And yet both of her brothers were dead because of this mad code of honour that, with a fierce suddenness she could not explain, now made absolutely no sense. As it was, her father couldn't work for fear of assassination. Until she became pregnant, Aliya had supported the family with begging and stealing. Now that she was with child and therefore a legitimate target under the rules of the Kunan of Lek Dukagjini, they all relied upon handouts from Mimoza, although how long her Turkish husband would tolerate this was anyone's guess. It was, Engelushjia thought, both desperate and mad to carry on like this. As tears sprang to her eyes for the second time that morning she said, 'This has got to stop! I'm going out!'

'But there is nothing you can do!' her mother cried and moved forward to try to stop her daughter from leaving.

'Leave it be, silly girl! This is men's work!' her father added sternly.

'I don't care!' Engelushjia cried, freeing herself from her mother's grasping hands and then breaking into a run. 'My brothers are dead! Rifat was butchered like an animal! I saw it, Mother – me! I can't lose any more of my family! I can't!'

'But—'

'No!' she screamed and flew out of the kitchen and down the stairs. Engelushjia looked back just once to see, through her tears, the blurred vision of her mother panting heavily in the hallway. But the sight didn't stop her. From the house she ran into the street. It was only when the cold winter air had filtered into her brain for a few minutes that she realised she didn't have a clue what she should do now.

'So you think that the family of the victim will go after this other clan,' Ayşe Farsakoğlu said rather more baldly than İkmen had intended.

'I think it's a real possibility,' he answered. 'Albanian blood feuds are notorious both for their brutality and the inevitability of the process. They all adhere to a set of rules known collectively as the Kunan of Lek Dukagjini. This states that blood on one side must result in the letting of blood on the other. If Rifat Berisha was killed by the Vlora family, we can expect their blood to flow very soon.'

'Does your informant think that Berisha's death was definitely the work of this other lot, sir?' Orhan Tepe asked.

The three uniformed officers turned towards him as he spoke. His question went to the heart of what İkmen was proposing they do. Staking out both the Berisha place and an address on Tahtakale Caddesi was not going to be cheap with regard to man hours and so there had to be at least reasonable suspicion regarding this other family.

'Forensics are not yet in on Rifat's body,' İkmen said and lit up a cigarette. 'And with no witnesses, as yet, there is no way we can even think about arresting any-one.' He paused briefly in order to cough. 'However, my informant does know that the feud between the Berishas and the Vloras is longstanding and serious. Whether the Vloras killed Rifat or not, the Berishas will probably think they did. That is enough, in my mind, to warrant us doing what we are doing today.'

'So what do you want us to actually do then, sir?' a young officer called Hikmet Yıldız asked.

'I want you to watch the properties, observe the comings and goings around them and note and report anything unusual or suspicious. By that I mean things like known faces turning up at either address or movements of people in or out of the buildings.'

'And if things get rough?' Tepe asked. 'For instance if we observe a Berisha attacking a Vlora or—'

'You contact me before you do anything,' İkmen said gravely. 'It's important that they remain ignorant of our presence and suspicions.'

'But what if they actually try to kill each other?' an older constable called Roditi inquired.

'Well, as officers of the law, you will have to prevent that,' İkmen said, 'but I would prefer it if you try not to arrest protagonists at the scene. We don't officially have anything on the Vloras and the last thing I want to do is compromise my informant. Now, do any of you speak Albanian?'

The three 'uniforms' plus Tepe looked sheepishly at each other. Then they all looked blankly at İkmen.

'I take it that's a "no" then,' he said as he moved behind his desk and sat down.

'We do know that the Berishas speak Turkish though, don't we, sir?' a frowning Tepe observed.

'Yes. As do the Vloras, but it would be helpful if we could understand what they are saying when they speak to each other. Unfortunately, we don't have any

Albanians on the force or they would be here now instead of you poor souls, so we'll just have to make the best of what we do have. İnşallah we will gain something useful from our efforts. Any more questions?'

For a few moments the occupants of İkmen's office looked at each other questioningly before, finally, Tepe said, 'No, sir, I think we're all clear.'

Various heads nodded in agreement.

'Good. Off you go then,' İkmen said with a wave of what some considered an imperious hand.

They started to leave, with the exception of Tepe who approached İkmen's desk.

'Sir?'

'Yes?'

'Is anything going to happen about that surgery Rifat Berisha had?'

İkmen put his cigarette out, lit another, and then looked up gravely at his junior officer. 'That fascinates you, doesn't it, Orhan?'

'Only inasmuch as I find the idea of selling your bodily organs repellent,' Tepe said as he, too, lit a cigarette.

İkmen sighed. 'I am planning to formally interview the Berishas in the near future,' he said, 'and I will raise the subject with them. It is always possible, you know, that he might have had his kidney removed legitimately. Even if he didn't, getting hold of the buggers who organise these deals is notoriously difficult. Not to mention the doctors who perform the operations.'

'They're usually based abroad, aren't they, sir?'

'Usually,' İkmen said, 'but we never know what life may throw at us, do we? And in this case, my dear Orhan, our surgeon might be home-grown.'

'Yes, sir.'

'Well, on your way then,' İkmen said in dismissal. 'Can't let the uniforms out on important business unescorted, can we?'

Catching just the edge of a twinkle in his boss's eye, Orhan Tepe smiled as he said, 'No, sir.'

His friend was, Balthazar Cohen thought as he watched Mehmet Suleyman stride purposefully into the living room, growing even more handsome with age. Tall, dark and grave, Mehmet was turning into one of those middle-aged heroes Balthazar remembered being so popular in films in the 1960s. Not of course that he would tell Mehmet this.

'You were very late last night,' he said as a visible leer crossed his features. Strange the way Mehmet was always late home when old Dr Babur Halman was out of town.

'I had some work to do,' the younger man replied.

'Oh, well, I hope you felt relieved afterwards.'

'Cohen!'

Even though the handsome eyes blazed in line with the sharpness of his voice, Cohen knew it was only a warning. They were old friends, they'd been here before.

Cohen lit a cigarette and watched with some amusement the rather laborious process Suleyman employed in order to get his tie just right. Finally, tiring of his

75

friend's fastidiousness, he said, 'Berekiah's going in to see the old man today.'

'Yes, I know, I'm taking him. Remember?'

'I hope he manages to persuade him to join up.'

Suleyman frowned. 'I don't think that İkmen's in the business of making the force appear sweeter than it really is, you know, Cohen.'

'My son needs a job, Mehmet,' Cohen said as he raised his dark-rimmed eyes to his friend's face. 'He can't work for Lazar for ever. I mean, if he were running the gold shop himself that would be one thing. But to be just an assistant and at his age – that's a job for a child and he's a man. He needs a man's job now.'

'Well, it's for Berekiah to decide,' Suleyman said with a sigh. 'İnşallah he will make the right decision.'

'Mmm.'

The telephone, which now that he was housebound sat permanently at Cohen's side, trilled into life. He picked it up with what Suleyman observed to be a very shaky hand.

'Yes?' he said into the instrument and then, looking up at his friend, 'Yes. He's still here . . . Yes . . . One moment.' He placed his other shaking hand over the mouthpiece and said to Suleyman, 'I think it's your father.'

'My father? But—'

'Just take the call, Mehmet,' Cohen said and handed the phone to him. 'Whoever it is, he wants you.'

With a shrug, Suleyman took the instrument from Cohen and walked towards the window.

'Hello?' he said cautiously. 'Can I help you?'

'Mehmet, it's me,' a familiar elderly voice replied. 'My son, you must listen, we need to talk.'

'I think we did that some time ago, didn't we?'

'Child, I need to see you before all this stupidity means we never see each other again!' There was a desperation in his father's voice that made Mehmet pay attention. 'I have been speaking to your brother,' his father continued, 'and I think that the three of us really do need to meet. I can reserve a table at Rejan's. Talk to Murad and pick an evening that suits you both. He can let me know.'

His father's tone was beginning to worry Mehmet now. He wondered why his father had suddenly chosen to move out from under his wife's harsh gaze and contact him again. 'Father, you and Mother are quite well, aren't you?' he asked as his heart began to pound inside his chest.

'There is nothing wrong with either your mother or myself,' his father replied. 'I just want an end to all of this bitterness in our family.'

'And Mother?'

'Your mother makes her own decisions, as you well know,' the old man said with a sigh. Mehmet could all too easily picture his thin, world-weary face.

'I know,' he replied with a smile. 'I will speak to Murad.'

'You will come?'

'If my brother comes, so will I.'

A faint sigh from the other end of the line signalled to Mehmet that his father was very relieved at this, albeit qualified, acceptance from his son.

'You know I've never felt any resentment towards you personally, don't you, Father?' Mehmet began. 'I—'

'We will discuss all things when we meet, my son,' his father interrupted. 'A man should eat with his sons and . . . Call your brother soon, won't you?'

'You have my word that I will,' Mehmet said, responding formally to what sounded almost like tears in his father's voice.

'Thank you, my son. We will speak again soon.'

'Yes, we shall,' Mehmet said with genuine gentleness for the old man in his voice. 'Goodbye, Father.'

'Goodbye, Mehmet.'

Had Berekiah Cohen not walked in resplendent in his older brother's suit just at that moment it is uncertain how long Mehmet Suleyman would have spent staring out of the window in the wake of that telephone call. But Berekiah wanted a man who had some dress sense to judge his ensemble. And the only man in the apartment who qualified was Mehmet.

For just a second, the aristocratic Turk frowned. 'Mmm,' he said, 'grey suit with grey shoes is,' he smiled suddenly and dazzlingly, 'very smart indeed, Berekiah, if a little too stylish for a police station. Not that I have ever allowed myself to be dictated to by the lowest common denominator.'

Estelle Cohen, who had been watching her son's entrance from just inside the kitchen door, moved forward rapidly to take his face between her hands. 'Didn't I tell you you looked just beautiful?' she said and kissed a slightly resistant Berekiah on the cheek. 'Nobody understands good dressing like Mehmet and if he says you're smart, well . . .'

'Mum, please, don't fuss.'

'As long as the Inspector likes him, that's all that really matters,' Balthazar said sternly. 'You be polite, respectful and show real interest, Berekiah. The Inspector is a great man and don't you forget it.'

'No, Father.'

Fearing that his friend might now be on the edge of one of his frequent eulogies about İkmen or his own days on the beat, Suleyman brought proceedings smartly to a close.

'Well,' he said, turning towards Berekiah, 'we'd better go.'

'Right.' Going first to his mother and then across to his father, Berekiah kissed them both before making his way towards the door.

'You will look after him, won't you, Mehmet?' Estelle asked with the kind of strained concern in her eyes Suleyman knew sprang from the fact that the Cohen's eldest son Yusuf now lived in an institution. His mind broken by months of fighting and anxiety in the eastern provinces, Yusuf would probably never come home again now, which left Berekiah to carry all of his parents' hopes, ambitions and fears.

Suleyman smiled. 'He'll be fine, Estelle,' he said soothingly, 'and you know that Çetin Bey won't force him to commit to something he's unsure about.'

'Yes.'

'Oh, will you let those boys go now, woman!' a frustrated voice called from its static position at the other side of the room. 'They have men's business to attend to!'

Smiling once more into Estelle's anxious eyes, Suleyman squeezed one of her hands and then left. Had he looked back a moment later, he would have seen the hardness in her face as she looked down at her husband. But it was not until he and Berekiah reached the front door that they heard her start.

'Don't you ever tell me what is and is not my business!' she yelled.

'I—'

'You have absolutely no right to tell me anything, Balthazar!'

Suleyman looked at Berekiah, who shrugged before saying, wryly, 'Families.'

'Indeed,' the Turkish aristocrat replied and then held the door open for his young friend 'Let's go.'

The apartment block İkmen's informant had named as housing the Vlora family did not, in Tepe's judgement, look like the sort of place either he or his temporary partner on this observation, Hikmet Yıldız, would feel comfortable living in. Of probably early twentieth-century vintage, it boasted a cheap clothing shop on the ground floor with even cheaper apartments above. Drab, by the look of it even in the summer, the place had a couple of boarded-up windows on the second floor, and a pile of litter and filth had gathered by the front entrance. Tepe could not help feeling that the building's kapıcı, if such a place had one, deserved to be beaten for such slackness.

Since the two officers had been observing the property, from early that morning, they had seen numerous people come and go: headscarfed women carrying empty baskets, on their way to shop in either the Mısır Çarşısı or amongst the local street traders; short, bundled up men wearing flat caps and smoking, heading for their various places of employment; and of course children, lots of them, running into and out of the building, laughing and shrieking as they went. The only constant in this shifting scene was the small group of middle-aged men who squatted companionably beside the steps up into the building. There were three of them and they had been where they were now when Tepe and Yıldız had arrived. Two of the men were small and dusky, while the third was of a rather different order, being tall and blond. Typically, the men spent their time talking, laughing and smoking. The officers didn't know whether or not they were Vlora men but they were almost certainly Albanian. A brief pass by Tepe across that side of the street had quickly established the lack of Turkish, Greek or any other recognisable language between them.

Yıldız looked down at the cards in his hand and then placed them face up on the table.

'I quit,' he said and emptied what was left of his tea into his mouth.

Tepe looked briefly at the cards in front of his partner and then laughed. 'This really isn't your game, is it?' he said.

'I don't like these places.' Yıldız looked around the plain, exclusively male interior of the kahvehane.

Tepe shrugged. 'But for our purposes, they're really

useful,' he said. 'After all, what else do men in kahvehanes do but drink tea, play games, sit and watch. We could quite easily sit here all day without attracting attention from anyone.'

'A pushover, our job, then,' Yıldız answered with a smile, 'what with one of these places on every street.'

'Oh, there are still plenty of nooks and crannies where those of subtle disposition can go to hide themselves away,' the older man said sagely. 'You'll learn all about that when you make the mistake we all do.'

'What mistake is that, sir?'

'The one you make when you underestimate people.'

'So did you . . .'

Tepe smiled. 'When I was in uniform I was assigned to a stake-out team led by Inspector İskender. He was young and inexperienced, as were we all. But we moved quickly and on what was good information to a house in Edirnekapı. When we got there, however, the place was quite empty save for the body of our dead informant, who had also been the dealer's wife. The previous evening, just before he left for Bulgaria, the dealer had decapitated the woman and then placed her head on a spike. It was the first thing we saw as we entered the building.' He sighed and folded his arms across his chest. 'I was quite sick, as I recall.'

Yıldız, who had been listening intently to Tepe's story, had nevertheless kept one eye on the goings-on across the road. And so it was he and not Tepe who first saw the small group of Albanians move quickly back inside their apartment building.

'I wonder what's making them shift so smartly,' he

said as he flicked his head in the direction of the retreating men.

Scanning the area with his eyes, Tepe could not immediately see anything that might obviously alarm the men. It was in fact his ears that first picked up something untoward. For what was approaching the men was, due to its small size, only noticeable by its voice, which was female, foreign and very angry.

It was not something the crowd around the owner of the voice wanted to be close to. And so they parted, revealing to the two officers the slight figure of a small headscarfed girl shouting the name 'Mehmet' in amongst a load of other completely unintelligible words.

Tepe stood and looked at the girl more closely. 'If I'm not mistaken,' he murmured, 'that girl is Engelushjia Berisha.'

'Are you sure?' Yıldız asked.

'Fairly,' Tepe replied. As he watched, one of the windows on the first floor of the apartment block opened and a man's mocking face appeared.

'Mehmet!' the girl shouted as she, too, saw the face. 'Mehmet Vlora!' Then flying into what must have been the most vitriolic Albanian, she nearly screamed herself hoarse. The mocking man in his turn yelled down what could only have been abuse at her.

'I think we should get out there, just in case,' Tepe said. He threw some banknotes down onto the table and retrieved his overcoat from the back of his chair. His partner, following in silence, kept his eyes firmly trained upon the girl who was now jumping around in her agitation.

As soon as Tepe opened the kahvehane door, the damp winter air hit him like a hammer. It made him wonder, briefly, how Engelushjia managed to survive in her thin cotton skirt – but then she had her towering anger to keep her warm.

'I wonder why Roditi and Farsakoğlu didn't warn us about this,' Tepe said as soon as Yıldız had joined him on the pavement.

'Perhaps the girl slipped past them,' Yıldız replied. 'Do you think that we ought to contact Inspector İkmen before we do anything, sir?'

'I don't know,' Tepe said as he watched the girl suddenly leap up the steps and into the apartment building. 'But right now I think that we should go and observe,' and he broke into a run.

When they reached the landing of the first floor, the two officers found Engelushjia Berisha standing with her back to them. In front of her, his hands placed arrogantly on his hips, was the man who had mocked her from the window, who the policemen assumed was Mehmet Vlora. Beside him was the other short, dark man who had, until the girl came along, companionably shared the front step with him.

Pausing only briefly to glance at the two men who had arrived at the top of the stairs, Engelushjia Berisha first spat onto the floor in front of the brothers and then took something from the pocket of her skirt.

Yıldız, who was standing rather deeper in the shadow of the stairs than Tepe, nevertheless had a clearer view of the scene before them. Leaning forward to whisper in his superior's ear he said, 'She's got a knife.' Which, given the obvious mirth this object elicited from the girl's intended victims, seemed somewhat incongruous.

Everything changed when Mehmet Vlora produced a rather larger weapon of his own. Looking briefly across at the two men in the shadows, a smirk just catching his coarse features, Mehmet Vlora raised the hunting knife high enough for it to be exactly level with the girl's throat. Then, slowly, he growled something out in Albanian. The girl's back visibly stiffened, as did the arm in which she carried her knife.

'I'm going in,' Tepe murmured to his partner. He drew his service revolver from the holster under his arm and stepped out of the shadows, holding his police ID out in front of him. 'Police!' he shouted 'Stay where you are!'

'Don't move and nobody will get hurt!' a similarly armed Yıldız added as he, too, moved out into the thin landing light.

And for a moment nobody did move. The girl, her mouth now open in shock, looked too confused to react, as indeed did the Albanian men – for just a moment. When the spell broke, movement came with wild rapidity. Using what seemed to be only the power in his eyes, Mehmet Vlora ordered his brother back into the apartment and slammed the door hard shut behind him.

Rushing forward to try to stop the door from closing, Tepe only narrowly missed getting his foot crushed in the process. Swearing with frustration, he took hold of the now screaming Engelushjia Berisha in one hand and waved his gun at the door with the other.

'Well, break the fucking thing down, Yıldız!' he shouted at his partner.

'Yes, sir!'

Two well-placed kicks were all that it took to reduce the poorly constructed door to broken panels and matchwood. The Vlora brothers were no longer behind it. As the two officers dragged a screaming and unintelligible Engelushjia into the Vloras' apartment, it was easy to see in the paucity of that place that the men were not there. The only occupant was a tiny old woman, her head covered in a thick, black veil.

'They must have gone down the fire escape,' a panting Tepe said to Yıldız and then, turning to the old woman, he barked, 'Where's your fire escape?'

'I imagine it's somewhere on the side of the building,' she replied in heavily accented but perfect Turkish. 'They usually are.'

Tepe shot the woman a vicious glare and told Yıldız to search all the rooms. While he was doing that, Tepe turned to Engelushjia Berisha for the first time. 'Bit of a mistake to come here, wasn't it? I—'

'Why are you here?' the girl screamed by way of reply. 'Why are you interfering in people's private business?'

'It's a good question,' the old woman said, 'and one to which I, personally, feel I deserve an answer.'

'Well, when people start threatening other people with knives,' Tepe began, slowly as if to an idiot.

'A scene you just obviously "happened to be passing",' the old woman jibed.

'Well, er . . .' Tepe stumbled. Knowing what İkmen

had said about not allowing the protagonists in this drama to realise that they were being watched did not make convincing this astute old woman any easier – not to mention the deeply suspicious Engelushjia Berisha. 'Yes, we were,' he said, 'and as—'

'Nothing at all on the fire escape, sir,' Yıldız said as he re-entered the main room, his revolver now held limply at his side. 'Given the time involved I reckon they must have climbed into another apartment and got out that way.'

'Is that what happened?' Tepe demanded of the seemingly amused old woman.

'Maybe. Maybe not,' she said with a shrug and then added slyly, 'Our men do as they wish, just as you people do.'

'Madam—'

'And besides,' she said, flicking her eyes across at Engelushjia before she continued, 'my boys were only joking with my young friend here, is that not so, young lady?'

'Well, yes. Yes, of—'

'Oh, so knives are some sort of toy now, are they?' retorted an increasingly agitated Tepe. 'Just having some sort of a laugh with sharp instruments, were you?'

A pause during which a frightened-eyed Engelushjia Berisha appeared to lose the power of speech passed in what felt to Tepe like a dangerous silence. Looking nervously across at Yıldız, he noticed that the younger man was eyeing the old woman with open revulsion.

'It is, I believe, up to this young lady,' she said at

length, 'to decide whether making a complaint against my three boys is appropriate. If it is not, then I think that you gentlemen will have to go.' And then smiling at Engelushjia she added, 'Well?'

'We were only playing, Mehmet and his brothers and—'

'So why did they run when they saw us?' Tepe snapped.

'I imagine it is because the Turkish police enjoy persecuting Albanians,' the old woman said, surprisingly calmly. 'My sons were afraid, an emotion exacerbated, no doubt, by the idea that you would completely misunderstand the game they were playing with Engelushjia – which of course you have.'

'Madam—'

'You people do not take any time to get to know us,' she said. 'You do not learn our language, you misunderstand our customs . . . Of course a few, a very few of my kind, do allow you the odd glimpse into our world.' Then looking up sharply into Tepe's eyes, she continued, 'One such is Mustafa Bajraktar.'

The name meant nothing to Tepe. He shrugged and was about to turn his attention back to Engelushjia Berisha when the old woman added, 'But then Mustafa is related by blood to one of your fellows.'

'What, a Turk or a police officer?' Yıldız asked.

The old woman laughed. 'Why, both, you stupid boy!' she said, flashing him what once must have been a very attractive grin. 'Mustafa, or Samsun as he is known here, has a cousin in your police force.'

'Oh? And?'

'And so,' she said, grinning widely at both officers, 'perhaps I am thinking that Samsun the catamite has perhaps spoken with his cousin, the son of Ayşe Bajraktar, the witch. You may know him, the İkmen boy. Samsun's relationship with him could explain your presence here now.'

Tepe's mouth opened unbidden, but he didn't speak – he was too shocked for that.

Chapter 7

İkmen, as was his custom when he was particularly agitated, was smoking furiously.

'So tell me again,' he said as he lit the end of a new cigarette off the butt of the old one, 'this woman, this . . .'

'Angeliki Vlora, sir,' Tepe said as he stood very straight in front of his superior's desk. 'She said that some person called Samsun is related to you and that your mother, Ayşe Bajraktar—'

'But I had never even heard of a family called Vlora until yesterday!' İkmen exploded, then added, more to himself than to Tepe, 'How this woman knows of my mother I can't imagine. I mean, I knew all of my mother's friends, not by name admittedly. Great crowds of Albanian women used to take us children to the hamam . . . Mind you, I suppose Mother did read cards and cast spells for many, many—'

'She was quite clear on this point, sir,' Tepe said, feeling the need to cut across İkmen's self-absorbed musings.

'Yes, well . . .' İkmen looked down at his desk with a troubled, almost haunted, expression on his face. When he looked up again, his face had cleared and, although still frowning, he appeared to be himself once more. 'So you have Engelushjia Berisha down in the cells, Tepe? Is that right?'

'She bit Yıldız on the neck,' the young man said. 'I—'

'Oh, it's all right, I do understand,' İkmen replied and wearily waved his sergeant in the direction of a chair. 'Sit down, will you, Orhan.'

He did as he was asked.

'Look, I know that her assault on Yıldız gave you really very little choice but to arrest Miss Berisha, but I did tell you not to intervene.'

'Well, if you'd told us your informant was a member of your family perhaps we wouldn't have!' Tepe answered hotly. 'Besides, that girl and the Vloras were armed with knives, sir! Serious knives! Somebody was going to get hurt at the very least.'

'Yes, yes, I appreciate all that, Orhan, but an Albanian blood feud is not a game, you fool! I was given confidential information about these families by an informant you may well have now put in danger.'

'Oh, come on, sir, that's hardly fair! Angeliki Vlora knew all about this Samsun person.'

'She speculated, Tepe! She saw policemen, thought about how we could possibly know about her family and made an educated guess. The Vloras are not obviously connected to the recently bereaved Berishas. The only way we could have known about the family link is if someone told us and the most likely candidate for that is someone connected to Turks in some way!'

'Well, the cousin of Aliya Berisha is married—'

'People "in blood", as they say, do not talk to police-men!' İkmen banged his fist down hard on his desk. 'No, it would have had to come from someone outside that situation. And because it would seem that every Albanian in the world apparently knows that Samsun and I are cousins, she is the most likely contender.' Cigarette still in his mouth, İkmen bowed his head and placed his hands on his ears. 'Oh, Allah!'

'Sir . . .'

'Oh, it's not really your fault at all, Orhan,' he said wearily. 'It was me. I didn't think through the implications . . .' And then to himself he added, 'Perhaps I should give this to Suleyman . . .'

'But we do have that witness statement now, don't we, sir?' Tepe said, alarmed at the way İkmen seemed to be berating himself. 'The old man who heard something heavy being thrown from a car?'

'You mean Enver Alpe? Yes, not that he actually saw anything in the fog. So we can't know that the heavy thing that was dumped out of that unseen car was without doubt the body of Rifat Berisha.'

'But it is a start, sir,' Tepe said, trying to be positive. 'It puts a time, possibly, on the disposal of the body. People are thinking, they are coming forward.'

'Yes,' İkmen said on a sigh. 'Though not to any great effect . . .'

There was a knock on the door.

'Come in,' İkmen said, and the door opened to reveal a very smartly dressed young man.

'Er, Inspector . . .'

'Oh, there you are, Berekiah,' İkmen said with a

broad smile. 'I'm so sorry I couldn't take you to lunch myself.'

'I do understand.'

'Please sit down,' he said, gesturing towards one of the chairs beside Tepe. 'This is my sergeant, Orhan Tepe.'

Briefly standing, Tepe exchanged a small bow with the younger man and then both of them sat down.

'Mr Cohen is the son of our old friend Balthazar Cohen,' İkmen explained to Tepe before turning to Berekiah once again. 'I should imagine that Inspector Suleyman took you somewhere a little more stylish than the places I would have chosen.'

Berekiah grinned. 'We went to Pandeli's.'

'There! What did I tell you? But don't get the idea that we dine like that every day, Berekiah.'

'No,' he laughed. 'Dad always had a saying, "Working lunch means simit on a street corner".'

'Your father is a wise and perceptive man.'

Looking first at Tepe, Berekiah moved his head a bit closer towards İkmen. 'I haven't yet made up my mind, though,' he began. 'I don't—'

'Nobody would expect you to make such a decision quickly, Berekiah,' İkmen said gravely. 'Mr Lazar pays you generously and treats you well. And although you would have a secure position within the police, I'm not going to lie to you and tell you how marvellous it is out on the streets. Sometimes we have to see awful things, the stuff of nightmares. Sometimes we are in mortal danger, and we're often either too cold or boiling hot. We're not liked, drug dealers from all around the world laugh at us as they do at every other police force on the planet, but . . .'

'My dad loved it.' As the young man looked up, İkmen saw that his eyes had just a slight liquid quality to them.

'Yes,' İkmen said, his face now a little taut around the memory of the unfortunate Cohen. 'Yes, he did.'

After a short pause, during which none of the men looked at each other, Berekiah said, 'Well, thank you very much for your time, Inspector İkmen, but, er, I had best be going now.'

The young man rose to his feet and first shook hands with Tepe, then extended his hand to İkmen. The older man, however, stood up from his chair and took the young man firmly in his arms.

'It has been my pleasure,' he said as they embraced.

'Thank you, Çetin Bey.'

İkmen went over to the door and held it open for his departing guest. As the young man left, İkmen added, 'You know that if you or your family need anything, you only have to ask.'

'Thank you,' Berekiah said with a smile.

Tepe was aware of İkmen's legendary generosity but, he wondered how in the world this poorly paid, incorruptible man with nine children could possibly be in any position to offer help to anyone. But then İkmen was of the old school – irreligious yet imbued with old Islamic notions of social welfare and generosity. Suleyman, in a rather superior Ottoman manner, was very like his old boss in this respect. As different as they were in status and background, İkmen and Suleyman were, Tepe was beginning to appreciate, really very alike. Once again he wondered if he would ever be able to occupy Suleyman's place in İkmen's scheme of things.

When he'd closed the door behind Berekiah Cohen, İkmen allowed himself some moments for deep thought and hard smoking before he spoke again. Although he had fully attended to his conversation with the young man, part of his brain had also been working along other, more work-based lines.

Eventually, looking up and smiling at Tepe, he said, 'I think I'm going to release Engelushjia Berisha now. Take her back to her parents.'

'Oh, but sir,' Tepe began, 'she—'

'I'm sure that, despite his injuries, Yıldız will survive her attack, Orhan.'

'She broke the skin, you know, sir,' Tepe said, frowning. 'He had to go and see the doctor.'

'Who will have given him several quite painful injections by this time,' İkmen said as he moved round to the front of his desk, 'all of which elicits nothing but sympathy from me. However, we must not lose sight of the fact that the main thing at issue for us is the unlawful death of Rifat Berisha. And if, in pursuit of the truth about that, certain other, less important offences are allowed to pass us by—'

'Sir!'

İkmen's face suddenly hardened. 'Look, it's like this,' he said. 'Those "in blood" don't want us getting involved in their world. The Berishas want to kill the Vloras and vice versa. They won't tell us anything unless we have something they want that we can give them first. I may be proved wrong, but Engelushjia's freedom may well be that thing.' Moving forward so that his face was almost touching Tepe's, he went on, 'I'm still not convinced that the Vloras killed Rifat anyway. But in order to find out who else might have done it, not to mention the circumstances of his recent surgery, we need to enter Rifat's world. And in order to do that, we have to somehow gain his family's confidence, which, given today's events, will not be easy.'

'No, sir, I—'

'However,' İkmen raised a hand to silence his deputy, 'if we give them back their daughter we may yet have a chance.' He retrieved his coat from the back of the door. 'Come on,' he said and moved smartly out into the corridor.

'But what about the Vloras, sir?' Tepe asked as he grabbed his coat from the back of his chair and hurried after İkmen.

'Oh, I haven't forgotten about them, Orhan,' a retreating İkmen boomed back at him, 'and in good time they will be dealt with, of that you can be sure.'

As soon as they had cleared the apartment of the Qerimi *fis* who lived below, Mehmet, Aryan and Mehti Vlora had split up. If the police were in the apartment, the 'boys' wanted to be elsewhere. Mehmet had briefly checked on their mother after the police had gone. But both she and the kokain she had secreted in the folds of her dress had been safe – Angeliki was nothing if not resourceful and, besides, the police hadn't come about narcotics anyway. Either they were following Rifat Berisha's sister or, more likely, as Angeliki had thought, they'd been tipped off to watch the Vlora apartment because of Rifat's death. Mehmet, his hands thrust deep into his tattered pockets as he walked along the busy Divan Yolu, knew that he was not, unfortunately, to blame this time. And since Aryan had been with him for the whole evening during which it was said that Rifat Berisha had died, that left only Mehti. Dull though he was, Mehti would surely have mentioned such a momentous event in his life. The only thing that could possibly top that would be the discovery of their brother Dhori's body. Everyone knew that Rahman Berisha had killed him – only a Berisha could be so cowardly as to conceal a body, thereby halting, until now, the progress of *gjakmaria*. But that was probably all by the way now, Mehmet thought as he passed in front of the grim façade of the Imperial Ottoman Tombs. Now the Berishas had, or thought they had, good reason to take out another Vlora man. He wondered how long it would be before Rifat's shirt hung in one of the upper windows of his parents' apartment.

As he weaved his way through the thick traffic choking Babıali Caddesi, Mehmet's eyes were distracted by an attractive woman wearing a long, dark coat. Young and pretty, she was standing talking to a far larger and considerably older woman. But although his eyes were drawn by the sight of the girl, it was eventually the older woman that he actually stopped and looked at. And as recognition dawned, his anger increased, for as his mother had said, if anyone within the fellowship of ex-patriot Albanians was going to tell tales to the police, it would probably be this cousin of a policeman.

Mehmet realised it would be unwise to take issue publicly with the unnatural Samsun Bajraktar on this busy street, but walking straight past her without a word was asking rather too much of his now mounting temper. And so he opted for a more subtle, if still satisfyingly vengeful approach. He moved up behind the transsexual and whispered in her ear.

'I know you've given information about us to your kinsman in the police,' he hissed as his victim started to turn round to face him, 'so you rest uneasily in your filthy bed, you unnatural fuck!'

Before Samsun Bajraktar could turn round to face him full on, Mehmet Vlora dived back into the crowds traversing Divan Yolu and was gone. It occurred to him later that it was just possible Samsun had not informed the police of anything. Perhaps they had, after all, been following Engelushjia Berisha. Either way, it didn't much matter. Catamites like her deserved everything that was coming to them even if that did mean being in blood with the Bajraktar *fis*. Perhaps taking on a really powerful clan like them would be the making of the Vloras. After all, had not the Bajraktars seen off all their enemies many years ago with astonishing ferocity? Mehmet pulled his jacket tight round his thin frame and marched determinedly towards Sultan Ahmet Square.

Working with the Berishas in a way that they would understand was, İkmen knew, the key to success with these people. And so, strange as it felt to be doing this, he kept an unwilling Engelushjia between himself and Tepe as he spoke to the parents. To them she was, he imagined, a police hostage of sorts.

'So tell me about Rifat,' he asked the grey-faced couple before him. 'What kind of young man was he?'

Rahman shrugged. 'As usual.'

'Meaning?'

'He liked to enjoy himself.' He looked up blankly. 'You know?'

'No,' İkmen said wryly, 'I don't. That's why I'm asking you.'

In return for this retort he got back silence. Briefly he looked across at a somewhat tense Tepe before he decided to take a different approach.

With what was usually a winning smile, he began, 'OK, let's get realistic about all this, shall we? I know that you are "in blood", as you say, with the Vlora clan.' He lifted a hand to silence Rahman Berisha whose mouth had suddenly filled with protest. 'How we know this is not your concern, just as why and to what extent you are in blood with the Vloras is not mine. My only concern, sir, is to catch the person who killed your son. Now if that is a Vlora—'

'Well, of course it is!' Aliya burst out, only to be slapped hard across the face for her indiscretion by her husband.

Tepe, instantly on his feet, was only prevented from intervening by one of İkmen's thin arms, which came out quickly to prevent his officer from doing something unwise.

'Now,' he said tersely, 'I suggest we all calm down. Hitting—'

'The woman spoke out of turn!' Rahman Berisha fumed.

'Look, Mr Berisha,' İkmen snapped as he motioned Tepe to take his seat once again, 'my job involves finding the truth about why people die unnaturally. Unless the Vloras did indeed kill your son, then I have no interest in them beyond establishing where they all were on the night of Rifat's death. They may or may not have killed him but until I have proof that they did I must look at every aspect of your son's life plus the forensic evidence as supplied by our laboratory.' Raising his hands to count out the various points he was making, İkmen continued, 'I need to know who his friends were, what his job was, whether there were any women in his life, what his health was like, what he liked to wear, eat, drink, do. Whoever killed your son nearly severed his head from his shoulders, Mr Berisha. This person is vicious and extremely dangerous. Now, are you going to help me catch him or am I going to have to avenge Rifat's death all on my own?'

By the time İkmen, Tepe and the other officers İkmen had drafted in to catalogue and remove all of Rifat's personal possessions finally left the Berishas' apartment, night had fallen. As the two men stepped out into the street, they both placed cigarettes in their mouths, which Tepe, watching İkmen rub his ungloved hands briskly together, lit. It was, the younger man observed, going to be a bitter night, a notion İkmen interpreted as an expression of his desire to get home.

'We'll sort through Rifat's stuff tomorrow,' İkmen said. He switched his mobile telephone back on again. 'You get on home now, Orhan.'

Tepe smiled. 'Thank you, sir. Quite a result getting Mr Berisha to allow us access to his son's possessions, wasn't it? Do you think he knows about your being, sort of, partly Albanian?'

'Who knows?' İkmen said with a dismissive shrug. 'I—' A beeping sound from his mobile indicated that he had a new message. He pressed various buttons to retrieve it. 'If you could just wait while I see what this is . . .'

'Yes, of course,' Tepe said as he watched İkmen put his ear to the telephone and listen.

It was quite a long message and from what Tepe could hear of it, it sounded like a woman. A rather shrill, if not hysterical woman. As the message progressed, İkmen's face became grave. When it finally ended, he clicked the phone back to receive mode and sighed. The harsh light from the streetlamp across the road emphasised the depressions under his eyes and cheekbones.

'That was my eldest daughter,' he said after a pause. 'Apparently she met my cousin Samsun Bajraktar when she was out shopping earlier today.'

'Oh?'

'And at the junction of Babıali Caddesi and Divan Yolu, as Çiçek and my cousin stopped to gossip, a small middle-aged man, speaking Albanian, first accused Samsun of being an informant and then threatened her. He was, so Samsun says, Mehmet Vlora. My cousin is apparently at my apartment now, distraught to the point of collapse, according to my daughter.'

'Oh, sir, I—'

'In trying to prevent an escalation of this blood feud, it would appear I have made matters very much worse.' İkmen started to walk towards the end of the street where his car was parked. 'I have implicated my own family.'

'You did what you thought was right,' Tepe said as he followed after him. 'You knew that the Berishas would go after the Vloras in the wake of Rifat's death. You also knew, as I do, that they didn't necessarily kill him and that until the truth about his death is established—'

'I think that the only way round this problem is for me to go and see Angeliki Vlora,' İkmen said gloomily, cutting across Tepe's loyal speech. 'I need to eliminate them from our inquiries, if that is possible. If I can speak to her and perhaps gain willing access to Mehmet and his brothers . . .'

'Do you want me to come with you, sir?'

İkmen paused. He didn't look as if he was actively considering what his sergeant had just said, but when he replied it was obvious that he had been. 'No, Orhan,' he said and patted the younger man gently on the shoulder. 'You go home to your wife and family now.'

'But . . .'

İkmen looked up at what was now a very large and bright full moon. 'No,' he said with a cracked laugh, 'those of us of Balkan origin should meet alone on nights like this.' He turned back to Tepe. 'If Angeliki turns into a werewolf, you, as a Turk, might be alarmed.'

'What?'

'Oh, come on, Orhan!' İkmen said impatiently. 'You must know that the world's most disordered legends have come out of eastern Europe. Werewolves, vampires, the fucking un-dead. Only they really understand this rubbish. I was simply saying that as someone who has received half his blood from such a source I am rather more adapted to deal with it than you are. It was, if you can appreciate this, something of a joke.'

'Oh.'

'But don't worry about that for the time being, Orhan. You just get off home now. It's OK, really.'

'Well, if you're sure.'

'I am,' İkmen said as he drew level with his car and unlocked the door. 'I mean, even if Angeliki Vlora should turn into a beast right in front of my eyes, how bad can it be, eh?'

And then with a twinkling smile that was almost evil, he slid into the driving seat, turned on the engine and left. It was only when he was halfway down the road that the memory of just how much his wife disliked his transsexual cousin came back to him. With Samsun in the apartment, even if she were being looked after by Çiçek, Fatma would be at the very least in a foul mood when he got home.

'Shit,' he said out loud and then burst into laughter as he tried to decide whether he would rather face his wife in a mood or Angeliki Vlora as a were-wolf.

He concluded that the latter possibility was less painful.

Chapter 8

Whether or not Samsun Bajraktar had learned to behave like a woman from watching too many Turkish historical movies was not known. That her femininity was of the nineteenth-century 'fainting with anxiety' variety was, however, evident to everyone in the İkmens' apartment that night. Not that this heightened emotion had a great deal to do with the threats of Mehmet Vlora now. No. Since being almost carried back to the apartment by her cousin's daughter, Çiçek, some hours before, Samsun had spent a considerable amount of fruitless time trying, without success, to contact her lover, Abdurrahman. He was not in his leather shop or their apartment, and she could not imagine where he could be. Even his mobile was switched off, which, for the technology-addicted Abdurrahman, was unheard of behaviour.

'If he's with some girl . . .' Samsun began as she accepted yet another glass of tea from the sympathetically attentive Çiçek.

'I'm sure he isn't,' Çiçek replied soothingly. 'From what you've told me, he sounds really very nice.'

'Why don't you peer into a bowl of oil and find out,' a sharp female voice from the kitchen retorted. 'It's what your aunt would have done.'

Çiçek moved towards the kitchen, her face set in anger. 'Mum! I—'

'Look, if Samsun's in danger, he's welcome to stay as long as he likes,' Fatma said as she appeared, red-faced and headscarfed, from the kitchen. 'I have never turned anyone in need of help away from my hearth. But if he's going to go on about his relations with other men . . .'

'Oh, I'm so sorry, Fatma,' Samsun said, turning to look up into her reluctant hostess's face. 'I know that I'm the most dreadful old—'

'Why has that lady got such big feet?'

As one, all those in the room, including eighteen-year-old Bülent İkmen who had been reading the paper up until this point, turned to look at the small boy now standing beside Samsun's outstretched legs. Fatma, her lips pursed in anger, simply cleared her throat.

Again it was Çiçek who rescued the situation. 'Some ladies do have big feet, Kemal,' she said with a smile at her grave-faced younger brother. 'Like some men have small feet.'

'Dad's got very small feet,' Bülent put in before returning to his paper.

'Yes, that's right, he does.' Then stretching her hand out to the youngster, Çiçek said, 'But we don't have to talk about that right now, do we? I mean, wouldn't you rather go and lie down?'

'No.' With such an odd woman around to stare at, life was far more exciting in the living room than it was in his bedroom.

'Gul's gone to bed.'

'Oh, for the love of . . .' Fed up with her daughter's

attempts to reason with an eight-year-old, Fatma bustled forward and with some determination took a firm grip on her youngest child's hand. 'You're going to bed now, Kemal, and that is the end of it.'

'But what about my dad? I—'

'If you haven't got used to the fact by now that you never see your father, there really is no hope for you,' Fatma said as she dragged the protesting youngster from the room after her.

As the living-room door slammed behind the two figures, Samsun, her eyes lowered, said, 'I am sorry. I appear to have caused quite a scene, don't I?'

'Police,' İkmen said as he thrust his identification into the old woman's face.

'Again?'

'Seems so.' He placed one foot across the threshold of Angeliki Vlora's sparse, fried potato-scented apartment.

The old woman first tucked the stray ends of her headscarf underneath her chin and then, her eyes dark with suspicion, moved out of İkmen's way.

'My boys are out, enjoying a drink together, if that's why you've come,' she said as she followed him into her gloomy living room.

'It's you I've come to see, Mrs Vlora,' İkmen replied.

'Oh?' Bending down to wrap up potato peelings that stood exposed on newspaper on the floor, Angeliki Vlora motioned for İkmen to sit down. 'Why?'

'Because you named certain members of my family to one of my officers this morning.'

Angeliki, straightening up, put one hand into the painful small of her back. 'Oh?' And then seemingly remembered the occasion in more detail. 'You are İkmen?'

'It's what it says on my ID, yes.' He lit a cigarette and leaned back into the damp, old chair she had allocated to him.

'Ach,' the old woman said tetchily, 'I don't read. No Albanian women of my age do.'

'My mother did,' İkmen remarked.

'Only because the Turk, your father, taught her,' Angeliki said, lowering herself onto the sofa opposite İkmen's chair. 'Ayşe Bajraktar didn't need to read, in any event.'

'Why?'

'Because the Bajraktars were the most powerful *fis* outside Ghegeria. There was a time when they were in blood with many rival clans. But, with their viciousness and the curses that your grandfather threw around like mountain snow, they defeated all-comers, even the Ndreks – but you know about that.'

'No.'

Her look of disbelief caught İkmen unawares. In fact, so shocked did she appear that her mouth hung open like a fish's. Only when she eventually extracted a rough hand-rolled cigarette from the folds of her clothing and placed it between her teeth did she close her mouth. But although her reaction seemed extreme to İkmen, he did not dwell upon it. The hour was getting late and as the fog gathered outside to create another frozen, impenetrable night, he knew that he must finish here soon and get home to whatever mayhem awaited him in his Sultan Ahmet apartment.

'You told Sergeant Tepe,' he said, 'that you thought that my cousin Mustafa Bajraktar may have informed the police about your feud with the Berishas.'

The old woman shrugged. 'Well, didn't he?'

'No. And I would prefer it if you did not, in future, throw such unsubstantiated assertions around without thinking.' He paused briefly to knock the ash from his cigarette into the large metal stand ashtray at his elbow before continuing. 'And you might also tell Mehmet that if I catch him threatening any member of my family again, I will personally see to it that he spends some time in our cells. There he might like to think on the error of his ways.'

'Mehmet's threatened nobody.'

'From which I deduce,' İkmen said sharply, 'that either you haven't seen your son since he ran away from my officers this morning or that the noble art of the Albanian lie is truly perfected in you.'

Impervious to the policeman's insults, Angeliki Vlora simply changed the subject. 'Well, if the catamite Samsun didn't tell you about us and the Berishas, then who did, eh? You answer me that, witch's boy!'

Stung by the sudden use of a term usually applied to him, but with affection, by his wife, İkmen snapped, 'As an officer of the law, I am not permitted to reveal my sources.'

'Unless I get my money out!' the old woman cackled sourly. 'Turkish men and money . . .'

'I don't take bribes, old woman!' he flung back at

111

her. 'Like my Turkish father, I am an honest man. I owe nothing, am in blood to no one.'

'As long as it pleases Emina Ndrek, or more to the point her surviving son,' she said with an unpleasant smile.

'What are you talking about?' İkmen said. 'Just keep Mehmet—'

'Emina's brother killed your mother, Ayşe Bajraktar.'

The world, for İkmen, became quite silent. Temporarily aware only of sight, he had the notion that his eyes were in fact peering out of something that had turned to stone, leaving him trapped in a body he did not know. He was suddenly and heart-stoppingly at one with the notion of men inhabiting forms not their own – the un-dead, the ghost, the werewolf . . . Indeed, when he found his voice again, its rough pitch and intensity was not unlike the growl of a beast.

'My mother died of heart—'

'Your mother's throat was cut! The Bajraktar were in blood to the Ndrek for the killing of Emina's brother.'

'No! No!' İkmen said, his heart pounding as he rose shakily to his feet. 'My mother had a heart condition, she died in her bed.' And then shouting he added, 'I was there! I saw . . .'

'Did you?' The old woman's face folded into something that now looked far darker than the visage İkmen had first seen – or so it seemed as she regarded him with contempt. 'Think back, İkmen,' she said spitefully, 'and try not to impose convenient Turkish lies on your memory.'

Normally, İkmen would have reacted immediately to

what Angeliki had said, to the insults she had thrown at him. But for just a moment he took a mental step back from her words and did not speak until he had regained his composure. What the old Albanian was saying was ridiculous, wasn't it? It had to be! Both his brother and his father had seen the body of his mother after death and neither of them had ever spoken of murder. Yes, the police had come to the house that terrible afternoon but then, as İkmen well knew, they did sometimes attend the scene of sudden death. And he could remember no blood. Cut throats produced a lot of blood. And victims of *gjakmaria* were always male, weren't they? The image of women going out and about on behalf of their besieged men made İkmen suddenly, and to the confusion of Angeliki Vlora, smile.

'Oh, very clever,' he said. 'You almost had me going there for a moment, Mrs Vlora.'

'I speak only the truth, I give you my word.'

'This from a person from a country where – how does the saying go? "You are free to be faithful to your word or to be faithless to it"?'

The old woman smiled. 'You know more of Albania than your Turkish father would have liked.'

'Just stop trying to distract me with malicious fabrications and make sure that Mehmet and his brothers present themselves to me tomorrow morning at nine.' He placed one of his business cards down in front of her. 'Your boys can, I take it, read.'

She glanced at it and shrugged.

'If they fail to appear, I will have them arrested,' he snapped and turned towards the door.

'Think about why your father always kept you away from your own kind,' Angeliki said as she stubbed her cigarette out in her ashtray. 'Consider why he might have done that.'

But İkmen, on the surface at least, ignored her words. 'Nine o'clock tomorrow, Angeliki,' he said, 'or your blood feud with the Berishas will end in my cells.'

And with that he walked out of her apartment and down into the now barely visible street below.

On several occasions since his father had contacted him that morning, Mehmet Suleyman had thought about telephoning his brother Murad. Sometimes he had been distracted from the task by other matters, but in the main he had not yet called because he really didn't know what to say. From what his father had told him, it was obvious that Murad was in favour of them all meeting up again. But it still felt odd and also somehow wrong to just cover over with a mere meal what for both of them had been years of deep parental disapproval. And even if their father hadn't been the prime mover in the Suleyman brothers' personal misery, he had undoubtedly acquiesced in their unhappiness. But it was late now, and all the psychological tricks Mehmet had employed earlier to keep himself from Murad had gone. His brother would most definitely be home – after all, where else could single fathers go at this advanced hour of the night?

He pushed a pile of as yet unattended paperwork to one side and pulled his telephone towards him. Just to talk to Murad wouldn't do any harm – he talked to him a lot, always had. Besides, he had promised his father he would and as a man of his word he would just have to do it. His fingers got as far as the receiver before he heard the knock on his door.

'Come in,' he said, his hands retreating from the phone.

The door opened to reveal a middle-aged man in uniform.

'Hello, Roditi,' Suleyman said. 'What can I do for you?'

'A patrol over in Ortaköy has found an abandoned Mercedes underneath the Boğaziçi Bridge.'

'Oh?' Suleyman prepared to return to his telephone. 'And this concerns me how?'

'The inside is drenched in blood, sir,' Roditi said, his voice betraying his discomfort with this image.

Suleyman frowned. 'And whose blood is it?'

'Oh, the car is empty, sir,' Roditi said. 'The men are searching the area for either a body or somebody who might be wounded.'

'I'd better get out there.' Suleyman slipped his jacket from the back of his chair and put it on.

'That's what I thought,' Roditi said as he watched his superior check his pockets for keys, cigarettes and the like. 'I mean, it might not be a murder, but from the description we've been given of the car's interior, I can't see how death in some form can't be involved.'

'Well, you'd better get ready to come with me then,' Suleyman said, moving across determinedly towards his colleague.

Roditi took a deep, hopefully calming breath before he spoke.

'Right, sir,' he sighed. 'I'll go and get my overcoat.'

'Oh well now, what a turn of events, eh, Mother?' İkmen said as he hunkered down in front of the small marble slab that was his mother's gravestone. 'I'm cold, it's dark, I'm not supposed to be here and it's foggy. I feel like I'm about to star in some sort of horror movie.' Shivering violently he added, 'But then after the things that ghastly old woman said to me, I just felt I had to come. Seeking inspiration I suppose. Closeness to you.'

Trying to keep his coat off the damp grass beneath him, İkmen leaned forward to touch the chilly tablet that announced that his mother, Ayşe İkmen, had died on 3 May 1957. A long time ago now – a time when the Turks lived without television and young men still spoke about their heroic deeds on the battlefields of Korea. Try as he might, İkmen had never been able to recall seeing his father's face on the day of his mother's death. All he could remember was how Timür İkmen had held on tightly to both his and Halil's hands at the funeral, standing grimly over this spot, his hair touched with hints of grey. Some people claimed that the grey hairs had arrived overnight, but perhaps his father had been going grey for some time before that. After all, what notice at that age, did the young Çetin take of his father? The man was usually out working and anyway it was Ayşe that he adored with all his soul, her that he really *knew*, or thought that he did.

'Mother, if someone killed you, I will need to find out who that was.' İkmen fought to choke back tears that had started to rise at the back of his eyes. 'I didn't see you on the day you died and so what that old bitch Angeliki said could be true for all I know. But then if it were, surely Timür or Halil would have told me about it? I mean why keep such a thing a secret after over forty years . . .'

Unbidden, tears of grief and frustration ran down his thin face.

'If only I could reach you, Mother,' he said, 'sometimes I know that I can but . . . I'm so lost. I just need an idea, somewhere to start . . . I don't care if this *gjakmaria* nonsense is part of your culture, it's wrong. If you died in blood then I need to know that. I need to understand and come to terms with that.'

Then standing up he called out to the cold winter wind. 'A young boy lies dead. Possibly killed just because of his name. And his people, *your* people, Mother,' he said as he looked down at the gravestone, 'are messing with my head. And because of what they know about you, and because I love you, they're succeeding!'

Away on the distant Bosphorus, a ferry sounded its fog-horn. As he looked across the top of his mother's stone, the faint smudge of numerous other tombstones made İkmen feel that he was at the end of the recognised world. Now, in some poisoned anteroom of death, he felt desolate in almost every respect: as a bereaved son, as a man wrestling with professional difficulties, as one possessed of enough knowledge to realise that one day either the earthquakes or the growling pain he felt now in his stomach from his ulcers would put him into this same rancid earth. As if bowing to the inevitable, he lowered his head to the harsh wind.

'It was Halil who found you,' he said to the gravestone, 'so I should, I suppose, go and talk to him. Not that he'll like it. We've always avoided talking about that day. It's too painful. But,' he shrugged, 'it would appear I have no choice. If he reiterates the tale we have always believed, I'll feel relief, as well as anger towards that Vlora woman. But if I do discover that Halil has been lying to me, well, I don't know what I'll do.'

Turning away from the gravestone, away from the wind, he pulled his cigarettes and lighter out of his coat pocket and lit up. It was, he felt, time to move on from this ugly, toxic place. His mother was dead. Only her bones remained, rotting now beneath the feet of her younger son. And, as he started to walk back towards the entrance to the cemetery, İkmen wondered why he'd even attempted this vast trek over to the Asian side of the city.

However, halfway down the hill, İkmen suddenly stopped. Whether the thought that came to him had, as he felt, been suddenly inserted into his mind or whether his fevered cogitations had just simply sifted the idea out from what was already there, he didn't know. But wherever it came from the thought was both helpful and logical.

Vahan Sarkissian. Of course! Like his sons, Arto and Krikor, Vahan Sarkissian had been a doctor. Indeed he had been the doctor who had come out to the İkmen house in response to Halil's request for help. Vahan it had been who, all those many years before, had declared Ayşe's life extinct. So logically Vahan would have been obliged to keep records of that incident – if, of course, such things still existed after all this time. Vahan had died only a few months after Ayşe İkmen. Who could know what may have become of his possessions after so many years? İkmen suddenly felt deflated. Well, either Arto or Krikor could have his things . . . But it was worth a try, rather than contacting Halil immediately. And so, thanking whatever power had allowed him to uncover this thought, he continued to stride through the dampness towards the cemetery entrance.

It was unusual for Arto Sarkissian to be up after 11 p.m. when he wasn't working. But his wife, Maryam, had watched a video of the film *Gladiator* earlier in the day, which, she had declared, had been very good. And so, as soon as Maryam had retired to bed, Arto had slipped the tape into the machine and then settled down on one of his enormous sofas with a glass of tea and a big bowl of aşure. The deranged son of the Caesar Marcus Aurelius was just descending into thoughts of incestuous perversion when the phone at Arto's elbow rang.

Pausing the tape, Arto picked it up. 'Sarkissian,' he said. 'Hello?'

'Hello, doctor,' the familiar voice of Mehmet Suleyman replied. 'I do apologise for disturbing you so late into the night.'

'It's not a problem, Inspector. I assume you require my assistance.'

'Not, happily, in person, no,' the younger man said and the doctor heaved a sigh of relief. 'I'm in Ortaköy at the moment standing beside an empty car, the interior of which is drenched in blood.'

'Oh?'

'Yes. There's no body, but I'm having it moved after forensic have taken samples for analysis. What I need from you, doctor, is a sample of Rifat Berisha's blood. Could you send it over to the Institute in the morning?'

'You think he may have died in your car of blood?'

Suleyman sighed. 'I think it's possible. We must, after all, explore every eventuality.'

'Well, I will certainly do as you ask,' Arto said and jotted a note to himself on the pad beside the telephone. 'Do you want me to contact you in the morning?'

'Please.'

'Well,' Arto said with a smile, 'you'd better get out of this dreadful fog and back to your home then. These conditions give doctors far too much work, in my opinion.'

'Thank you, doctor, I will bear that in mind,' Suleyman said. 'Goodnight to you.'

'Goodnight, Inspector,' Arto replied and replaced the receiver.

So Suleyman wanted some of Berisha's blood for comparison, did he? Although he was holding the video remote control, Arto didn't press the 'play' button – not yet. Professional interest swinging in whether he wanted it to or not was a common occurrence in his life. A man with one kidney struggling for life in a car full of blood was a disturbing image – if indeed that was what had happened. If so, there would have to be glass, if in small quantities, present too. Now that he'd had a chance to examine the small shards properly, he'd noticed how very thin and brightly coloured they were. Almost pretty really, and definitely not the sort of material a murderer would jam into a dying man's face. Unless, of course, the glass constituted a message of some kind. Like the message the Italian Mafia sent to the families of informants when they stuffed their dead mouths full of banknotes. It was interesting and also vaguely morbid to speculate on these issues – not unlike, Arto felt, creating aspects of a character for a novel. However, he was not destined to muse for long. The ringing of his doorbell, plus the knowledge that the housekeeper had gone to bed many hours before, forced Arto from his seat and out of the living room.

Cringing against the sound of his own slippers slapping against the marble floor of the hall, Arto moved in a leisurely manner befitting a man of wide stature. Now that he was on this side of his enormous mansion, he could hear that the weather outside had taken a turn for the worse. Fog had apparently given way to driving rain. He switched the outside light on before unlocking and opening the door. For a moment he thought that the small, drenched Turk who stood on his doorstep was a rather alarming-looking beggar. That was until he saw first the smouldering cigarette in his right hand and then the familiar manic expression around the eyes.

'What in the name of God are you doing here,

Çetin?' Arto asked as he pulled his friend into his house.

'It's a long story, Arto,' the Turk replied. 'It may well take me all night.'

Chapter 9

Orhan Tepe was engaged in sorting through the considerable possessions of the late Rifat Berisha when he noticed a familiar pale face pass by the window in his office door. Using this as an excuse to do something other than marvel at the convoluted picture he was building up of the Albanian's world – old railway tickets, expensive trainers, cheap aftershave, foreign artefacts – he left his desk and ran out into the corridor.

'Çöktin!' he called to the back of the other man's drooping red head. 'What are you doing here? I thought you were ill!'

Turning, a thin smile on his pale lips, İsak Çöktin walked slowly back towards Tepe, stopping occasionally along the way in order to cough.

'I've returned,' he said 'gasping somewhat over his words, 'as much to visit the pharmacy and get some proper medicine as anything else.'

'Haven't you been taking aspirin?'

'No, but I have been given a variety of drink and food designed many hundreds of years ago to alleviate symptoms such as these.'

'Your mother,' Tepe said with a knowing smile.

'Yes,' Çöktin replied, 'wishing only a speedy recovery for her son.'

'She makes you eat and drink Turkey's past.'

Çöktin's smile encouraged Tepe to usher him into İkmen's office. Had Tepe known that what Çöktin's mother had given him was not a Turkish but a native – to the Çöktin family – Yezidi remedy, he might not have behaved in quite such a friendly fashion. Although ethnically Kurds, the Yezidis are not Muslims, they worship a version of a redeemed and restored Satan they call the Peacock Angel. In common parlance they are called the Devil Worshippers and Tepe, unlike his rather more enlightened superiors İkmen and Suleyman, would have been very disturbed to know that Çöktin was one of their number. Not that Çöktin ever spoke of his faith himself, even to İkmen and Suleyman. It was a known but unspoken fact that existed only between the three of them in a sort of silent agreement to maintain yet further silence.

'Do you have a fever?' Tepe asked as he rummaged in the top drawer of his desk.

'Yes,' Çöktin replied, dragging forward a chair and sitting in front of Tepe's desk. His eye caught on some of Rifat Berisha's possessions scattered there. 'What's all this?'

'I've got aspirin, which will bring your temperature down,' a still very medically minded, Tepe said, 'or there's some stuff in sachets which is supposed to be specially for influenza. Tell me which you would prefer.' Holding the medication aloft, he assumed a grave expression as he offered it to the other man.

'Just some aspirin will be fine for now,' Çöktin said with a smile. 'So what is all of this stuff on your desk?'

Tepe poured some water out of one of his drinking bottles into a glass and handed it and the tablets to Çöktin before replying.

'It belongs to an Albanian we found dead in the road down in Eminönü,' he said. 'Twenty-five years old, name of Rifat Berisha. Whoever killed him cut his throat literally from ear to ear.'

After swallowing the water and the tablets, Çöktin thanked Tepe before advancing the idea that perhaps Rifat had died a gangster's death.

Now sitting down opposite his colleague, Tepe said, 'It's possible, yes, and in fact we have discovered that Rifat's family are currently feuding with another family of Albanians. However, there are complications.'

'Complications?'

'Yes.' Tepe picked up several small items from the top of a pile of papers on the left side of his desk and passed them to Çöktin. 'Look at these, will you, and tell me what you think.'

'If it will help.' Çöktin took hold of the items and then coughed heavily once again.

As he sifted through what turned out to be a stack of picture postcards and some rather unusual tickets, Çöktin listened to Tepe's account of how Rifat's body had been discovered, how Dr Sarkissian had found that the young man had recently undergone kidney removal, and the difficulties both he and İkmen had faced when questioning the Berisha and Vlora clans.

Çöktin looked up. 'So why do postcards of London complicate things? I don't understand.'

'There's a possibility that Rifat had his kidney removed abroad,' Tepe said as he offered his colleague a cigarette and then lit it for him.

'And so?'

'And so we have pictures of London.'

'You only need to check the visas in this man's passport,' Çöktin said as he let yet more smoke irritate his bronchioli.

Tepe sighed. 'His passport is missing. His parents, although acknowledging that their son sometimes went away for several weeks at a time – womanising, the father reckoned – claim to know nothing about any foreign trips.'

'So check with the British Consulate.'

'Yes.'

'Then at least you'll know whether the man actually went to that country or just received postcards as a present,' Çöktin said with a smile.

'True.'

'And anyway, as far as I can see, we don't know whether the removal of this man's kidney has any bearing on his death.'

In the small silence that followed, Çöktin picked up the unfamiliar tickets and frowned. 'Mind you,' he said, 'these are English tickets, or at least they are written in that language.'

'Are you sure?' asked Tepe.

Pointing at some words on the small orange-edged card, Çöktin said, 'Yes. Look, here it says Kensington – that's in London.'

'Is it?'

'Oh, Kensington is most certainly in London,' a deeper and far more sonorous voice replied.

Both younger men turned to look at Suleyman who had just entered the room.

'Sir.'

Holding his hand out to Çöktin, Suleyman took the ticket from him and looked at it.

'Yes,' he said, 'this is certainly from England. It is, I think you'll find, a ticket for the London metro.'

In spite of the fact that all of his children who still attended school or were due to work that day had gone to their various places of study or employment, Çetin İkmen's apartment still echoed to the sound of more than one voice. As he moved wearily across the threshold, İkmen thought at first that perhaps Fatma was watching television. It was only when he entered the living room and saw his wife sitting about as far away as she could get from someone who looked like a life-stained, and far taller, version of Marlene Dietrich that he realised Samsun was still with them.

'Oh, and who might this be?' Fatma said as she caught sight of her husband drooping in the doorway. 'Could it be that mysterious stranger I occasionally encounter in the kitchen?'

'Highly amusing, Fatma,' İkmen countered with first a scowl and then an apologetic smile. 'I'm really sorry I didn't ring you.'

'Oh, that's all right.' Fatma rose to her feet, tightening the scarf round her head as she moved. 'After all, I've not been bored without you. As well as the usual thousand problems presented by our children, plus the fact that Squeaky has died, Samsun here has been wanting to speak to you for most of the night, haven't you?'

'Well, er . . .' the rapidly reddening transsexual began.

'But now that you are here, Çetin,' Fatma told her husband, 'you can, I am sure, be of assistance.' Moving past İkmen towards the hall, she added, 'For myself, I have hamster shopping and a hundred other things to do.'

'May it come easy,' İkmen said, quoting the standard formula appropriate to his wife's activities.

An annoyed grunting noise was all that İkmen received by way of a reply – that and the sound of the front door slamming.

'I'm ever so sorry, Çetin,' Samsun said as she took a tissue out of her pocket and dabbed her mascara smeared eyes. 'If I'd been able to contact Abdurrahman . . .'

'Oh, it's my fault for being out all night,' İkmen said. He flopped down onto the sofa beside Samsun. 'I should have rung Fatma. But,' he shrugged, 'I was otherwise engaged and absorbed.'

'With?' Samsun asked, her natural curiosity, especially with regard to anything salacious, piqued.

Laughing, İkmen lit a cigarette before replying. 'With nobody you'd find particularly interesting, Samsun.'

'Oh, not a . . .'

'No, not another woman. I have quite enough trouble with the one I've got.' He descended into silence for a few moments as he smoked in a very committed and concentrated fashion. And although Samsun wanted to raise some of her fears regarding both Mehmet Vlora and the seemingly elusive Abdurrahman, she did not feel that this was appropriate at the moment. Çetin İkmen looked too distracted and even upset to listen to her problems. His own, if his face was anything to go by, were far more serious than hers.

'What's the matter?' she asked, touching the side of his face in order to get his attention. 'Do you need me to read your cards?'

'No.' He smiled. 'No, but thank you anyway.'

'But?'

İkmen sighed before he started. Samsun, he knew of old, would not stop questioning him until she got some answers – not that even an entire night spent first at the cemetery and then with Arto Sarkissian had provided any. Angeliki Vlora's story still nagged away at him, unsubstantiated and unresolved. Perhaps he should tackle Samsun about what she could remember of Ayşe İkmen's death – if he could find the will or the energy to do so.

'I went to sit at Mother's grave,' he said at length. 'I needed to sort my thoughts out.'

'In the middle of the night?' Samsun's eyes widened in shock. 'Weren't you scared?'

'Well, of course I was!' İkmen exploded. 'I'm half Albanian, I see ghosts everywhere!'

'Çetin!'

He turned towards her, his face serious. 'Look, Samsun,' he said, 'I am not best pleased with your

129

people right now. Yesterday I met the Vlora family matriarch, Angeliki.'

'And?'

'Angeliki told me that my mother was murdered in an act of *gjakmaria*.'

'Auntie Ayşe died of a heart attack. We all know that, Çetin.'

'Do we?' Puffing heavily on the dying butt of his cigarette, İkmen quickly lit another to take its place. 'I'm not so sure. I will have to raise that event with my brother, which I really don't want to do.'

'Why not?'

'Because we've never spoken of it. Because as the older brother he bore the brunt of it, which has scarred him. And different though my brother is from me, he's a good man and I don't want to hurt him.'

'Then why don't you just forget about it?' Samsun said lightly as she opened her handbag to look for her cigarettes. 'The Vloras are, as anyone will tell you, liars and thieves.'

'Angeliki said that she knew my mother.'

'All Albanians ultimately know each other,' Samsun said with a dismissive wave of her now lit cigarette. 'They bitch, lie to and curse each other. It's another way of getting at you, Çetin. They know that you'll have to investigate them in relation to this Berisha thing. They suspect, as Mehmet Vlora so eloquently told me, that I told you about that particular feud. They don't like it. Mehmet in particular, I should imagine, is probably worried in case you discover his drug-dealing activities.'

His interest diverted temporarily by this snippet of information, İkmen said, 'He deals? What?'

Samsun shrugged. 'Whatever you want, or so it's said. Not, of course, that you heard that from me.'

'No.' İkmen smiled and then instantly frowned once again. 'I've asked Arto Sarkissian to look amongst what is left of his father's papers.'

Looking genuinely perplexed now, Samsun said, 'Why?'

'Because Vahan Sarkissian came out to confirm that Mother was dead. And because I have never been able to find anything at all relating to her death amongst my father's possessions.'

'Except everybody's certainty that your mother died of a heart attack,' Samsun said with not a little irony in her voice. 'And besides, as I think I've told you before, Çetin, the Bajraktar have not been in blood with anyone since we left Albania. And even if we had been, Auntie Ayşe would not have been killed.'

'Why? Because she was female?'

'Yes, and as such she did not come, as men do, from the Tree of Blood.'

'The what?'

'Look,' Samsun said, 'according to tradition, men are descended from the Tree of Blood and women from the Tree of Milk. This means that only the killing of men can result in blood feud. Angeliki Vlora would know this – she would also know that you, as a Turk, would not know this and would therefore take her story at face value. The Vloras set out to frighten and disturb all of us and in that they have been most successful.' She smiled. 'I for one will pray that evidence may be found to connect them to the death of Rifat Berisha, whether they are guilty or not.'

'Which reminds me,' İkmen said as he looked down anxiously at his watch, 'I have an appointment with Mehmet and the others at nine.'

Samsun frowned. 'The Vlora boys made an *appointment* to see you?'

'No.' He rose to his feet, stretching hard as he did so. 'I told Angeliki that if they didn't turn up at nine, I'd have them arrested. I was a little resentful about what she had told me regarding Mother at the time.'

'Oh, well done!'

İkmen, who was only now beginning to feel the full effects of a night without sleep, yawned. 'I can give you a lift, Samsun.'

'Oh, yes, I suppose I'd better get out of here before Fatma returns, hadn't I?'

İkmen just smiled.

Rising to her considerable feet, Samsun replaced her cigarettes in her handbag and pulled her thin pink cardigan up onto her shoulders.

'I guess the only way I'll find out where or with whom Abdurrahman has spent the night is to go home,' she said mournfully.

'You think Abdurrahman might be seeing someone else?' İkmen asked.

'I don't know,' Samsun replied with a shrug. 'But if he is I'll kick the shit out of him – that is, of course, after

I've thrown his mobile telephone down the toilet and fed pizza into the video recorder. I've had all night to think about this stuff and anyway, as an Albanian, could I do any less?'

İkmen, laughing, opened the door leading into the hall. 'I'm sure there is a reasonable explanation for his behaviour,' he said. 'Come on.'

Once out of the apartment and down in the cold street again, İkmen's face resumed its previous troubled expression. Samsun, shrouded against the winter in full-length red fake fur, sashayed along behind him until they reached İkmen's 'new' car, a 1981 Mercedes.

İkmen suddenly turned to face her. 'I suppose some-one else who would know would be Uncle Ahmet.'

'Know what?'

'Know the truth about how Mother died.'

Samsun's breath clouded the cold air as she said in exasperation, 'Çetin, how can my father know about something there is nothing to know about? Don't you think he would have told me if there were?'

İkmen, turning the key in his car door, sighed. 'Yes, I suppose so.'

'Look, I think I might walk home,' she said abruptly. 'After all, we can't have one of our senior police officers party to an act of domestic violence, can we?'

He smiled. 'Don't be too vicious, will you?' he said as he climbed into the car. 'Remember how expensive lawyers are in this city. Let that guide your actions. And keep away from places frequented by the Vlora brothers, for the time being at least.' And then with a smile he drove off.

Once the car had turned the corner into Ticarethane Sokak, Samsun took her mobile telephone out of her handbag and punched a number into the keypad. Thirty seconds of waiting and stamping of feet against the cold later, somebody answered.

With a very serious expression on her face, Samsun said, 'Father? It's me, Mustafa. Listen, there's something we need to talk about. It concerns my cousins, the Ikmen boys . . .'

'So Rifat Berisha died in his own car?'

'Not necessarily,' Suleyman said, stirring two lumps of sugar into his tea. 'What I am saying, though, is that the vehicle is registered to Berisha. I've sent Roditi around to the parents to tell them. Further, the car has the correct blue number plates, is taxed, was driven by a man who possessed a Turkish licence, and is therefore entirely legal. In short, a very expensive toy for a man whose sister I saw begging on the Galata Bridge less than an hour ago.'

Tepe leaned back in his chair and looked thoughtfully up at the nicotine-stained ceiling. 'Rifat's parents said that he was unemployed.'

'Exactly.'

'He could have obtained the money for the car by selling his kidney to someone.'

'Possibly in London,' Suleyman said as he regarded the ticket bearing the name Kensington.

'Where would he have been tested for tissue suitability?' asked a flu-thickened voice from across the room.

'Here,' said Suleyman.

'So one of the hospitals could have a record of the tissue comparison,' Tepe said.

Suleyman shrugged. 'Theoretically, yes. But Rifat or the purchasers of the organ could have given the medical staff a fake ID.'

'Right.' Briefly deflated, Tepe sighed.

'Anyway,' Suleyman said, 'what we need now is for forensic to finish their work comparing Rifat's blood with that in the car and, if Inspector İkmen agrees, we need to work on finding out where Rifat purchased this vehicle.'

'And possibly trace how it was paid for and by whom via the dealer?' Çöktin asked.

'Yes,' Suleyman replied. 'But not until I've spoken to Inspector İkmen. It is, after all, his case and he may have different ideas in light of this evidence.'

'Sure.'

'Inspector İkmen went to see the old Vlora woman last night,' Tepe said.

'What, alone?' Suleyman asked, frowning.

'Aliya Berisha admitted there was bad blood between the two families and so the Inspector thought it might be an idea to speak to those on the other side of the dispute.'

'The Vlora men wouldn't have been happy to see him.'

'The Inspector reasoned that after Yıldız and I went in, the Vlora men would make themselves invisible for a time,' Tepe said. 'Since the Inspector is part Albanian himself, he must know what he's talking about. And besides, when he started on about werewolves and vampires I admit that I got a bit lost.'

'Werewolves and vampires?' Çöktin inquired. 'What about werewolves and vampires?'

'Because he and the Vloras and the rest of them are from eastern European backgrounds, Inspector İkmen reckons that these things are familiar to them,' Tepe answered with a smile. 'As a full-blooded Turk he reasoned I'd find it difficult to cope should the old woman turn into something revolting.'

'In other words, he wanted to go there alone,' Suleyman said, laughing in spite of himself.

'Perhaps you should suggest to the Inspector,' said Çöktin as he rose unsteadily from his seat and walked towards Tepe, 'that from now on silver bullets should be issued as standard.'

'Eh?'

Both Suleyman and Çöktin laughed at Tepe's obvious confusion.

'I think you should perhaps get out to the movies a little more often,' Suleyman said as he stubbed his cigarette out and rose to leave. 'In the meantime, I think I should get back to my work and Çöktin should go home.'

'Oh, but—'

'Your mother's potions may not always cure you, İsak, but neither will they harm you,' Suleyman said. 'You are fortunate to have a mother who cares so deeply for you.' He looked a little sad. 'Value her.'

İkmen's interview with the Vlora brothers, Mehmet,

Aryan and Mehti, did not last very long. The 'boys', particularly Mehmet, were not exactly happy to be in his presence but, they did accede to his demands. As well as taking possession of a knife that Mehmet said was his, İkmen wanted forensic to inspect their apartment, with the boys' consent. He was certain that neither Mehmet nor Mehti really understood the true import of this, but he thought Aryan probably did; he asked what substances would be used to expose suspect stains. All the more encouraging then that the boys agreed so gracefully – and far more convincing than their predictable story regarding having been together all the time on the night of the murder.

İkmen did, however, wonder just how much Aryan Vlora really knew. He was, after all, only an unemployed immigrant. Clothes, carpets and walls that had been washed entirely clean of blood could yield damning evidence these days. Once in contact with almost any other substance, blood, it would seem, stuck. Rather like the Albanians' feuding rituals, it never really went away.

Before the interview with the Vloras, Tepe had passed İkmen some information Suleyman had uncovered regarding a car that had apparently belonged to Rifat Berisha. This, together with some postcards and tickets from London, were what Tepe considered to be the most significant pieces of physical evidence, apart from the body itself, so far. However, whilst acknowledging that the car was indeed important, İkmen was less certain about the London artefacts. After all, someone could have given him the postcards and, he thought cynically, he could have obtained the tickets whilst picking tourists' pockets. True, they indicated that Rifat could have travelled to London, but even if he had, whether he had sold his kidney there was unclear. And besides, in terms of Rifat's death, there was nothing to connect the sale of his kidney with his murder. What İkmen needed to do now was to sift through Rifat's possessions himself. Perhaps his take on their importance would be different to Tepe's. As far as the papers relating to Rifat's car were concerned, he would put money on it that Rifat's documents were forgeries. He held the same opinion about the victim's mysteriously absent passport – opinions that, he knew, many would condemn as unnecessarily harsh and unfairly stereotypical. And indeed perhaps if Angeliki Vlora hadn't brought up the subject of his mother, if Mehmet Vlora hadn't victimised Samsun, he might have been rather more open-minded. But these things had happened and, yes, he was prejudiced.

When his telephone rang, İkmen's hand sprang out nervously to grab it.

'Hello, İkmen.'

'Hello, Çetin, it's Arto. I've got that toxicology on Rifat Berisha for you.'

'And?'

'Nothing beyond the ubiquitous nicotine,' he said with a sigh. 'As far as I can tell, he was a very healthy young man whose one remaining kidney was working most efficiently. Did you ask his parents about hospital admissions?'

'They said they knew nothing about either hospital admissions or trips abroad, although his ownership of a very nice car plus a few artefacts from England does make me wonder,' İkmen replied. 'Apparently, Rifat would sometimes be absent from the family home for weeks at a time, doing what his mother described as "men's business".'

'Did they say whether their son had been ill?'

'Rifat was apparently, as you have indicated, a very healthy young man.'

'Which all seems to make the kidney for sale hypothesis more likely,' the doctor said.

'Yes,' İkmen agreed. 'Although we don't know whether that transaction has any bearing upon his death.'

'Anything that morally bankrupt has to be suspect surely.'

İkmen shrugged. 'Possibly.'

A short pause ensued, after which Arto Sarkissian asked, a little tentatively, 'And this blood feud thing . . .'

'I'm still pursuing that, yes.'

'You know, Çetin,' the doctor began, 'what we were talking about last night . . .'

'Yes?' His voice was now eager.

'I will, as I promised, sort through Father's papers tonight. However, I think that in the meantime you should attempt to put this thing about your mother from your mind, Çetin. It was all a very long time ago.'

'But the woman said that Mother was murdered, Arto!' İkmen exclaimed, shocked by his friend's seemingly calm stance on the matter.

'Yes, forty years ago, Çetin! Too long ago even for

139

you to find her killer now – if indeed there was a killer, which I doubt.'

'Yes, but don't you see, I must be sure?'

It was said with such a plaintive tone that Arto's unease about İkmen's seeming irrationality left him. Of course if one thought one's parent had been murdered one would have to act. Twenty minutes or forty years before, it didn't really make any difference. One's blood was one's blood and that was that – though clearly it wasn't compelling enough to make İkmen go and see his brother. Although Çetin was sometimes quite openly aggravated by his older sibling, when it came to that event forty years ago, Halil was both an heroic and a sacrosanct figure. And in any event, hadn't the thirteen-year-old who discovered his mother's body on that balmy May afternoon suffered enough?

'I can see what you mean, of course I can, Çetin,' Arto said.

'Then all I ask is that if you find something – anything – amongst Uncle Vahan's papers, you will be absolutely truthful with me.'

'Of course,' Arto Sarkissian replied. 'Do we not love each other as true brothers?'

'Yes.'

'Then I will do everything I can to help you as I know you would assist me if this sad matter belonged to my family.'

İkmen smiled. 'Thank you, Arto. I appreciate this.'

'It's nothing,' the doctor said. 'Now I really do need to get on with my paperwork. Perhaps you could assist me by telling Mehmet Suleyman that comparative tests between Rifat Berisha's blood and that found in the car are under way.'

'Of course,' İkmen said. 'I'll go and see him now.'

'Thank you.'

'So I will speak to you later then, Arto?'

Noting, yet again, the neediness in İkmen's voice, Arto Sarkissian said a very firm, 'Yes,' followed quickly by, 'Goodbye, Çetin.'

'Goodbye, Arto.'

As İkmen rose from his chair to go and see Suleyman, he reflected that although he trusted his oldest friend to keep his word and look through his father's papers, he wasn't sure that he would indeed be entirely honest about what he found there. After all, Arto Sarkissian was a doctor and they did not always, as everybody knew, tell people everything they thought they needed to hear. Doctors sometimes tried to protect people, even if that was against the knowledge of the ravages of time and their own biology. Still, there was nothing İkmen could do about this. He would just have to take Arto's word for whatever he found. It was either that or insult him and risk their friendship, and that was something he certainly didn't want to do.

Chapter 10

Although in recent days the residents of Kutucular Caddesi had become rather more accustomed to the appearance of unfamiliar people entering number 32, they had not reckoned on the sight of this huge vehicle blocking their street. Gold in colour and as Mimoza's husband Dilek the landlord would say to his coffeehouse friends later, upholstered in the finest leather, the Rolls-Royce represented a lifestyle completely unknown to Kutucular's residents. In spite of the best efforts of the chauffeur who stayed with the vehicle after the young lady had gone into number 32, the crowd that gathered around the Rolls was male and envious. Even discreetly fingering the small pistol Mr Evren had given him with orders to protect his children at all costs did not make Hassan the chauffeur feel any more secure.

Inside number 32, however, things were calmer than in the street, if no less strained. The girl, or rather woman as became apparent if one stood close to her, had entered asking to see 'Rifat's family'. Her tiny, twisted frame was swathed in black from head to toe and she spoke in the same halting fashion as the Berishas themselves, as if she, too, were not native to the Turkish Republic.

Aliya Berisha, predictably, had been hostile towards this unknown and ugly-looking person.

'What do you want with Rifat's family?' she had asked. 'Who are you?'

'My name is Felicity Evren,' the woman replied, her voice soft and quite deep. 'I was a good friend of Rifat's. His sister telephoned yesterday with the terrible news of his death. I said that I would come.'

'What? Engelushjia?' Aliya looked nervously at her daughter.

'Yes, Mum, I invited her,' the youngster explained as she moved forward to solemnly shake hands with the stranger. 'I had a number for Miss Evren. Rifat gave it to me some time ago.'

'Gave it to you!' her mother cried, slipping back into Albanian in her agitation. 'Why did I not know of this – relationship?'

'There were lots of things you didn't know about Rifat,' Engelushjia said, stoically speaking in Turkish. And then taking this odd and, at close quarters, facially disfigured woman by the hand, she led her into the living room and sat her down.

Following, Aliya and Rahman muttered agitatedly to one another.

Only Mimoza Özer smiled. 'This must be one of Rifat's conquests,' she whispered into Aliya's ear. 'One with money, by the look of it, cousin.'

'I have come to pay my respects,' Felicity Evren said. 'It is all I can do for beloved Rifat now.' And then she burst into tears, her tiny frame threatening to fall apart with every miserable convulsion. 'I'm sorry!'

The Berishas, admittedly with half an eye on the great golden car outside, sat down beside her, with the exception of Engelushjia who went to the kitchen to prepare tea. The older Berishas sat and watched the stranger cry for quite some time.

'Do you think she wants something?' Rahman asked his wife in the Albanian they spoke when addressing each other, trying, as he did so, to work out whether this odd stranger had lumps on her face or whether parts of it were paralysed.

'If Rifat had sex with this one then I think that the mystery about those trips he took and where he got his car from are solved,' Mimoza commented acidly. 'A man would have to close his eyes and think only of money in order to pleasure such a thing without vomiting.'

'Oh, please do not speak of that cursed car again!' Aliya said. 'When that policeman told me they'd found it out in Ortaköy and I, in this grief, had to act as if I knew nothing about it . . . A car, full of my son's blood . . .'

'We don't know that it was Rifat's blood,' Rahman said gravely. 'It—'

'Rifat took me to some beautiful places,' the strange woman cut in. The Albanians stared at her. 'Even though he was a foreigner too, he'd lived here a lot longer than I have, so he knew where to go. Monuments, parks and restaurants were quite unknown to me until I met Rifat.'

'Which is why that boy gained so much weight lately, I suppose,' Mimoza mouthed into Rahman's ear.

'You're not carrying his child?' Aliya asked her guest with a directness that caused Engelushjia who was now entering with the tea glasses to nearly drop her burden.

'If only I was,' Felicity Evren said with a sad little shrug, 'then at least there would be something left of Rifat. But that was never – couldn't be – possible.' And then she started crying again.

'I expect she's too old and dry for motherhood,' Aliya said as she turned towards her cousin.

'Must be older than you,' Mimoza answered knowingly, then added, amazed, 'What can your Rifat have been thinking of?'

'Perhaps he just enjoyed the lady's company,' Engelushjia snapped at the older women. Then, turning to the weeping stranger, she said, 'I have made you some tea, miss.'

'Oh, that's very kind of you,' Felicity said and attempted to compose herself enough to dry her eyes. 'Thank you. I'm sorry. I'm so, so sorry!'

As she solemnly handed a small glass of tea to their guest, Engelushjia reminded her Albanian audience of their obligations vis-à-vis a guest – any guest. Using the words of the despised Lek Dukagjini – a man's house belongs to Allah and the guest – she effectively brought to a close her family's more offensive and prurient questioning of this stranger in their midst. She also obtained some satisfaction from using their own code of conduct against them.

And so an hour passed amid tea and tears. Rahman, Aliya and Mimoza smoked incessantly while Felicity told them how kind and special Rifat had been to her. Although she did not exactly say that she had loved him, it was possible to infer this from her words, if little else. Where and when she had met Rifat and what, if anything, her family had made of him were not topics that the Berishas were enlightened about. Indeed, at the end of Felicity's visit they found that they didn't even know where she lived or what kind of 'foreigner' she was. She just came, paid her respects and then with a hug only for Engelushjia she left. She didn't know that the young Albanian girl knew things about her that made her feel distinctly uneasy – things she didn't feel she could tell her parents.

'I really think that we should let Sergeant Tepe know that she's been here,' Engelushjia said as she started to clear the tea glasses and ashtrays away.

'I don't,' her father answered. 'Why do they need to know about your brother's conquests?'

'They need to know everything about Rifat if they're going to catch his killer,' Engelushjia answered.

'Yes, but we know who killed your brother,' Aliya started. 'It—'

'No, we don't!' her daughter insisted. 'Not for certain.'

'Oh, so you went over to see the Vloras just for a little talk, did you?' Rahman sneered. 'With a knife in your pocket.'

'I always carry a knife, as well you know!' Engelushjia retorted. 'In case people threaten me.'

'Which they did.'

'Yes! But I went there just to talk. To try and sort

this stupid mess out.' Then looking at the expressions of disbelief all around her, Engelushjia tossed her head and said, 'Well, don't believe me, I don't care. But what I say is true whether you like it or not.'

Mimoza, laughing now, said, 'You don't have to cover up your lust for the Turkish policeman to us, girl! You should set your sights on a Turk, they have money and they've always liked our women.'

'Sergeant Tepe is married actually,' Engelushjia said and looked down her nose at the vaguely dissolute face of her mother's cousin. 'And even if he were not, I would have more respect for both him and myself than to just offer my body to him. I want to be with a man that I love and who loves me.'

'Then you're a bigger fool than I thought you were,' Aliya Berisha said as she moved slowly towards the kitchen. Then, stopping and turning to face her daughter, she said, 'You want to look like me at thirty-nine years old?'

Silently, Engelushjia lowered her eyes.

'I thought not,' her mother said bitterly and left the room.

'Never mind,' Mimoza laughed. 'When your father's avenged Rifat, I'll persuade Dilek to make a party.'

'What, a death party?'

'No!' Mimoza laughed even harder. 'I'll think of something, some excuse. I'll get Dilek to bring his friends. They're all Turks. You're bound to find some- one you want amongst them.'

'Right,' said Engelushjia heavily. Just the thought of Dilek's largely drunken friends was enough to make any rational girl opt for celibacy. But the irony in her tone was lost upon Mimoza, who now followed Rahman and Aliya into the kitchen.

Alone now, Engelushjia Berisha thought again about how much she wanted all this morbid trouble to be over. She wanted Rifat to be at rest in his grave, she wanted her father to stop planning the murder she knew was coming, and she did indeed want to see Sergeant Tepe once again. It wasn't every day that a man treated her like a human being, much less a lady – even when she had bitten his partner.

Engelushjia laughed gently and then went out into the hall to retrieve her shoes.

'I'm going out for a while,' she said as she threw a cardigan on over her dress and opened the front door to the apartment.

But none of those in the kitchen heard her either call or leave. They were too busy with their own plans and the demands of blood.

It was hard to decide whether she wasn't fully attending to the boy because of the inanity and sheer self-indulgence of his condition or because her mind was already fixed upon the task she had set herself when the appointment was over. By rights she should have been concerned. After all, it wasn't as if he was improving. The mannered morbidity he had been exhibiting for the last three months was in fact deepening.

Peering from inside his many sweaters, the boy, his kohl-rimmed eyes haunted and black, cleared his throat. 'Doctor?'

Ashamed to have been caught out in a moment of reverie by one who shared her native language, Zelfa Halman shifted herself up a little straighter in her chair and smiled.

'So fear of becoming obese is not what motivates you,' she said, referring hastily to some notes she had written several minutes before.

'I would hate to be fat,' he replied, his pinched face forming a scowl, 'but no. It's more philosophical than that, it's—'

'You do know that the end of this process results in loss of muscle tone, teeth and hair, followed by excruciating pain.'

'As the body in an attempt to live digests its own organs,' he said brightly. 'Yes. My father told me about it. But I do eat, I assure you. I've eaten since I last saw you two days ago – several times actually. Honestly, my father does panic . . .'

'He cares about you, Ali. He wants you to be well.'

The boy smiled in a way she found totally confusing. 'Yes.'

After a short pause she continued, 'You tell me you like old horror films and books – Dracula and Frankenstein, that sort of stuff.'

'Yes, but if you're going to say that my appearance is due to my interest in the supernatural—'

'No, I wasn't.'

'Because I know that I'm only a teenager and that we are prone to obsessions of this type, but it's really rather more complicated than that, doctor. As I've said, it's philosophical . . .' He turned away, smiling into a corner of the room. Intent, no doubt, Zelfa thought, as many of his kind could be, upon romantic notions about things of a dark nature. It was something she found very European, but then the boy had lived in England, which was apparently his mother's country. 'Gothic' kids were common there. The British, just like the Irish, could afford such frippery.

'You know that the vampire's inability to see himself in a mirror encapsulates our fear of becoming inhuman and the loss of identity a transformation to a more powerful primitive state may bring,' he said in what over the few months she had been seeing him Zelfa had come to recognise as his precocious intellectual mode.

'Which book did you read that in, Ali?' she inquired.

'My sister read it actually,' he replied. 'Yesterday.' And then he said more to himself than to Zelfa, 'Some sort of alternative explanation, I suppose.'

'Yes, but that doesn't pertain in any way to your own situation, does it? You, like me, are real and so you, like me, can see yourself in a mirror.'

He sighed a trifle sadly before replying, 'Well, yes, we are currently boringly mortal, you and I.'

'A condition we cannot change,' Zelfa said with a smile. 'However, if you don't eat properly or talk to people outside your family you may eventually think that you're something you're not.'

'Oh, I don't believe that's likely to happen, do you?' he said, his face now comically aghast. But there was bitterness behind it too.

'Well, I've known odder things happen,' Zelfa replied firmly, 'so don't push it. Your mind is a delicate organ that is highly susceptible to outside influences. So, before you see me again, try at least to engage in some sort of conversation at school and eat one more item per day. Will you try that?'

'I'll give it a go,' he said, looking down sulkily at the floor. And then with his head still bent he rose to his feet. 'So will it be Thursday then?'

'We do need, I feel,' she said, looking up at him, 'to explore some more of the issues that may lie behind your unhappiness.'

'I'm not unhappy.'

'Your father feels—'

'My father wants to put me in an institution.'

Zelfa only just managed to stop herself from smiling at what was, she knew, a case of teenage over-exaggeration. Although a little rough around the edges, the boy's father had seemed, in the short time she had been with him, to be a most concerned individual.

'Ali, your father only wants you to get well.'

'Oh, well, you'll see,' he said with a dismissive shrug.

Zelfa changed the subject. 'Perhaps next time we can be really brave and return to the subject of your mother.'

He took his jacket off the back of his chair and put it on.

'Maybe,' he said. 'I mean if you would find it of interest.'

'My needs are not really relevant here, Ali. Although if you would like me to have such an interest . . .'

'Yes.' He smiled, revealing a set of white, even teeth. 'Yes, as an exercise in the exploration of annihilation, I think you might benefit from it, doctor.'

'Then I will see you on Thursday, Ali,' she said and rose to escort him out of her office.

'I'll look forward to it,' he said, still smiling as he left.

When he had gone, Zelfa Halman sat back down heavily behind her desk. So often with anorexics, even of an indulgent borderline variety like Ali, it was a game. But this notion he had that he was somehow doing her a favour was a new one. Convoluted and really quite intellectual for one so young, she thought. Interesting. But not so interesting as to blind her to the fact that she would quite like to speak to the boy's obese father soon. For all his posturing, it was, she felt, important that Ali learn from the horse's mouth, as it were, that his one surviving parent was on his side.

In the meantime, and before her nerve deserted her, she had to make another phone call, the one she had been wanting to make all day. The one to Mehmet Suleyman. Her face reddened as she dialled his mobile number. 'Bloody menopause!' she muttered.

When, several seconds later, he answered, she did not for once refer to either her condition or say something deliberately cynical. But as she spoke to him she knew that it was far too late to go back on what she was doing. As they said back home, she would just have to 'spit it out and be damned'.

'Where are you, Mehmet?' she asked after he had thanked her profusely for calling and therefore brightening up his day.

'I'm just getting into the car,' he said. 'Going over to the Forensic Institute.'

'So you're not driving yet? And you're not with anyone else?'

'No. Why?'

She smiled. Here it came and he, apparently, didn't have a clue. 'You're sitting down now, in the car?'

'Yes. Zelfa—'

'Mehmet,' she said, and slowly savoured what was now the moment of affectionate torture she had always envisaged, 'dear Mehmet, I have decided, after much consideration, to accept your offer and become your wife.'

The strange strangled noise that came from the other end of the line made it quite apparent that he had heard her, but she did say his name a couple of times anyway, until he answered.

'You do know,' he said when he had recovered his voice, 'that you have just made me immeasurably happy, Zelfa.'

'Yes, foolish boy,' she said as she quickly wiped gathering tears from her eyes, 'although in comparison to my own joy, well . . .'

'Look, why don't you come over tonight so that we can tell people?'

'What, to Cohen's?'

'Yes,' he laughed. 'They will be so happy for us! Almost as happy as I am, my darling.'

She smiled. Sometimes, despite the fact that he was on the edge of middle age, Mehmet still behaved like an excited schoolboy. It was one of the many things that she loved about him.

'OK,' she said, quickly glancing at the diary that

lay open on her desk. 'I'll be finished here at about six.'

'I'll come and pick you up!'

'You—'

'I don't want my beautiful wife to walk the streets in the cold, dirty fog!'

Resisting the temptation to say something about how it had been good enough for her when she was his mistress, Zelfa just smiled and then assented to his request.

It was only when she finally put the phone down and asked for Mr Turkeş to be shown into the surgery that she thought properly about what she'd just done. 'Oh, shit!' she giggled as her patient walked uneasily through the door.

İkmen looked first at the small piece of paper in his hands and then shifted his gaze to Tepe's face.

'So you don't think that Miss Berisha is playing games with us then, Orhan?' he asked.

'No, sir,' Tepe replied.

'Despite the fact that when she went to the Vloras' apartment armed to kill she then joined forces with her enemy to lie to us about that.'

'She says she went over there to try and talk to Mehmet. She only took the knife, she says, because she apparently takes it everywhere.'

'She says,' İkmen muttered, echoing what he considered to be the most important element of his colleague's speech. Then suddenly smiling broadly he said, 'So is Miss Berisha still with us or has she run off back to her parents' place?'

'She's still here, sir,' Tepe said. 'In fact, I'd go so far as to say she's quite reluctant to leave.'

'How very odd.'

'Perhaps she's keen to find out whether you will telephone Felicity Evren and, if you do, what the outcome of that might be.'

İkmen raised the telephone receiver and dialled. 'Let us not disappoint her,' he said and then waited for someone to answer.

After several seconds the monotonous sound of an unattended phone was broken by a male voice.

'I would like to speak to Miss Evren, please,' İkmen said.

'Very well,' replied the male, who sounded quite young. Then he called out to someone in what İkmen immediately recognised as heavily accented English.

'Miss Flick!' he shouted. 'Miss Flick, some man on telephone!'

'What does he want?' an extremely English female voice replied.

'I do not know,' the man replied. 'Here, take.'

Shuffling sounds as the telephone receiver changed hands crackled in İkmen's ear. Just before the woman spoke, the policeman lit a cigarette.

'Flick Evren,' the woman said breathily into the receiver. 'Yes?'

'Hello, Miss Evren,' İkmen replied with what even Tepe recognised as a very good English accent. 'My name is Inspector Çetin İkmen. I work for the İstanbul Police Department.'

'Oh. Yes?'

'Yes. I am telephoning, Miss Evren, about the death of a young man I believe was a good friend of yours.'

'Oh.' He could almost see her gaze drop sadly towards the floor – her grief encapsulated in one small paravocal expression. 'How did you . . . ?'

'Mr Berisha's family are, as I hope you can appreciate, helping us with our inquiries. And because Mr Berisha's death has been declared unlawful we are bound to interest ourselves in all his contacts.'

'Of course.'

'And so anything that you, as a friend, could tell us, Miss Evren, would be appreciated.'

He heard her sigh. 'Now?' she said. 'I—'

'We could make an appointment for the near future,' İkmen said and rapidly looked at the back of his cigarette packet, which served as his diary for the day. 'Perhaps around five o'clock?'

'Today?'

'Yes.' It was always as well, İkmen thought, to be quite clear about what you wanted from those you wished to question. Such gentle bullying allowed everyone to understand the reality of their position within the process – even if words like 'you will' or 'you must' were never actually used.

'Well,' the woman drawled, 'do you want me to come in?'

'I can drive out to your home if you wish,' İkmen said.

'Oh, no. No, I'll come to you,' she said and then added through the filter of a tense little laugh, 'I'll get Hassan to drive me. It won't be any trouble.'

'Excellent. Thank you.'

'Right.'

He gave her the address of the station plus directions up to his office. She, in her turn, stated that she was looking forward to their meeting, which struck İkmen as odd. But then with Miss Felicity Evren being so very obviously English, this was perhaps not so strange. Old Timür İkmen always used to say that the British were polite to the point of irrationality. Once again, İkmen thought grimly, his late father had probably been right. In view of recent events, however, it was perhaps unwise to be thinking about his parents. In an attempt to divert himself he looked up sharply at his junior and said, 'Perhaps you could take Miss Berisha home now then, Orhan. No sense in her sitting downstairs indefinitely.'

'No, sir.' He stood up.

'You can tell her that everything is in hand with regard to Miss Evren,' İkmen said. 'You don't need to go into detail.'

He turned his attention back to the pile of papers he had been considering when Tepe first entered his office. But his mind refused to concentrate on the task in hand. His mother's death now haunted both his days and his nights, and he had begun to think that perhaps putting off talking to his brother was more an act of cowardice on his part than genuine care for Halil. After all, if, as Arto Sarkissian seemed to think, there was nothing relevant to his mother in Vahan Sarkissian's papers, he would have to contact Halil anyway.

With a sigh he lifted the telephone receiver and

dialled his brother's number. After what seemed like an eternity, a smooth voice answered.

'Halil, it's Çetin,' İkmen said quickly, aware of the very real danger of losing his nerve at this point. 'I need to see you.'

The reply he got was full of concern. 'What's wrong, brother? Is it Fatma or . . .'

'No, Fatma and the children are fine – as is, as far as it ever could be, the money situation,' İkmen said, effectively covering the usual reasons for calling on his brother.

'Then . . .'

'Look, Halil,' İkmen said, knowing that he was being unaccountably tetchy, 'I just need to talk to you, OK? I mean, are you busy this evening?'

'Çetin, this is really worrying me.'

'Yes or no, Halil!' İkmen said, his temper flaring. 'I can come to you or we can go out.'

'Çetin—'

'Halil, I need to speak to you about our mother!' and then furious that he had disclosed the subject of his anxieties before he was ready, he added, 'It's a conversation we should have had forty years ago!'

'*What?*'

Responding instantly to the panic in his brother's voice, İkmen said, 'Can we talk of these things or not? Can I come and see you?'

'Tonight?'

'Yes! Yes, I need to do this, Halil, I—'

'All right! All right!' In his mind's eye İkmen could see the long, heavily ringed fingers of his brother's hands flying into the air in agitated submission – hands, if not the gestures that they made, so like those of Ayşe İkmen. But then everybody said that the older İkmen brother had inherited his mother's good looks while the 'little one' had gained much from her magical personality.

'I will be finished with these figures at around seven,' Halil said, 'so if you want to come after that, I will ask Mrs Kemal to prepare dinner for two.'

'There's really no need,' İkmen said as he recalled the contemptuous looks his brother's housekeeper had given him the last time he had visited. But then what did he expect? His brother, as a successful, childless and now divorced accountant, lived, dressed and ate well. Çetin, on the other hand, as a married policeman with nine children, looked exactly like what he was – a stressed-out chain-smoker with several barely controlled stomach ulcers.

'Well then, I will see you later,' Halil said with a resigned sigh.

'Thank you, Halil.'

'It's nothing.'

But it was, and Çetin İkmen knew that they both knew it. The one thing that the subject of Ayşe İkmen could never be was nothing. Though dead for over forty years, the witch of Üsküdar had always been the focus of passionate speculation to those interested in such dark things – and, of course, to her two sons, between whom, although they never spoke of her, İkmen often thought, she stood immovably, like one of the harsh mountains of her birthplace.

*   *   *

She hadn't expected to find someone like him in a place like this. Tall, slim and quite spectacularly handsome, the man was locking the door to what she assumed must be his office. And, because he was so obviously leaving, Felicity Evren had to assume that this attractive man couldn't possibly be the inspector she had spoken to on the telephone. He was, in all probability, a colleague whom, had she felt more confident of her Turkish, she would have asked about this İkmen fellow, simply to speak to him. But as quickly as he had appeared, so Inspector Suleyman, or so the plate on his door would have it, had gone, leaving Felicity alone with the door opposite – the one belonging, so its plate said, to Inspector Çetin İkmen.

A single tap on the glass brought a short, wiry man to the door. First, slightly bemused, his face quickly resolved into a really very pleasant smile.

'Hello, Miss Evren,' he said in perfect English as he extended a small hand towards her. 'Thank you so much for coming so promptly.'

'Anything I can do to help . . .' She shrugged, the upward motion of her shoulders accentuating the pronounced puffiness that İkmen observed on the left-hand side of her face, and the barely concealed discolouration of the flesh.

'Please sit down.' İkmen pulled his hand free from her grip and motioned her towards the chair in front of his desk.

'Thank you.'

She sat, her tiny form almost disappearing from view behind piles of paper.

'Can I get you some tea?'

'No. Thank you,' she said and smiled in a manner almost as disconcerting as her shrug.

İkmen, ever the perfect host, took his cigarettes and lighter from his pocket. 'Cigarette?'

'No, thank you,' she said, 'but please, if you want to smoke then don't let me stop you.'

He nodded by way of thanks and lit up.

'My father smokes quite heavily,' she said as she watched İkmen light his cigarette and then exhale with pleasure. 'Like all of you, really.'

İkmen frowned. 'All of you?' he said. 'Meaning, Miss Evren?'

Laughing, she answered, 'Turks, Inspector. My father, like you, is Turkish.'

'Oh. And you?'

'Like my mother, I am English,' she said, 'but then that is something that I think you knew already.'

He smiled.

'You speak the language so well, Inspector, and with such a perfect accent.'

Ever embarrassed by flattery, İkmen looked down at the desk in front of him. 'My father taught English, French and Russian at the university. Many years ago now, however.'

'My father lived in London all his life until now, but he doesn't speak the language as well as you do,' she replied.

'Thank you.'

And then, for a moment, a silence descended upon them. Felicity Evren, feeling that she might perhaps have over-flattered this unknown man, looked away. İkmen, too, though for other reasons, sought out something upon which to pin his gaze. This, conveniently, turned out to be Rifat Berisha's file.

'So, Miss Evren, how long did you know Rifat Berisha?' he asked.

'For about eighteen months.'

'Right.' İkmen turned the pages of the thick file and came to the postcards and tickets from London.

'And where did you meat Mr Berisha?'

'I bought a very delicate cup and saucer from him,' Felicity Evren said with a smile of remembrance. 'He had a stall, with some other men, at the Ortaköy Sunday market.'

'These other men,' İkmen asked, 'were they Albanian too?'

She shrugged. 'I imagine so, yes. I couldn't understand anything they said.'

'And then?' İkmen prompted with a forward movement of his shoulders.

'We became friends, Inspector,' she answered, smiling that awful crooked smile of hers. 'He showed me so much of this city. We had a lot of fun together. I've only lived in İstanbul for two years, since I came here with my father and brother.'

'So your mother . . .'

'Is dead, Inspector.'

'Oh, I'm sorry.'

She just shrugged and, taking this as his cue to move

163

on, İkmen said, 'When did you last see Mr Berisha, Miss Evren?'

She paused to think. 'The morning before the night of his death. We had lunch together.'

'Where?' İkmen put his cigarette out and then immediately lit another.

'At the Yeşil Ev,' she replied, naming one of the ever increasing number of Ottoman Mansion Hotels.

İkmen, frowning, observed, 'Expensive.'

'Yes,' she said simply. 'I'd been shopping. It was a nice way to finish my trip.'

İkmen took a long drag on his cigarette. 'And so, Miss Evren, did Mr Berisha, at either that luncheon or before, give you any reason to think that he might be in some kind of danger?'

'No,' she replied without, this time, pausing to consider her answer. 'Although he didn't talk very much at lunch.' She smiled. 'I'm afraid I tended to go on a bit about my purchases. I always hogged the conversation.'

'And yet you and he had a lot of fun.'

'Yes, we did,' she said with a sudden, quite aggressive sharpness. 'Rifat liked the way I was with him. Our friendship was good!'

'Yes,' İkmen said in as conciliatory a way as possible. 'Yes, there are plenty of things that men and woman can . . . do . . .'

'We did not have . . . have sex, either,' she added, still quite obviously fuelled by anger. 'I loved Rifat and I will miss him bitterly, but not in . . . in that way.'

'No.' İkmen nodded. 'Quite right.'

Another small silence followed, which was again eventually broken by İkmen.

'So did you and Rifat ever go further afield, outside the city?'

'We spent a day in Bursa together,' she said, 'just before the earthquake.'

'No other trips then?' İkmen asked as he looked down once again at the postcards and tickets in Rifat's file, 'You didn't go abroad?'

'Abroad?' She laughed. 'Are you serious? Rifat was Albanian, Inspector İkmen, they're not welcome in a whole lot of places, you know – especially in Europe which is where I tend to go when I leave Turkey.'

İkmen frowned. 'So you have no idea where he might have obtained these?' he said as he pushed the postcards and tickets towards her.

Felicity Evren looked down at them briefly and shrugged. 'No. I suppose I may have given him the postcards at some time but I don't remember doing so.'

He smiled. 'And you have no idea where else he might have got them from?'

'No.'

İkmen took the cards and tickets back. 'Do you know how Miss Berisha came to have your telephone number, Miss Evren?'

'She didn't say. It must have been amongst Rifat's things.'

'No, he memorised it actually,' İkmen said blandly. 'Engelushjia Berisha told my sergeant that her brother gave her your number when he went abroad with you last year. He didn't know where he was going to be

165

staying, but he wanted her to have the number just in case anything should happen to him.'

Felicity Evren turned her face away.

'Miss Berisha also told my sergeant,' İkmen continued, 'that while he was abroad with you, Rifat had surgery. He gave you one of his kidneys, didn't he, Miss Evren? Before you answer, remember that I can order you to be examined to verify this.'

'You have no idea,' she said, still not looking at him. 'I had kidney disease . . . It's . . .'

'And in return you gave Rifat a very nice car.'

She turned back to face him again, her features red with anger. 'That was not why I gave him the car!' Her voice trembled with emotion. 'Rifat helped me because he loved me. I gave him the car because I am rich and I loved him. No money ever changed hands!'

'Free donation of an organ is not illegal,' İkmen said. 'You must understand that when our doctor discovered that Rifat had only one kidney—'

'You thought the worst!' she snapped.

'Well, considering his parents were entirely ignorant of the matter . . .'

'It was his body! He could do what—'

'But you must agree, Miss Evren, that the apparent secrecy surrounding his donation does look suspicious – we were bound to investigate.'

Her poor twisted face now attempted a smile. 'I know.'

İkmen felt quite sorry for her. 'But now that you have told us the truth, that is fine,' he said gently, 'though I will of course have to check with the British authorities.'

'Yes, yes. Please do,' she said distractedly, obviously now chastising herself. 'We obtained a visa for Rifat at the consulate and . . . I'm so very sorry that I lied to you, Inspector İkmen. I just thought that with Rifat's death you would think all sorts of things and . . .'

'Well, as long as that is all, miss.' He paused briefly in order to give her some time to vouchsafe more information. But she didn't. 'Perhaps you would be good enough to give me a statement to that effect.'

She sighed. 'Of course.'

But then something subtly changed. Felicity Evren suddenly leaned forward and pointed to her face. 'You know, although he helped me beyond all measure, I didn't need Rifat, as some women might have done, to feed my ego. I mean, looking the way that I do, why would I?'

Taken aback, not quite understanding what was expected of him here, İkmen simply said, 'No, miss.'

'Had I wanted Rifat to love me, I would have had no difficulty in securing his affections. One doesn't when one is beautiful, does one?'

'I wouldn't know,' İkmen said with great honesty. 'But if that is your perception . . .' He shrugged.

Felicity Evren smiled, crookedly. İkmen turned away. Was she being ironic or was she just delusional? At a loss, he returned again to the day of Rifat's death, taking a kind of refuge there.

'So after you had lunch with Mr Berisha . . .'

'I went home and Rifat, to my knowledge, went to his home,' she said.

'And he didn't seem either nervous or worried?'

'No. I invited him to dinner at my home, next Friday, and then we parted company.' She shrugged. 'Very normal.'

'Right, well,' he said as he gathered various bits of evidence back into Rifat Berisha's file, 'we'll need all the details about your trip to England in your statement.'

'You want me to do that now?'

'I'll take you down to one of our interview rooms in a moment, yes,' he said.

'Very well.'

İkmen stood up. 'Then that will clear up at least one part of our investigation, will it not?'

'Yes.' She rose too and smiled as he held the door open for her. 'Thank you.'

'You're very welcome.'

Of course her story made perfect sense, and İkmen had no doubt that the British authorities would confirm the details. But he wasn't particularly happy about it. Rifat's parents had had a right to know what he had done, even if Rifat himself hadn't wanted them to. What if he had become ill upon his return to the Republic? What could poor little Engelushjia have been able to do about that? And anyway, it was an abuse of power as far as he was concerned. The rich could buy anything and everything they wanted. He knew it was how life was, but that didn't mean that he necessarily liked it.

There were other issues here too. Like Felicity's appearance, and her attitude to it. Also, if she had been so concerned about the matter of Rifat's gift of a kidney to her as to lie to the police about it, what else might she or her family want to conceal about what had happened over in England?

Chapter 11

Grunting against the steep gradient that fell away sharply behind the white BMW, Zelfa Halman pushed the car door open and eased her feet down onto the pot-holed road surface below. She turned to look at the small Fiat that had pulled up behind them.

'Isn't that your brother?' she called across the car roof to Mehmet Suleyman.

'Yes,' he replied, smiling. Joining her in the road, he took one of her hands in his. 'I wanted Murad to be with us when we told people. You don't mind, do you?'

'No. Of course not.' And then squeezing his hand encouragingly, she walked with him down to where a slightly plump man of medium height was extricating himself and a toddler from the Fiat.

'Murad!'

The face that looked up from behind the tangle of beribboned hair on the little girl's head was as affable as it was tired looking. Although shorter than his younger brother, Murad Suleyman would have shared Mehmet's good looks had it not been for the weakness of his chin. It was a feature many put down to the significant amount of imperial blood that ran in his veins.

'Hello, Brother,' he said as he tried vainly to prevent

171

his daughter, who was now stretching her arms out towards her uncle, from over-balancing out of his arms.

Letting go of Zelfa's hand, Mehmet grabbed the little girl from his brother's arms with a laugh.

'Oh, this is a lovely welcome from a lovely girl!' he said as the little one wound her arms round his neck, burying her face in the thick collar of his coat.

'Well, you are Edibe's only uncle, so what do you expect?' Murad said and then turned his tired eyes towards Zelfa. 'Good to see you again, doctor.'

'Thank you.'

He smiled breifly at her before addressing his brother once again. 'So is this just a social invitation or something more?'

'When we get inside, I will tell you everything,' Mehmet replied. He caught Zelfa's eye and smiled.

'Not anything to do with Father's invitation then?' Murad said.

'No, but . . .'

The two brothers exchanged what to Zelfa looked like a strained gaze.

'But what, Mehmet?'

'But now is not the time to talk about that,' the younger man said, breaking once again into a smile directed solely at Zelfa. 'Tonight is about happy, hopeful things that lie not in the past but in the future.'

'How very mysterious!'

Murad's words were not, to Zelfa at least, in any way convincing. He was, she felt, not only ready for the news but judging by the champagne bottle poking out of his overcoat pocket, prepared for it too.

As they all moved forward towards the Cohens' apartment block, Zelfa smiled at this small, and kindly, deception.

In some families it is easy to see resemblances. In others there is little or nothing to denote blood connection. The İkmen brothers, Çetin and Halil, appeared not only unrelated but like foreigners. As Halil's housekeeper left after serving the two men with tea, Çetin İkmen, now alone with this virtual stranger, began to feel the alienation most acutely. It wasn't that he didn't love Halil – in fact quite the reverse was true – more that he felt awkward in his company, especially if *that* subject was to be discussed. As soon as he'd arrived at Halil's pleasant Emirgan house, he had, erroneously he thought now, launched into the subject of their mother. That Halil had been reluctant to talk about his family in front of Mrs Kemal had been obvious from the straight-faced silence with which he had greeted Çetin's opening remarks. Now, however, with only the silence of the night to bear witness to their conversation, the words still stuck in Çetin's throat.

Looking across at the well-dressed man sitting back, seemingly comfortably, in his armchair, Çetin shuffled precariously on the edge of his seat and cleared his throat. He took his cigarettes and lighter out of the pocket of the coat he was still wearing and held them aloft for his brother to see. 'May I?'

'There's an ashtray on the table,' Halil answered with a shrug.

Smiling, Çetin leaned forward to offer his brother a

cigarette. With a small bow of the head and the placing of one hand over his heart, Halil refused.

Çetin, a little more relaxed now he could light up, noticed for the first time that the hair around his brother's ears and temples was quite white. It was one of those rare moments when one realises that those close to one are no longer young. Counting upwards from his own age, Çetin İkmen discovered that his brother was now fifty-seven. It was a strange, half-known shock that took a little time to recover from.

In the silence, Halil finally spoke. 'So what is it exactly that you want to discuss about Mother's death?'

Çetin took a deep drag on his cigarette before answering.

'I want to know what happened that day,' he said. 'I want to understand.'

'You were there—'

'I was ten years old, Halil,' Çetin cut in sharply.

'Yes, and I was thirteen.'

'You walked into that room. You stood in front of me. I saw only your back.'

Halil leaned forward in his chair and clasped his hands between his knees. 'You were my little brother, Çetin. I wanted to protect you. I knew that Mother was dead.'

'How?' He took a nervous drag on his cigarette and attempted to catch Halil's eyes which seemed to be trying to avoid his own. 'One thing I do know is that she was lying on her bed. Couldn't she have just been asleep?'

'Çetin, she was dead.'

'Yes, but how—'

'I don't know how I knew! It all happened a very long time ago!' He got up quickly from his chair and walked across to his brother, took a cigarette out of the packet in his hands and lit up.

'If Mother did indeed die of a heart attack, there couldn't have been all that much to see surely.'

Halil halted in his progress back to his seat and turned to face his brother.

'I don't know,' he said. 'I don't remember. Perhaps you should speak to Arto about the possible post-mortem condition of a cardiac patient.'

'All I'm saying is—'

'Çetin, I don't know,' and then with a long drag on his cigarette followed by a sigh he sat back down in his chair. 'And I don't understand why these old miseries are suddenly so important to you. Mother died when we were both children. Father had a terrible, hard life for many years after that. I thought that you and I had decided to consign all of that to the past.'

Halil's observations were not, Çetin knew, unreasonable. Life had indeed been very difficult for the family in the wake of Ayşe İkmen's death. Their father had had to carry on working in order to support his boys, but at a price. Keeping house, cooking and doing the laundry were not activities that two intellectual and intense boys wanted or enjoyed. They would both fall exhausted into their beds at the end of days spent cleaning, cooking, going to school and doing their homework. Late into the night, every night, their father Timür would work on his lecture notes, prepare the soup for the following morning and, in the winter months, go out into the garden to gather wood for the fire. Not once during that time did his eyes so much as touch upon another woman, even though he was still a youngish man at that time and must have been terribly lonely.

But notwithstanding all of this bitter old pain, Çetin knew that if he were ever to get the vision of Angeliki Vlora's vindictive face out of his mind, he would have to somehow root out the truth. Besides, with his mother's death weighing on his mind plus the connection he had with the Albanian community via Samsun, Çetin felt that he was becoming compromised with regard to the Rifat Berisha case. The sooner this question regarding Ayşe's death could be cleared up, the better. And so he told his brother everything: about Angeliki Vlora, about *gjakmaria*, about the unfortunate involvement of their cousin. The only thing he omitted was Angeliki's allegations about the manner of their mother's death, reasoning that if that were correct, Halil would know about it anyway.

When he'd finished, Halil took another cigarette from his brother's packet and leaned back thoughtfully in his chair.

'So you see, Halil,' Çetin said, lighting up also, 'I do need to know. It's affecting my work . . .'

'Yes, well . . .' Halil replied, 'I do see that it is important that you know, Çetin.'

'But?'

Halil smiled. 'But if Arto can't find anything in Uncle Vahan's papers, I think you may very well be at a dead end.'

'But Halil, you were—'

'Yes, I was there, Çetin, and yes, I called Uncle Vahan and got you looked after by the neighbours.' He leaned forward in his chair, his eyes intense and also a little moist. 'But the truth is that even if you threatened me with death I could not tell you what I saw in Mother's bedroom.'

For Çetin who, on his way over to Halil's, had struggled with various theories regarding what if anything his brother might have been concealing from him all these years, this empty revelation came as a shock. It also, for the moment, puzzled him.

'So now when you think about going into that room . . .'

'I see only blackness,' Halil replied. 'Nothing.'

'Nothing? At all?'

'Çetin, I can't even recall what Mother looked like unless I get my photographs out!'

'But you look so like her.'

'Then perhaps that is why I do not linger at the mirror in the morning! Perhaps it all hurts too much!'

They lapsed into silence. Çetin tried to order his thoughts. If Halil had expunged the memory of their mother's death from his mind, what did that signify? This was not, Çetin knew, unusual in those who had suffered severe trauma. But as time progressed such memories generally either returned or the person suffered some other problems resulting from the sublimation of the unacceptable, which usually led to that person seeking psychiatric help. As far as he knew, neither of these things had happened to Halil. So had his brother seen something so terrible in that room that what appeared to be a permanent curtain had been brought down on the sight? Could it be that he had seen their mother lying there with her throat slashed open – the gash deep and liverish like the one that had taken Rifat Berisha's life? Could there be truth in what Angeliki Vlora had told him?

'Halil—'

The sound of his mobile ringing interrupted him. With a brief apologetic nod at his brother, Çetin took the instrument out of his coat pocket and pressed the receive button.

'İkmen.'

'Inspector, it's Orhan,' a rather breathless voice informed him.

İkmen frowned. 'Is there a problem?'

'I'm afraid Samsun Bajraktar has been admitted to hospital with stab wounds.'

The guilt washed across İkmen's mind like a tidal wave. It had to be the Vloras. One day, he had always known, his job would damage a member of his family. Now it had happened.

'How is he?' İkmen said as he nervously lit a new cigarette off the butt of his old one. 'And where?'

'Well, the good news is that he is conscious. A Zabita officer actually witnessed the end of the attack . . .'

'Where did it happen?'

'Near the Kapalı Çarşı, I don't know where exactly.'

'Did the Zabita manage to apprehend the assailant?'

Halil moved over to his brother. 'What is it? What—'

A sternly upheld hand cut him off and Halil watched

in silence as Çetin's face registered what seemed to be further bad news.

'No, he didn't,' Orhan Tepe answered, 'although apparently he thinks he can give us a reasonable description of the man.'

'Good.' İkmen would have liked to ask at this point whether the description fitted Mehmet Vlora but he moved on to what was really the more important issue right now. 'So where is Samsun, Orhan?'

'He was taken to the Cerrahpaşa,' Tepe said, naming, to İkmen's relief, the excellent teaching hospital that, as luck would have it, happened to be the nearest medical facility to the site of the incident.

'I'll get over there right away,' İkmen said, rising to his feet.

'I should imagine that he's probably receiving treatment now, sir.'

'Well, I'm going anyway,' İkmen replied. 'As well as being a crime victim, he is also my cousin.'

Halil's eyes widened and he mugged furiously at his brother in order to elicit more information. Çetin turned away, intent upon the telephone call.

'Is anybody with him at the Cerrahpaşa?'

'Only the Zabita at the moment, although I have sent one of the uniforms, Roditi, over there to relieve him. I've asked him to send the Zabita back here so that I can take a statement.'

'Good. I'd better get moving myself now.'

'Are you at home, sir?'

'No,' İkmen replied with a sigh, anticipating the not inconsiderable journey to the hospital, which was across the Golden Horn in Aksaray. 'No, I have to come from Emirgan. I'm at the home of my brother.'

'Oh.'

'But if I leave now, it shouldn't take me too long.'

'OK.'

'I will see you after I've been to the hospital, Orhan,' he said and then added, if a little distractedly, 'Oh, and thank you for what you've done. I don't know why you're working so late but—'

'I'll see you later then, sir,' his inferior cut in.

'Yes.' And with that İkmen pressed the end button and shoved the telephone back into the pocket of his coat.

'So what is it?' his wide-eyed brother asked as he followed Çetin to the door. 'What has happened?'

'Our cousin Samsun Bajraktar has been attacked,' Çetin said as he stepped into the wide hall at the centre of his brother's house. 'And it's all my fault.'

'But . . .'

Çetin strode out through the front door and into the coldness of the night. As Halil stared after him, his heartbeat loud with anxiety, he could not help noting that it had been many years since he had seen his brother actually run.

High heels and fish-tail skirt notwithstanding, Samsun Bajraktar was still a sizeable and muscular prospect to take on in a fight. The assailant had been much smaller than Samsun and even the element of surprise would not have given him much advantage. The knife had sliced quite deeply into Samsun's buttocks but the fact that the transsexual was not dead was largely a tribute to her greater size and power. Once her wounds had been stitched, Samsun did not, of course, allow this opportunity for high drama to pass her by.

'The blood loss was so great,' she said as İkmen pulled a chair up to her bed and sat down, 'that I simply fainted into the arms of that Zabita.'

'That must have been an interesting experience for him,' replied İkmen, who had now met the man and knew him to be young and attractive.

Dr Alptekin, who had treated Samsun less than an hour before, smiled.

'Actually,' he said, 'your blood loss was not really that great. You didn't need a transfusion. But then,' he added kindly, 'we all know that that stuff really spreads, don't we?'

'Oh, absolutely,' İkmen agreed. 'Just a spoonful of blood can look like an ocean.'

'I'll leave you alone now,' a still smiling Alptekin said as he left, closing the door behind him. The noise of the heaving hospital outside abated.

'He's downplaying it,' Samsun explained as soon as the doctor had gone.

İkmen smiled. 'Probably for the best,' he said and then, sighing deeply, changed tack to more serious matters.

'So, was it Mehmet Vlora who attacked you?'

'Oh, I couldn't possibly answer that, Çetin,' Samsun said, looking intently at the white bowl that stood on the table beside her bed. 'It all happened so quickly. I was out looking, like the stupid, besotted girl that I am, for that faithless bastard Abdurrahman—'

'The Zabita officer,' İkmen cut in before Samsun's attempts at blinding him with superfluous details really took hold, 'is at this moment giving one of my officers a very comprehensive description of the man involved.'

Samsun looked at İkmen sharply. 'Oh?'

'He got a very good view of everything,' and then smiling into the lie he added, 'including the man's face.'

'Oh.'

'So if you do know who did this, you might as well tell me.'

Samsun, who with her hair scraped back harshly from her face looked more like a man than usual, distracted herself by playing with what was left of her chipped nail polish.

'Samsun?'

She looked up from her fingers. 'Yes?'

'Look, if you're worried about reprisals . . .'

'Çetin, if the Zabita clearly saw who attacked me then I can't really see why I need to add my observations to his. I mean, as an officer of the law—'

'He needs all the help he can get,' İkmen said. 'They're only market police, the Zabita. People view them as little more than glorified security men. Yes, they are observant and yes, they do have a good knowledge regarding thieves and dodgy dealers in their particular area. But they are not accustomed to serious acts of violence, a fact that will be known to any lawyer the assailant might engage.'

Samsun turned a shocked face towards her cousin. 'You mean that the Zabita might not be believed? That my attacker might get away with it?'

'It's possible.'

'Oh, well then,' she said and painfully pushed herself up a little straighter against the pillows, 'if that happened, I'd have to sort it out myself, wouldn't I?'

'Reverting, no doubt,' İkmen said as casually as he could, 'to the laws laid down by Lek Dukagjini.'

'Well, yes, I—'

'So your attacker was Albanian then,' İkmen said through a glaze of barely concealed triumph.

Samsun, her eyes once again rooted to her nails, spat the word 'Bastard!' at him before returning her now hostile attention back to his face.

İkmen smiled. 'If your description matched that given by the Zabita, it would be very helpful. That sort of evidence, where people observe similar clothes, colouring, height, is very compelling.'

'So I don't actually have to give a name.'

'Oh, no.' İkmen smiled again as he slowly reached into his pocket for his notebook and pen. 'Just an outline of what the man looked like to you.'

'And I don't have to talk about his nationality either?' Samsun said, her voice now wavering both from the effects of the painkilling drugs she had been given and from the strain of this delicately oblique conversation.

'No,' İkmen replied. 'Just tell me *exactly* what he looked like and what he was wearing.'

As if pulled by invisible cords, Samsun's eyes turned quickly towards the door of her room, her features exhibiting some nervousness about what might be beyond it.

'I won't let anything happen to you, you know,'

İkmen said. 'One of my men is going to be outside that door until you leave this hospital.'

'And then?' Actively she searched his face for reassurance.

'By that time the culprit should be in my cells and his family under close observation.'

'Do you mean it, Çetin? I mean, you're not just saying this to—'

'I give you my word,' İkmen said, his face now serious. 'As your cousin as well as an officer of the law, I guarantee that nothing bad will happen to you.' Briefly, he took one of her hands in his, an action that made her slowly smile.

'Oh, well,' she said after a pause, 'I suppose I can give a description . . .'

'Good girl!' İkmen enthused. He opened his note-book. 'So?'

'Well,' Samsun began.

Although attending to every word she said, some of which quite surprised him, at least half of İkmen's mind wondered how on earth he was going to deliver on his promise to protect Samsun from harm. After all, it wasn't as if she was inconspicuous – and that was apart from the problem of how he'd ever find enough manpower to stake out the home of her attacker. But then he consoled himself with the notion that as a Turk he should really trust to the fickle arms of kismet; the fact that he didn't actually believe in fate was, he decided, of no importance.

Chapter 12

Dawn came late that day, as is its custom during the winter months. For Çetin İkmen the reduction in daylight hours was a blessing. For, as he stood outside the entrance to the Vloras' Tahtakale Caddesi apartment, the pistol that only he knew was unloaded in his hand, he was grateful that the long hours of darkness had allowed him to deploy so many men around the building. Inside could be any number of people who might offer armed resistance to the police – something that he knew would not be affected by whether or not he smiled at the obviously nervous Orhan Tepe at his side, but he did it anyway. It cost him nothing and was worth the tense little grimace that he received in return. Then looking up at the two uniformed officers now holding the battering ram up against the flimsy door that young Yıldız had so recently kicked down, İkmen mouthed the word, 'Go!'

In the confusion that followed, the sound of the splintering door and the officers' announcement of their presence melded with the screams of the women and the noise of the Vlora men's bare feet slapping against the floor. All this enveloped in an odour which İkmen instantly recognised as the sharp smell of cannabis.

'Mmm,' he said as his officers cleared a path for him through to what had earlier been identified as the sleeping quarters. 'Drugs and violence.' Then, looking up at Tepe, he added, 'Whatever next, eh, Orhan?'

Smiling by way of reply, Tepe strode out ahead of İkmen, following the uniformed officers into the room.

They were all there with the exception of Aryan Vlora who some of the other officers were already talking to in the kitchen, along with the boys mother Angeliki.

Mehmet and Mehti were, or rather had been until the police had broken in, otherwise engaged. The woman in Mehti's bed, with her white skin and ash-blonde hair, was of western European appearance, and the tiny dark creature cringing beside Mehmet was probably Albanian. Maybe she was his wife.

'What do you mean breaking in here like this!' Mehmet Vlora shouted as they entered. 'We had you in here yesterday. Men in white coats, taking things away . . .'

'Forensic, yes, about Rifat Berisha's murder. They're outside again now, waiting to come and do a bit more. I believe you were expecting them, though perhaps not quite yet if the smell of this place is anything to go by. But I haven't come about that or indeed to talk to you, Mehmet. I've come to speak to Mehti,' İkmen said with a smile in that man's direction, 'about a very unpleasant attack upon one Samsun Bajraktar. It happened yesterday evening.'

'He was here with us!' Mehmet growled, more to the

large constable who now had one hand on his shoulder than to İkmen.

'What's going on?' the blonde woman said in what İkmen immediately recognised as English.

'It concerns a violent crime your boyfriend may have committed, miss,' İkmen replied in English, 'and also, now that I'm here, possession of cannabis.'

'Well, it's got nothing to do with me!' the woman snapped back harshly, pulling a rather greasy looking sheet across her naked body. 'And he isn't my boyfriend if that's what you think!'

İkmen, smiling, said, 'That's probably just as well then, isn't it, miss?' He turned to Mehti, speaking Turkish again. 'Unfortunately for you, Mehti, the young Zabita officer who probably saved Samsun's life gave a very good description of you, including,' he tipped his head towards an emerald-green puffa jacket lying on the floor, 'your clothes.'

'But—'

'I want the whole lot of them brought down to the station,' İkmen said, addressing his team.

'Get dressed,' Tepe ordered the two Albanian men.

Silent and now seemingly afraid, Mehmet and Mehti began to put on their trousers, socks and shirts, whilst quietly urging their women to do likewise. Although the English-speaking girl was still obviously outraged, she complied without further comment.

As he made his way back into the hall, İkmen reminded his officers that Mehti Vlora's clothes would be needed for forensic analysis and that that gentleman should be encouraged to take spare garments with him for what could be a rather long stay in the cells. Once out in the hall, however, İkmen's earlier arrogant bonhomie faded under the searing glare of an old woman's infuriated eyes.

'You pig!' Angeliki Vlora spat at him as she struggled to free her clawed fingers from the restraining arms of a thickset constable.

'We found cocaine on this one,' the constable said.

'Oh dear,' İkmen replied as he bent down to look into the woman's furious face. 'That is not good, Angeliki.'

'None of my sons were involved in the attack on the catamite! None of them!'

'Did I say that they were?' İkmen said with feigned innocence. 'I think not.' He looked up at the constable holding the woman and asked, 'Did anyone tell Mrs Vlora why we are here while you were in the kitchen, Bilgen?'

'No, sir.'

He turned back to the old woman. 'Well then, Angeliki, either you can now hear through a lot of noise and thick walls or things are truly getting worse and worse for you.'

'Witch's child!' the old woman hissed at him. 'I know why you're persecuting us!'

'Oh, and why is that?'

'Because you're lazy! Because my boys are convenient culprits for the Berisha boy's murder! And because I told you the truth about your mother's death which you just cannot take!'

Stung by her words, İkmen rounded fiercely upon her. 'For your information,' he said through gritted teeth, 'I'm just about the most diligent detective you'll find in this city. I could have arrested your boys within twenty-four hours of Rifat's death if I'd wanted to, if I'd been convinced of their guilt. But I'm not. I'm not convinced of their innocence either.' He paused then, taking just a moment to light a cigarette, his eyes not leaving hers as he did so. 'And as for my mother, so far your story is substantiated by no one.'

'And you won't take the word of an Albanian woman, oh no!'

'Not if that woman is both a harbourer of criminals and a drug dealer, no. Would you?'

She shrugged. 'If you asked the right people . . .'

'What do you mean?' he said, staring into her crafty yellowing eyes, searching for yet more deceit.

'If Ahmet Bajraktar is still with the living . . .'

'My uncle?'

'The witch's brother, yes. He knows, İkmen.' A smile broke across the dryness of her lips. 'He knows everything.'

'What—'

'Do you want this lot downstairs now, sir?' Tepe asked as he, the other officers and their prisoners effectively broke the spell that had briefly existed between İkmen and Angeliki Vlora.

İkmen turned away from the old woman and looked up into his sergeant's questioning face.

'Yes,' he said and then seemingly gathering both strength and resolve from his separation from the old woman, he added, 'Yes, take them down to the cars.

Don't let them talk to each other. Oh, and you can tell forensic they've got the place to themselves.'

'Right.'

As the officers and their prisoners moved out of the apartment and into the communal areas of the building, İkmen put one unsteady hand up to his head and then wiped away the small bead of sweat which, despite the current freezing conditions, had formed upon his brow.

Breakfast was not a meal that often featured in Zelfa Halman's day. A cup of coffee and three cigarettes was the usual form. This morning, however, and in the face of what felt alarmingly like sickness, she felt that she should really try to force something down. Must be the effects of drinking that champagne the previous night, she thought. OK, she'd had only two glasses, but then she hadn't been able to drink like she used to in the old days for many years. She hadn't attempted five pints of Guinness followed by several large whiskies for a long time – if she had she might have felt that her hangover was justified, but it wasn't and so it was with a bad grace that she ordered breakfast and tea in the little café opposite her office.

When it arrived, although the cheese, honey and bread looked reasonably appetising, the sight of the hard-boiled egg made her feel even worse. Cringing, she picked it up, wrapped it in a napkin and dumped it on the empty table beside her. She took a sip of her tea and then checked her watch before she attempted to deal with the food that remained on her plate. She had half an hour before her first appointment, which was enough, hopefully, to inject a little humanity back into what felt like a toxin-wracked body. Shakily she picked up her knife.

'Hello, doctor.'

It was a young, male voice and one that, with its perfectly accented English, she recognised immediately.

'Hello, Ali,' she said and tried not to be shocked at the hollowness of the eyes that now regarded her with what seemed to be amusement. 'What are you doing here?'

'I came in for some tea,' he said as, unbidden, he lowered himself into the chair opposite hers. And then as if answering some silent question he could see forming in her mind he said, 'I do drink, you know.'

'But no food,' Zelfa said, cutting into her cheese without enthusiasm.

'Maybe later.' He smiled. 'But not now.' Leaning forward, he said, 'I know you telephoned my father last night and I know what you said.'

Zelfa sighed. 'Then you'll know, as I do, that he is very concerned and wants the best for you.'

The boy looked across at her paltry efforts at eating with something Zelfa recognised as smugness.

'That's what he told *you*,' he said as he watched her chew disgustedly on the cheese. 'He told *me* that he's sick of my madness and that if I don't conform to what he wants me to be he'll have me put away.'

'I'm sure he didn't mean it.'

'Yes, he did! I know him!' His eyes took on an even more intense aspect. 'He isn't a nice man, my father. Sometimes he hurts people. He hurt Mum with

191

his indifference and lack of understanding. But then,' he added sadly, 'we all had our part to play in that drama.'

'Ali,' Zelfa said gently, 'we've talked about your mother's death and you know that I feel there is work to be done there. Your feelings of guilt are totally disproportionate. You were a child, what could you have done? Your mother was, as I understand it, a very unhappy woman.'

'What do you know about it?' he snapped. 'I don't want to talk about that! Death. I don't have to go there! I want to talk about me and I want you to make certain that my father doesn't put me in some stinking institution!' Then looking deeply into her eyes he pleaded, 'You won't let him, will you, doctor? I mean, I'm not mad.'

'I certainly couldn't and wouldn't hospitalise you at the present time, Ali, no,' Zelfa responded calmly, hedging, as doctors do, her bets for the future.

Not that the boy seemed to have heard. 'Because unlike my mother I have no intention of taking my own life. I just wish to live my life in a way that I find appropriate to the creature that I am. I am not a cheap gangster like my father, I am a gentleman. I have manners, I protect the honour of my beloved sister, I dress plainly and well.' He looked arrogantly around the café at the other diners, contempt written all over his features.

His verbal fluency coupled with his school uniform gave Zelfa momentary pause. Perhaps that other bright boy, Mehmet Suleyman, had affected people like this when he was a schoolboy? Serious, charming, mannered

– although without the obvious fevered disorder that characterised this child's hollow eyes. Her lover, her man, soon to be her husband. She made a conscious effort not to smile at the thought before she spoke again.

'Look, Ali,' she said and laid her knife on her plate, 'all your father wants you to do is to eat as normally as you can and make yourself agreeable to your peers. I know that you experience problems with sleep, but if you won't take the tablets that I've given you—'

'But I like the night, doctor!' he cried excitedly. 'My sister and I have always stayed up into the night, as I've told you before. It's beautiful at night with her,' he smiled, 'and anyway it was difficult for her to go out in the day back in England.'

'Because of your mother's illness?' Zelfa recalled the conversation she'd had with Ali about his much older sister when he first started coming to her.

'Partly.' He looked away.

'You do know that you can't really live in a horror story, don't you?' Zelfa persisted. 'You may feel as if your life so far has been full of horror—'

'Mum read *Dracula* when she was pregnant with my sister.'

'Meaning?' Zelfa frowned.

'Oh, it was just an observation,' he said, shrugging into what appeared to be sulky teenager mode. 'Mum liked that stuff. So did my sister, it wasn't just me.'

It was not, Zelfa thought, probably the best material for a suicidally depressed woman to read whether she was pregnant or not. It made her wonder what the woman had been perusing when she did finally take her own life.

'Your mother was always depressed, wasn't she?' she said. 'That's hard for all concerned. Depressed people can have an effect on those around them, pulling them, often unwittingly, into their own dark world.'

'You really don't understand at all, do you?' he said wearily.

'No, I don't, but if we talked more about these issues—'

'Mum is not the reason my father wants to put me in an institution.'

'I agree,' Zelfa responded evenly, 'but I do think that you have issues with your mother's suicide which are impacting upon your current behaviour. And things are not, as yet, improving, Ali. I mean, this latest fixation about becoming institutionalised . . .'

'But he does mean to do it to me, doctor! It isn't a delusion! You must believe me!'

'Whether I believe you or not is not at issue here, Ali,' Zelfa said. 'That you believe it is what concerns me. We need to look at why you think it is even a possibility. I believe the issue is intimately connected with unpleasant things that have gone on in the past.'

He moved his head downwards, pushing it into his thin shoulders, like a miserable little child. And although the sight of this made Zelfa want to put her arms round him to give some comfort and warmth to his starved body, she resisted this unprofessional urge. Instead, and against the better judgement of a psychiatrist with a full appointment book for that day, she said, 'Look, Ali, you're obviously very agitated today so why don't you come and see me when you finish school? We can talk more comfortably in my office.'

'But won't my father have to pay—'

'I'm sure your father won't mind when he realises how important this is to you. He does, after all, want you to get well.' Feeling a little less nauseous now than she had been when Ali arrived, Zelfa took a long drink from her tea glass.

Ali still looked uncertain.

In an attempt to break through his misery, Zelfa said, 'Look, why don't I just see you with no charge? Your father is paying for Thursday anyway.'

'Are you sure, doctor?'

'Yes.' This was a sick boy who, if she was right, might be getting sicker; anything she could do to help him she should – even if that meant being out of pocket. And besides, the boy intrigued her, she had to admit. There was something unusual here, he interested her in the academic sense. Obviously possessed of his own version of reality involving a fear of being 'locked away' coupled with gothic fascination with the macabre, Ali Evren put Zelfa in mind of Edgar Allan Poe.

Smiling now, the boy rose to his feet. 'Then I will see you later on this afternoon, doctor,' he said, punctuating his words with a small bow.

'OK. But promise me you'll try to speak to at least one of your classmates.'

He responded sharply, 'I don't talk to base creatures, doctor.'

And then he left. Zelfa looked again at her watch

before sinking back into thoughts about her lover and what it might mean to be his wife. There was, she knew, a meeting planned between the Suleyman brothers and their father, who probably already knew of his younger son's 'good news' from Murad Suleyman. Where that left things with regard to Mehmet's mother, Zelfa didn't know. Perhaps she, like her own father, was currently living in blissful cluelessness. *You must*, her guilt told her firmly, *get around to telling the old man soon* . . .

'I don't know that I'm entirely happy with this, you know, Çetin,' Mehmet Suleyman said as he walked with İkmen towards the interview rooms. 'I mean, if this man is the main focus of your investigation . . .'

'Which is why I want Tepe to give his brothers a good grilling,' İkmen replied with vigour. 'And anyway, as I've explained, I need you.'

'Yes.'

The two men lapsed into silence. İkmen needed the space to try to banish the unwanted demons that surrounded the subject of his mother's death; Suleyman was grappling with what the older man had told him – that İkmen now felt that his preoccupation with his mother was beginning to distance him from what was truly important in this investigation, the death of Rifat Berisha. With little beyond paperwork at the present time to occupy his mind, Suleyman was well placed to help keep İkmen focused. If only, thought Suleyman, Tepe wouldn't take all this personally . . .

Just before they entered Interview Room 1, İkmen's lugubrious face broke into a smile. Holding his hand out to his colleague he said cheerfully, 'Oh, and lest I forget, Mehmet, congratulations on your forthcoming marriage.'

'Thank you,' Suleyman replied, taking the outstretched hand warmly in his own. 'I meant to tell you myself yesterday but—'

'I was otherwise engaged,' the older man said and pushed open the door to the interview room. 'Cohen phoned me.'

'Oh.'

Mehti Vlora looked even smaller than usual as he sat hunched in his chair, glaring at the guard who viewed him impassively from across the other side of the room. Several hours had passed since Mehti had been brought into the station, and knowing that his need would now be great, İkmen threw a half-full packet of cigarettes onto the table in front of him, indicating that he should help himself. With very bad grace, Mehti did so.

As the lead officer, İkmen reminded his prisoner that he was entitled to have a lawyer with him during his interview, a service that Mehti, yet again, refused. Once all the preliminary tasks regarding the exposition of rights and the setting up of tapes were over, İkmen began what appeared at first to be a somewhat laborious line of questioning.

'So,' he said, 'tell me about this feud you have with the Berishas.'

'I thought I was brought here because of the attack on the catamite,' Mehti replied.

İkmen smiled. 'We'll get to that in due course. For the moment, Mehti, why don't you give me a history lesson? I mean, I presume this feud started back in Ghegeria.'

'Yeah.'

Suleyman, who had no idea where or what Ghegeria might be, kept his face impassive, his eyes fixed upon their prisoner.

'Go on,' İkmen prompted.

Mehti Vlora shrugged. 'So they hate us and we hate them. What's to tell?'

'What has happened with regard to this feud since you've been in this country would be a good start,' İkmen replied.

'Why are you asking me this!' Suddenly animated, Mehti jumped up from his chair only to be instantly pushed back down into it by the guard.

İkmen leaned across the table towards him. 'Because it seems to me,' he said, 'that ever since Rifat Berisha's death all I've heard about are feuds between Albanians! Samsun Bajraktar is an Albanian—'

'Yes, and you are of his *fis*!'

'Let's leave me out of this, shall we?' İkmen growled through gritted teeth. 'I've had quite enough of hearing about my own supposed involvement in this melodrama! I want to know how this feud has progressed since you came to Turkey.'

'Then you'd better ask Rahman Berisha, hadn't you?'

'Why?'

'Because he killed our little brother Dhori, that's why!' Mehti said and pounded his fist on the table in what looked like triumph.

Suleyman, who up until this point hadn't felt equipped

to add anything to the proceedings, cleared his throat. 'And so this "murder", Mr Vlora, when did it happen?'

Seemingly exhausted by his recent outburst, Mehti muttered, 'I don't know. Before the beginning of last year . . . In the summer . . .'

'Nineteen ninety-nine?'

'I guess.'

İkmen looked questioningly at Suleyman, who just shrugged.

'I don't think that either my colleague or I remember the case,' İkmen said.

Mehti looked İkmen straight in the eyes as he replied, 'Well, that's because Rahman hid the body.'

Suleyman, feeling yet again that this was getting beyond him, nevertheless asked, 'Why?'

'I don't know! Ask Berisha! We've searched and searched for Dhori ever since that time, but . . .' He hung his head again in an attempt to hide eyes which were now filling with tears. 'But we never find him.'

İkmen, knowing that asking why the Vloras didn't contact the police when their brother first vanished was a useless question, instead turned his attention to possible alternative explanations for Dhori Vlora's disappearance.

'But couldn't Dhori have just gone away to another city?' he asked. 'Or couldn't someone else have killed him?'

'Dhori had no enemies beyond the Berishas!' Mehti replied hotly. 'He was a good boy. Everyone liked him. He even had an old woman who wanted to spend money on him!'

'A European?' İkmen inquired tartly, recalling Mehti's English girl.

'Why?'

'Because you, at least, seem to possess a fascination for such women,' İkmen replied, and then recalled Rifat Berisha's friendship with Felicity Evren. 'Like so many of your men,' he added.

Mehti didn't react to this. All he said was, 'I don't know who she was, I never met the woman. Dhori kept a lot to himself, you know.'

İkmen leaned back in his chair and looked fixedly at the wall in front of him, leaving it to Suleyman to ask what had to be the logical next question.

'Assuming that Rahman Berisha did kill your brother,' he said, 'there must have been a reason why he did it.'

Mehti Vlora lowered his gaze to the floor. '*Gjakmaria*, the blood . . .'

'Which, according to your custom,' Suleyman continued, 'means that your family must have spilt Berisha blood prior to your brother's death.'

Mehti didn't answer.

'That is something else we might ask the Berishas about, don't you think, Inspector?' İkmen, now roused from his reverie, asked his colleague.

'Yes, I think you're right,' Suleyman said with a smile.

'Rifat Berisha only got what was coming to him.'

Both İkmen and Suleyman looked at their prisoner.

'Oh, did he?'

'And did you give him what was coming to him, Mehti? Was that the reason why you tried to silence

Samsun Bajraktar? In case he told me too much about your history with the Berishas – like why Rahman may have killed your brother?'

For a moment it seemed as if Mehti Vlora had decided to ignore these questions. His mind appeared to be elsewhere. When he did finally speak, his words were mumbled.

'I want to do a deal,' he said.

İkmen leaned forward, frowning.

'Would you care to repeat that please, Mr Vlora?' he said. 'Just so that we can understand it on the tape.'

'I want to do a deal with you,' Mehti said, his voice clearer. 'I'll give you Rifat's murderer if you let my family go.'

İkmen first looked across at Suleyman and then sighed deeply.

'Well,' he said, 'let's have the details and then I'll see what, if anything, I can do.'

Mehti Vlora's statement was taken in the form of a dictated script because his writing skills were poor. As a gesture, rather than as part of the deal, Aryan Vlora and the two younger women were released from the cells just before Mehti began his story. Unlike Angeliki and Mehmet Vlora, neither Aryan nor the women had had any drugs on them when they were arrested, so, in any event, İkmen only released those he possessed the power to release anyway.

According to his statement, Mehti Vlora had been watching Rifat Berisha for some months before he finally killed him. He knew that he'd left the city for some considerable time at one point and that he routinely saw a foreign woman with a 'twisted face' in smart and expensive parts of town. On the night of Rifat's death, Mehti followed him to this woman's house and then waited for him, hiding himself in the back of Rifat's car. When Rifat came out, Mehti allowed him to drive for a few kilometres before he revealed himself and ordered his victim to pull over to the side of the road. Then he killed him with one deep slash of his knife. He drove the car containing the now dead Rifat Berisha back to Eminönü where, under cover of the fog, he dumped the body near to where it was found by the ferry piers. Thus far, if one discounted the bravado in the phrase 'one deep slash', it was all very believable given the history between these two families, although İkmen would have found Mehmet Vlora a more convincing killer – Mehti, it had to be admitted, possessed a certain lassitude of spirit which made him an odd murderer.

Where Mehti's story faced problems was in the details surrounding what happened after he had dumped Rifat's body. To drive back towards Felicity Evren's house in Bebek and then dump the vehicle in Ortaköy seemed pointless. Leaving the blood-soaked car outside the Evrens' house, thereby involving them with the police right from the start would, surely, have made much more sense. Although Felicity and her family would not have been implicated directly, the police would, at least temporarily, have concentrated their efforts away from Eminönü and the Vloras. When asked why he had performed this seemingly illogical move, Mehti simply replied that he had been scared and hadn't really known what he was doing at the time, which was indeed possible. However, the fact that he knew where the car had been dumped was significant – or at least it would have been had İkmen not known how quickly such information could have been spread from the Berisha family to the rest of the Albanian community.

Other points of interest involved the old Fiat Mehti claimed he had stolen in order to follow Rifat that night. He had, he said, left it opposite the Evrens' house when he jemmied his way into the back of his victim's Mercedes. Bebek, İkmen knew, was the sort of district where people reported dumped cars, particularly if they were old and scruffy-looking, and so asking the Traffic Division for some information on that was high on his agenda. He was also a little disappointed that Mehti had not yet made any mention of either the shards of coloured glass in the victim's face or of the curtains in which the killer had wrapped Rifat's body. These could be just oversights, or they might signal that he had chosen to fabricate his story, perhaps to please his punitive and aggrieved relatives. If so, the price of life imprisonment he would soon be obliged to pay was very high. There was still, as yet, no forensic evidence to confirm Mehti's story. Various items had been removed from the Vlora place but the apartment had yielded only old bloodstains. These would still need to be processed but they were unlikely to have come from Rifat Berisha. Whether Mehti's fingerprints or any of his blood or other detritus was amongst the evidence gleaned from Rifat's car also remained to be seen.

With so much hinging upon past events alleged to

have taken place between the Vloras and the Berishas, İkmen took the decision to go with Tepe back to the Berishas' Kutucular Caddesi apartment. There, hopefully, a conversation with Rahman Berisha might prove instructive. Suleyman, for his part, set off to follow Mehti Vlora's directions to the Evrens' Bebek residence. It was, he and İkmen had agreed, important to ascertain whether or not the Evrens' had seen anything untoward outside their house that night. Felicity particularly needed further work. The last she'd seen of Rifat, so she'd told İkmen, was at lunch on that final day. But if Mehti Vlora was telling the truth, that had to be wrong. According to Mehti, Rifat had gone to the Evren house that night. If he hadn't gone to see his girlfriend, what was he doing there?

Chapter 13

'He came here to see me,' İlhan Evren said impassively.

'Why did he do that, sir?' Suleyman asked.

Evren, who was an obese man, shifted uncomfortably in his seat before replying, 'He wanted money.'

It wasn't easy trying to hold a conversation with a man who so pointedly did not offer one a seat. But Suleyman comforted himself with the thought that he had the advantage in terms of position; awkward though it might be to stand all through this conversation, it was Evren who had to look up at him in order to communicate.

'And did you give him money?'

'Well, of course not!' Evren retorted angrily. 'He'd already had a car courtesy of my daughter! He was getting nothing more from me! Nothing!'

'Nothing more from you, sir?' Suleyman asked, emphasising the second word.

Evren took a fat cigar out of the top pocket of his jacket before replying.

'I paid for that boy to come to London with us; bought his flights, new clothes, everything.'

Recalling what İkmen had told him about Felicity Evren and her seeming reluctance to discuss that trip, it struck Suleyman as surprising her father was being so forthright about it.

'Why did you take Rifat to London, Mr Evren?' he asked as he watched the man's thick lips attach themselves to the end of his cigar.

Evren puffed to get his smoke going, then briefly inspected the lit end of the cigar before continuing.

'Mr Berisha kindly donated one of his kidneys to my daughter. She's already given a statement about it to another of your lot.'

Despite Felicity's statement to İkmen, after so much talk back at the station regarding the possible trade in human organs, such a bald statement from Evren came as a shock to Suleyman. Not, of course, that Evren had said that he had actually paid for the kidney.

Out of patience with Evren's boorish manners, Suleyman sat down unbidden in one of the chairs opposite his host.

'So your daughter—'

'My daughter has multiple health problems,' Evren said impatiently. 'I was happy for her to receive dialysis here but I wanted her to have her surgery in London. I wanted her to have the best. I know Mr Collins, I've done work for him in the past. I trust him.'

'Mr Collins?'

'The consultant who removed Mr Berisha's kidney and put it into my daughter's body. It's perfectly legal for a person to willingly donate one of their organs. No actual money ever changed hands.'

'Except for Rifat's expenses and that Mercedes your daughter—'

'Felicity did that of her own volition!' Evren roared. 'Nothing to do with me! I warned her against it. I said it would set a bad precedent, and it did!'

Suleyman frowned. 'Meaning?'

'Meaning that the car gave him ideas.'

'What sort of ideas?'

'Well, that he'd been paid for his fucking kidney, of course!' Evren shouted. 'That sort of thing is illegal in Britain, which is exactly what Rifat Berisha said to me when he came here that night to try and extort money from me!'

One of the doors that led out of what Suleyman felt was a spectacularly ugly room opened, revealing the man he had passed in the hall when Evren had reluctantly shown him into his house.

Catching sight of this figure, Evren suddenly smiled. 'I won't be much longer, Alexei,' he said. 'Get yourself a drink, have caviar, enjoy.'

The man laughed briefly before departing. It was a thick and yet at the same time brittle noise which, Suleyman thought, was almost as alarming as the excessive width of his shoulders.

He turned back to Evren. 'Go on, sir. Were you surprised, shocked, by Berisha's behaviour?'

'Not really. He told me originally that he was willing to give Felicity one of his kidneys because he was in love with her. Now, I'm not a fool and I knew that could not be true.'

'Why not?'

'He was Albanian,' Evren barked. 'They have this clan thing. They indulge in blood feuds. Carry all sorts of hardware to protect themselves. They only marry their own and anyway, have you seen my daughter?'

'Yes.'

'Then you'll know that she isn't the type of woman a man could love!'

'I—'

'Felicity is a nightmare!' With much determination, if some difficulty, Evren leaned forward towards Suleyman, his face red with fury. 'She always has been! Born like a freak! If Mary, my wife, hadn't produced my son, well . . . Not that he's much use any more . . .' He looked down and away, towards the legs of Suleyman's chair. 'Of course I've never told Felicity that, I've always tried to boost her confidence, especially since her mother's death, which she took badly. I've given her everything, even entertained useless, blackmailing young men in my home.' He flicked his gaze up to Suleyman once again. 'Oh, Berisha wasn't the first, no. As soon as we arrived in this city the bastards started coming! Neighbours to dinner, sniffing out our money. But he was the only one who ever got really in here, ever paid, albeit in cheap flesh, for all the largesse I have allowed my daughter to squander over the years.'

For the first time Suleyman managed to detect something approaching pain in this man's face. It made him feel a modicum of sympathy.

'Your daughter's version of these events was, according to my colleague, Inspector İkmen, somewhat vexed,' he said. 'She was at first most reluctant to admit to the kidney transplant and seemed a little, shall we say, optimistic with regard to her physical attractiveness to men.'

'Felicity lives in a fantasy world.'

As if by reflex, Suleyman looked behind him.

'Oh, you don't have to worry, Inspector,' Evren said. 'My daughter is out spending my money at the moment.'

'Oh.'

'Not that I have ever discouraged my daughter's fantasies,' he continued. 'In fact I frequently promote them myself – tell her that she's beautiful, you know. Felicity needs her delusions in order to survive. Just don't believe too much of what comes out of her mouth is all I will say to you.'

'Where was your daughter when Rifat Berisha came to call, Mr Evren?'

'She'd gone to bed, as had my son.' He puffed on his cigar before adding, 'He takes pills to make him sleep. I let the boy in. We had a conversation in this room, it was about ten o'clock, and then I threw him out.'

'Did you actually see Rifat get into his car?' Suleyman asked.

'No, but I heard him drive off. Then I went upstairs to bed.'

'You didn't hear any other cars drive up around the time Rifat arrived?'

Evren shrugged. 'I don't know. Not that I remember.'

'What about cars abandoned in the street the day after Rifat's death?'

'None that I noticed. But then we are quite a way back from the street here.' A walled drive led up to his house. 'Why?'

Suleyman smiled his particular closed, professional smile. 'Just a line of inquiry, sir,' he said.

Hopefully the uniformed officers who were currently doing house-to-house inquires in the rest of the street would discover someone rather more observant than Mr Evren. Although these properties were not as select as those that actually fronted the Bosphorus, they were still highly desirable places where the residents generally kept their cars on their drives. A dumped vehicle, particularly a scruffy green Fiat like the one that Mehti Vlora had described, would be very noticeable. And if the Traffic Division came up with something also . . .

'What do you do for a living, Mr Evren?' Suleyman asked, changing tack to a subject which, given the external splendour of the house in contrast to the cheap, almost greasy interior, was one that he found interesting.

Evren's darkly sagging eyes narrowed. 'Why?'

As if on cue a big, gold-coloured Rolls-Royce pulled up underneath the window of the living room. 'Because whatever it is that you do, Mr Evren, seems to afford you a comfortable living. And you did mention that you had done work for the surgeon who performed your daughter's operation.'

'I'm a legitimate businessman,' Evren said as he stubbed his cigar out in his ashtray. 'I deal in works of art. I obtained several items for Mr Collins. I only handle good pieces . . .' Someone turned a key in the front door of the house and let themselves in. Just briefly a shade of nervousness seemed to cross Evren's face before he continued, '. . . aimed at the western European market. I import them.'

'From eastern Europe?' Acknowledging the question in Evren's expression, Suleyman explained, with a hint of İkmen-ism, 'You called your friend Alexei which, I believe, is a Slavic name. Rightly or wrongly, I made a connection.' He smiled. 'The state pays us to do that.'

'I deal with the Russians, yes,' Evren said, shrugging his stiff, fat shoulders, 'but it's all quite legitimate. I'm not one of those who sends gangsters into small village churches to pillage their icons. If people want to sell to my agents – who, by the way, always give them a fair price – then that's up to them.'

'Quite.'

'And anyway,' Evren said, continuing to justify what Suleyman was beginning to regard as a rather dubious operation, 'we're not talking about very valuable works. The Russian government grabbed all that from their aristocrats years ago. In fact I buy the really valuable stuff here.' He gave an odd grim little smile. 'You'd be surprised at how many of our own ex-imperial family still have enough good jewellery to put their kids through university.'

'Would I?' Suleyman replied, wrestling with the bitterness he knew was in his voice. Although it was doubtful that Evren had ever had dealings with his own family, somebody like him had purchased his grandfather's precious collection of jewelled cigarette cases. Somebody like him who had not given his, at the time, desperate father anything like 'a fair price'.

He was just about to ask Evren whether this antique Turkish jewellery as well as the icons went across to western Europe when the door behind him opened. Seeing her reflection in the large mirror that hung directly in front of him, Suleyman recognised Felicity immediately. Although he had only caught a glimpse of her outside İkmen's office the previous afternoon, Felicity Evren's appearance was so disturbingly startling that it was not one a person easily forgot.

'Daddy, there are lots of policemen in the street,' she said, using what Suleyman recognised was probably more comfortable for this essentially English woman, her own language. Spotting the policeman in her own house, she smiled with something like pleased recognition.

'Inspector . . .' Evren snorted as he struggled to remember Suleyman's name.

'Suleyman,' the policeman offered.

'Yes,' Evren said, his speech now in English, his eye distinctly jaundiced with regard to his 'guest', 'Inspector Suleyman has come to ask questions about your friend Rifat.'

'Oh.' She smiled and then moved to the plastic covered window seat which placed her directly between the two men. 'I thought I told Inspector İkmen everything that I know yesterday,' she said mildly, 'but if there is anything more, Inspector Suleyman . . .'

'I told him about Rifat giving you his kidney,' Evren said quickly and, seemingly, harshly.

Although she didn't display any sort of reaction to her father's words, Felicity Evren remained silent for a few moments following his statement. It was not the sort of silence, Suleyman felt, that anyone but Felicity should break.

When she did finally speak, her words were slow and deeply sad.

'I loved Rifat. There is a hole in my life where he once was.'

'There will be other young men, my precious angel,' her father replied, and then added an observation that Suleyman felt was wildly at odds with reality. 'After all, who could not love you, my beautiful little soul?'

'Indeed.'

Felicity Evren then looked across at Suleyman, her twisted face forcing her eccentric collection of muscles into a smile.

Only Engelushjia and Rahman Berisha were in the apartment when İkmen and Tepe arrived, Aliya having gone next door to tell Mimoza the dreadful thing Rifat had done to his body for that foreign hag. When it became apparent that İkmen had come to question Rahman, Engelushjia left too. And, although the hard, grey sky of winter was pouring copious amounts of rain onto the city, Engelushjia did not go to join her mother. Instead she took herself up to the flimsy awning on the roof which, in summer, the family used as a way of escaping from the stifling heat indoors. There, pulling her barely adequate cardigan across her thin chest, she watched as the tough city pigeons squawked and jostled for supremacy over the crumbling Eminönü skyline. The greyness and with the animals' aggression combined to underline the feeling of foreboding that mention of that one awful name had sparked inside her mind. As she'd been closing the door on her father and the policemen, she'd heard the older officer say the words 'Dhori Vlora', and there on the landing she had felt her heart beat so hard she thought she might die. Her father had killed Dhori Vlora, taken his blood for Egrem's. Everybody – well, everybody who was Albanian – knew it. The police had probably learned of it through that Bajraktar creature, although what they could do about it without Dhori's body, Engelushjia couldn't imagine. Perhaps there were ways, maybe even cruel, painful ways, in which they could 'persuade' Rahman to give up his knowledge regarding Dhori's whereabouts.

Engelushjia herself didn't have a clue, either about where Dhori was or why her father had concealed his body. All she knew was that after Egrem's murder, as she looked down into that hastily dug hole on some rough ground out by the airport – waste land where her family's poverty had obliged them to inter her beloved brother – her father had sworn to take Vlora blood. When, sometime later – she didn't remember now how long afterwards – Dhori Vlora had disappeared, word naturally went around that her father had killed him. And indeed Rahman, although never offering any information on that subject himself, had seemed calmer and almost more fulfilled afterwards. Until, that was, Rifat joined Egrem in death.

How long she sat up on the roof, Engelushjia didn't

know. But when she did finally see the two policemen, the old one and the nice, clean young one, step out into the street again, her hands and her feet had turned blue. Swaying just a little at first on her numb and woolly feet, Engelushjia made her way back inside, slowly climbing down the ladder onto the landing.

Her father was still in the kitchen where she'd left him. And although his head was propped wearily between his hands as he leaned forward on the table, his face was not overtly anxious.

Slipping quietly into the chair opposite him, Engelushjia watched him light the cigarette that hung between his lips and then, coming straight to the point, she said, 'They asked you about Dhori Vlora, didn't they?'

Rahman tipped his head almost reflexively to one side. 'Yes.'

'What did you say, Father? What did you tell them?'

'All that I know.'

Engelushjia threw a hand up to her mouth in an attempt to stifle the scream that was aching for release. At the same time, the pounding in her chest started again and tears sprang into her eyes. If her father had indeed told them 'everything' . . .

But Rahman, even in the face of her obvious distress, just smiled.

'Father . . .'

'I told them I know nothing about Dhori Vlora's death.'

'So you lied!' Placing one calming hand across her chest, Engelushjia closed her eyes, muttering, 'Praise be to Allah.'

Rahman looked at his daughter. 'No,' he said.

'What?'

'No, I didn't lie to the policemen.' He watched the threads of confusion knit themselves across his daughter's face. 'I told the police the truth. Much as I would have liked to have killed Dhori Vlora, I didn't do it. I've never actually killed anyone in my life, Engelushjia.' He rose slowly from his chair. 'I don't have the courage.'

'So who did?'

'I have no idea who killed Dhori Vlora,' Rahman said, pushing his chair back against the table, 'or where his body is.' And then he left the room.

Engelushjia, for whom the last hour or so had been an enormous strain, burst into tears.

By the time İkmen returned to his apartment that evening, he knew that the only person who could categorically state that a green Fiat had been abandoned outside the Evrens' Bebek home was Mehti Vlora. The car certainly wasn't there now, having seemingly become as invisible as Dhori Vlora's missing corpse – if indeed that young man was a corpse. That he had disappeared was indisputable but the manner of his disappearance remained unproven, as did the identity of Egrem Berisha's killers. The fact and manner of Egrem's death could, in theory, be established, but in practice there were problems. Yeşilköy, which is where Berisha had said he had buried Egrem, had been one of the areas most violently devastated by the earthquake. With so much rubble removed from that area, not to mention bodies taken away for burial, the chances of actually locating Egrem were thin. And even then his identity would have to be proved somehow. İkmen knew from experience how problematic that could be.

In the meantime, and against Mehti Vlora's expectations, his drug-dealing brother and mother remained in İkmen's cells. And, on the face of it, the investigation into Rifat Berisha's death was over. Mehti had admitted to the crime, had provided details that were consistent with most of the facts. True, the issue of the green Fiat still nagged at him, as did Mehti's omission regarding the wrapping up of Rifat's body. But then perhaps he had simply forgotten – such things were not unknown even in those who had actually been seen committing a crime. But Mehti had also failed to mention, or explain, the fragments of coloured glass found in Rifat's face. On reflection, perhaps a further talk with Samsun about the Vlora brothers might prove instructive. It would also give him the opportunity to talk to his Uncle Ahmet, Samsun's father, who was due to arrive from İzmir sometime in the morning. Anxious to see his wounded child, the old man probably wouldn't be happy talking about the circumstances surrounding his sister's death but, selfish or not, İkmen was going to ask. Angeliki Vlora had said that Ahmet 'knew the truth' and İkmen intended to confront him outright and hope that if Ahmet attempted to lie, he would know.

Fatma poured some water into her husband's glass and then placed his meal on the table in front of him. As ever she had cooked far too much and, although pide with egg was one of his favourites, the sheer quantity was off-putting. Not, of course, that he could tell her that.

Busying herself with various small cleaning tasks, Fatma watched her husband slowly begin his meal and then said, 'Hulya said that the girls' bedroom shook for a few seconds last night.'

'It was only four point four,' İkmen replied. He hadn't noticed the small tremor the previous night but it had been widely reported in the media.

'There were little ones like that last time,' Fatma said.

Deducing from the strained expression on her face that his wife was yet again entering a state of extreme earthquake anxiety, İkmen first took a large bite out of his pide, chewed and swallowed, and then said, 'So did you get another hamster?'

'Yes, but—'

'Well then, we have nothing to worry about, do we?' he said with a smile. 'The animal will wake us up and—'

'Don't you dare patronise me, Çetin İkmen!' Fatma roared as she waved a cleaning cloth furiously at him.

Slamming his pide back down onto his plate, İkmen countered, 'Don't shout at me when I'm eating, woman!'

She was just about to shout again when what was rapidly turning into an argument was interrupted by the door buzzer.

'And who is that at this time of night!' Fatma said, rolling her eyes in frustration.

'Well, how should I know?' her husband replied. 'Why don't you go and find out?'

'I will,' she said and stomped angrily past him towards the kitchen door. 'But not because you tell me to do so!'

When she had gone, İkmen looked down at his not even half-eaten meal and pushed his plate impatiently to one side. Rarely an enthusiastic eater, the argument had put him completely off his food now and so he did what he always did at times like these and lit up a cigarette.

A few minutes later he heard footsteps come back down the hall and inwardly braced himself for yet another round of strife. But the person who entered the kitchen was not, thankfully, Fatma.

'Hello, Çetin,' Arto Sarkissian said as he smiled his way into the room.

'Arto!'

'No, don't get up.' The Armenian waved his friend back down into his chair. 'Finish your meal.'

Looking briefly at the rapidly cooling pide, İkmen scowled. 'I have,' he said.

'Ah. Well, that won't please Fatma very much.'

'What a pity,' İkmen replied acidly.

For a few seconds, Arto watched his friend as he smoked in what seemed to be distracted silence, then he extended his hand towards the plate and said, 'Give it to me.'

İkmen, laughing, pushed the plate in his friend's direction and then slouched back into his chair.

'Just like old times,' he said softly.

'Yes, except that these days I shouldn't really be eating anyone else's food.' Arto took a large bite of bread and egg. 'I sometimes think that one of the reasons I'm so fat now is because I used to eat your food whenever you came to our house.'

İkmen shrugged. 'You were always very willing.'

'It was a mystery to my mother how you remained so skinny.'

'Did you ever tell her the truth?'

Arto smiled. 'No. But then sometimes people do keep things from others for very good reasons, don't they, Çetin?'

There was a look in his friend's eyes that made İkmen sit up straighter – it was the kind of look he knew Arto used just before he was going to tell somebody something important or unpleasant.

'You found something amongst Uncle Vahan's things, didn't you?' İkmen said, his whole body tense.

Arto took another bite of the pide and then put it down. 'Yes.'

İkmen waited, if not patiently, until his friend had finished chewing. 'And?'

'The official line on your mother's death,' Arto said gravely, 'was suicide. I'm very sorry, Çetin.'

'But that's impossible!'

Looking at the table as opposed to his friend's outraged face did, Arto found, help his progress through this nightmare slightly. 'I'm afraid the report is quite specific. There was even a note. Your mother cut her own throat.'

İkmen put his hands to his head and got to his feet, knocking his chair over as he did so. He began to pace distractedly across the kitchen. 'But I was only a child, Arto! How could she do that to us?'

'I don't know, Çetin. Her note, apparently, stated nothing beyond her intentions, and my father's report didn't go into any psychological specifics, if indeed they were known at the time. Zelfa Halman might be able to come up with some theories if you ask her. In fact I tried phoning her office late this afternoon but apparently she'd gone home after her last appointment, she didn't feel well.'

'If this is the case,' İkmen said, totally ignoring what his friend had just offered, 'my brother and my father lied to me.'

'Well . . .'

'All that stuff Halil came out with the other day about how he couldn't remember anything about Mother's death, about how every time he tries, it all goes black . . .'

'Çetin . . .'

'They lied to me, Arto! Uncle Vahan lied to me too, and to you!'

'I expect your father was just trying to protect you.'

'Yes, at the time, I can see that,' İkmen said as he put one cigarette out and lit up another. 'But why didn't he tell me later on? And as for Halil . . .'

'Now, Çetin, I know that in your work you have sometimes seen what can happen when people are confronted with information or sights that they just cannot bear.' Standing up too now, he moved over to where his friend was pacing and put a hand firmly on his shoulder. 'They blank them out.'

'For over forty years!' İkmen roared.

Fearing that if he didn't establish a firm hold upon this

situation soon, Çetin would spin out into hysteria, Arto changed his tone to one of stern and brutal honesty.

'Your brother,' he said, 'walked into a nightmare the day he found your mother! You know what people look like when they've had their throats slashed – imagine coming home and finding the person who loves you most looking like that! Imagine Fatma looking like that!'

'Arto . . .'

'He knew she was dead! He could see that there was nothing he could do for her and so he did the next logical thing, he made certain that you, his little brother, didn't have to endure it too.' Without taking his eyes off İkmen's face, Arto bent down and picked the fallen chair up off the floor. Then he told his friend, or rather ordered him, to sit down. Strangely, for he was still very agitated, İkmen complied.

'The fact that Halil has never spoken to you of these things before,' Arto said as he, too, seated himself, 'is, I believe, because he genuinely doesn't recall them. I suspect, although I don't know this of course, that as soon as our fathers and the police arrived and the pressure was off Halil, he wiped the image from his mind. I certainly remember being told of your mother's death on the day that it occurred and of being fed what became the official line, that she'd had a heart attack. Neither Krikor nor I ever knew any different, until today.'

'But Father knew.'

'Our fathers both knew, Çetin, as did the police. But I think that once they realised that your brother had expunged what he had seen from his mind, they made a decision to change the details regarding Auntie Ayşe's death into a far more palatable lie. We were all very young at the time.'

'Halil will have to know now, won't he?'

Arto sighed. 'I think we need to take advice on that, Çetin,' he said. 'Psychiatric advice.'

İkmen, although somewhat calmer, frowned.

'Halil has over forty years of denial to come to terms with,' Arto said gravely. 'It was in fact with him in mind, rather than you, that I called Zelfa.'

They lapsed into a silence born, on İkmen's part at least, of exhaustion. Arto had not wanted to bring this news to his friend and, in truth, had he made the discovery when not under instruction from İkmen he might have kept it to himself. İkmen had asked him to find out whether or not his mother had been murdered and he had brought him news of something almost more difficult to bear. After all, with murder there was, even if the culprit was unknown, another person out there somewhere upon whom one could pin one's fury, but with suicide there were just loss and confusion and, worst of all, rejection.

'So,' İkmen said finally in a voice that appeared to have reasserted some control over its tone, 'can I see Uncle Vahan's report?'

'Of course.' Arto reached inside his jacket pocket and retrieved a couple of yellowing sheets of paper. 'But your mother's note isn't with it, Çetin. I don't know where it might be or even if it still exists.'

Wordlessly, İkmen took the papers from Arto's hands and spent the next few minutes reading what was written there. Once he wiped a tear from his eye with the cuff of his shirt. When he had finished, he handed the papers back to his friend.

'Thank you, Arto,' he said, once he felt able to speak again. 'I appreciate your doing this for me, it can't have been easy for you.'

'I'm just sorry that that spiteful Albanian woman caused us both to search for what we should never, really, have known.'

'Mmm.' And then slowly frowning as if something even more troubling had occurred to him, İkmen said, 'If our fathers were so keen to keep her suicide a secret from their children they must have lied to mother's friends and family too.'

'I should imagine so, yes,' Arto agreed. 'They would have to have done to ensure that we didn't learn anything from an unguarded tongue.'

'And yet Angeliki Vlora, who cannot surely have known about this, still maintains that my mother was murdered with a knife and that my Uncle Ahmet knows all about that.'

'Well then, you'll have to tell your uncle what I have told you today and ask him what he knows about it.'

İkmen leaned forward onto the table and placed his head in his hands. 'Oh, Arto,' he said, only now beginning to weep in earnest, 'what am I going to say?'

By way of reply, Arto went out into the hall and retrieved Fatma who had been patiently waiting outside. As soon as she entered the kitchen, she flung her arms round her husband's shoulders and stroked his hair until his tears began to subside.

Chapter 14

Dr Babur Halman watched closely as his daughter joined him at the breakfast table. Still wearing her bathrobe, she sat down heavily in the chair opposite.

'Still not feeling well?' Babur inquired as he watched her unnaturally white face scowl at the food laid out in front of her.

'I think it must be anxiety,' she said, attempting with a grimace to drink the small glass of tea her father had poured for her earlier.

'Wedding nerves,' her father said sagely. And then he smiled. He'd been so pleased about her news when she'd told him the previous night and obviously still was now.

'No, I think it's about that case I told you about last night actually,' she said. 'I feel the patient in question might be sliding down into something – I don't know what. Full-blown psychosis?'

'Patients do sometimes intimate things that test our ability to protect their confidentiality – particularly your type of patient.'

'It's not that this person,' she said, 'has intimated to me that he wishes to hurt someone. It's just that his world view is so macabre. I feel, well, almost stifled in his presence.'

Babur forked a little tomato and cheese into his mouth before asking, 'And so?'

'If what I'm being told is true, then it could be that my patient's home situation is really quite unhealthy.'

'In what way?'

'I can't say that I really know,' she said. 'The way he talks is characterised by seemingly paranoid thoughts and concealment. He's scared, as if there's something or someone after him. There is also, I'm sure, a sexual element although whether that is real or just adolescent fantasy I don't know.'

'Mmm. Freudian elements.' Babur, who didn't hold with psychoanalysis, smiled. 'Perhaps your patient is playing games with you.'

'Well, exactly!' she replied, excited now that her father had, seemingly, arrived at the same conclusion as she had. 'I mean, I can hardly accuse others of things if it's all a delusion.'

'No, but this person could be in danger.'

'At psychological risk,' she corrected.

Babur shrugged. 'Same thing.'

Zelfa sighed, after which both father and daughter sat in silence for some moments. Until, that is, her fingers agitated against the tablecloth.

'I've asked my patient to come back daily for the time being,' she said. 'But the family member who pays the bill isn't willing to engage with the process. This person just wants their relative better, which I can appreciate, but it does mean that the door to further information about the home situation is difficult to access. There's a sibling too, but I don't begin to understand that. It's as if the sibling is loved, protected but my patient is not.'

'You could suggest a home visit,' Babur offered. 'You could say that since you want to see your patient so frequently, a home visit might help to relieve some of the pressure you know this can cause to someone who is unwell.'

'Mmm.' Zelfa smiled. 'That's not bad, actually.'

'Old doctors still have their uses,' her father replied and then leaned forward across the table towards her. 'Only one of which is to know when my own daughter is physically ill.'

'Eh?'

Babur spread white, unsalted butter on his bread as he spoke. 'Well, I appreciate that you are worried and preoccupied about this patient, but I also know, and have done for some time, that you have no colour in your face and you are weary all the time.'

'Well, the menopause—'

'That's your explanation for anything and everything.'

'But—'

'Just have a blood test, Zelfa,' he said rather sternly. 'The menopause, if that's what it is, can affect your iron levels. Get something done. I don't have to tell you what the consequences of iron deprivation can be, do I?'

Like a small child bowing under the weight of her parent's anger, Zelfa lowered her head. 'No.'

'So do what far too few of us actually do in practice and go and see a doctor, doctor!'

*   *   *

Once she had been assured that Mehti Vlora and his brother Mehmet were absolutely, definitely residing in police cells, Samsun Bajraktar was only too willing to talk to İkmen about them.

Originally there had been five Vlora boys – Mehmet, Aryan, Mehti, Dhori and Leka who had, it was said, died of typhus when he was a child. Dhori, who it was widely believed had been murdered by Rahman Berisha, had been the baby of the family. Born when his mother was well into her forties, there had been a gap in excess of twenty years between Dhori and his eldest sibling, Mehmet. Addicted to women and drink, young Dhori had been, according to Samsun, an amiable enough lad – he rarely fought and was generally pleasant. With regard to brains, however, Dhori had not been over-endowed, that particular honour falling to Aryan who Samsun felt had always been out of place in 'that family'.

'Aryan thinks about things,' she said as she ground her cigarette out in the sick bowl beside her bed. 'It makes him much more cautious than the others. I mean, I'm not in the least bit surprised that you didn't find any drugs on him.'

'And Mehmet?' İkmen asked. 'What of him?'

'Mehmet is a psychopath,' Samsun replied venomously. 'He's violent, he's manipulative, he deals . . . I really thought it had to be him when I was attacked. If I hadn't seen that it was Mehti with my own eyes I wouldn't have believed it. Mehti Vlora is nothing,' she said with a dismissive wave of her hand. 'Always has been.'

'Mmm.' With Mehti's recent confession to another,

far more serious crime in mind, İkmen asked, 'Do you think it's possible that Mehti might have mounted his attack to try and impress the rest of his family?'

Samsun shrugged. 'Who knows? But if Mehmet asked him to do it then you can be certain that he wouldn't dare not do it. As I said, Mehmet's a psychopath.'

'Of whom the others are afraid.'

'Yes.'

Further discussion of the Vlora brothers was cut short at this point by the entrance of a tall, elderly man wearing a thick sheepskin coat over a pair of loose-legged şalvar trousers. But although clad in the garments of a peasant, it was obvious to even the most casual observer that these were very good peasant clothes – indeed they were rather like those items wealthy tourists might buy. His heavily lined face was still handsome, and the resemblance he bore to both Samsun and İkmen's brother Halil was striking.

'Hello, Father,' Samsun said when she saw him.

'May it pass quickly, Mustafa,' the old man replied, using the standard phrase one uses to the sick.

'Thank you.'

İkmen, rising to his feet, gently embraced the newcomer.

'I trust your journey was a good one, Uncle Ahmet?' he said as he led the old man over towards his own chair.

The old man raised one long, limp hand in a gesture of weariness. 'The bus came, I got on it, I arrived,' he answered and sat down heavily.

'I'm so sorry to have given you this trouble, Father,' Samsun said, lowering her long-lashed eyes in an expression that was genuinely sorrowful.

Ahmet Bajraktar sighed. 'Though you choose to walk about like a painted odalisque, you are still my son,' he said gently. 'You are my blood.'

Not relishing another conversation involving Albanian blood, İkmen said that he would give Samsun and her father some time alone together. Later, he added, he would return to take his uncle back to his apartment. Even Fatma, who was far softer in her approach to the world since his distress the previous night, fully understood that the old man, however 'Albanian' he might be, could hardly be expected to stay at the apartment Samsun shared with the now strangely absent Abdurrahman. In fact, Fatma had even offered to prepare a corner of the living room for Ahmet's use, an unprecedented piece of hospitality when it came to anyone called Bajraktar. Unfortunately, none of this would ease the pain İkmen knew Ahmet would feel when he broached the subject of his mother's death with the old man.

As he stepped outside the warmth of the hospital and into the cruel dampness of the winter air, İkmen told himself that was something that would happen later. Right now, he had work to do. He was still waiting for forensics on Mehti's clothes and on the old blood discovered in the apartment, but in the meantime there was Mehti to deal with. The man and his story warranted rather more 'attention' from him before he came up in front of a judge. Even with confessions, one had to be careful, and İkmen felt that this confession in particular called for caution. After all, if Mehmet Vlora really was a psychopath he'd have no problems either getting his brother to kill Rifat for him or committing the murder himself and making his weaker sibling take the blame for it.

Pausing only to light a cigarette, İkmen headed back towards the station.

Divan Yolu, though cold and morbid in the drizzly winter rain, was still one of the better places to beg. Even in winter, tourists came to the city and, as Engelushjia Berisha had discovered on quite a few occasions of late, a living of sorts could be obtained provided you kept away from the fat Anatolian peasants selling their knitting and the religious woman who beseeched passersby to have mercy upon her for the love of Allah. With her tight, shadowed features and thin, twelve-year-old's body, people felt sorry for Engelushjia. That her brother had once owned a car worth hundreds of millions of lire was an irony that, though not lost upon Engelushjia, would happily remain unknown to the passing trade.

And so she sat, just beyond the step up to the cheap jewellery shop, feeling the almost ceaseless rumble of the trams as they headed towards Eminönü reverberating up her spine. On the mud-slicked ground in front of her lay a small open bag – the receptacle for donations from the generous. Since she'd started, just over an hour before, Engelushjia had received two million lire and a loaf of bread with a packet of olives. The money had come from tourists while the food, all of which she had eaten, had been donated wordlessly by a stern-looking Turkish housewife. It had, Engelushjia had to admit, made her feel, if not happier, at least a little warmer inside.

In truth, not much could actually make her happy at the present time. Rifat was dead and, even though her father said that the police now had Mehti Vlora in custody for his murder, she could find little comfort in that fact. For, even though her father had told the police that he had had no hand in the disappearance of Dhori Vlora, she knew they would still be watching him. And for what? For a stupid deception designed, she imagined, to convince their countrymen that the noble course of *gjakmaria* was being faithfully pursued. Dhori had disappeared, everyone assumed that Rahman was responsible, and he had not disabused them of that notion – until now. Allah alone knew where Dhori Vlora might be – or rather where his body might be rotting.

Engelushjia looked down at her bag with fury in her eyes. Stupid, stupid, stupid Father! And she probably would have remained looking downwards had someone not first waved a ten million lire note under her nose and then placed it in her bag.

Anxious to discover who could so casually part with such riches, she snapped her gaze upwards.

'You!'

'Yes,' Aryan Vlora said as he bent down again towards her. 'Me.'

'What do *you* want?' Engelushjia hissed, careful not to create the kind of scene that might put potential benefactors off.

'I want to talk to you,' Aryan replied.

Engelushjia's hand flew to her bag to retrieve his note.

Seeing that she intended to give him his money back, Aryan said, 'No, I don't want it, Engelushjia, I—'

'Take it!' she snapped and pressed the money into his hand. 'I don't want it!'

'No, you don't understand,' he said as he moved still closer towards her. 'This note is to pay for your time. I need to speak to you.'

'After your brother killed our Rifat?' She laughed bitterly. 'I don't think so!'

'But Mehti didn't—'

'That isn't what the police are saying! They—'

With a speed that took Engelushjia by surprise, Aryan Vlora grabbed the top of her arm in a vice-like grip.

'Aiyee!'

'Now listen to me,' he said through gritted teeth. 'I don't know how long the police are going to keep my brother Mehmet and my mother in their cells so I really don't have time to play any stupid games!'

Her face contorted with pain, Engelushjia squeaked, 'You're hurting me!'

'Yes, and I won't stop hurting you until you come with me!' Aryan pulled her to her feet. Then with a quick glance around to make sure that no passersby were particularly interested in what he was doing, he bent down to pick up the bag and then dragged Engelushjia in the direction of the Pudding Shop.

*　　*　　*

'So what does the coloured glass symbolise then, Mehti?' İkmen asked.

'Eh?'

'Smashed coloured glass, from a bottle or some other decorative item – is it a message of some sort? Some kind of warning to other members of the victim's *fis*?'

Mehti Vlora leaned back from the table and scowled. 'I don't know what you're talking about,' he said, looking at İkmen as if he was mad.

'Oh, that's a surprise.'

'Yes,' Tepe, sitting beside his boss, agreed. 'It is.'

Frowning, Mehti Vlora examined both of the faces in front of him with deep suspicion.

'So how did you get into Rifat's car?' İkmen said changing, as he had done so many times before, the course of the interview apparently on a whim.

'I forced the lock on one of the back doors.'

'Which back door?' Tepe asked. 'Left or right?'

'I don't know.' He shrugged. 'I don't remember now.'

İkmen smiled. 'You know I own a Mercedes myself,' he said pleasantly. 'Not like Rifat's. An old one.'

Mehti Vlora looked down at the floor, feigning boredom.

'But old as it is,' İkmen continued smoothly, 'one thing that my car retains is its robustness. I always buy Mercedes because of that. It's something that someone like myself who routinely goes into the most unsavoury parts of the city must take seriously. After all, I don't want somebody to steal my car, do I? That would be most embarrassing.'

In spite of the fact that Mehti Vlora didn't respond to any of this, Tepe carried on where his boss had left off.

'However,' he said, 'unlike Inspector İkmen's car, Rifat's was alarmed.'

'Not of course when *we* found it,' İkmen put in.

'No.' Tepe smiled at Mehti. 'But it did possess an alarm which would have sounded when you forced the door.'

'It must have been switched off!' Mehti shouted, now suddenly agitated.

'Mmm, well,' a markedly unruffled İkmen observed, 'that may be so, but . . .' he paused here to light a cigarette and then offer his packet to Tepe, who took one. Neither man offered the packet to Mehti. 'Try as they might,' İkmen continued, 'forensic cannot find any sign of forced entry on any of the car doors.'

Mehti Vlora jumped to his feet, knocking his chair over.

'I slashed Rifat's throat with a knife! I dumped his body down on Reşadiye Caddesi! I described his clothes – just right, you said! We were in blood and I'm glad that I alone finally avenged Dhori's death!'

'Yes,' İkmen said in a voice whose calmness was in stark contrast to the Albanian's outburst, 'we know all that, Mehti. But now the time has come for you to tell us the details of your crime.'

'I was angry! I wanted to taste his blood!' He stared at İkmen. 'Mad, you know!'

'Yes.'

'And you don't remember too much when you're like that, do you?'

'No, but there's usually a little more evidence that you've done it, though,' İkmen said and rose swiftly to his feet. 'Which is something you might like to think about after we've gone. Personally, I believe you're full of shit, Mehti.' He smiled. 'Come along, Tepe.'

'But . . .' Mehti Vlora began.

'We can talk again later,' İkmen said, and called to the guard outside.

The door opened and the two policemen left.

Out in the corridor, İkmen leaned heavily against the cold cell wall and sighed.

'Mehti Vlora has motive, seeming opportunity, he knows enough about Rifat's movements that night to have been there . . .'

'But either he didn't get into Rifat's car or Rifat let him in,' Tepe reasoned. 'Or someone else was involved.'

'Someone he is unwilling to name.'

'Perhaps because an admission regarding the use of an accomplice would damage his pride.'

İkmen closed his eyes against the pain that was building up in his head.

'Inspector Suleyman told me that none of the Evren family can remember anything about a second car pulling up outside their property, confirming what Traffic have told us' he said, opening his eyes. 'İlhan Evren also confirmed Felicity's story about Rifat's trip to England.'

'Oh?'

The two men started to walk towards the stairs.

Several unseen prisoners banged on the metal doors of their cells, demanding their lawyers, food, their mothers or wives.

'Yes,' İkmen said, raising his voice against the cacophony. 'And according to him, no money changed hands. Felicity gave Rifat the car as a present and everybody was happy, or so Evren thinks, until Rifat decided to try blackmail to make some money out of his organ donation. On the night of his death, he went to the Evren house to put this to the father and the old man threw him out.'

'Do you think that Mr Evren could have killed him?' Tepe asked, mounting the stairs ahead of his boss.

'Well, it has to be possible,' İkmen answered, flinging what was left of his cigarette onto the stairs. 'But then logically if he had done so it would have been to his advantage to say that he saw a green Fiat outside. I mean, Inspector Suleyman was obviously following a line of inquiry which didn't implicate him.'

'Felicity Evren is a curious-looking woman, I have to say, sir.'

'Yes,' İkmen puffed, one flight up and already fighting for breath. 'She's a . . . a bit of a, er, fantasist, according to her father, but, um . . .' He came to a halt on the stairs. Halfway up the second flight was his limit. Bracing his hands against his knees, he put his head down and puffed hard. Tepe, smiling at what in anyone else would give cause for alarm, knew that İkmen's physical state was simply part of him rather than a life-threatening condition. At least that was how it was for the moment.

'So she lies?'

'I think it's more changing facts that she doesn't like.'

'Lying.' Tepe said firmly.

'Well . . .'

On the move once again, İkmen heaved himself up the final half flight of stairs and then rested with his hand on his chest for a few moments.

When he had recovered his breath sufficiently to speak again, he said, 'Inspector Suleyman was of the opinion that Mr Evren was some sort of gangster. He intends to make a few calls to London, where the family used to live, about him.'

'Why, was his house "tasteless"?' Tepe asked, spitefully emulating Suleyman's tight-lipped delivery of the word.

'Yes,' İkmen replied mildly, 'it was. But then Evren is an art dealer with many eastern European contacts. You know the scene, Tepe. Give the starving peasant a loaf of bread for his dead wife's gold jewellery and then sell it on in London for a quarter of a million dollars. That kind of art dealer.'

'Oh.'

'And Tepe,' said İkmen with a note of warning in his voice, 'don't mock your superiors to me. Inspector Suleyman may be an aristocrat but that doesn't make him a fool.'

Tepe lowered his gaze. 'No, sir.'

'Treat him with respect,' İkmen continued as he made his way along the corridor towards his office. 'How would you have coped had the Evren woman leered at you?'

'Did she?'

'What woman doesn't?' İkmen said, making use of his knowledge regarding Tepe's extramarital affair with Ayşe Farsakoğlu – a woman still besotted with Suleyman.

In an effort to try to answer his superior's question without losing his temper, Tepe stammered, 'Well, I, um . . .'

'You don't have to answer that,' İkmen said as they entered his office. He sat down, and from behind the vast paper mountain that was his desk, he added, 'Spite breeds spite, you know, Tepe, and you don't want people to start talking about you, do you?'

Tepe, who had now seated himself at his own, far less chaotic desk, switched on his computer terminal and said miserably, 'No, sir.'

'By the way,' İkmen's disembodied voice said as he rapidly changed the subject back to business, 'how did Mehmet Vlora react when you told him that Mehti had confessed to Rifat Berisha's murder?'

'He reiterated that both he and Aryan were with Mehti all the time on the night of the killing, but he looked rattled.'

'Did he?'

'Yes.' And then after pausing for a moment in order to collect his thoughts, Tepe said, 'Sir?'

'Yes?'

'Do you think it might be possible that the truth lies somewhere between Mehti's story and that told by the Evren family?'

'Oh, Mehti has told us enough to make me believe he

was there,' İkmen said, 'as were Evren and his children. And unless Rifat was attacked on his journey home by someone as yet unknown, one of them probably murdered him.'

'Yes, but if Evren did kill Rifat, why was he so co-operative when Inspector Suleyman went to visit him?'

'Perhaps Evren himself didn't kill the boy,' İkmen said. 'Maybe he really does know nothing about Rifat's death. His children might, though.'

'What, that weird, twisted little woman!' Tepe frowned with disbelief. 'No! Dr Sarkissian said the murderer, if not necessarily strong, would have to be determined and have a strong stomach.'

'Evren also has a young son and a very fit-looking chauffeur,' İkmen replied.

'But why . . .'

'Well, that we don't know,' İkmen said as he lit a cigarette. 'Beyond attempting to extort money from Evren, Rifat seems to have been the model friend to poor Felicity. But then we don't possess the full picture yet, do we?'

'No.'

'Somewhere in the triangle that exists between outraged Albanian blood, a woman's fantasies and the growing wants of a greedy young man lies the answer,' İkmen said and then picked up his telephone and dialled a number.

'What are you doing, sir?' Tepe asked.

'I'm going to ask Commissioner Ardiç to allow me enough manpower to assist us in the formal interrogation of the Evrens and their chauffeur. And, when that is done, we will reinterrogate the Vloras, including Aryan, and also Rahman Berisha. By that time forensic should—' His call was answered and İkmen turned away. 'Hello, sir,' he said. 'Yes, it is . . . Yes . . .'

Tepe didn't really hear anything more of İkmen's conversation with Ardıç, his mind was stuck on both the stern reprimand his boss had given him earlier and the truly enormous amount of work that was mounting up for all of them. And in view of the fact that they already had a confession, albeit a suspect one, he found his enthusiasm flagging.

'You started it!' Engelushjia Berisha spat out across the cup of coffee he had just bought her.

'No, I didn't!' Aryan Vlora countered hotly. 'The ignorant peasants who were our ancestors started it!' Bending forward across the table, he continued in a low voice, 'I have never even been to Albania, do you know that? Much less the town we spend all of our time fighting about!'

'Well, I was born in Kukes,' Engelushjia answered, naming the place where they all originated. 'My father saw your cousins kill his uncle! So when we came here and found another branch of your accursed *fis*—'

'Engelushjia . . .'

'Why should I talk to you when everyone knows that you killed Egrem?'

'My *fis*, yes, but not me, not personally.'

'You know who did it though, don't you?' Engelushjia persisted. 'You must.'

241

Aryan looked briefly around at the other people in the Pudding Shop. Most of them appeared to be tourists; they obviously had money, if their clothes and neat hair were anything to go by. There were Turks as well, who also looked clean and well-fed. Only he and Engelushjia with her mud-stained skirt broke this ordered pattern. Poor slaves to their own insistent, costly blood.

'If I tell you who killed Egrem,' Aryan said gravely, 'will you believe me when I say that Mehti did not kill Rifat?'

Engelushjia looked at him suspiciously. 'I don't know. We've always believed he was useless. Rifat laughed at him . . .'

Aryan folded his thin, gnarled hands in front of him on the table. 'I won't lie to you and tell you that I was with Mehti on the night of Rifat's death,' he said. 'I wasn't. The truth is that I don't know where Mehti was that night.'

'The police say he followed Rifat out to the house of his girlfriend.'

'Yes, and I wouldn't argue with that,' Aryan agreed earnestly. 'He did sometimes follow your brother – as I know you know. He never spoke or actually did anything. Mehti felt the loss of Dhori more keenly than anyone, he wanted to punish your *fis* for that. But I know that he didn't kill Rifat.'

'How?'

Aryan shrugged. 'Because I know.'

'That's no answer,' Engelushjia retorted angrily. 'Why should I believe that?'

'Because when I came home one evening to find

Mehmet crouching over your brother Egrem's body with a bloody knife in his hand, Mehti was hiding in our bedroom with a blanket over his head covering his ears with his hands!'

For just a moment it was almost as if she hadn't heard him. Her eyes, strangely impassive, even flicked up as one of the old shoeshine men came in for tea and rice pudding. Only when the jolt that his words had given her passed did she begin to cry, softly and silently like one already drained of tears.

'Mehti screamed at me to stop Mehmet, but it was too late,' Aryan continued. 'Your brother was dead and my mother had already started helping Mehmet move Egrem over towards the fire escape.'

'We all knew that Egrem was dead when he didn't come back that night,' Engelushjia said in a voice that was now chillingly calm. 'We'd even talked about how Mehmet might kill him . . . And then in the morning your neighbour, Ahmet Qerimi came . . .'

'Your father and mother brought a handcart to carry your brother away from the rubbish tip at the bottom of our fire escape.' He looked down at his hands again, which were clenched into fists. 'My mother smiled . . . And then your father killed Dhori, and Angeliki didn't smile again.'

'Except that my father didn't kill Dhori,' Engelushjia murmured, as if she was afraid to allow her enemy to hear her admission.

Frowning, Aryan said, 'What? But I thought—'

'Oh, yes, you thought!' Engelushjia said bitterly. 'Just like everyone else, just like me! But Father didn't kill

Dhori – how could he when he was too frightened to leave the house? When could he have done it? Rifat was young and silly and bold and Mother and I could go out any time that we wished, but Father?' Crying properly now, she struggled to keep her voice down, causing it to tremble with emotion. 'Father is a coward, he told me, he—'

'All right! All right!' Aryan reached across the table and took her cold hands between his fingers. 'So where is my brother Dhori? He was a simple, friendly man. Who else but your father, Engelushjia, could have killed him?'

'My father has never killed anyone,' she sobbed mournfully. 'Even when your father killed my grand-father, it was left to my Uncle Muhammed to take revenge.'

'Upon my father,' Aryan said with a sigh.

'Yes, and so on and so on down to Egrem and Rifat and . . .' The catalogue of death seemed to exhaust her and Engelushjia lapsed into silence.

After a moment, Aryan said, 'Drink your coffee, it'll get cold.'

The girl silently did as she was asked, her throat occasionally spasming with unshed tears. Aryan watched her with what an outside observer would have deemed a hard intensity. In truth, however, his eyes were not hard so much as searching, seeking out what he hoped might be a growing sympathy within her. And when he felt that the time was right, he resumed their conversation.

'Look, Engelushjia,' he said, 'whether we believe what the other has said or not, if we can start from the

244

idea that your father and my brother Mehti are innocent men, then – hear me out, please!' he said when she attempted to protest.

For a moment she looked searchingly into his eyes and then she shrugged and was silent.

'The only thing we know for certain is that Mehmet killed Egrem,' Aryan said softly lest anyone in the Pudding Shop was Albanian. 'Mehmet is crazy but now that he is finally in a police cell perhaps there might be a way of keeping him there. And Mother.'

Shocked by this apparent lack of *fis* loyalty, Engelushjia said, 'But Mehmet is your blood.'

'Yes, and I have loyally kept silent about his excesses for long enough! I have covered up, lied and cheated for Mehmet for most of my life, but like the rest of my brothers I have done so out of fear. I'm only here with you today because Mother and Mehmet are down in the cells! Mehmet is insane, he frightens me and Mehti – he used to frighten Dhori too.' He rubbed his eyes wearily with his fingers. 'Look, I know for certain that Mehmet ordered Mehti to beat up Mustafa Bajraktar – he fancies a war with them, the fool! Luckily, however, Mehti is weak and frightened, and Bajraktar is big and vicious.'

'So you think Mehti is incapable of murder?'

'I know it!' Aryan replied passionately. 'Like I told you, I've seen him hide from Mehmet's excesses.'

'So was it Mehmet?'

'No, he was with me all the time on the night of your brother's death, and that is the truth.'

'But if neither of your brothers killed Rifat, who did?' Engelushjia said mournfully.

'I don't know,' Aryan replied, 'but maybe if we look into your brother's life a little harder we can work it out.'

'We?' she asked, her eyes narrowing.

Aryan cleared his throat. 'If you let me try and prove Mehti's innocence, I will go to the police and tell them how, when and where Mehmet killed Egrem.'

'*What?*'

'Mehmet has to be locked away for good! He's an animal! And anyway, all of this has got to stop, this bloodshed. We have a chance now, Engelushjia! With Mehmet and Mother in custody, we have a chance to finish this thing for good! Don't you want to live a normal life like all the other people in this restaurant?' He swept an arm round to illustrate his point. 'Well?'

Chapter 15

Against her better judgement, for she felt that he might feel she was forcing her company on him, Zelfa Halman decided to offer her patient a lift home at the end of his session. His home in Bebek was further north than her own house in Ortaköy, but it was raining and he did look so very tired. Besides, if his family were in, it might give her a chance to assess his situation at first hand.

For one so young, Ali Evren seemed to carry a lot of guilt. Much of it appeared to revolve around his mother and the manner of her death. Mary Evren had suffered from depression for most of her life. She had been sectioned to several British psychiatric hospitals before she took her own life nearly three years ago. Whether Ali's guilt arose from her suicide or from conversations that had taken place within the family subsequently, Zelfa didn't know. Although he had what would have been described in the past as a 'morbid nature', which was something that he had obviously shared with his horror-aficionado mother, the exacerbating factor in Mary Evren's illness had not been Ali but rather his sister Felicity. Mary felt guilty about the heavy responsibilities she placed upon her daughter even though, according to Ali, Felicity wanted to take care of Mary. Felicity – a beautiful girl, Zelfa understood – had been a slave to her mother's illness, a sickness Mary could neither control nor curtail. And so Mary had killed herself – an act of both selflessness and selfishness. An act that would not apparently go away.

Ali's guilt was not the main cause of Zelfa's concern, however. It was a common enough byproduct of the death of a loved one. No, what really worried her was Ali's increasing fear. Not all of it could be attributed to his father; it ran through every aspect of Ali's life. He feared people because of the disclosure that closeness to others encouraged; he feared sleep because of the lack of control that state requires; and he feared losing the one person who empathised with him – his sister. Felicity, apparently, understood. A conversation with her would be most interesting, Zelfa thought.

'You know the Aya Sofya?' the boy said when he finally decided to break the silence between them.

'Yes,' Zelfa answered as her brand new Renault glided under the grey bulk of the Boğaziçi Bridge.

'You know that it used to be a church?'

'Yes.'

'Well, I went there today, on a school trip, and it made me feel weary and sort of oppressed.'

Zelfa smiled wryly. 'Like a wicked, unholy vampire, you mean?'

'No,' he responded with what Zelfa felt was admirable calmness. 'It was not, you will recall, me who was born in the shadow of Bram Stoker's epic, but my sister.'

'Does she experience trouble in churches then?' Zelfa asked.

'I don't know.' Out of the corner of her eye she saw him frowning. 'But then she doesn't go into them – at least not with me. She's never ever been to the Aya Sofya. Perhaps I should take her sometime.'

'Perhaps you should and then if you find that God doesn't strike either of you dead you can both feel a bit more certain about who and what you are,' she said even though she knew that she was making fun of a delicately constructed and desired delusion.

Ali Evren did not react badly; in fact he smiled.

'Oh, I'm pretty sure my sister would feel something, doctor,' he said. 'In spite of what she says, Felicity has no reflection.'

For rather longer than was strictly safe, Zelfa took her eyes off the road and stared at him. 'What did you say?'

'You heard what I said,' her patient responded calmly.

'But Ali—'

'I don't want to talk about this any more,' he said with finality. 'So we won't.'

Resisting the urge to press him further, Zelfa concentrated on her driving. With so much rain coming down, it was difficult to see and the road required her full attention. But it wasn't easy, what with this strange boy and his invisible sister and her appointment earlier with Dr Aksu. It was one thing talking about being menopausal; having it confirmed by tests was something else. She wasn't at all sure how she would face the clinical fact. Perhaps she might do something mad like go back to Ireland without telling anyone . . .

'It's the next on the left,' Ali said.

The small street in which Ali lived branched left off Kuçuk Bebek Caddesi. Though no residents of Bebek were poor, it was not one of the better streets. Architecturally a mish-mash of styles, the houses encompassed nineteenth-century Ottoman cottages through to the strangely clinical curves of the Art Deco villa that, apparently, belonged to the Evren family. Zelfa assumed that the property was supposed to be white, they usually were, but time and the elements had ensured that the house now matched the present grey colour of the sky. But this far up in the hills behind Bebek proper there was really only one reason why a person would purchase a house, any house. Even through the rain, Zelfa could see that the view was spectacular – a raging torrent of Bosphorus directly below, and beyond it Asia stretching on and on to strange, shut-away China. Instant romance in just a glance.

Her mood changed when she went into the house. It was dark and cluttered in a way that Art Deco houses should not be; the place was littered with items that looked cheap even if they weren't. The telephone in the hall, an 'antique' china and gold leaf affair, was a typical case in point.

Insisting, as she knew he would, that she stay for tea, Ali escorted Zelfa to one of what appeared to be two living rooms. Here, seated in front of an enormous bay window, she found herself looking not at a beautiful view, for she was on the wrong side of the property, but at a very vulgar gold Rolls-Royce which was parked directly outside the window. Hating her own hypocrisy, she made some admiring comments before Ali left to go and get the tea. When he had gone, she turned her attention to other parts of this horrid room. It contained overstuffed furniture, nasty, cheap kilims, a large gaudy mirror and a smattering of quite staggeringly lovely eastern European icons.

'Hello.'

The suddenness combined with the clipped Englishness of the greeting made Zelfa jump.

'Jesus Christ!' she said as she placed a calming hand on her chest.

The woman was tiny and dressed entirely in black. At first Zelfa thought she must be either very young or very old. In fact she was neither. What she was, however, was extraordinarily misshapen, hunched over to one side and with a face that could have been lovely, had it not been stretched and distorted by an agglomeration of ugly red lumps.

'I'm sorry I startled you,' she said and extended a small hand out towards Zelfa, 'My brother told me you were Irish.'

'Oh, right,' Zelfa replied, also in English, as she took and encompassed the hand in hers. Strangely, though tiny, it was firm and sinewy. Christ, Zelfa thought wryly, if this was Ali's beautiful sister, she would hate to see someone Ali considered ugly.

'I am Felicity,' the woman said, 'David's sister.'

'David?'

The strange face attempted a smile. 'It's what Ali

was known as back home,' she said. 'I still use it myself. Habit.'

'Oh.'

'Yes.' She pulled back from Zelfa, her face grave. 'Nice though it is to meet you, doctor, I'm afraid that I will have to ask you to leave.'

'Oh?'

'We are expecting the police here any minute.'

'Nothing wrong, I trust,' Zelfa began. 'I—'

'Nothing that any of us can do anything about now,' Felicity Evren answered cryptically. 'A family matter. Of no concern to those outside, if you know what I mean.'

'Of course.'

Felicity swung an arm towards the door. 'Then let me escort you out,' she said, 'and thank you for so kindly bringing David home.'

'Oh, it's nothing, really . . .'

But Felicity was already moving off towards the hall and the front door. Zelfa wondered if the poor woman ever ventured out through it. For herself, she was certain that if she suffered from whatever it was that afflicted Felicity, she wouldn't have needed the excuse of a sick mother to make her stay indoors. People could be so cruel about such things. No wonder Ali was so stiflingly protective of her, so weirdly kind – though also at times almost bitter too. Maybe this was part of his strange, multifaceted problem. Perhaps Felicity simply *wanted* to disappear. Zelfa could see why.

When they reached the front door, Felicity again attempted a smile before opening the door.

'You know, I'm really quite concerned about your brother's condition,' Zelfa said as she stood in the doorway. 'He has some unusual and, I think, not always helpful perceptions of events.'

'Oh.' She lowered her eyes. 'Is that so?'

'Yes. And although I can't actually tell you what they are because of client confidentiality, a talk with you about him might be useful.'

Felicity nodded gravely. 'Well, of course, whatever I can do to help David . . .'

'Perhaps you could call me,' Zelfa dug in her bag for one of her business cards, 'soon?'

'Yes, of course,' Felicity said with another of her twisted smiles.

'Sometime tomorrow perhaps?'

'Yes . . . possibly . . . Now I must say goodbye, doctor,' she said and began to close the door.

'Oh, er, yes. Goodbye. Thank you.'

The door slammed shut.

As Zelfa turned towards her car, her eyes widened at the sight of Mehmet Suleyman standing in the rain on the driveway.

'I suppose I shouldn't ask you why you've just left that house,' he said as he suppressed the urge to smile at her.

'No,' Zelfa replied, 'you shouldn't.'

'Not unlike the seal of the confession, the doctor/patient confidentiality thing,' İkmen said as he joined Zelfa and Mehmet Suleyman. 'Is that not right, doctor?'

'It is,' she smiled and then turned back to her fiancé. 'I'll call you later.'

'Make sure that you do.'

'Yes, sir!' With a laugh gurgling at the back of her throat, she made her way over to her car. As she passed Suleyman, he gently squeezed one of her hands, and they shared a look, just briefly. But it was significant enough for the people watching from inside the house to notice.

Since Angeliki, Mehmet and Mehti had been out of the apartment for a while the place somehow felt cleaner. And although Orhan Tepe knew that this perception was probably quite irrational, there was no doubt that some physical features of the place had changed since he had last burst through the front door. For a start, with just Aryan in residence, there was a lot less cigarette smoke, while vegetable peelings, the traditional preserve of Angeliki, were entirely absent. What was totally unexpected was the presence of Engelushjia Berisha.

'I don't suppose your parents would be very pleased if they knew where you were,' he said to the girl as he sat down in the chair next to hers. Engelushjia bowed her head and reddened.

'I do hope that nothing is, er, happening here,' he added, looking at Aryan Vlora.

'Miss Berisha and I are simply trying to find a way to help my brother Mehti and discover Rifat Berisha's killer,' the Albanian replied with what Tepe felt was remarkable calmness.

'It's true, Sergeant Tepe,' the girl put in. 'Both Mr Vlora and I want the same thing.'

'But your brother has confessed to the murder of Rifat Berisha,' Tepe pointed out.

'Do you have any forensic evidence to connect my brother to Rifat's murder, Sergeant?' Aryan asked.

'Not yet.'

'Well, you won't find any.'

'Why not?'

'Because he didn't do it,' Aryan replied simply.

With a sigh, Tepe took his pen and notebook out of his jacket pocket and opened it. 'It's about the night of Rifat's murder that I've come to speak to you, Mr Vlora,' he said as he wrote something Aryan couldn't see at the top of one of the pages. 'I want you to tell me what you and your brothers were doing that evening.'

'What, again?'

'Yes. You must appreciate that if a story changes, as it has done in this case – first Mehti was at home all night with you and then he wasn't – we have to check it out.'

Aryan shrugged. 'All right.'

'So what happened?'

'We all ate together – we usually do. Our mother likes that, she . . . Well, at about seven Mehmet decided he was going to get drunk.'

'He didn't take any of his drugs then?' Tepe asked.

Aryan sighed. 'No. He doesn't always do that. In fact most of the time he prefers to drink and anyway, as I know you know, Sergeant, good drug dealers rarely sample their own products. At any rate, Mehmet sat down in front of the television with a bottle of rakı while I did what I usually do.'

'Which is?'

'He draws,' Engelushjia Berisha said. 'People and streets and stuff. He's good.'

Tepe looked up from his notebook and raised his eyebrows in surprise. It was difficult to imagine any sort of artistic pursuit in such a squalid, seemingly barren place. But then Inspector İkmen had said that he'd been told Aryan Vlora was not in the usual mould of unemployed immigrant. 'I'll show you,' said Aryan. He left the room briefly and came back with one of his drawings.

Tepe was impressed. He could see that Aryan had considerable talent and acute observational skills. The picture, which was of his mother, had managed to capture much of Angeliki's character, even down to her overriding spitefulness. Tepe expressed his admiration and then pulled his interview back on track.

'So,' he said, 'Mehmet was drunk and you were drawing.'

'My mother fell asleep and at about eight o'clock Mehti went out.'

'Did he say where he was going?'

'No, although,' he hesitated, as if undecided about what he should say next, 'although I knew that since Dhori's disappearance he spent a lot of time standing around in the vicinity of the Berishas' place. I'd seen him myself.'

'But he never did anything,' Engelushjia interjected. 'I remember Mother saying she saw one of the Vlora boys outside a couple of times – she thought it might be Mehmet and was afraid. But Rifat wasn't, he said it was only Mehti and then he laughed. It would explain why he was so fearless.'

'So it's well known that Mehti is no threat?'

'Yes,' Aryan replied.

'And yet you, as a family, seem to have quite a reputation,' Tepe said. 'Miss Berisha's parents are frightened of you and the attack on Mr Bajraktar can only have increased their fear.'

'A *fis* in blood either rules through fear or it perishes,' Aryan replied gravely. 'The Vlora boys are feared but in reality it has always been my mother and Mehmet who have been the most enthusiastic.'

'But if you didn't approve, Mr Vlora—'

'Oh, you think it's easy to just say you don't want to play this game any more, do you?' Suddenly roused to anger, Aryan stood up and started pacing across the room. 'Sergeant Tepe, do you have any idea what my brother Mehmet would do to me if he came in here now and found Engelushjia here?'

'Well . . .'

'He would kill me! Our rules, the Kunan of Lek Dukagjini, demand it! We cannot be cowardly, we cannot show mercy, we cannot even discuss our differences!' His hands visibly trembling now, Aryan lit a cigarette before sitting back down in his chair. 'And that suits a madman like Mehmet just fine.'

'What about Mehti?'

Aryan put his head in his hands. 'Mehti would like to be like Mehmet but he just isn't. He's a fool and, yes,' he raised his head, 'I know that he attacked Bajraktar and that he hurt him. But I believe he only did it because he couldn't bring himself to kill Rifat Berisha – as well as to punish Bajraktar for being an informant. He also did it to impress Mehmet who wanted him to do it. He was actually proud that he had put us in danger from the Bajraktars. Mehmet, I know, relishes being in blood with them. They are a very powerful *fis*, as your Inspector İkmen well knows.'

The connection between İkmen and the transsexual was not something Tepe wanted to discuss right now and so he simply cleared his throat.

'Mr Vlora and I are thinking about other people that Rifat might have known – people who might have wanted to kill him,' Engelushjia offered.

'And yet,' Tepe persisted, 'Mehti left this apartment at about eight in the evening and returned when?'

'The following morning, yes, but—'

'So he had both motive and opportunity, Mr Vlora.'

'But I know he didn't do it, Sergeant!'

'How do you know?'

'I just do,' Aryan said lamely.

'Mr Vlora, I understand that you love your brother and want to help him. But you must see that the case against him is strong, even without his confession. We also have good reason to believe that he was in the same place as Rifat the night he died.'

'If it's all so hopeless, Sergeant, why have you come to speak to me?'

It was a reasonable question, and the answer, that Mehti Vlora's story was not entirely consistent with the facts, was not one that Tepe felt it would be prudent to give at this point.

The silence was broken by Engelushjia who walked over to Aryan and crouched down beside him. 'Why don't you tell Sergeant Tepe about, you know, what we were talking about earlier?' she said.

'Look,' said Tepe in frustration, 'how exactly did you two suddenly become best friends? You say you're working together but frankly I find it hard to—'

'Sergeant!' Aryan Vlora's voice was loud and commanding but as he spoke he didn't take his eyes from Engelushjia Berisha.

Tepe noted how they were looking at each other but did not read very much into it. He was just annoyed that he had been shouted at by a civilian.

'Yes, Mr Vlora?' he threw back angrily.

'If I give you someone who is a real murderer, will you listen to me about Mehti?'

'Can you give me Rifat's murderer?'

'No,' he said, 'I cannot. But I can give you Egrem Berisha's killer and a description of how Mehti reacts around violence.'

'Go on,' said Tepe cautiously.'

'When my brother Mehmet killed Egrem Berisha, Mehti screamed and sobbed like a child.'

Tepe leaned back sharply in his chair as if pushed by the force of this information. 'Were you actually present at the time, Mr Vlora?' he asked gravely.

'Just after I was, yes.'

'And you didn't report it to the police?'

Aryan looked down at the floor. 'No.'

Tepe sighed. 'Well, I hope you understand the implications of what you've said, Mr Vlora. For yourself as well as for your brother.'

Strangely, given the gravity of the situation, Aryan smiled. 'Oh, yes, Sergeant,' he said. 'I know what I've done. It's something I should have done a long time ago.'

Taking hold of Tepe's chair by the arms, Suleyman moved it across to İkmen's desk and sat down. Outside, night was already beginning to fall and in the silence that preceded their conversation both men listened to the sound of the relentless rain, the occasional ship's foghorn and the rapid footsteps of people who didn't possess umbrellas. With some displeasure Suleyman observed that his shoes were quite disgusting, what with the ever present mud and the rancid food and tainted puddles of old İstanbul.

Nothing so trivial was bothering İkmen. 'You know,' he said, having inserted himself deftly behind his great desk and lit up a cigarette, 'although there is nothing I can actually tell you about the Evren family that gives me cause for alarm, I'm not happy about their involvement in this case. To use a word that Zelfa would approve of, I don't feel comfortable about the "dynamics" between that man and his children.'

Suleyman shrugged. 'İlhan Evren is a gangster. The Metropolitan Police in London say he has one conviction for fraud and there is evidence, if not proof, that he arranged for refugees to sell body parts to rich Europeans. There are also rumours of violence. Such people and their families routinely live lives circumscribed by secrets and deception.'

'Yes,' İkmen said with a frown, 'and that's what bothers me. If your assessment of him is correct, Evren is probably a most accomplished liar. But he was quite open about his feelings about Rifat, and the daughter, too, has been quite helpful in her own weird way. There's been no attempt to hide their involvement with Rifat on that night.'

'No.'

İkmen paused to puff heavily on his cigarette and stare at the smoke-stained ceiling. 'The only thing I really didn't like,' he said, 'was the way the young son always looked at his sister before answering questions. Smiling, sly. Something about it gave me the creeps. It was odd. I mean, had he been a small child I could have understood it. But not a teenager.'

'You think he should have been more confident?' Suleyman smiled. 'Perhaps back in England he was told about how monstrous the feared Turkish police can be.'

Smiling too, İkmen said, 'Maybe.'

Suleyman took his cigarettes out of his jacket pocket and lit up. 'So what do you think about this present Evren now says Rifat brought for his daughter? Seems he used it as a sort of excuse to gain entry. At least that is what I assume he did.'

'Yes,' İkmen said, 'although he apparently left with it, whatever it was.'

'Mmm.' Suleyman sucked thoughtfully on his cigarette. 'It's a pity we don't know what it was.'

İkmen nodded in agreement. 'In particular, whether it was a coloured glass item. It would be interesting to discover what precisely was smashed so venomously into Rifat's face.'

'If it was the gift for Felicity, it would open up various possibilities.'

'Yes.' İkmen smiled. 'Perhaps the lady involved didn't like the gift.'

'Or another lady was consumed with jealousy.'

İkmen pushed back on his chair and rocked it on its two back legs. 'But with absolutely nothing to go on with regard to other women we are thrown back onto the Evren family. Just because Felicity and her brother were supposed to be asleep when Rifat was at the house doesn't mean that was so.'

'In that case,' Suleyman said, 'why did Felicity Evren lay herself open to discovery by presenting herself at the Berisha house?'

'She was invited by Engelushjia Berisha. The girl informed her about Rifat Berisha's death. I don't suppose she imagined Engelushjia would report her visit to us. After all, as far as Felicity was concerned, Engelushjia might have been aware of her friendship with Rifat but she didn't know he'd told his sister about going to London. And quite honestly I don't think Engelushjia would have reported it if she wasn't sweet on Tepe. Besides, Felicity would have had to visit the Berishas, wouldn't she, as soon as she saw the story in the papers. After all, she did love Rifat.'

'Even though she and he were never lovers.'

Ikmen laughed. 'Oh, the cynicism written on your

face is a joy to behold!' He clapped his hands in appreciation. 'When I first knew you, you delighted in letting me know that in your opinion sex was really quite an unimportant aspect of human activity. There were lots of things people could do without that, you said.'

'OK! OK!' Suleyman, smiling in spite of himself, rubbed a tired hand across his face. 'I was very young.'

'And oh so traditionally repressed,' Ikmen said with obvious glee in his voice. After all, love and respect Suleyman as he did, the younger man was still part of the 'old order' and therefore a legitimate target for a peasant like himself.

Suleyman did not take offence or even react to this minor slight; he simply, as was his custom, returned to the subject that concerned him.

'I suppose if Mehti Vlora really was outside the Evrens' house on the night Rifat was killed – and I believe he was – he might have seen something of significance.'

Ikmen's face resolved into a scowl. 'Possibly. But we'll have to get past his desire for family approval and his Albanian machismo before he'll tell us. Unless, of course, Mehti is doing all this under orders from the unsavoury Mr Evren. Not, of course, that we have established any connection between the two.'

'No.'

'No. But I must say that I do like the idea of Rifat's gift being smashed into his face. It indicates spite. Although I can't see why the apparently bereft Felicity would do such a thing and I doubt whether that brother of hers could do it.'

'Evren's Russian friends probably could.'

İkmen inclined his head to one side. 'True. And dumping a body near to its home is a very mob thing to do . . . If only we had some hard forensics.'

'Indeed.'

'But we don't,' İkmen said with a sigh, 'so we must work with what we've got, which, at the moment is an unsound confession. I think some further investigation of Mr Evren's associations is called for. Although Rifat apparently donated one of his kidneys to Evren's daughter of his own free will, I can detect a certain unsavouriness in that business, which has little to do with old suspicions regarding İlhan's involvement in the organ business.'

'Yes,' Suleyman agreed, 'I do too. Like why would Rifat do it? But then perhaps we need to ask ourselves whether we would feel like this if Felicity Evren were young and pretty.'

İkmen smiled. 'Well, he got a car out of it and a holiday.'

'In hospital?' Suleyman said acidly. 'How delightful.'

İkmen allowed his chair to fall forwards with a thump. 'Which reminds me,' he said, looking at his watch, 'I need to go to the hospital and pick up my uncle.'

Suleyman put his cigarette out in İkmen's ashtray and asked, 'So how do we proceed then, Çetin?'

İkmen removed his jacket from the back of his chair and stood up. 'We still need to find out what Roditi discovered from the chauffeur, as well as looking into Mr Evren's associates. I've asked the British consul to contact me. Perhaps Rifat was working for this "British" businessman.' He shrugged. 'I also think that perhaps Mehti Vlora should be appraised of the worst-case scenario with regard to his current situation.'

'You mean you want him really frightened.'

'Yes.' İkmen shouldered his jacket. 'Perhaps when Çöktin returns in the morning you might speak to him about it. After all,' he added, his eyes twinkling wickedly, 'if one of Shaitan's own can't frighten a man, who can?'

Suleyman was about to respond to this somewhat controversial observation when Tepe, unannounced, burst into the office.

'Sir,' he said as he fought to catch his breath, 'sir, we've got something in the Berisha case!'

'Aryan Vlora has given details of the exact manner and location of Egrem Berisha's death,' said Ayşe Farsakoğlu, almost hidden from view by Tepe's considerable height.

İkmen frowned. 'That's Rifat's brother.'

'Yes! Aryan Vlora says that Mehmet Vlora definitely killed him.'

'And how does Aryan know this?' a far calmer Suleyman inquired.

'He knows because he was there, Inspector,' Ayşe Farsakoğlu said as she pushed herself past Tepe into the room. 'A fact the sergeant here very cleverly got out of him.'

'Oh, indeed,' İkmen said, fighting against the discomfort he was feeling being in a room with a woman he knew had slept with both of his colleagues. 'And why would Aryan allow him to do that?'

'Why don't I tell you on the way?' Tepe said as he held the door open for his superior.

'He's here, is he?' İkmen asked wearily.

'Yes.'

'And Engelushjia Berisha,' Ayşe added. She looked triumphantly at Suleyman. 'It's quite a story.'

'I expect it is.'

With a sigh, İkmen took his mobile telephone out of his pocket and keyed in a number he knew by heart.

'Well, if I'm going to have to listen to yet more confessions of guilt, I'd better arrange for someone else to pick up my poor uncle,' he said and waited for the familiar voice of his eldest son to come on the line.

Chapter 16

Uncles, or rather the opinions of a particular uncle, were very prominent in Zelfa Halman's mind as she dragged herself wearily into her cold bed that evening. It wasn't even nine o'clock yet but she felt weary and even though she knew she had promised to telephone Mehmet, she just didn't feel up to it. And as if having a body that felt like lead were not enough, the telephone call she'd received from her Uncle Frank had upset her. Virtually demanding that she tell her father about her engagement, which was something Zelfa had in fact now done, Father Frank had also gone into far too much detail about an aspect of his work she had always found particularly disturbing.

There was, apparently, an unquiet spirit in the house of one of Frank's parishioners. Manifesting itself as a tall, grey man, this 'ghost' had caused great consternation to the elderly lady who lived there; so much so that Frank, without even thinking to consult his superiors, was fully intending to wade in with bell, book, candle and lots of Holy Water.

Zelfa, who failed to see how anybody with even the minutest grasp on reality could believe in such bullshit, had told her uncle that she thought he was being most irresponsible.

'This lady could be mentally ill, for all you know!' she'd snapped at her now rather offended uncle.

'Oh, don't talk so ridiculous, Bridget! Mrs Morgan is as sane as I am.'

Reigning herself in from vocalising the obvious riposte, Zelfa had instead said, 'But she could still be having an autoscopic episode – anyone can have one of those, particularly if they're under stress or—'

'What the hell are you talking about, girl?'

'Autoscopic experiences are about the mind making something appear to a person when that thing isn't really there. It's often a form of wish fulfilment. Like for instance if a woman's husband dies and then, three months later, she starts seeing him in her bedroom.'

'Oh, for the love of—'

'It's true, Uncle Frank. It rationally explains such phenomena.'

'To prove there's no such thing as the spirit, I suppose!' he had retorted angrily. 'You and your science. Jesus God, as if it isn't bad enough that you're marrying a heathen . . .'

As soon as he'd said it, she could tell by his sharp intake of breath that he wished he hadn't. But by then it was too late, a fact Zelfa made very plain by slamming the phone down on him.

Now, some two hours later, Zelfa was still troubled. Heathens and ghosts and medieval ceremonies – it was all the stuff of ignorance and prejudice. Like the notion of evil, these things had no place in the modern practitioner's therapeutic armoury. But still they persisted, if in perhaps more clinical guises. After all, wasn't young

Ali Evren in a sense 'haunted'? Guilt plus fear, which was a common combination in bereavement, particularly after suicide, were high on Ali's agenda. Perhaps it was his dead mother's 'ghost' that made him behave so strangely – wanting her son to die or go mad so that she could make contact with him again. Scary echoes of *Wuthering Heights*. But on a more mundane level, poor shrunken little Felicity Evren was enough to frighten the shit out of a gladiator. Creeping around like some portent of doom. Despite everything her brother might believe, she was not, unfortunately for her, either lovely or invisible. But then if she had really been invisible, Ali would have been sad. After all, he loved his sister. A simple and laudable emotion.

Zelfa wondered what her beloved 'heathen' Mehmet had been doing at the Evren house. As far as she was aware, he was not currently engaged in anything apart from assisting İkmen in some homicidal Albanian feud. They didn't talk about their respective professions very much. For both of them there were far too many rules around security and confidentiality to allow any real freedom of speech. Still she wondered why he had been there and which member of the household he had gone to see. After all, the presence of the police could mean criminal activity, which in turn could point towards a far more earthly reason behind Ali's fears than the ghost of his dead mother or his invisible sister.

It was too bad she couldn't simply ask Mehmet. Maybe if she approached the subject obliquely or posed hypothetical questions . . . But then perhaps not. Zelfa sank still deeper into her bed. She didn't feel like talking, not even to Mehmet, not even about Ali Evren. Old priests and her own vestigial religious indoctrination were at work inside her mind tonight. As well as feeling unwell she was bothered, she had to admit, by a trace of guilt. It seemed that the word 'heathen' had struck home on some sort of level. Born of a heathen and now marrying one too? Why had she not detected the vicious prejudice underneath Uncle Frank's usually kind words before? After all, tonight had obviously demonstrated what he really thought. Stupid that she'd never considered that before. And hadn't her own mother left her heathen father in order to go off and screw around with all those lovely Catholic boys? More pertinently, hadn't her grandmother approved? Yes, by her silence she had. But perhaps there had been more to it than that. Right now Zelfa didn't feel up to exploring this particular line of thought. Medieval superstition! She leaned across the bed to switch off her reading light and then lay awake in the darkness, wishing that her lover was there to help her fight the gargoyles that kept on entering her mind.

Sınan İkmen had long since returned to his home in Fener when his father Çetin finally entered the Sultan Ahmet apartment. Charged with the task of bringing his father's uncle back from the Cerrahpaşa Hospital, Sınan had done so and more besides – after all, he could hardly refuse his mother's offer of a meal, could he?

By the time Çetin İkmen got home, Fatma and the children were in bed. Only Uncle Ahmet, who was apparently engrossed in a music programme on the television, was still conscious. And so, after bringing them both bottles of Efes from the kitchen and asking after the rapidly improving health of his cousin, İkmen sat down beside his uncle and wondered how he might broach the subject of his mother's death. After all, if Uncle Ahmet had indeed known the truth for all these many years, İkmen felt he was due an explanation, if for no other reason than to finally dispel Angeliki Vlora's stories of bloody Albanian murder.

When he eventually felt that he'd drunk enough of his beer to both warm his body and give him courage, İkmen turned to the old man and said, 'You do know that I know Mother didn't die of a heart attack, don't you, Uncle?'

Ahmet placed his now empty beer bottle on the table and sighed. 'Mustafa told me that you had been asking questions.'

'Oh, so Samsun knew.'

'No! No of course not. Mustafa, poor creature, knew only that he should always tell me if either you or your brother asked. He didn't know why – he never asked why. I suppose it is possible that his kind, maybe above all others, know the true value of not asking that which should not be asked.'

Now that the music programme was over, a quiz show of what İkmen felt was quite staggering banality came on. And as he half listened to the questions the ultra-smooth host posed to the nervous contestants, he wondered why he wasn't on the TV winning a couple of months' salary in what for him would have been a very short space of time.

But he wasn't on the TV, he was in his apartment with his uncle, a man who had kept his secrets for long enough.

'So how did you find out the truth about Ayşe's death?' the old man asked.

'A woman called Angeliki Vlora t—'

'That daughter of Shaitan!' Ahmet cried malevolently and spat on the floor. 'She told you?'

'Yes.'

The old man's head sank down onto his chest.

'Uncle Ahmet . . .'

'Of course I am aware that Emina Ndrek still moves amongst the living.'

İkmen recalled that Angeliki had mentioned the name Ndrek in connection with his mother's death, but her name on Ahmet's lips still came as a shock. His uncle seemed to be assuming that Angeliki Vlora had told him the truth. But Angeliki had said his mother was murdered, which meant that what Arto Sarkissian had discovered was incorrect. İkmen suddenly felt very, very sick.

'Uncle, Emina Ndrek—'

'With the death of your mother, all debts were paid,' Ahmet said. 'When I was told what had been done, I went to see Emina's father, he called me, and between us we came to a solution. May my fathers forgive me, but I didn't even try to follow Salih back to Albania, though it made my eyes weep.'

İkmen could only mumble, 'But uncle, the suicide . . .'

Finally hearing as well as seeing the lack of understanding on his nephew's face, Ahmet Bajraktar shook his head wearily and took one of İkmen's hands in his.

'Oh, but you don't know, do you, Çetin?' he said softly.

'Know?'

'You've heard only what you imagined was a rumour from Angeliki, plus the supposed truth your father and his Armenian thought they had discovered.'

His heart beating very quickly now, his lips dry as leaves, İkmen could only whisper, 'So?'

The old man took a deep breath before replying. 'Just over a month after I killed Işmail Ndrek, his younger brother Salih murdered your mother.' With a small crooked smile upon his face, he looked at İkmen and said, 'So perhaps you should arrest me now, officer? Eh?'

İkmen only stared in horrified silence, wrapt by the vision of a face he thought he had known.

'Oh, it was *gjakmaria*,' the old man continued, now seemingly at ease with the subject matter. 'But with the death of your mother all that stopped. It had to. Even Emina was shocked at what was done.'

İkmen snatched up the TV remote control and turned the hideous sniggering quiz show host to blackness. 'I don't understand. She was a woman . . . I mean, how . . .'

Uncle Ahmet squeezed his nephew's hand between his bony fingers. 'You and I need to speak to Emina Ndrek. Only between us can we give you the explanation you probably deserve now, Çetin.' He sighed. 'I will fix it.'

'You . . .'

'I'll take you to see Emina. She still lives in Üsküdar – with her son and her memories and with a distant view of the back of your old house, where my sister lay down willingly on her bed and had her throat cut.'

As İkmen, in an effort to distract himself from this horror, tried to focus his thoughts upon any aspect he could still remember of his old wooden home, his uncle curled into his chair and wept. It was, the policeman thought later, almost as if Ahmet had never cried until this moment. It was desperately sad, or at least it would have been if İkmen had been able to feel anything other than fury. He'd had enough of these people – the Berishas, the Vloras, his own family. For the first time in his life he wanted to be someone else doing something else. He didn't care what, as long as it took him away from all Albanians.

Slowly he rose from his seat and made his way towards the door.

'Turn the light off when you've finished,' he said coldly.

'Çetin . . .'

But he didn't stay to hear whatever else his uncle might have to say. As quietly as he could, he crept towards the comfort of his bed and the Turkish woman who waited there for him.

Aryan Vlora had never imagined that once he had given his statement to the police, İkmen would let him go. After all, by being present during the last moment of Egrem Berisha's life and not reporting it, he was an accessory to murder. But then İkmen was of Albanian stock himself, so there was probably some level of understanding there. And anyway, if he had reported Egrem's murder at the time, he would now almost certainly be dead – and İkmen knew it.

Not that freedom was going to do him very much good for very long. As soon as that idiot Mehti decided to come to his senses with regard to his ridiculous confession, it wouldn't take him long to contact the relatives back in Kukes and arrange for his brother to disappear. Neither Mehti nor the other relatives would take kindly to Aryan appearing in court to give evidence against Mehmet. But he was still glad that he'd done it. A drugs charge would only hold Mehmet for a while but a murder conviction would put him away for good, and that, after all, was where he needed to be.

Engelushjia Berisha had waited patiently for hours in the police station while Aryan gave his statement. When he eventually emerged, she looked up at him and smiled. They left the station together. Dressed only in her thin mud-stained skirt and multiple unravelling jumpers, her poor little face looked blue in the misty light from the streetlamps beside the Yeni Valide Cami. Aryan wanted to wrap his arms round her so that she might share some of his body heat. But he knew he couldn't do that. After all, even though he was now patently her hero, he was still a Vlora and a man old enough to be her father.

'I'd better go on alone from here,' she said as she looked into the dense maze of streets that made up the Eminönü bazaar quarter.

'Of course,' he answered with a smile and then, taking

her small hand in his, he shook it gently. 'But thank you, Engelushjia, for staying with me.'

'We have to finish this stupid thing, Aryan,' she replied firmly and then darted forward quickly to lightly brush his cheeks with her lips. 'Thank you.'

And then she was gone. What she would say about the events of that day to her father, Rahman, Aryan couldn't imagine. He just hoped that Berisha didn't conform to the usual behaviour exhibited by *fis* in blood when their children are found associating. He could do nothing about that, of course. Men had certain rights over their daughters and that was unchangeable. Aryan just hoped that Rahman didn't put Engelushjia in hospital.

Chapter 17

'You can't arrest someone for buying curtains,' Suleyman said as he eased himself down onto the edge of İkmen's desk.

'I know that!' İkmen snapped. It wasn't the first time he'd been short with his colleague that morning. Suleyman was making efforts not to react. İkmen looked and sounded dreadful, and silently Suleyman wondered what might have happened in İkmen's private life to cause such a reaction.

'And anyway,' Suleyman continued, 'the Evrens' chauffeur didn't actually know what Felicity had bought. It was only when Roditi suggested curtains—'

'Roditi shouldn't have suggested curtains then, should he?' İkmen growled. 'If only people would just use what little intelligence they have.'

'Oh, come on, Çetin!' Suleyman said, finally out of patience with İkmen's bad humour. 'Roditi was just making suggestions in the face of what he perceived to be sullenness.'

'He should not have led that man!' İkmen lit yet another cigarette. 'It makes my return to the house all the more difficult.'

'But you said you wanted to search—'

'I do, but some degree of certainty around allegations received would help!'

'Less than a minute ago you were going to arrest the woman!'

Quite how İkmen and Suleyman had come to be eyeball to eyeball like this was no longer entirely clear. To Suleyman it seemed that the route had been one of irrational leaps of faulty logic from an especially agitated İkmen. Uncharacteristically excited by the idea of Felicity Evren having bought the curtains she would later wrap Rifat's body in on the day of his death, İkmen did not seem to have thought about how innocuous the simple act of buying curtains was. In itself it proved nothing, especially in light of the fact that Hassan the chauffeur didn't have a clue about where 'Miss Flick' had purchased the material. And since he had obviously been led by Roditi, Hassan didn't really know that what she had bought were curtains anyway. None of this made a great deal of difference to İkmen in this mood.

Having smoked furiously for several silent seconds, İkmen finally took his cigarette out of his mouth before saying, if a little more calmly, 'Well, whatever, but that family is hiding something, I'm certain of it. And after what I've experienced recently I should know what a devious family looks like, shouldn't I?'

'If you are measuring the Evrens against the Vloras—'

'Ah, but I'm not,' İkmen replied as he stared intently into Suleyman's face. 'I don't need to stray that far from home in order to find such behaviour.'

Suleyman sighed. 'Çetin,' he said, 'if we are, as I

think we are, talking here about the issue surrounding your mother—'

'Her family, *my* family,' İkmen said, vehemently jabbing his chest, 'together with some other hellish Albanian clan, killed my mother. There!' He hurled himself backwards into his chair. 'There's a family secret for you, forty years old.'

'Çetin, are you certain?'

'No!' With a gesture of hopelessness, İkmen spread his hands in the air and then let them drop limply into his lap again. 'And that is the agony of it, if the truth be told. There have been so many lies, who knows or even cares about the truth? But then that is not unlike this case, wouldn't you say? One person confessing to a crime, another unbidden providing evidence that runs counter to it, strange transactions involving supposed love and still pulsing body parts . . .' He brought his head down briefly to meet his hands. What was left of his cigarette fell to the floor.

Knowing that any allusion to İkmen's state of mind would be neither appreciated nor helpful, Suleyman opted to do what he did best and took a dignified, practical stance. Bending down to pick up the still smouldering cigarette, he said, 'Well, at least we now know that the blood in that car was definitely Rifat's. And although forensic have not yet completed the tests on the traces of blood found in the Vloras' apartment, they have established what group it is and it is not Rifat's. So we know that he died in or near the car, which we know from both Mehti and the Evrens themselves was at the Evren house on the night of his death.'

'So what do you think then?' İkmen said through the lattice of fingers across his face.

Suleyman first put the dying cigarette out in one of the ashtrays and then lit up one of his own. 'I think that Evren is not the sort of man who is accustomed to controlling his anger. I also feel that he is very protective of his daughter.'

'Isn't killing a somewhat excessive reaction to what was probably a very clumsy attempt at extortion? And anyway, why even admit that Rifat was there that night? We only suggested we had information that he had been there. Evren could easily have denied that.'

Looking now into a fully exposed if slightly reddened face, Suleyman put his head on one side as he considered these points. 'Perhaps Evren felt, in light of the fact that he didn't know who had given us the information, that to deny that Rifat had been there might be risky. After all, he could have been to the house, left and then met with his killer later on. Both Evren and Mehti place themselves near Rifat at ten o'clock. From then until the time of death, which Dr Sarkissian reckons was between midnight and two a.m. is a long time.'

'Indeed.' İkmen lit up a fresh cigarette. 'I can't see Evren spending all that time wrangling over money he never intended to give the boy, can you?'

'I can see him calling on a group of thugs to do it for him,' Suleyman said. 'The art world at his level seems to make frequent use of such contingents.'

Remembering what an outraged Suleyman had told him about Mr Evren's dealings with, amongst others, the former Turkish aristocracy, İkmen smiled.

'If Evren is in league with eastern European heavies, they would surely have had a bit of fun with him before they killed him? I know his body was bruised but most of that occurred post mortem. And that glass in his face suggests a woman to me.'

'Possibly.' Suleyman shrugged.

'So what's happening with Mehti Vlora?'

'He'll have to appear before a judge tomorrow.' Suleyman eased himself off the edge of the desk and stood up. 'As you suggested, I have arranged for Çöktin to go over his story yet again this morning.'

'You have, I trust,' İkmen said some grim humour in his voice, 'emphasised the urgency of some sort of conclusion to Çöktin.'

'I've told him that provided nothing physical occurs he can do whatever he thinks fit in order to obtain the truth.'

İkmen smiled, but not with pleasure. Although in reality a naturally passive individual, İsak Çöktin had during his time with Suleyman proved himself invaluable as a hunter of truth. His methods were hardly subtle but they were never physically cruel even if they did at times overstep the boundaries of psychological harm. Neither İkmen nor Suleyman felt comfortable about that but sometimes, despite İkmen's lifelong battle against police brutality, someone like Çöktin was necessary. Like now when they were running out of time – and when Mehti Vlora could very well be condemning himself to life imprisonment for something he only wished he'd done. After all, İkmen thought grimly, with these Albanians one had to remember that the honour of the *fis* was paramount. For his mother, apparently, it had been stronger even than her love for her husband and children. She had laid down her life for something he for one didn't even begin to understand.

'Who was that ringing so early in the morning?' Balthazar Cohen said tetchily as his son replaced the receiver.

'It was Zelfa for Mehmet,' Berekiah replied. 'I told her he's already gone to work.'

'Yes, which is where you should be if you don't want Lazar to start complaining.'

In an attempt to try to find a comfortable position for what was left of his legs, Balthazar began to wrestle with one of the cushions underneath his backside. As he did so he muttered angrily between gasps of pain.

Unable to tolerate witnessing this struggle, Berekiah moved across the room towards his father. 'Dad, if you'll just let me—'

'No!'

'But—'

'No!' Balthazar repeated with even more vehemence. 'Keep away! If I want your help I will ask for it!'

'But Dad, you allow Mehmet to help.'

'Mehmet is my friend and he is a man!' his father said as he finally managed to remove the offending cushion.

'Yes, but I'm your son!'

Balthazar threw the cushion onto the floor, presumably for either his wife or his son to pick up at some point.

'Dad?'

Balthazar looked up sharply and without any apparent affection in his expression. 'While you do the work of a child, you cannot be a man,' he said harshly. 'Get yourself a man's job and then perhaps we can talk as equals.'

Cut to the bone by this brutal judgement upon his current employment, Berekiah turned away from his father's hard gaze. So here they were, talking about joining the police again. Ever since Berekiah had visited İkmen and talked to both him and Mehmet Suleyman about police work, his father hadn't stopped. To both Berekiah and his mother's embarrassment, it had even come up when Zelfa and Mehmet had announced their intention to marry. And although Berekiah was now quite close to having made up his mind about his future, he was not going to be pushed into a hasty decision – not even by his sick father. So he did as he so often had to do in these days of bad moods and tearful nights and just smiled at Balthazar, saying, 'Well, Dad, as you said, I'd better go now if I don't want to be late.'

'Perhaps you should speak to Mehmet again when you get home tonight.'

'Maybe,' Berekiah smiled. 'In the meantime, I've got to take some more leaf over to the Aya Sofya today.'

Although not really interested, Balthazar managed a muttered, 'Why?'

Berekiah took his coat off the back of his chair and put it on. 'For the restoration work,' he said. 'Professor Apa and his team are working on the mosaics in the dome. We provide the gold for the project.'

'Images of false messiahs!' Balthazar raged.

Berekiah finally lost patience with his father. 'Since when were you so religious?' he snapped. 'God, I've never heard anything so hypocritical in my life! I think I preferred you when you were running around after cheap women half your age!'

'Oh, yes!' Balthazar countered bitterly. 'Go ahead and remind me about being stuck in this chair.'

Berekiah shrugged. 'You don't need me to do that,' he said, moving towards the door. 'You're quite capable of doing that for yourself.'

'Berekiah!'

But all he received by way of reply was the sound of the door slamming in the wake of his furious son. The boy would, as was his custom, calm down during the course of the day. In the meantime, all Balthazar could hope was that Estelle, who he thought must be in the kitchen, hand't heard. But as the door to the living room opened sharply once again, he felt his hope fade. Standing in the doorway with her hands on her hips, Estelle Cohen was clearly once again about to give him a piece of her mind about his treatment of her unhappy son.

Hassan Cıva hadn't expected Miss Flick to get into the car with her brother. Not known to be an early riser, she didn't usually join the boy on his journey to school in the morning. She had the look of one who had scarcely slept the previous night. Her face looked positively grey.

But perhaps that was only to be expected, thought Hassan as the boy and the woman climbed into the great gold Rolls. Mr Evren had telephoned him the previous night to tell him the police had been to the house and to warn him about their imminent appearance at his apartment. But unfortunately his call had come too late. Some ugly, fat cop had already asked him all sorts of weird questions that Hassan hoped he had answered the way Mr Evren would have liked. Not that the questions seemed to pertain to anything sensible – after all, what possible use could information about Miss Flick's shopping habits be to anyone? So she'd bought some material. He hadn't known what it was for even though he'd agreed with whatever ideas the cop had put forward. Who cared?

As far as he could tell, all of this police activity was somehow connected to the death of that Albanian Miss Flick had been so keen on. The police had the idea that this man had been at the Evren house on the night that he died. Hassan had no idea about that. He didn't lodge with the Evren family and, although they did undoubtedly live in some style, he was quite pleased about that. The boy Ali was weird and nervous and Miss Flick, though obviously considerate of and loving to her brother, had a peculiar relationship with both him and her father. It was almost as if, Hassan sometimes thought, she controlled the men as opposed to them controlling her. It was only Miss Flick who could interrupt her father when he was in one of his business meetings with men from overseas – hard, frightening men. This wouldn't have suited Hassan. When his daughter grew up she would obey him, she wouldn't run around with Albanians, oh no.

'I'd like you to take us to Sultan Ahmet, please,

Hassan,' Mr Ali said when he had settled himself into the back of the car.

Before Hassan could answer the boy, Miss Flick spoke in a low but agitated fashion to her brother – in English as usual.

When she'd finished, Mr Ali turned back to Hassan and said softly, 'Did you hear me?'

'Er, yes, Mr Ali. Sultan Ahmet.'

'That's right,' he answered. 'Sultan Ahmet.'

'Not the school?'

'No, I'm not going to school today.' Mr Ali sat back in his seat. 'Please drive now.'

And so Hassan did. Occasionally, he glanced at his mirror to see what the two of them might be doing behind him. But he saw only frozen silent faces, looking not at each other but at the snow that had just started to fall across the city. The Evren children were obviously preoccupied with their own thoughts. Hassan comforted himself with the fact that beyond driving and protecting these two, their problems were none of his business.

Chapter 18

'Do you know what an F-type prison is, Mehti?'

To Mehti Vlora it was not only the man's tone but also his look that was threatening. Red-haired and yet possessed of such dark, slanted eyes – the man obviously came from the east of this wretched country, the place where everyone said there was always trouble. With İkmen and even with that tall, rich-looking detective, Mehti felt that he was in touch with some sort of humanity, if of a hostile nature. But alone with this man plus the blank-looking guard over by the door, he felt as if he was facing a whole new set of risks.

Having failed to elicit any sort of response from Mehti, Sergeant Çöktin proceeded to answer his own question.

'An F-type prison is one where men are kept in cells of two or three people. Unlike the old wards, the new arrangement doesn't allow for the formation of the sort of gangs we used to have at Bayrampaşa, which we destroyed. In other words, it is unlikely you'll be able to find anyone willing to protect you, particularly if we put you into a cell with people like yourself.'

Mehti looked up. 'Albanians?'

Çöktin smiled. 'No. I mean soft men. Men who have

to offer their arses to the more punitive prisoners – if they want to stay alive.'

Mehti moved forward in his seat, his eyes blazing with anger. 'You—'

The heavy hand of the guard flashed forward and pulled the Albanian back.

'Have you ever been forcibly buggered, Mehti?' Çöktin looked briefly into the Albanian's eyes and then continued, 'It's really very painful and if the other man is big, it can damage a person for life. Even if you are incarcerated with your brother, I doubt very much whether he would be able to help you. We've got people in our jails who make Mehmet look like a saint.'

Realising finally, through the fug of his slow-moving mental powers, that he was being deliberately wound up, Mehti narrowed his eyes.

'What do you want from me?' he said.

Çöktin shrugged. 'I don't know yet. But with no tape in the machine I can do just about whatever I feel like.' He looked up at the guard. 'Is that not so, constable?'

'Yes, sir.'

'I could gain some satisfaction from beating you senseless . . .'

'You're not supposed to do that!' Mehti cried. 'What about all that stuff about police station walls being made of glass now?'

'Empty rhetoric, I think you'll find.' Çöktin leaned forward until his nose almost touched that of his victim. 'After all, we are Turks, your enemies. You know how cruel and ruthless we are.'

Mehti's eyes were filled with real fear now. If this man didn't, as he said, want anything tangible from him, then what exactly was he doing here? Was it, as he said, to enjoy beating him up? Or maybe all that talk about buggery hadn't been just some sort of ploy to get him to say something he didn't want to say. Perhaps this Turk wanted to bugger him. Maybe the guard would hold him down and . . .

'Take him back to his cell.'

In his panic, Mehti hadn't noticed that Çöktin had stood up and was standing with his back against the wall of the interview room.

With rough alacrity, the guard grabbed Mehti by his cuffed hands and dragged him towards the door.

Stunned by the speed and apparent senselessness of the whole procedure, Mehti could only gape helplessly as he was pulled out of the room. The last thing he saw was that sinister, red-haired ape grinning at him.

As soon as Mehti Vlora had gone, the smile on Çöktin's lips faded and he lowered himself slowly into his seat again. Although very good at playing the part of the sadistic, pervert cop, he did sometimes wonder whether he went too far. His 'character' was like something out of the movies or, more sinisterly, like those engaged in organised crime. Something deep inside Çöktin shuddered.

But then he pulled himself together. He looked at his watch and decided to give Mehti Vlora an hour. Then maybe, if they were lucky, terror would lay bare the truth of the matter – if indeed anything could.

*　　　*　　　*

Zelfa made the call just after her first patient had left.

'Hello, darling,' she said when she heard the familiar sound of his voice on the line. 'I'm sorry I didn't call you last night. I was very tired and then Uncle Frank called. We argued – I'll have to call him to put things right. He's an old man now . . .'

'I'm sorry,' Mehmet Suleyman replied, still with, she noticed, some weariness in his voice. 'As it happened, I had to work late. And then when I got home Cohen wanted to talk – you know how it can be.'

'Yes.'

'We're both very busy people,' he continued with a sigh, 'but things will get better when we're living together. Then we'll at least meet up occasionally in your father's kitchen.'

Zelfa laughed. To be like an old married couple was a strange concept for her; she had never lived with any man except her father.

She came to the main point of her call. Trying to sound as casual as she could, she said, 'So, you spent some time at the Evrens' home yesterday . . .'

'Yes.' A pause followed.

'And?'

'Don't try to lead me where you know I cannot go, Zelfa,' he responded sternly. 'You haven't been asked to consult on this case and just because a member or members of the family are your patients doesn't mean I can discuss them with you.'

'Mehmet, I only ask in order to get a clearer picture of the home situation of my patient.'

'Would you give me information about this patient if I asked for it?' he asked. 'No, you wouldn't, would you? You respect your patients' right to confidentiality.'

'Yes, but you know I would have to break that rule if there was a safety or legal issue involved,' she countered.

'Is that the case with this patient then, Zelfa?' Mehmet asked.

Realising that she had effectively boxed herself into a corner, Zelfa retreated. 'No, there's no safety issue involved,' she admitted.

'Good,' he said, and changed the subject. 'Since you've called, can I take you to lunch? How does Pandeli's sound – at about one?'

'It sounds like you're spending the money for our wedding,' she said lightly, 'but what the hell! I'm a psychiatrist and you're an aristocrat, between the two of us we can probably manage an entrée plus coffee – provided we share.'

Mehmet laughed. 'I'll ring you at twelve thirty, just in case something comes up – for either of us.'

'You have a date.'

She put the phone down and, still smiling, turned to the stack of files on her desk. Mr Gürel, paranoid delusions, was her next patient. Persuading him that his apartment wasn't bugged was a rather more modern problem than the gothic ramblings of Ali Evren. But then perhaps Ali's delusions simply reflected his British background – after all, it would be unusual for a Turk to be taken with stereotypical vampire images, an essentially European/Christian phenomenon. Nor would an Albanian; the Albanians, like the Turks, were, in the main Muslims. But then the Balkans were another matter altogether. Zelfa had been there once, many years ago – a holiday in sunny Yugoslavia – Dubrovnik. A place now scarred by years of ethnic violence. She'd sunbathed on the beach and got drunk in the bars when she was there. Uncle Frank had shared that holiday. Poor old man, she'd been far too hard on him . . .

Although Fatma İkmen was not in the habit of getting too involved in the lives of her husband's family, she had noticed that Ahmet Bajraktar had not been himself when he came in for breakfast that morning. He'd been quiet, which was not his usual way, and had looked sad. She'd never had a great deal of time for these odd foreign relatives, but this made Fatma feel for him. She assumed that Çetin must have told him the truth about Ayşe's death. It must have come as a shock; after all, even in the twenty-first century suicide still carried a stigma. All well and good to die fighting for Islam but lonely acts of self-violence committed in darkened rooms were considered unholy and unnatural. It was something the Bajraktars and the İkmens would have to learn to live with.

'Would you like another egg, Uncle?' Fatma said as she placed some more food on her own plate.

'No thank you, Fatma dear,' the old man replied. 'I don't really have the time.'

'Oh?' She sat down opposite him. 'Are you going to the hospital?'

Ahmet sighed. 'Mustafa can go home today. Although

quite where that is I don't think even he really knows.'

'Well, he has an apartment up by the Kapalı Çarşı,' Fatma said, without thinking.

'Yes,' Ahmet replied drily, 'so he does. But it isn't his, is it? It belongs to this, er, this other character who was a wrestler . . .'

'Oh, yes.' Fatma lowered her gaze to the table, 'A younger man, I believe.'

'Well, anyway, whatever the situation, I must take my son somewhere,' the old man said as he pushed himself up from his chair, 'even if that has to be back to İzmir with me.'

'I'll get your hat and coat,' Fatma said, rising from her chair and moving past the old man into the hall. 'It's started snowing so please do be careful on the pavements, won't you, Uncle?'

'If Allah wills I shall arrive at the hospital whole,' he said.

Holding the coat up for him, Fatma helped the old man slot his thin arms into the garment and then she gave him his hat.

'Will you be staying with us again tonight, Uncle?'

'It all depends upon my son,' Ahmet replied with a shrug. 'But if it is not a trouble, I will return. I need to speak to Çetin again before I go.'

'Of course.' She smiled. 'Your being here has been a comfort to him.'

Ahmet raised a wry eyebrow. 'Has it?' he said. 'I wonder.'

Fatma looked at him questioningly. But when nothing was forthcoming, she opened the front door.

'May Allah reunite,' she said as he walked slowly across the threshold.

'If it is His will,' the old man responded.

Fatma watched him until he reached the door at the bottom of the stairs which, when he opened it, allowed the snow that had been building up against it to spill into the lobby. Fatma hated that – sloppy wetness everywhere, people slipping and sliding about all over the floor. The younger children would love it of course, but the older ones wouldn't be so impressed. Hopefully that lazy dog Aziz, the kapıcı, would clear it away from the building pretty soon. If he didn't, she and some of the other women in the block would have to do it. If Çetin slipped in the lobby she'd never hear the end of it, particularly in his present mood. She wondered whether he and his uncle had argued. Maybe Ahmet had problems believing what Arto Sarkissian had discovered. As far as she knew, her brother-in-law Halil had not yet been told about the suicide. She could understand this. As Arto had said, because Halil had discovered Ayşe's body all those years ago, telling him had to be handled carefully. Perhaps Ahmet and Çetin had disagreed about this.

All she did know was that life at present was even harder than usual. What with Çetin being so upset, various children catching colds, Uncle Ahmet's appearance plus the occasional visit from Samsun, there seemed to be no immediate end to her problems. Not, of course, that she could afford to dwell upon such things, not now that the snow had come. Diving briefly back into the apartment, Fatma covered her head with a scarf and grabbed a broom from the kitchen. OK, she was doing somebody else's job, but if she hung around for Aziz to do it she would only spend the rest of the morning worrying about it.

'Do you want me to pick you up?' Mehmet Suleyman said into his mobile telephone. Down here in the cells it was much colder than up in the main body of the station. Now that it was snowing, his mind naturally drifted towards thoughts of warm, comforting things.

'Well, I know you enjoy their lemon vodka, Father,' he said, 'and it's no trouble to me.'

A key-swinging constable passed him in the corridor and saluted. Suleyman returned the gesture.

'All right then, Father,' he said and smiled into the instrument, 'I'll see you at Rejan's at eight . . . Yes, Mrs Papas is picking Edibe up at six so Murad will come to my place first . . . Yes . . .' Spotting Çöktin leaning against the wall at the end of the corridor, he gestured for him to come and join him. 'All right, Father,' he said into the telephone again. 'Look, I must go now. I'll see you this evening.'

As Çöktin drew level with him, Suleyman switched his phone off and put it back into his pocket.

'So, how did you leave him?' he asked his younger colleague as they simultaneously rubbed their hands against the encroaching cold.

'Well, I know he was confused,' Çöktin said. 'I wasn't with him for very long. I think if you go on and on planting suggestions into someone's mind they eventually become inured to them.'

'You're probably right.' Suleyman offered Çöktin a cigarette, which the Kurd declined.

'I gave him the impression that he wasn't safe with me,' Çöktin continued as the two men started walking in the direction of Mehti Vlora's cell. 'Some of the suggestions I made were quite nasty.'

'I don't think I really want to know,' Suleyman said.

'No, sir.'

'I think that if you and I now go over Mehti's statement with him, the seeds you have planted might bear fruit.'

'How do you want to play it then, sir?' Çöktin asked.

'Interview Room Three is empty. Have him brought up there and set the tape. I'll ask the questions while you,' he smiled, 'just sit next to me looking sinister.'

Çöktin scowled. 'Very well, sir.'

Laughing now, Suleyman said, 'You do it so well, İsak. Look upon it as a gift.'

'Yes, sir.'

As they passed Mehti's cell they were silent. Although they knew he couldn't possibly hear what they were saying, they both felt uncomfortable – outnumbered. The two cells directly opposite Mehti's contained his brother Mehmet and mother Angeliki. An Albanian invasion seemed, at times, to be in progress.

When the officers reached the guardroom, they were offered tea by the duty officer, which they both accepted. They then acquainted the guards with what their plans were vis-à-vis Mehti Vlora. It was decided that the same guard who had been in with Vlora when Çöktin had spoken to him earlier would be present this time too. Hopefully, Mehti would interpret this in the way they wanted him to.

Chapter 19

The Church of the Holy Wisdom, Aya Sofya, has always been one of the most violently disputed buildings on earth. But, despite the fact that only a minority of its visitors have a clearly defined faith, reports of spiritual uplift among those who pass through its doors are common. The place is now a museum, and though dark inside, the luminous quality, some say, of the representational mosaics filter through the thin light like visitors from another dimension. Across vast ranges of time and space, strange imperious figures, crusted with priceless jewels, commune with images of a dusky Greek divinity. Old world in the extreme, this is Christianity with an opulent, almost pagan face. And looking upwards towards the high arched windows and then beyond into the heaven-like distance of the dome, one can be forgiven for imagining that one sees the smoke and smells the perfume of incense. Even for the most cynical the pressure exerted by over one thousand five hundred years of often fanatical devotion is undeniable. And Ali Evren, for one, was of their number.

Now, with the snow falling heavily across the great, soaring dome, Aya Sofya looked more Russian than

Turkish to Ali. But then hadn't the Russians taken both their religion and aspects of their architecture from the Byzantines? Nothing was, after all, new in this world even if this place was, as yet, unfamiliar to the boy's sister. But would not be so for long and, once she was inside this most holy of structures, he would know for certain what she was. He would know whether or not she had been lying to him. After all, those who disappeared from mirrors died in churches and as Dr Halman had told him only the day before, the only way that he could be really certain that Felicity was truly what he thought and wanted her to be was to take her to a church. And now it was very important that he know the truth. Why hadn't he thought of it before? He would, of course, have to bear his own increasing discomfort in this place, but it would be worth it in the end. If she died he would know and if she didn't he would also know. And much as he loved her, that knowledge was far more important to him now than she was. As Felicity herself knew, he had gone way beyond her power or control.

Walking through the almost entirely white gardens, both Ali and Felicity hurried to get out of the cold. Stepping first into the exonarthex and then into the narthex, Ali shook snow from his coat onto the floor. Then entering via the Imperial Gate, he paused to appreciate the swathes of space, rendered crystalline by the snowy light from outside. It was amazing. The scaffolding erected up into the dome by the academics and artisans who were currently restoring the frescoes looked like a modern-day Tower of Babel, attempting but not quite succeeding in reaching up to unknowable heaven. But already his breathing was coming hard as the place exerted its strange, toxic hold over him. Looking back to where Felicity was still standing beyond the main door out in the snow, he beckoned her towards him.

'Come in,' he gasped, attempting an encouraging smile. 'It's really very impressive.'

But she just shook her head in that eccentrically deformed way of hers and continued to stand out in the snow.

That, to Ali, was encouraging. But for him to really see what was what, she had to come inside. He walked back towards her, his head clearing a little as he approached the outside world.

'What's the matter?' he said. 'Are you afraid that something might happen to you in here?'

'No,' she answered simply. 'As I told you after Rifat died, David, that was all a game I created around something that's happened to me, something I can't explain. It doesn't affect how we feel about . . . each other.' She looked down sadly at the ground and then said, 'I just feel that after what has happened, I shouldn't be in a place like this. And anyway, you should be at school.'

'Oh, come in for just a moment, Flick,' he pleaded. 'It's really very wonderful. And besides,' he added, his voice hardening with what sounded like rising anger, 'Dad and I have always protected you and so why should I not do that now?'

'Well . . .'

'Come on, Flick,' he said as he held one hand out towards her. 'You've paid to come in, so come in.'

And she did. Walking unevenly in front of her brother she, too, observed the nave with awestruck eyes. What she did not do was burst into flames or crumble to dust. Ali's face was pale as he watched her. He had built his world around a sick woman's lies. He had become what he had strived so hard to become only to discover that he was now entirely alone. His sister, his love – she was just a lie.

'Why don't I take you up to the gallery?' he said breathlessly and took hold of her thin arm. 'You'll get a better view up there.'

'If you like,' she said with a smile, 'just so long as we don't have to talk about vampires any more. I hope that finished with Rifat.'

'Yes. You know it did.' He ushered her forward towards the door at the end of the narthex, which led to the famous Aya Sofya cobbled ramp. 'Now that he's gone, you're mine again, so that's OK.'

The fact that there are no actual stairs to the upper galleries of Aya Sofya speaks eloquently of Byzantine social mores. Unlike the traditional western European idea of Christian women, Byzantine ladies of high status were frequently veiled. Indeed, it is said that the Ottomans conceived the idea of the harem from the Byzantines. As in life, so in religion women and men were kept separate – the body of the church for the men, the gallery for the women. However, in view of the fact that these were noble women, the wives and daughters of emperors, they weren't expected to walk. Instead, they were taken up to the gallery in heavily curtained litters – presumably, so Felicity Evren thought as she puffed and struggled up the unevenly surfaced ramp, carried by armies of poor slaves who probably wished they were dead. At the top of the ramp she stopped for some time to catch her breath. Her brother, who had preceded her, was also panting heavily, which indicated a lack of fitness that gave Felicity a moment of concern.

But then as he ushered her forward to look at the view of the nave from the gallery rail, her concern turned to delight as she beheld the vastness of the space both above and below.

İkmen had been mildly surprised when he discovered that the person calling him from the British Consulate was actually the consul himself. Usually it was an underling who was given such tasks, but not in this case.

'İlhan Evren doesn't, officially, have a police record,' the consul said smoothly.

'Really?' İkmen, who already knew that Evren did have a police record, was puzzled.

'But there is what is now a spent conviction from nearly twenty years ago.'

Oh, so that explained it. 'What was it for, sir?'

'Fraud. Basically it involved arranging fake marriages for illegal immigrants. Evren himself is a legitimate UK subject of Cypriot origin. Apparently he used other Cypriot UK passport holders to act as brides and bridegrooms.'

'And his connections with the art world?'

'They are more recent,' the consul replied, 'and seemingly legitimate. He lives here on a residence permit, as I expect you know, Inspector. He made a lot of money back home in England and, I believe, has powerful friends there.'

İkmen frowned. 'Powerful friends, sir?'

'Art lovers, Inspector. Prominent doctors, lawyers, actors – people like that.'

Including, as Suleyman had told him, the doctor who performed the kidney transplant from Rifat to Evren's daughter. It made İkmen wonder whether in fact Evren had paid for the operation at all. Had it been a favour owed for maybe providing the doctor with some particularly fine Selcuk silver? It was a sobering possibility.

'Evren has been back to the UK a few times since he came to live here,' the consul cut into İkmen's thoughts. 'He also, as you suspected, made a visa application for an Albanian national.'

'Rifat Berisha?'

'Yes.'

'Which you allowed.'

'Yes.' İkmen heard the consul smile. 'We do occasionally, Inspector,' he said, 'especially if that person can be vouched for by a UK national and we have a firm departure date.'

'This was given to you?' İkmen asked.

'Yes indeed, as was an address in London which is I believe the family's UK base.' İkmen heard him smile again. 'It's in Holland Park,' he said and then expanded, 'It's the sort of place where a million pounds will just about buy you a garage – the apartment will cost you considerably more.'

'Oh, I see.'

The consul couldn't give him anything more. In

Britain, Evren was, it seemed, clean in the eyes of the law with regard to his art dealing. With most artefacts in the former eastern bloc as well as the jewels of the old Turkish aristocracy apparently legally up for grabs, Evren was free to do business with whoever he liked. And if this included leather-jacketed men with Russian names, that was his affair.

What was of interest to İkmen was the apparent scale of Evren's wealth. In UK sterling terms he was a millionaire, which meant that he was a very rich man indeed. He could have given Rifat several hundred million lire and not even noticed. So why hadn't he? wondered İkmen. Perhaps he didn't want to set a precedent for future extortion, or maybe money wasn't the issue at all. Had Rifat wanted to be paid off for something other than donating his kidney to Felicity? Perhaps, İkmen thought with a shudder, he had given the strangely deformed woman something no man had yet been able to face?

'So,' Suleyman said as he looked down at Mehti Vlora's statement, 'you say here that you arrived at the house of Rifat's girlfriend at about ten p.m.'

'I thought we'd done this,' Mehti said as his eyes, unbidden, flashed across to the grinning face of İsak Çöktin. 'We've done this now, I've put it there!'

'Yes,' Suleyman said and then frowned. 'Unfortunately there appear to be some inconsistencies.'

'Oh, not the Fiat.'

'Not *only* the Fiat is actually more to the point, Mr Vlora.'

'Only?'

'Perhaps if we run through the sequence of events again things will become clearer to me,' Suleyman said.

'But . . .'

'You say that you stole the green Fiat from outside a jeweller's on Babıali Caddesi at around about four p.m.'

'Yes.'

'What did you do with this vehicle before you followed Rifat Berisha to Bebek later that evening?'

Mehti shrugged. 'I drove. I picked up a girl . . .'

'Was she European, this girl?' Çöktin, who had until this point been silent, asked.

Mehti briefly looked at the person who had become for him the principal object of his fears and muttered, 'Yes.'

'Did you fuck her?'

Mehti just sat there with his mouth open.

'Is that question really necessary, Sergeant?' Suleyman inquired, frowning.

'It would mean that we might be able to track down someone else apart from Mr Vlora who actually saw this Fiat, sir.'

'But then I took it home,' Mehti said. 'My brothers—'

'Oh, so your brothers saw it, did they?' Suleyman asked. 'That's new.'

'Yeah, I showed it to Mehmet and—'

'But not to Aryan?'

'He was out. He didn't come back until it was time to eat.'

'Strange that Mehmet hasn't mentioned seeing this vehicle, don't you think, Mehti?' Suleyman said.

'Well, I often go and get cars. I can't afford one of my own. And anyway, Mehmet's trying to protect me.'

'Or you're protecting him,' Çöktin said with a sneer.

'That's not true! I've confessed to it, me! What more do you want?'

Suleyman leaned forward across the interview table. 'We want to make sure,' he said, 'that we have the right man. Because the person who killed Rifat Berisha will spend the rest of his life in jail. That will mean no women, unpleasant food, no chance of escape and, even though they try their hardest, no guarantee that the prison authorities will be able to protect you from some of their more brutal inmates.'

'But I did it!'

'Oh, well, if you did then that's OK,' Suleyman said. 'You deserve everything you're going to get.'

Çöktin's silent laugh was not lost on Mehti Vlora.

'So, moving forward in time,' Suleyman said, 'you followed Rifat Berisha to Bebek at about eight thirty.'

'Yes.'

'And once he had gone inside Mr Evren's house . . .'

'I let myself in the back of his car.'

'How?'

Mehti Vlora looked blank.

Suleyman cleared his throat. 'What I'm trying to get at, Mehti, is that at your original interrogation you said that you jemmied one of the back doors open. However, when it was pointed out to you that none of the back doors had been tampered with, you said that the door must have been unlocked. Which version am I to believe?'

With a shrug of his shoulders Mehti said, 'The door was open. I let myself in.'

'You're sure?'

'Yes.'

'OK.' Suleyman wrote this down on a piece of paper he intended to add to the original statement. 'You will get an opportunity to read this,' he explained to Mehti, 'and sign it if you agree with its contents.'

The Albanian didn't answer, seemingly fixated on Çöktin.

'Now,' Suleyman continued, 'you say in your statement that you waited for Rifat Berisha in the back of his car. Is that correct?'

'Yes.'

Suleyman smiled. 'So perhaps you'd like to tell me why it is that despite an exhaustive search of Rifat's car our forensic colleagues have been unable to identify even one fingerprint that matches yours?'

'Well, I was wearing gloves,' Mehti said. 'It was cold.'

'You didn't mention gloves in your statement, Mr Vlora. Would you like me to addend gloves to your original version?'

Mehti shrugged again. 'Well, yeah.'

While Suleyman wrote this on the addendum sheet, Çöktin fixed his eyes firmly on Mehti's face. Then he smiled. The Albanian looked away.

Suleyman put his pen down on the table. 'Forensics have gleaned numerous fibres, hairs and fluids from the vehicle that will be subjected to genetic testing which is totally accurate. If you remember, we asked you for a sample for this purpose, from your mouth.'

Mehti first scratched his head and then rubbed his face with one of his cuffed hands.

'So if that stuff doesn't match my genetic stuff . . .'

'Then you were never in that car, Mr Vlora,' Suleyman said. 'It's that simple.'

In view of the snowy conditions, Miss Flick had given him the rest of the day off.

'Ali and I can make our own way back,' she'd said as she'd got out of the car in Sultan Ahmet Square. 'Get home now, Hassan, before this snow gets any worse.'

'What about your father?' he'd asked.

'Oh, I don't think he'll be going anywhere today,' she replied as she shivered on the pavement. 'He's far too old for weather like this. Just leave the car in the drive and go home. I'll take my father out if he needs to go anywhere.'

But Hassan had been unsure. Knowing from experience that if Mr Evren wanted something and didn't get it people tended to suffer, he resolved to check with him first. He had to take the car back to the house anyway, so he might as well go in.

He parked the car out in front of the house and was about to let himself in when a man came running towards him from across the road. It was one of Mr Evren's Russian friends, Dimitri something or other.

'Hey, you!' he called as he approached, his leather

jacket flapping against the snow. 'Is your master with you?'

'No, I think Mr Evren is in the house,' Hassan replied and took his door keys out of his pocket.

'No he isn't!' the man snarled. 'I've knocked and knocked and there's nobody in. I'm supposed to be having a meeting with him at ten thirty.'

Hassan shrugged. 'Maybe he's gone out to get something,' he said, although not with any conviction. Evren rarely if ever went out without the car, as Hassan well knew.

'I'd better come in and wait then,' the man said.

Hassan felt that it probably didn't matter. This man was, after all, a known associate of his employer. Not that he had a choice anyway because as soon as he unlocked the door the man pushed into the house and made his way to Mr Evren's living room.

Hassan headed for the kitchen. If Mr Evren did have an appointment with this man, he'd be back soon. He could then ask him whether or not he needed the car and tell him about Miss Flick's plans – Mr Evren liked to know about those. In fact the various activities of his children was always the first thing Mr Evren asked about when Hassan returned from taking them somewhere in the car – which made his absence now all the more noticeable and strange. But like other mortals Mr Evren was subject to shifting circumstance. For some reason he'd had to go and that was that.

In the kitchen, Hassan went straight for the refrigerator. There was a bottle of real Scotch whisky in there which, provided he didn't take too much, served to supplement his meagre wages. Topped up with Coca-Cola it was pleasant and warming. Hassan started to relax after his stressful drive through the snow and swung his feet up onto the kitchen table.

Although later he claimed to be unable to recall the sound of Dimitri's footsteps running towards the kitchen, Hassan had no trouble remembering what the Russian's hands had looked and smelt like. Thrust under his nose like horrific trophies, they smelt strangely of musty iron and were as red as the deepest arterial blood – which was what they were smothered with.

Chapter 20

She was, he thought as he watched her gaze across at the great tower of scaffolding that clung, spider-like, to the other side of the nave, disturbingly fit. Unlike his own breathing, hers was steady and although sad around her eyes, she didn't appear to be very distressed any more. She had been very fond of Rifat but he had never given her real love, only fucking, and he had been a most greedy young man, so she was better off without him. It would have been nice to believe that she had no heart, but he didn't. Ali scowled. Her calm demeanour made him feel angry, cheated and, most importantly, alone. It was, he felt, somewhere he shouldn't be, somewhere he had never been before, except that he had because Felicity had lied. Oh, she'd told him the truth after Rifat's death, but he hadn't really believed her until now. It was too big and too scary a concept to take in. Death – she could die. And now he alone was this thing . . .

'I actually don't feel that bad now I'm here,' she said, turning her twisted face towards him. 'I thought I might feel guilty.'

'What for?' He put his arms round her shoulders and smiled. 'You didn't do anything, did you?'

She looked down at the floor, the hard grey marble squares so far below.

'Not to Rifat, no,' she said quietly, 'but I do nevertheless feel responsible. I mean "vampire" was just a way for me to express what is really inexpressible, David.'

'Mother was reading *Dracula* when you were born.'

'That's irrelevant,' Felicity said, turning to look into her brother's eyes. 'You shouldn't make so much of it, David. Christ, you still don't believe me, do you! Mother was ill and I, well, to me it was, as I've said, it was a way I could express what I was experiencing to you. You were, after all, very young.'

'But it was still a deliberate lie, wasn't it?' He tightened his grip on her shoulders. 'After all, Flick, it was you who encouraged me to stay up all night with you.'

'I was lonely. You've always been so good for such a young boy,' she said as she looked across the nave once again. 'I've always had problems sleeping, especially when I've been in pain. Your precious love, my sweetheart, helped me pass the time.'

'You who said that perhaps in time I would become a vampire too and together we would live for ever. No death, Flick, not for us.'

One of the men on the scaffolding opposite smiled at her as he began to descend towards the floor. Felicity nervously returned the smile.

'Until . . .' Her throat was dry, she swallowed hard. 'Until Rifat . . . I didn't know that you were . . .'

'Serious? Obsessed with you?' He laughed. 'I told

you I'd all but given up eating, and why! I was already going to that doctor Dad insists on sending me to! But it was OK because all I could think of was you.'

'David . . .'

'I loved you, but first you betrayed me with that Albanian and now I find that you're this . . . nothing! A lie! I suppose that next you're going to tell me that you only realised what I was doing when you saw me lick up Rifat's blood!' he said as he moved one of his hands slowly and sensuously up her back and towards her neck. 'Liar!' Suddenly he pinched her skin between his fingers, causing her to shriek.

'David!'

The man Felicity had smiled at on the scaffolding turned to look. Felicity hoped he could see the expression on her face, which was now one of frozen fear. But as she watched, the man simply turned his head and moved on down the scaffolding.

'What you have to understand, Mehti,' Suleyman said, 'is that Mehmet is going to be tried for murder whether you like it or not.'

'But I told you that it was me and not Mehmet who—'

'Oh, I'm not talking about Rifat Berisha now,' Suleyman cut in. 'I'm talking about his brother Egrem.' He leaned forward to emphasise his point. 'You know, the one Mehmet killed in your apartment. The murder you watched.'

'Ah, but he didn't though, did he, sir?' Çöktin interjected with a smile.

'Oh, no, of course not!' Suleyman said. 'No, you were huddled on your bed in the next room at the time, weren't you, Mehti? Screaming.'

'No!' But his eyes, which were now huge with fear, told another story.

'Oh, yes.'

'No, that's a fucking lie!'

'Your brother Aryan came to see us. It was most illuminating.'

At the mention of his brother's name, Mehti Vlora first looked confused and then, once he had fully taken in what Suleyman had said, furious.

He tried to rise to his feet, but after being pushed back down again by the guard he just fumed, his face dark with rage.

'You're a fucking liar!' he spat at Suleyman. 'Blood would never talk to the police about blood.'

'Oh, no?' Çöktin sneered as he watched his superior calmly wipe Albanian spittle from his jacket lapel. 'So how do we know, Mehti?'

'Know what?' the Albanian shouted. 'Lies!'

'Oh, it could be, I grant you.' Suleyman replaced his handkerchief in his pocket. 'But you will know whether this story is true or not, won't you? You hardly need us to tell you.'

'Lies!' His eyes had started to water now, making him look as if he was crying.

'Yes, so you keep saying,' Suleyman observed, 'although whether that is for our benefit or whether you are just attempting to convince yourself I really don't know.'

'There's nothing wrong with being disgusted by murder,' Çöktin said with a smile. 'Unless, of course, if you're supposed to enjoy it.'

'Which Aryan thinks that you don't,' Suleyman added. 'But then that always has been your problem, hasn't it, Mehti? You want to do what your family dictate but the reality is that you just can't stomach it.'

'I killed Rifat Berisha!' Snot and spittle sprayed as he attempted to communicate through his anger and his misery. 'Blood demanded blood and I was there!'

'So tell me everything about it then.'

'Wh . . .'

'Tell me what he looked like, how you felt, what you did!' Suleyman leaned forward. 'Come on! Tell me!'

Through choking sounds that he would have been loath to admit were sobs, Mehti Vlora said, 'Well, he was in the car . . . he . . . I put my hand on his shoulder . . .'

'And his face? What about his face?' Suleyman demanded. 'What was that like? Was he afraid?'

'Yes!'

'And? What else? What did he do, this frightened man you were about to kill? Did he plead? Did he blubber? Well?'

'Well, no . . . yes, he was . . .' Mehti shrugged. 'He was scared . . .'

'Yes?'

'It's in my statement.'

'Was he well-groomed?' Çöktin put in. 'Or was he rough and hard-looking? We've only seen Rifat's corpse, Mehti. Tell us.'

'Well, he was like he always was!' It came out in a rush, without thought or order. 'Pretty, like a girl. Scared of me, his eyes sort of black with it and . . . But when I cut him that put a stop to that, that made him ugly and I liked that! When blood splashes all over the face . . .'

'So he didn't have any blood on his face before you cut him?'

'Well, no, of course he didn't, why should he?'

'Rifat's dead face,' Çöktin explained, 'was covered with lots of small cuts, many of which had bits of glass in them. If you recall, Inspector İkmen did ask you about coloured glass before.'

'Yeah, so?'

'So his face was damaged prior to his death, Mehti. Quite a mess. Odd you didn't notice. Odd you didn't respond when you were asked about this. You see, whoever killed Rifat would have known about it.'

The colour had left Mehti's face. He opened his mouth to speak but seemed incapable of forming the words.

'Well then,' Suleyman said and turned to face his red-headed colleague. 'Just possession of cannabis and assault on Mr Bajraktar then, Sergeant Çöktin.'

'But . . .'

'Hardly worth a tape for just that, sir,' Çöktin said as he pressed the eject button on the tape recorder.

'No,' Suleyman said and then rose to his feet and without another word left the room.

Çöktin, smiling, looked down at the man who was now a very low-grade prisoner.

'You see, Mehti,' he said as he shoved the tape into one of his pockets, 'we didn't dig too deeply into your confession until Aryan came to see us. But after that, the little details that had simply niggled before turned into very big issues indeed.' Shrugging theatrically he added, 'Families, eh? You try your best to impress them and they just go and piss on you!'

When he reached the floor, Berekiah Cohen looked up to where he'd seen the strange woman and the boy. They were still there, pressed against the side of the guard rail. Too far away now to be able to see the expression on the woman's face, he was nevertheless uneasy about her. For some reason she had shrieked in panic and, for just a second, he thought he had seen real fear on her face. No one else had responded to the cry, but then Professor Apa and his colleagues were always so absorbed in what they were doing. Even when he'd handed over the gold leaf the professor had done little more than mutter his thanks. Berekiah understood why. It was so fabulous up there inside the dome, suspended as it were with the angels. Indeed the mosaics upon which the team were currently engaged depicted Michael and Gabriel, their faces unearthly and serene, their wings spread against the great expanse of gold that enveloped their figures. It was, he thought as he made his way towards the guard who stood by the exit, a privilege just to be able to deliver gold to such a place. It was something he wanted to do more of, whatever his stupid father might think. History was interesting and as Professor Apa had told him when they'd first met, it was alive too. A great empire like that of Byzantium didn't just disappear, it echoed relentlessly down the centuries, in the faces of modern İstanbulis, in the city's architecture, in the almost live quality of these pictures of faith, these mosaics. Berekiah felt invigorated just being in the building.

He turned his thoughts back to the woman. She hadn't made a sound since that first shriek but he still wasn't entirely happy about what might be taking place in the gallery.

'There's a boy and a woman up in the gallery,' he said to the cold-looking guard by the open door. 'I think they might be having an argument.'

The guard, a thickset man with a bored expression, shrugged. 'So?'

'I think the woman might be in trouble!' Berekiah said with some passion.

The guard first suppressed a yawn and then shuffled his no doubt cold feet. 'Which part of the gallery are they in?' he said. 'It's a big place.'

'Just above us, actually.' Berekiah pointed towards the roof of the narthex. 'In the Gynekoion.'

'The women's gallery, typical,' the guard said and moved slowly towards the cobbled ramp. 'I expect this woman's just nagged the poor boy half to death. Wanting to see everything, asking stupid questions all the time, not listening. I see it every day – foreigners, our own people. Always the same.'

'Do you want me to come with you?' Berekiah asked, watching the man's slow progress forwards.

'No, you stay here,' he said with a sigh of resignation. 'I'll do it. I'll sort it out. I always do.' And with yet another sigh, he mounted the step up to the ramp and began his no doubt slow ascent to the upper gallery.

Berekiah, now alone save for the thin smattering of tourists entering the narthex, leaned back against one of the porphyry-dressed walls and closed his eyes. Porphyry, he knew, came from Egypt. Mr Lazar, his tiny fox-faced employer, had once remarked that the stone had in all probability been hewn by the ancient Israelites, erstwhile slaves of the great Egyptian dynasties. With a laugh, Lazar had then said that by rights the Jews should have at least some of this now very valuable material and that perhaps Berekiah might like to try and lift some off with a knife one day when no one was looking. Mr Lazar said that the dark purple stone would look stunning in a white gold or even platinum setting. Berekiah smiled. Lazar might be old but at least he was still amusingly anarchic, not unlike the old communist antique dealer he knew in Beyoğlu. Still wearing that 'uniform' of the 1950s, a beret and black jumper, Mr Orga even had a painting of himself in full Che Guevara kit over the entrance to his tiny, dusty empire. It had been there even during the Cold War years. He was tenacious, funny and challenging, just as Berekiah's father had once been – before the earthquake, before Berekiah's brother Yusuf's mind splintered into fragments in a place very far from home. A place Berekiah didn't want to remember.

He opened his eyes just as the guard, now in rather more of a hurry than he had been, emerged at the bottom of the ramp.

'So was it all right?' Berekiah asked him.

'We're going to have to clear the building,' the guard said in a voice that was not a great deal above a whisper. 'But now I must call the police.'

Berekiah's face creased with concern. 'Why? What's going on? Is the lady hurt?'

The guard turned. 'You'll have to go back up the scaffolding and tell the professor and the team to come down,' he said and then shaking his head in disbelief he added, 'We can't take the risk of anyone doing anything to upset that boy up there.' And then he hurried forward again, muttering, 'I'll have to get the police . . .'

Berekiah laid a hand on the guard's retreating shoulder. 'What's wrong? Please tell me.'

The guard turned again, his wide eyes expressing what he felt about what he had just seen. 'The kid has a knife', he mouthed. 'OK?'

'Right.' Berekiah took a deep breath and quickly made his way back into the nave and up the scaffolding.

He made a point as he climbed not to look at the Gynekoion. By the prickling on the back of his neck, he knew with every step precisely where the women's gallery and its occupants were.

İkmen had to bend down and turn his head to see İlhan Evren's face. Twisted to one side, the art dealer's head lay on a small stack of his personal stationery on top of his desk. Slackened by death, his jowls spread limply across paper and pens, all of which were covered with his blood.

İkmen straightened and looked once more at the

scissors that stuck out of Evren's back. They would, he imagined, have to be long in order to have killed someone of Evren's bulk. But unless Arto Sarkissian found another more subtle cause of death, it was the scissors that had killed İlhan Evren – or rather, more precisely, the person wielding the scissors.

'I don't suppose the chauffeur has any idea where this Dimitri character may have gone,' İkmen said to Tepe who was, for some reason, regarding his own profile in what remained of the smashed mirror over the fireplace.

'No. Apparently he just cleaned his hands on a towel and left.'

'Do we have the towel?'

'Yes.' Tepe turned away from his image and looked at İkmen. 'And I've taken quite a good description from Hassan. The Russian did regular business with Evren so there could be correspondence or financial details pertaining to him.' And then frowning he said, 'I wonder why only the mirror is damaged. Nothing else is broken.'

'Apart from Evren.'

The sound of a car drawing up outside momentarily distracted the men's attention. Only İkmen went to look. The vehicle was a large black Mercedes.

'Dr Sarkissian has arrived,' he told his colleague. 'I'd better let him in. You go back to the kitchen. I'll join you when I've finished here.'

Hassan the chauffeur had drunk more of his employer's whisky since the last time Tepe had seen him. Not that he was inebriated; in Tepe's experience, people in shock could often drink a lot without getting drunk. Perhaps the extra adrenaline they produced ate up the excess alcohol – or something.

'Did Mr Ali give you any idea when he and his sister might be back?' the policeman asked as he sat down at the table opposite the chauffeur.

Hassan shrugged. 'No.'

'And you've no idea where they might have gone?'

'Somewhere in Sultan Ahmet. I don't know. That boy likes to wander around the monuments sometimes. So does Miss Flick. Or at least she did occasionally when she was friendly with the Albanian.'

Tepe leaned back in his chair and reached into his pocket for his cigarettes. 'So what did you make of Rifat Berisha the Albanian then, Hassan? Did you like him?'

'I liked it that he helped Miss Flick.' Hassan poured himself another glass of whisky. 'He was nice with her.'

'But?'

'But I knew he didn't fancy her. I mean, who could? She, of course, wanted him to want her.'

Tepe offered the chauffeur one of his cigarettes, which he took. 'So did there ever come a point when Rifat made that apparent to Miss Evren? Do you know?'

'No.' Hassan lit up and then offered his lighter to Tepe. 'But then it would have been very difficult for him to do that, wouldn't it? What with her giving him that car and anything else he wanted. And anyway, she has this strange attitude that makes telling her things like that very difficult.'

'What do you mean?'

'Well, she sort of talks about herself like she's beautiful. I mean, at first I thought she was just making a joke,' his eyes widened at the memory of it, 'but Allah in his mercy made sure I kept my mouth shut which is why I still have this job – if I still do.'

'Presumably keeping your job was the reason why you didn't tell Constable Roditi anything about these matters when he spoke to you.'

Hassan lowered his head. 'Mr Evren was still alive then.'

'Right.' Tepe frowned. 'So do you think that Miss Evren is suffering from actual delusions about her looks?'

'I don't know.' Hassan took a good long swig from his glass and then banged it back down onto the table. 'She's a weird woman. Her and that boy—'

'Her brother?'

'Yes. They talk all the time when they're together. Always in English, which I don't understand very well.' He leaned forward across the table conspiratorially. 'If Mr Evren were still alive, I wouldn't be saying this, but I've always thought there might be something unnatural going on between those two. Something about the tone of their conversations . . . Not that the boy seemed unhappy about whatever it was.'

'But if Miss Evren wanted Rifat . . .'

'Oh, I don't mean that Miss Flick and Mr Ali were fucking! Well, I don't know, maybe . . .' Hassan, his eyes now glazed with drink, laughed. 'No, it's more like there's some sort of control thing going on. Sometimes it's him, sometimes it's her. I don't know. Like today I think she would have liked him to have gone to school, but he said no. He refused. And she just went along with it.'

Tepe sucked thoughtfully on his cigarette. 'You don't know why he didn't want to go to school, do you?'

'Perhaps because he's not been well. Not that I've ever known him really fit.'

'But if Ali is ill, surely he would want to stay at home?'

'If I'd taken them up into Taksim I'd have said he was going to see his doctor.'

'His doctor?'

Hassan tapped the side of his head with one of his fingers. 'Doctor for the brain,' he said darkly. 'Crazy doctor.'

'You mean a psychiatrist?'

'Yes. Some other English woman or something.'

No, Irish actually, Tepe thought as he recalled hearing about İkmen and Suleyman's meeting with Dr Halman on this very doorstep. They had wondered at the time who the psychiatrist had come to see. Now they knew.

'So did you see Mr Evren this morning when you came to pick his children up?' Tepe asked, changing the subject back to one that was more relevant to current events.

'No, they just came out of the house when they saw me arrive.'

'Is that usual?'

'I generally manage a glass of tea between getting out of my car and starting up the Rolls.'

'But not this morning?'

'No.'

'Mmm.' Tepe put his hands up to his lips and frowned. According to Hassan, Dimitri the Russian said he'd knocked on the door to no avail before Hassan arrived in the car, so Evren could already have been dead by then. Maybe he was dead even before his children left the house. In fact, he could have been dead since the previous night.

'Hassan,' he asked at the end of these musings, 'you don't know whether the door to Mr Evren's office was open when you came in with Dimitri, do you?'

After thinking this over for a few seconds, Hassan said, 'I don't know is the honest answer. That Russian pushed in front of me and so I came straight down here. Mind you, even if it had been open, I wouldn't have been able to see anything because Mr Evren's desk is round the corner from the door.'

'So his children wouldn't have been able to see that their father was dead unless they actually went into his office?'

'No.'

If they hadn't needed to speak to their father about anything they could have left the house with no idea he was dead. It was, Tepe felt, an eerie thought and one that the Evren children, once tracked down, would probably find shocking. If, that is, Evren had indeed been dead when they left. After all, there was still the issue of the now absent Russian.

As it turned out, Tepe didn't have to wait very long for these issues to be addressed. İkmen put his head round the kitchen door and called him into the hall.

'What is it, sir?' the younger man asked as he observed the grave expression on İkmen's face.

'The doctor thinks that Evren died some time ago,' İkmen said, 'possibly in the early hours of this morning or even late last night. We need to know whether or not he had visitors and we need to find those children of his fast.'

'Hassan says Ali Evren didn't go to school today,' Tepe said. 'He took Felicity and Ali out to Sultan Ahmet this morning, he doesn't know why or what for. He did tell me, however, that Ali is one of Dr Halman's patients. So I suppose he could be a bit, well, you know what they can be like.'

İkmen did. 'Well, it might be worth giving her office a call,' he said. 'It's just possible Zelfa might have some idea where they might go.'

'Yes.'

İkmen gave Zelfa Halman's office phone number to Tepe who punched it into his mobile telephone. Then, as it started ringing, the two men waited in silence for someone to answer.

The thickness of the snowfall had, if anything, increased since he'd last looked outside. Moving back from the window, Mehmet Suleyman placed Mehti Vlora's latest statement on his desk and smiled as he recalled what Çöktin had told him about the green Fiat. In reality it had been dumped just round the corner from the Vloras' own apartment. Having driven around aimlessly in it all night Mehti had abandoned it when it had run out of petrol. How very incompetent and thoughtless. How very Mehti.

Suleyman looked at his watch and then walked across his office to where his overcoat hung on the back of the door. He'd only left himself twenty minutes to get down to Eminönü and Pandeli's. He didn't want to keep Zelfa waiting, not in this weather. He'd have to hurry.

Pausing only to light a cigarette, he closed the door of his office behind him and then made his way towards the stairs. Although rushed, he was looking forward to this meal. He hadn't had an easy morning with Mehti Vlora and although it now seemed that they had finally arrived at some sort of truth about his involvement, or lack of involvement, in Rifat Berisha's death, they still did not know who had committed the crime. It was troubling. The murderer was still at large and could, conceivably, kill again. It was a frightening thought and one that he knew his usually less than sympathetic superiors would share. Burglaries and car crime were one thing, but unsolved murders were quite another. They made the public nervous, got into the newspapers, sat on your service record like tombstones . . .

Lost in thought, he didn't really register that Çöktin had come alongside him, much less notice that the Kurd was panting.

'Sir, we've got a hostage situation,' he puffed.

'What?' Suleyman turned towards him, his eyes still clouded by his earlier thoughts.

'You've got to come. We've got a woman taken hostage!'

Suleyman's heart began to pump faster and he felt the familiar sensation of adrenaline release clear his mind.

'Where?'

'In the Aya Sofya,' Çöktin said. 'The guards have cleared the museum.'

'Right.'

Perfectly in step now, the two men ran into the squad room and called out three of the constables who were lounging in there.

'Do we know who the victim or the perpetrator are?' Suleyman asked as he took his phone out of his pocket and punched a well-used number into the keypad.

'No,' Çöktin replied.

'OK.'

As a body the five men moved towards the door out of the squad room, Suleyman with his ear pressed to his telephone.

'Zelfa?' he said. 'Look, I've got to go to something. There's been an incident at the Aya Sofya. Sorry.'

Running now, the small squad of men pushed through the crowd of sad-eyed peasants, weeping women and disgusted businessmen who clustered around the front desk. For some reason, extremes in the weather, of whatever sort, seemed to lead to increases in reported crime.

Not that any of this registered on Suleyman who was now frowning fiercely into his mobile. 'No, I don't know who is involved!' he said as he pushed his way through the crowd after his colleagues. 'Yes, it could be . . . Well, yes, Zelfa, if Çetin says the Evrens were taken to Sultan Ahmet . . . Yes, I will bear it in mind . . . Well, I think that's all rather psychological . . .'

As the door to the station opened, a sharp blast of icy air hit the hurrying officers, including Suleyman. Faced with the choice of either continuing to talk to Zelfa who seemed to be convinced that the couple in the museum were Felicity and Ali Evren, or pulling his coat more closely round his body, Suleyman chose the latter option.

'Just let me deal with it, will you, Zelfa!' he said and then clicked the end button with a determined finger.

The guards hadn't made any attempt to try to control what was happening up in the gallery. It had taken all their powers of persuasion to get the visitors and the restorers to leave quietly. As one of the men said to Suleyman as he escorted the squad of policeman up the cobbled ramp, nothing like this had ever happened before and they had no idea what they should do. This guard in particular, looked rattled and, once the officers had arrived at the top of the ramp, he quickly made himself scarce.

Even assuming that the assailant had seen the policemen enter the building, Suleyman didn't want to walk straight up to the couple without surveying the scene first. The Gynekoion is a wide and very light part of the upper gallery which is covered by a patterned cradle vault. Light comes in via arches set into the outer walls of the building, which correspond with similar structures across a wide corridor. These allow views into the nave below. There was only one way up to the gallery but it would still be possible to position men on both sides of the archway in which the couple were standing. Preventing the boy with the knife from tipping them both down into the nave would not be easy, however. After a few moments' thought, Suleyman decided to position Hikmet Yıldız in the northern part of the gallery opposite where the couple were standing. He could report on anything happening from that clearer vantage point and his presence, armed as he was, might be a deterrent – depending of course on the state of mind of the assailant.

Suleyman had just sent the young man about his business when he caught his first sight of the couple's faces. They had moved slightly away from the guard rail and their profiles were visible. Her strange, misshapen face was unmistakable. Suleyman did not recognise the boy but he was speaking English, which was enough to identify him.

Suleyman ushered his team back behind the door of the ramp and said, 'I know these people. Felicity and Ali Evren. They're brother and sister.'

'Sergeant Tepe and Inspector İkmen went out to the house of someone called Evren this morning,' Constable Avcı said. He was the sort of man who made it his business to know everything about everything other people were involved in.

'Do you know why?' Çöktin asked.

Avcı shrugged. 'I'm only a constable,' he said a trifle moodily. 'Why should they tell me?'

Suleyman turned towards Çöktin and said, 'I think

Ali Evren is one of Dr Halman's patients. She had an idea they might be here.'

'Ah.' Çöktin offered no further comment.

'I'd better call her. Any background she can give us might be useful,' and then to Avcı Suleyman added, 'Get downstairs and tell the guards to expect the doctor, will you.'

'Yes, sir.'

'Oh, and you might prepare them for the arrival of Inspector İkmen too,' he said as he keyed Zelfa's number into his mobile. 'He spoke to Dr Halman earlier about the Evrens.'

'Do you want me to call him, sir?' Çöktin said as he watched Avcı move quickly back down the ramp.

'Yes,' Suleyman replied as he listened to Zelfa's phone ring, 'but keep your voice down.'

Beyond the door, in the gallery, a male voice shouted something that neither of the officers could understand.

İkmen took his telephone out of his jacket pocket and pressed the receive button.

'İkmen.'

'Inspector, it's Çöktin,' an urgent, whispering voice responded.

'What do you want?' İkmen turned away from the sight of Arto Sarkissian removing bloodied surgical gloves.

'Inspector Suleyman and I are at the Aya Sofya, with Ali and Felicity Evren.'

'Oh, good, I've been trying to find them,' İkmen

replied. 'I even asked Dr Halman if she knew where they might be.'

'Well, she does now, sir,' Çöktin said in tones İkmen now recognised as anxious. 'She may be joining us soon. Ali Evren is threatening his sister with a knife. He's with her in the gallery.'

'Why the fuck would he be threatening his sister?'

'Inspector Suleyman and I may be about to find that out.'

'I'll join you,' İkmen said decisively and ended the call. He turned towards Tepe. 'I need you to stay here while I go to Sultan Ahmet,' he said.

'Right.'

Arto Sarkissian rolled his sleeves down and walked towards his anxious-looking friend.

'Problems?' he asked.

İkmen sighed as he pulled his overcoat on and wound his scarf round his neck. 'The Evren boy might know rather more about his father's death than we thought.' He riffled in his coat pocket for his car keys and pulled them out. Then he left without another word.

'Are you going to kill me?' Felicity said as she felt the edge of the knife press into the flesh at her throat.

'I loved you,' her brother replied as he let his breathless gaze drift around the margins of the enormous building. 'We were going to live for ever.'

'If you put the knife down and let me go, everything will be all right. I'll take care of you.'

'Like you did when you went off day after day with Rifat Berisha? When you allowed him to ruin you?'

'David,' she said, 'Rifat never touched me in the way you think. I keep telling you but you—'

'This building is very quiet now,' he whispered close to her ear. 'Do you think they've cleared it? Do you think they've called the police?' He smiled. 'You'd like it if they've called that Inspector Suleyman, wouldn't you? You like him. You'd like him to—'

'David, for Christ's sake!'

He pulled her in hard towards his chest. 'This is how it's going to be,' he said. 'First, I'm going to see whether you will die and then I'm going to leave here, with or without you. Either way, I'm on the run from death.'

Just as he tensed his arm to slash her throat, he heard a noise from the gallery opposite. He looked up.

'Police,' he said, 'or somebody.' And then, suddenly childlike, his face crumpled and he seemed on the edge of tears. 'They're going to try and stop me, Flick. What am I going to do?'

'David, we need to talk about this! You and I can both die. I know we've always said that we won't but the reality is . . .'

He wasn't listening. His eyes were everywhere, scanning for danger. He knew now he should have killed her immediately. But she was his sister and more, and he loved her . . . Lying bitch. But not even those harsh words inspired him and Ali Evren began to cry.

Chapter 21

Although technically he shouldn't even have been near the scaffolding, Berekiah Cohen was one of the last people to climb back down to the ground. Professor Apa, the project leader, had been impressed for some time by his enthusiasm and had actually promised to demonstrate his use of Mr Lazar's gold leaf to Berekiah when the young man told him that he and his team must leave the building. Boys threatening women with knives was not a matter for academics or for men who worked in gold shops. It was a matter for the police and maybe for doctors too if the boy proved to be unbalanced – which seemed possible. After all, who but a madman would attempt to threaten someone in such a public place? Reflexively, Berekiah's mind turned towards the subject of his brother Yusuf. In the fear and misery that attended his paranoid delusional state, Yusuf had attacked his doctor, meaning to kill him. After that he had been heavily medicated for a very long time. Then he'd tried to kill himself. He had hoarded some of his sleeping tablets and then locked himself into one of the bathrooms. He'd taken the lot. And when the doctors had eventually managed to revive him, Yusuf had cried – because he was in pain, yes, but mainly because he was still alive, a state Berekiah knew his brother found intolerable.

Once down on the ground, Berekiah and the scientific team were quietly escorted out of the building. Consigned to lurking in the snowy gardens, Berekiah took his hat out of his pocket and put it on. He then lit a warming cigarette, which he smoked while he and all the others watched a taxi pull up in front of the main entrance to the museum complex. But rather than stare as others were doing at the occupants of the car, Berekiah turned away in order to pursue his thoughts in solitude.

The notion that the boy he had seen up in the gallery was unhinged in some way was pervasive. Berekiah found himself wondering what the lad was going through – what motivated him, how he felt now that he was in this situation. What he might feel when confronted by the police. When Yusuf was particularly agitated, it was almost as if he was struggling with something inside, something devilish even. When asked by the medical director of the institution where her son lived what she understood about Yusuf's condition, Estelle Cohen had said that he was 'haunted'. By what, she didn't know. But Berekiah thought that he did. After all, things seen in combat could not then be unseen, as he well knew himself. It was all to do with whether one was overrun by the ghosts or only, as he was, bothered on occasions. Like now.

Just before what turned out to be the lone occupant of the taxi entered the building, Berekiah looked over his shoulder briefly to see what was happening. The visitor, who was now talking to a short, stout guard, was a woman. She had blonde hair and he recognised her immediately. Zelfa.

'That boy'll wish he'd never been born before the day's out.'

Berekiah looked round and found himself in the presence of an elderly man in the now familiar uniform of a museum guard.

'If of course he survives this day,' the man added as he rubbed his bare hands together against the bitter weather. 'Mad, of course, which is why she's here.' He tipped his head towards Zelfa and then whispered, 'Psychiatrist. And now that the police are here . . .' He shrugged. 'If you ask me they should all be locked up.'

Resisting an urge to disagree violently with this opinion, Berekiah just said, 'Oh.'

'Well, it's no good for our business, tourism,' the guard continued, 'and anyway, it can only end badly, can't it? I mean, if he means to do it, he'll do it. It's kismet. I can't even start to think about the mess.' Then he walked away to talk to one of his, no doubt, equally disgruntled fellows.

Berekiah sat down on the hard, cold ground and tried not to think about what Zelfa might shortly have to witness.

Although Felicity Evren was far from being a willing hostage, she was so very tiny that it was easy for her brother to pull her along with him as he darted out into the centre of the gallery.

Suleyman unclipped his radio from his belt and called Yıldız.

'What's he doing?' he asked. 'Can you see?'

'I think he saw me, sir,' the younger man replied, his voice sibilant with hushed tones. 'There's no way round above the mihrab, he's moving into the southern gallery which is a dead end.'

'Perhaps he's frightened we might try to come in behind him.'

'Probably. Do you want me to line him up?'

'Yes, but don't even think about taking a shot. Inspector İkmen is on his way – take your mark only from him or myself. Is that understood?'

'Yes, sir.'

Suleyman signed off and replaced the radio on his belt. He looked across at Çöktin and a middle-aged cadaverous individual known as Constable Güney.

'Ali Evren is English, he will communicate more effectively in his native tongue,' he said, and shrugged. 'So it would appear I'm going to have to employ my knowledge of that language.' He looked at Çöktin. 'I know that you're reasonably fluent, İsak.'

'Yes, sir.'

'Güney?'

'I can do "please" and "thank you" and I can ask for beer, tea and girls.'

Suleyman smiled. 'I like your priorities, Güney,' he said, 'but I think it might be safer for all of us if you remain silent. Sergeant Çöktin and I will translate anything we think you might need to know.'

'Very well, sir.'

'Good.' He slipped one hand underneath his jacket and felt his gun. He did not intend to draw it, he just needed to know it was there. And then with a smile he said, 'Gentlemen?'

The other two officers silently signalled that they were as ready as they were ever going to be.

And then mounting the top of the ramp, Suleyman stepped out into the Gynekoion.

Ali Evren, his right hand pushing the blade of his knife hard up against his sister's throat, was standing with her opposite an ornate three-columned break in the symmetry of the inner gallery wall. Felicity's eyes were wide with fear.

'The Byzantine empresses used to watch the religious ceremonies from that place,' Suleyman said, tipping his head in the direction of what was in effect a royal box. 'Whether Christian or Muslim, men and women have always been very separate in this place.'

Although there was a pause between Suleyman speaking and Ali's reply, when the boy did respond it was in a surprisingly firm voice.

'Yes,' he said, 'that is true. Although if they were related, men and women could get together after church. A lot of the Byzantine emperors were very close to their sisters and mothers – that's what my history teacher said. We came here on a school visit.'

'Yes.'

'Some of them even killed their female relatives,' he said and then, looking down into Felicity's frightened eyes, he added, 'Particularly if they were treacherous and told lies.'

'I have never lied to you, David!' Felicity gasped. 'Never!'

'Oh?' His grip upon her throat and shoulders tightened. 'What about death? What about that? What about the way you cheated on me with the Albanian?'

Suleyman, resisting the urge to move too far forward, said, 'Now I do not know what any of this is about or why this is happening—'

'I only want my sister to apologise to me,' the boy interrupted. 'We've done some terrible things together, things that maybe I wouldn't even have considered if it hadn't been for Flick.'

'What things?'

Ali and his hostage had been moving slowly backwards for some moments; now he accelerated, dragging his sister rapidly towards the marble doorway known as the Gates of Heaven and Hell. Beyond that lay the southern gallery proper and, as Yıldız had said earlier, eventually a dead end.

'Where are you going?' Suleyman asked as both he and Çöktin stepped forward to keep pace with their quarry. 'You're moving in the wrong direction for the exit.'

'Not necessarily,' the boy replied with a smile. Bracing his back against one of the ancient marble doorposts, he looked down into the great space that constituted the nave of the church. 'There are other ways.'

'You can't fly, David!' Terrified, Felicity followed her brother's gaze. 'Tell him he can't fly, Inspector!'

Suleyman, though confused by this, did so. The boy

didn't appear to be listening. He made a tiny surface cut on his sister's throat and caught the blood on one of his fingers. Then he placed his finger in his mouth and sucked it. He did it with very obvious pleasure.

Although the original plan had been to go straight up to the gallery in company with Avcı, Zelfa had to pause at the entrance to the exonarthex. Dizzy, her head pounding, she thought she might throw up.

'I just need a moment,' she said to Avcı and doubled back into the museum garden again.

'Are you all right, doctor?'

'Yes!'

Luckily he didn't follow her and although there were a lot of people gathered about outside, no one seemed to notice her. Not that she was actually sick. As soon as she sat down and took a few deep breaths, she began to feel better. But the fact that she was sitting in what was now quite deep snow didn't register for a few moments. This alone made her realise that she was probably quite ill. That or she was just frightened. If, as she suspected, Ali Evren was testing out his hypothesis regarding his sister, it was she herself who had put that idea into his mind. 'Take Felicity to the Aya Sofya with you and see what happens.' She had left the resolution of Ali's delusion about his sister up to him. She had, in effect, given him permission to do this. And the testing of hypotheses regarding suspected vampires could, if her memory of *Dracula* served her well, be quite drastic. They included such life-threatening procedures as driving a stake through the subject's heart, burning, and of course cutting off the head. Ali Evren had, so Mehmet had told her, a knife to his sister's throat; clearly, Ali was not impressed by the fact that Felicity had survived all of those religious crosses on the walls of the museum. Or perhaps, having discovered Felicity's true and obviously mortal nature, he now felt duped and angry with her. After all, she had lied to him, hadn't she? A stupid and pointless lie, in Zelfa's opinion. Everyone has a reflection – everyone.

'Zelfa?'

The voice, which was deep and rich, was instantly familiar.

'İkmen?' She looked up into a pair of dark, intelligent eyes and attempted a smile.

'If you don't mind my saying so,' he said as he hunkered down to her level, 'your face is as white as the snow.'

This was not an issue Zelfa wanted to address just then.

'What are you doing here, İkmen?' Behind him she could see a large number of uniformed officers spreading out around the perimeter of the ancient building.

'I suspect the same as you.'

'The Evren children.'

'Yes, Çöktin called me. I brought this lot,' he said, gesturing at the officers. 'In case young Ali should decide to run. I was at the Evren house actually.'

Zelfa recalled the somewhat cryptic conversation she'd had with Tepe earlier. 'Yes. What were you doing there?'

'Attending a crime scene.' Seeing that she was now

struggling to stand up, he offered her his hand. 'The family chauffeur found the body of İlhan Evren this morning.'

Zelfa's eyes widened.

'He had a pair of scissors sticking out of his back.' İkmen took Zelfa's arm and gently moved her back towards the museum. 'I have some ideas about who might have committed the crime but no hard evidence,' he said. 'Right now what we need to consider is whether to tell that pair in the gallery.'

Zelfa looked up at the great soaring dome dwarfing the entrance they were now passing through.

'I think,' she said gravely, 'that will depend upon what is happening up there.'

Nobody actually now knows which side of the Gates of Heaven and Hell relate to which aspect of the afterlife. But considering the fact that the portal had almost certainly been named by a man, Mehmet Suleyman reasoned that the heaven side probably related to the Gynekoion – the women's gallery. This meant that they were now pursuing Ali Evren into the southern gallery and Hell. So it was with some satisfaction that Suleyman spotted Yıldız in the northern gallery just before he passed through the portal with Çöktin and Güney. If Ali Evren did lose it completely, there was always Yıldız.

'I think that maybe we should talk, Ali.'

'But you want me to let go of my sister first, right?' Ali Evren smiled – a genuine smile, in no way ironic. Totally at odds with his words. 'I don't think so.'

'If you let your sister go,' Çöktin said slowly, 'Inspector Suleyman will talk and nobody will be hurt.'

'How much money will my father have to give you to just forget all of this? Eh? Anyway,' he said, his face flushing as he became more agitated, 'you can't kill me and so why should I worry? One way or another, my sister and I are leaving this place today, you know. She may very well leave here dead . . .' he paused briefly to gasp for air, '. . . but that is something she should have thought about a long time ago.'

'David, I—'

'When you look in a mirror, Felicity, tell me what you see!'

'I—'

'Tell him, Felicity.' Zelfa Halman was standing next to Mehmet Suleyman, her shaking hand resisting the temptation to touch him.

'Tell your brother, Felicity,' she said calmly. 'It's all over now.'

'But I can't!' Her voice was horse and, Zelfa noticed, she had blood dripping down the side of her neck.

'Felicity . . .'

'I can't see my own reflection! I have no idea how to describe myself!'

'Would you like to tell me what this is about?' Suleyman asked Zelfa quietly, his eyes never leaving Ali.

'It was just a game to humour you!' Felicity cried until her brother's hand tightened round her throat.

'You're trying to be a vampire, aren't you, Ali?' Zelfa said with what Suleyman felt was remarkable sang-froid. 'Felicity told you she can't see her own reflection in mirrors and you wanted to be like her, didn't you?'

'It's all about beating death, doctor,' the boy replied. 'The only way.'

'Yes, but it's just a game, as we just heard, Ali. Felicity is not a vampire.'

'She told me she was!' He looked fiercely down at the top of his sister's head. 'She said she could no longer see herself – ages ago! Then Mother died . . . Flick still couldn't see . . . I said that perhaps she and I were vampires and she said yes and I said that that was such a good way to beat death! Because,' he fixed his eyes hard upon Zelfa now, 'death isn't very nice, doctor! I've seen it and I want none of it!'

'For yourself, yes,' İkmen said, moving uneasily from foot to foot behind his colleagues. 'But as a vampire you have to take the lives of others, do you not?'

The boy opened his mouth to speak but was pre-empted by his sister.

'No, he hasn't, he doesn't, he—'

'Rifat's death had nothing to do with that!' Ali shouted, disgust at such ignorance evident in his voice. 'He said horrible things to Flick, he tried to take what was mine. He deserved to die! I only drank his blood because it was there, it was a natural thing for me to do, because of what I am – I didn't plan to do it!'

Felicity was crying now. Her brother, clutched her still more tightly to his chest and took three steps back.

'Where are you going?' Zelfa asked him.

347

'I told you, I'm leaving.'

Suleyman glanced quickly across the nave to the northern gallery, his eye catching something moving very quickly over there.

İkmen cleared his throat. 'Ali,' he said, 'I apologise for being slow but vampires, as I understand it, must drink blood, they cannot exist in the light and—'

'My transformation is not yet complete.'

'But if Felicity isn't, as I assume you now know, really a vampire then why should you believe a metamorphosis is happening within you?'

'I just told you, I drank Rifat's blood! And I've drunk hers,' he said as he swung his sister out in front of him, turning now so that his back was towards the outer wall of the church. He was moving away from the vast drop to the floor of the nave, which could mean Suleyman thought, that he had seen Yıldız on the gallery opposite. Either way, his new position made it impossible for the young officer to get a clear shot at the boy.

'My father has wanted to put me in a madhouse for a long time,' he said over the top of his sister's muffled crying. 'But he's as guilty as I am and—'

'Oh, David, don't!'

'Shut up!' He transferred the knife from his right hand to his left and looked down the length of the gallery towards the dead end. As in the northern gallery, there was a door, as Ali Evren knew. Old, and blackened with age, it was secured with a padlock. The boy pointed first at İkmen and then at the door.

'Open it,' he said, 'right now.'

*   *   *

In the few brief seconds during which Ali Evren looked across at İkmen's struggles with the padlock, Zelfa whispered to Suleyman, 'We can't let him just go through that door! The men outside will kill him!'

'You know some of these doors don't actually lead anywhere, don't you, Ali?' İkmen said as he made very convincing play of trying to undo an already broken padlock. 'I don't know why that is,' İkmen continued when the boy didn't reply. 'Perhaps it was some sort of Byzantine joke.'

'That it leads out is enough,' the boy replied.

'Yes, but if there's a big drop . . .'

'Well, I won't die!'

Now beyond thought, Felicity Evren stared ahead of her with hopeless intensity.

'Ali, it doesn't have to be like this,' Zelfa began. 'If you will just come with me now—'

'Your lover will beat me up,' he said, looking at Suleyman, 'and then you will put me in the loony bin!' He laughed. 'I do know that is what will happen, doctor! My father told me as much last night. He said he wasn't prepared to cover up for me any more. He said he was going to call you. He said that the fact that he helped me would never come out because I am mad and so who would believe me?'

'What do you mean he helped you?'

'Father's dead, David.'

It was said so calmly and with such certainty that for a moment İkmen's hands stopped working at the broken padlock.

Ali twisted his sister round in his grasp and looked into her face. 'Dead?'

İkmen glanced across at Suleyman who slipped one of his hands inside his jacket. Yıldız was completely unsighted now and they both knew it.

'I finally told him about my part in . . . in how you are, David,' Felicity said, her chin cringing away from the knife at her throat. 'And he didn't like it.'

'Did you drink his blood?'

'No!'

His eyes blazing, the boy snapped his gaze away from his sister's face and across to İkmen. 'Get that padlock off now or I'll slash her throat!'

İkmen pulled the rusted lump of metal out of its hasp and threw it to the floor.

'Now move away from it!'

'Ali—'

'Do it!'

İkmen moved over to the other side of the door.

Ali swung his sister round again to face the officers and the doctor whom he now fixed with a fierce gaze.

'You know that it's your fault we're here, don't you, doctor?' he said. 'You suggested this test for my sister and she failed.'

'Ali, I know that in your reality vampires exist, but—'

'Oh, I am going to cheat death,' he said. He moved over to the door and pushed the handle down. 'I don't want to die and so I won't. I'll do anything to avoid that.'

As the door swung outwards, a gasp of freezing,

snow-bearing air billowed into the building. From where Zelfa was standing, only a swathe of seal-grey sky, was visible.

'This is no way out,' İkmen said as he looked down at the huge drop beneath the now gently swinging door. 'You'll kill yourself.'

'No I won't.' Ali stepped forward into the frame of the door. 'I'll only kill the false vampire, the love cheat, the woman who can die.'

'Oh, Jesus,' Felicity murmured. 'Oh, Jesus, God . . .'

'And all the time I thought you were a daughter of Satan!' The boy tightened his grip on her throat, cutting off her air supply.

And then Ali looked behind him at the whitening drop below.

Suleyman drew his gun as İkmen reached across to grab hold of Felicity Evren's wrist.

Çöktin threw himself at İkmen's legs. Not that the dead boy still had a hold on his sister's throat, but the momentum of the bullet plus the weight of both Ali and Felicity had been enough to pull İkmen right to the very edge of the sheer drop. Quite how he had kept hold of Felicity's wrist he had no idea.

Amid a strange, frenetic silence, Çöktin and his fellow officers pulled and heaved both İkmen and Felicity Evren back from the door and dragged them, gasping for air, to the safety of the gallery floor. And then still in silence they watched them as they attempted to regain control of their bodies. Felicity, her head and shoulders smothered with her brother's blood, stared vacantly at the mosaic representing the Byzantine Empress Irene, a woman of remarkable, blonde beauty. The contrast between the luminous glory of the artwork and the misshapen woman covered with gore was not lost upon those in the gallery who could still think straight.

'Christ!' Zelfa murmured as she walked shakily over to the doorway. Looking down, she let her eyes follow the long streak of scarlet that cut its way through the snow, staining various small projections on the outside of the building. A crowd of people had already gathered below. And although she knew that Ali Evren was down there somewhere too, the fact that she couldn't see his body – yet – was disturbing.

'You'd better get outside, doctor,' she heard İkmen's surprisingly steady voice say.

Zelfa turned. Çöktin and Güney, who had now been joined by Yıldız, were escorting Felicity Evren's weeping figure towards a step where she could sit more comfortably. This was just opposite the Deesis mosaic, a representation of John the Baptist and the Virgin Mary interceding on mankind's behalf on Judgement Day. The Catholic part of Zelfa's mind smiled at this irony before her Turkish eyes looked up at the figure of Mehmet Suleyman who had his back to her, talking on his mobile telephone. The pistol he had fired at Ali Evren's head was still in his right hand.

A touch of fingers against her shoulder alerted her to İkmen's presence.

'I'll come with you,' he said.

'What?'

'Somebody needs to declare that boy's life extinct,'

İkmen said as he gently moved her away from the gaping nothingness beyond the door.

Zelfa's eyes were filling with tears. 'But I'm not a pathologist.'

'But you are a doctor, so you're more qualified to do this than I am.'

'Yes . . .'

'Listen,' he said as he took her hand in his, 'the only way around something like this is to keep working. I know, believe me.' And then, amazingly given the situation, he gently laughed. 'Listen to me, giving advice to the psychiatrist!'

Suleyman had finished his call and was putting his telephone back into his pocket when they drew level with him.

'İskender is on his way,' he said to İkmen, referring to a senior officer who would no doubt be given the job of investigating the circumstances surrounding today's 'incident'.

İkmen looked down at the gun in his colleague's hand and noted that the safety catch was back on again.

'You'll have to surrender your weapon,' he said, aware that Suleyman would know this but saying it anyway, just for something to say – for something to put off the moment when Zelfa spoke to her fiancé. Not that he succeeded.

'You killed him,' Zelfa said as she looked up into the cold, tense eyes of her lover.

'Yes.'

'I needed more time to talk to him . . .'

'Ali Evren forced the pace of events.'

'Which you failed to control!'

Suleyman's response was immediate and his tone and demeanour demonstrated why his ancestors had been men of power.

'No, I failed to understand, doctor!' he said icily. 'I walked into a hostage situation involving a madman, somebody you knew was insane even before Rifat Berisha was murdered!'

'No! No, he was referred . . .'

But Suleyman was walking rapidly away from them now, back towards his small team of officers and a much quieter Felicity Evren.

İkmen squeezed Zelfa's arm. 'I'll talk to him,' he said as he guided her past the men and the blood-soaked woman. 'It's shock. We must all settle now and think rationally about what has just occurred.'

'But Mehmet killed that boy, he—'

'Inspector Suleyman had no choice,' İkmen responded sternly. 'Ali Evren was going to launch himself into space and take his sister with him. We were going to have two very public deaths on our hands.'

'Couldn't you have just made a grab for her arm?'

'Ali would never have let go of his sister's neck while he remained alive. She was starting to turn blue. Think about it, Zelfa,' İkmen said as he led her to the top of the cobbled ramp. 'I only know a little of what was going on in that boy's mind, but you just think about what you know of his internal universe and then tell me what you would have done in Mehmet's place.'

She looked at İkmen with mobile, blank eyes.

Chapter 22

'This is the second time in your career that you've thrown yourself into a hostage situation without adequate preparation,' Commissioner Ardiç said sharply. 'You are impetuous.'

'Sir, with respect,' İkmen said, looking across at Suleyman as he spoke, 'Inspector Suleyman's involvement in that earlier case came about because the assailant specifically requested his presence at the scene.'

'Yes.' Ardiç looked at İkmen, his large face drawn. 'But that doesn't apply to this incident today, does it, İkmen?'

'No.'

'Today we received a call from a very public place which Inspector Suleyman responded to with rapidity, which was commendable, but also with a lack of forward planning I find unacceptable.' Turning his fierce gaze upon Suleyman, he said, 'You attended the scene with a small group of officers, deploying only one man to mark the assailant from another part of the building. Your lack of knowledge about the geography of the museum meant that you did not make provision for getting behind the assailant, which resulted in the boy effectively taking charge of the situation.'

'The boy was insane, sir,' İkmen offered, 'and actually under treatment.'

'From Dr Halman, yes. I know.' Although calm in tone, Ardiç was actually really dangerous now. 'Dr Halman who is an occasional police consultant and who is engaged to be married to Inspector Suleyman. Looks good, doesn't it, İkmen?'

'Sir—'

'Ali Evren was a dual Turkish–British national. Which means,' Ardiç said round a large cigar, 'that the United Kingdom authorities are going to want to know everything there is to know about this incident. And rightly so. While they are in most respects a friendly ally of our country, their misconceptions about our policing methods are the same as those shared by all the other members of the European Union. In addition, their pressmen are some of the most ruthless and unscrupulous in Europe. Between them and the Italians . . .' Ardiç shook his head.

İkmen knew better then to interrupt at this point.

'And to say that we are not all vicious bastards will not do, İkmen! We tried saying that when fucking Leeds United came to play Galatasaray and look what happened – death and chaos ensued. We were accused of complacency then; now we'll no doubt be accused of – I don't even dare think of what! We all know that there are good and bad officers and I know that both of you are basically decent, truthful men. But the British don't know that! All they'll see is him,' he pointed rudely at Suleyman, 'with a gun in his hand shooting a child!'

'With respect, sir,' İkmen countered, 'neither I nor

Inspector Suleyman considered any of these issues at the time because an officer's first duty is to the hostage. I am convinced that once all the evidence is in, you'll see that Inspector Suleyman really had no choice. That padlock should never have been in that state in the first place. If the door hadn't been accessible we would have had much more time. The psychiatrist—'

'Dr Halman will have to submit her clinical notes on the Evren boy to the investigating officer.'

'Inspector İskender?'

'No, me,' Ardiç replied. 'The international aspect means that I must take personal charge. You're lucky it's not the Director General himself,' he added ominously. 'We must do this right, İkmen. I want written reports from every officer at the scene on my desk by this evening.'

'Yes, sir.'

Ardiç cleared his throat. 'Now, the Evren woman – where are we with that?'

'She's under guard and sedation at the Cerrahpaşa, sir,' İkmen replied. 'The psychiatrist – not, I should add, Dr Halman – says that we can speak to her tomorrow morning.'

'Not before?'

'No. She's incoherent.'

'And the woman's father?'

'A forensic examination is taking place as we speak,' İkmen said. 'Dr Sarkissian has now removed the body to the mortuary. It was obvious from what was said at the Aya Sofya that Miss Evren, if not her brother, was aware of his demise.'

Ardiç leaned back in his chair and fixed his eyes, once again, on the colourless face of Mehmet Suleyman. 'I see. Think she did it, İkmen?'

'I don't know, sir. But I'll find out. From the little I know about the family, it appears that delusion and madness informed much of their actions. Things that don't, sir, conform to what may normally be classified as logical.'

'Psychological stuff,' Ardiç said with undisguised disdain.

'Yes, sir.'

'May Allah have pity!' He looked down at his desk. 'Well, you'd better go and write your reports. Take some leave, Suleyman.'

The younger man winced. 'Sir—'

'It's better this way, Suleyman,' Ardiç said gruffly. 'When this gets out, the British press will be looking for someone and I don't want them to find you. Bastards! When the dust has settled you can come back, hopefully with rather more respect for procedure and restraint.' He then pointedly turned his attention back to a file he had been perusing when they entered and İkmen and Suleyman were dismissed.

Out in the corridor, they both lit up immediately.

'Well, that's the end of my career,' Suleyman said bleakly.

İkmen placed what he hoped was a comforting hand on his colleague's shoulder. 'No, I don't think so. Ardiç wants you back, he said so. He also said that you're a good man, which I know he doesn't ever say lightly.

No, I think that once we've established that the Evren boy was insane—'

'What difference does that make? I shot him, Çetin.'

'You had no choice! I caught your eye, I knew what you were going to do! I'll put that in my report.'

Suleyman managed a smile as he thanked İkmen.

'Zelfa's notes should bear out the insanity hypothesis,' İkmen said as they walked along the corridor towards their offices. 'Had we been able to consult her about Ali Evren before this incident, I think things would have been very different. But we were not in a position to do that.'

'No.'

'Professional confidentiality,' he smiled, 'is not always helpful.' He raised his hands in a gesture of supplication. 'Kismet!'

'Indeed.'

And then with a brief embrace the two men parted and Suleyman went into his office to write his account of the day's events.

İkmen meanwhile sauntered slowly back to his base. He was confident that, even given Zelfa's connection to Suleyman, her evidence would be taken into account. The boy had clearly been unbalanced although for how long or to what extent he didn't know. Zelfa had tried to explain the boy's fixation with vampires to him on their way up to the museum gallery, but there had been so little time, he hadn't really understood. Something about the sister being a vampire, reflections in mirrors – other Balkan nonsense. As if he hadn't already had enough of that. Not that now was the time to ponder yet again on his mother. Now he must try and help Mehmet Suleyman and also disentangle this abortion of a case. If Ali Evren had indeed killed Rifat Berisha, possibly with the help of his father, İkmen wanted to know why. Just to drink the Albanian's blood didn't seem sufficient reason – although as he now knew from his experiences with the Berishas, the Vloras and even his own family, paltry or stupid reasons did not stop people from committing murder. Quite the contrary. And then there was Felicity's relationship with Ali to take into account. From the little that he had seen up in the gallery of the Aya Sofya, plus what Tepe had told him about the chauffeur Hassan's perceptions of the pair, İkmen felt the siblings' private life warranted a closer look. His mind baulked at the prospect.

The task of telling the Berisha family that murder charges against Mehti Vlora had been dropped fell to Orhan Tepe. And indeed by the time he set off for the family home, Mehti had formally withdrawn his confession. Whether he had done this in response to what must have seemed to him the treachery of his own family in the shape of his brother Aryan, or whether Çöktin had frightened him into it, Tepe didn't know. But he was glad about it, especially in light of what the drama in Aya Sofya had revealed. Some sort of substantiation was still required but it seemed that one or maybe both of the Evren children had murdered Rifat Berisha.

However, as he was quick to point out to a deeply suspicious Rahman Berisha, charges relating to the death of his son Egrem were still pending against Mehmet Vlora.

'Aryan Vlora has agreed to testify against his brother,' he said as he stood over the crumpled little Albanian sitting at his kitchen table, 'so it does look good, Mr Berisha.'

'Well, if he wants my thanks, he can want for ever,' Rahman replied bitterly as he rolled what was left of his cigarette between his fingers. 'Anyone could have told you that my youngest son was murdered by Mehmet. As far as I am concerned we are still in blood with the Vloras.'

'Well, that is your affair and your choice,' Tepe answered stiffly. 'However, I should warn you that any action taken against the Vloras by yourself will be viewed most harshly. Like it or not, you are now involved in a legal process, Mr Berisha. This involves proof, something which Aryan Vlora is helping us with.'

Perhaps beyond speech for the moment, Rahman Berisha just shrugged.

'What would be useful, though,' Tepe said, 'would be if you could give us an item of Egrem's clothing – if of course you still possess—'

'Why?' The eyes that looked up at Tepe were shot with blood and dark shadows hung under them.

'Because some old blood samples were recovered from the Vloras' apartment, around the area Aryan says Mehmet killed your son. They don't belong to anyone else in the apartment or even, I should add, to your other boy Rifat.'

'So?'

A little tired of what seemed to be almost wilful lack of comprehension, Tepe sighed. 'Well, Mr Berisha,' he said, trying to be patient, 'if samples of DNA in the blood match those found in perhaps hair samples on Egrem's clothes, that together with Aryan's testimony will prove Mehmet Vlora's guilt beyond most reasonable doubt. We're talking legal processes here again.'

Rahman coughed and then said, 'Well . . .'

It is possible that he may have said more but, as Tepe later felt quite strongly, it was probably more likely that he would have lapsed into silence again. After all, for this man the only justice that was in any way real was that meted out by the *fis*. But it was not Rahman who spoke next. His daughter had appeared at the kitchen door, the hand she held protectively across her damaged mouth failing completely to disguise the bruises around her eyes.

Shocked by her appearance, Tepe simply stared.

'We still have the shirt Egrem was wearing when he died,' she said with some difficulty as she tried to control what sounded like a swollen tongue. 'Will that do, Sergeant?'

'What are you doing out of your room?' Her father, enraged, rose to his feet, his hand moving as if to strike her. It was not a giant leap for Tepe to connect the girl's current appearance with the hand now raised in her direction. And unhampered as he was this time by his boss, he caught hold of Rahman's arm and twisted it up behind the Albanian's back.

Engelushjia's eyes widened in alarm.

Tepe, blessed with the kind of strength in his hands that only military service can develop, smiled at the girl and said, 'Yes, that will be perfect, Miss Berisha. Perhaps you'd like to get it for me.'

'Oh, er, yes. Right.' She moved painfully out of the room.

Tepe waited until he thought she couldn't hear before turning his attention to her father.

'Looks like you just stopped short of putting her in hospital,' he said, pulling Rahman's arm further up his back.

'Arrrgh!' Rahman yelled. 'She's my—'

'She isn't yours to kill!' Tepe said and eased the pressure slightly.

'Would you have a daughter of yours give herself to her brother's killer!' Rahman yelled. 'Putting ideas into her head about the innocence of Mehti Vlora.'

'Not ideas, Mr Berisha. The truth!' Tepe put in forcefully.

Rahman was too enraged to listen. He didn't even notice when Engelushjia re-entered the kitchen carrying a bloodied shirt in her hands.

'She let him fuck her, I know!' Rahman waved a hand dramatically. 'So now she's ruined and—'

'How many times do I have to tell you, Aryan and I did nothing bad!' the girl said, tears running down her swollen cheeks. 'We both just want to stop this stupid—'

'Liar!' Rahman wrenched his arm free of Tepe's loosened grip and launched himself at her. It gave Orhan Tepe the excuse he needed. His blow lifted the Albanian up off his feet and deposited him on the floor in front of the sink. And there he stayed, pathetic and humiliated looking up at Tepe's powerful form.

Engelushjia did not rush dutifully to her father's side; she simply placed the shirt in Tepe's hands and walked out into the hall.

'I'll contact you again when the tests are complete,' Tepe said to the man on the floor. 'You will be obliged to give evidence at Mehmet Vlora's trial.'

Rahman Berisha did not answer and Tepe walked out of the room to join a silent Engelushjia in the hall.

'Do you want me to do anything for you?' he asked her.

'No,' said her mother, Aliya, who was standing in the doorway to one of the bedrooms. 'Just go.'

'I was speaking to your daughter, not you,' the officer responded roughly and turned back to the girl. 'Engelushjia?'

She turned her tear-stained face up towards his and said, very distinctly, 'I want to leave this place.'

'What? Now?'

'Yes,' and then looking her mother straight in the eyes she said, 'Perhaps you could take me to Tahtakale Caddesi.'

'To your lover, Aryan!' her mother spat.

'That'll be enough of that!' Tepe warned Aliya with a rudely upraised finger. 'Are you sure, Engelushjia?'

'I want to go there, Sergeant,' she said, her eyes bright with conviction. 'I want to be safe.'

'You'll never be safe with the Vloras!' her mother sneered. 'They'll kill you. They have to, it's blood.'

'You'd better get a coat,' Tepe said, ignoring the older woman. 'It's still snowing.'

And despite the pain of her bruised face, Engelushjia Berisha smiled.

For once, İkmen had actually managed to telephone Fatma in order to let her know when he was going to be home. This, at the time, had seemed to please her. But when he did finally arrive at his apartment he found that not only Fatma but all of his children were absent. He experienced a moment of panic. Could it be that she had finally lost all patience with his erratic lifestyle and left for good? Or had she, in a rush of overwhelming earthquake panic, decamped to Konya and a more spiritual existence? The first indication that she hadn't in fact deserted him was a large plate of hot dolma with fresh bread set at his place on the kitchen table. The second came from his Uncle Ahmet as İkmen was about to cut into the leathery vine leaves that surrounded Fatma's very own 'secret' dolma mixture.

'Your wife has taken the children over to her sister's for a few hours,' Ahmet said as he smoked his way into the kitchen and sat down.

İkmen put his knife and fork back down on the table and crossed his arms over his chest.

'In the snow?' he said incredulously. 'Has she gone mad? Or have you just driven her out with your bloody stories about death and revenge?'

'She has indeed gone out because of me, yes,' the

old man said with a smile. Then he tipped his head towards İkmen's plate. 'But eat now, Çetin. When you have finished your food, all will be made clear to you.'

Unbeknown to Ahmet, İkmen was, after the day that he had had, a little tired of having to wait for answers to anything, particularly things which, like this, seemed to promise only further aggravation. After all, if Uncle Ahmet could be believed, the man was a self-confessed murderer. Not really, İkmen felt, the sort of person he wanted to talk to when he got home from a frightening and emotional day at work.

'More revelations about my mother, is it then, Uncle?' he asked bitterly, 'you and her and acts of genocide back in the old country, perhaps?'

'Çetin, I can see why you're bitter—'

'I'm a policeman, Uncle Ahmet, and you're a murderer!' İkmen pushed his wife's lovingly prepared food to one side and lit up a cigarette. 'What do you want me to say? Well done? As for my mother—' He stopped suddenly, his eyes widening as he stared towards the kitchen door.

The old man turned to follow his nephew's gaze.

'Oh, Emina,' Ahmet said with a smile and beckoned the elderly, overweight woman forward. 'Please, do come in. This is my nephew, Çetin.'

'Ayşe's younger boy, right?' the woman asked in a voice that was both deep and heavily accented.

'Yes.'

The old man pulled a chair out so that she could join them at the table.

'You have your mother's eyes,' she said as she sat down, staring intently at İkmen. 'I can see witchcraft there.'

'Oh, he has that, Emina!' Ahmet laughed. 'Oh yes! Unlike his brother, may Allah protect him, this one is in touch with forces.'

'Yes, the police force!' İkmen snapped, but he managed to smile at the woman with something approaching warmth. 'I take it you are the Emina Ndrek of whom I have heard?'

She inclined her head, which was wrapped in a headscarf.

'And so tell me, why are you here?'

'I'm here to tell you the truth about your mother. To clear away the poison spread about by that whore Angeliki Vlora.'

'I see.' İkmen leaned back into his chair and sighed. 'And which version of the truth am I to be treated to today? The heart attack, the suicide or the—'

'Your mother was murdered, young man! Ahmet here, in obedience to the laws of *gjakmaria*, killed my brother İsmail, and in response my other brother, Salih, killed your mother Ayşe.'

'Yes, I've heard all of this!' İkmen said with a quick and furious glance at Ahmet. 'What I don't understand is why your "inviolable" laws suddenly allowed the killing of a woman.'

'When a woman is pregnant with a male child it is permissible. The male makes her part of the Tree of Blood.'

In the stunned moment that followed this statement,

none of the occupants of the kitchen so much as drew breath. When sound and movement did eventually come, they were quick and violent.

'No!' İkmen shot up from his chair and started to leave the room.

'Çetin . . .'

'No! No, this is too much now,' he narrowed his eyes to peer venomously at his uncle. 'I don't know why you people have decided to torture me, but . . .'

'We are telling you nothing but the truth, Çetin,' Emina Ndrek said as she rose to go up to him.

İkmen flinched away from her. 'Don't touch me! You're sick. Don't speak to me! Get out of my home!'

'Çetin!'

'My mother would never have harmed a child, especially not her own! It's all lies!'

'My boy, I can, believe me, understand why you cannot accept this,' Ahmet began, 'but . . .'

'Get out of my house!' İkmen screamed, his eyes now streaming with tears. 'Get out!'

Ahmet rose to join Emina, 'Çetin it's true. On the Holy Koran.'

'No!'

'She was carrying a male child,' Emina said sternly, 'a being of bone and of blood.'

'No!' İkmen said as he moved agitatedly back towards the table again. 'You're lying! It's nonsense. Apart from anything else it was 1957. Doctors couldn't determine a baby's sex in those days.'

'Ah, but your mother was different,' Ahmet said, 'she didn't need doctors, your mother was a witch!'

'Oh, for . . . Look . . .' İkmen raked his hand through his hair and then banged his fist down on the table.

'If you will silence the policeman and allow the Bajraktar in you to listen, you will both know and understand,' the old woman responded firmly. 'I have a story to tell you, witch's child, which is both true and,' she looked briefly at Ahmet, 'in the end a thing of goodness for us all.'

Nodding his head in agreement, Ahmet muttered a few religiously inspired words in Albanian.

Emina Ndrek moved back towards the table and sat down. She then crossed her small, crinkled hands in front of her and looked İkmen squarely in the face. 'Are you going to listen, young man?'

The violence of his outburst at an end, İkmen just shrugged as he lit yet another cigarette. Taking this as acquiesence, Emina said, 'Well sit down. You too Ahmet. I can't keep on looking at you both, I don't have the strength.'

The two men, pointedly looking away from each other, did as she asked.

The old woman smiled. 'Good,' she said, and began her story.

'I won't go into how or why Ahmet here killed İsmail. Like all instances of *gjakmaria*, it all goes back far further than any of us can remember. But with İsmail's shirt hung in our windows, your *fis* knew that it was only a question of time before the Ndrek retaliated. Now, as I know you are aware, men are usually the targets in our tradition. And that means all males,' she raised a finger to emphasise her point, 'including boys. The male members of the Bajraktar in this city at that time were your uncle, your cousin Mustafa, your grandfather, who was by that time confined to his bed, you and your brother.'

'But my father was Turkish!'

Emina Ndrek waved a dismissive hand. 'I know, and your father meant nothing, but you and your brother meant a lot. You were the witch's children, still are. The magic was passed down to you through your mother from your grandfather. It was something that my brother Salih would have liked very much to destroy.'

'Your mother let it be known that she was pregnant,' Ahmet interjected sadly, 'and she made contact with Salih.'

'Your father never knew,' Emina said, watching the play of emotion on İkmen's face. 'Ayşe and Salih came to an arrangement – her life and the life of her unborn child for the lives of you and your brother. That afternoon, while your father was at work and you and your brother were at school, Ayşe Bajraktar lay down upon her bed and offered her neck to Salih Ndrek, like a sheep at Kurban Bayram. He slit her throat with one sure and swift movement of his knife.'

İkmen, his face now grey with distress, wiped a stray tear from the corner of his left eye.

Ahmet reached across the table to take his nephew's hand. 'Your father always believed it was suicide – Ayşe even wrote a note – and so did your father's doctor. They both took that belief to their graves.'

'Did you know?' İkmen said, suddenly turning violent

eyes upon the two old people in his kitchen. 'Did you know about this arrangement?'

'No, we didn't,' the old woman said, 'not until it was all over. Salih told us. But when we did learn . . .' She shook her head. 'Even my father, may Allah preserve his soul, was shocked when he heard of it.'

'Ali Ndrek called me to his house,' Ahmet said. 'Of course at first I was suspicious but . . . when I discovered what Ayşe had done . . .' His eyes filled with tears. 'What had been done to her . . .' He closed his eyes against the pain of the memory.

'Salih went back to Albania,' Emina said matter-of-factly, 'where he eventually died. But neither Ahmet nor your grandfather went after him. We all decided – my father, Ahmet, your grandfather – that with the death of your mother and her child, that was enough. It was too terrible. It had to finish.' She lowered her gaze to the floor and then reached across to take Ahmet's free hand. 'And so it did.'

'Neither the Bajraktar nor the Ndrek have been in blood since.' Ahmet looked at Emina with what appeared to İkmen to be affection. 'People like the Vloras occasionally have a go at us, like that pathetic attack upon my Mustafa, but nothing serious. Only old people like us remember these things now – and that includes Angeliki Vlora, of course.'

'That bitch being the only one to speak of it in all these years!' Emina said hotly. Turning to İkmen she added, 'It was an ill-omened day when you were called to her home, Çetin. She used her knowledge of what you should never have known to hurt and confound you.'

İkmen put his face in his hands. 'But if what you say is true,' he said his voice muffled, 'then she was only doing what my mother did for us. She was only protecting her children.'

'Yes she was,' Ahmet replied, 'in her own way.'

For a few moments they all sat in silence, the sound of cars and trams, deadened by the thick snow on Divan Yolu, reaching them faintly from outside. İkmen, wrestling with feelings of disbelief and disgust, tried to digest the horrible details of what he had just been told about his mother. Allah, if she had been pregnant, what kind of hellish sacrifice was that! The poor child, unrealised, unborn and . . . He couldn't think about it! It was so awful he really couldn't think about it!

How could you do it, Mother? he screamed inside the wild tumult that was his brain. How could you do that to your baby? Why . . . But you did it for us, didn't you, Mother? For me and for Halil. For your children, your live babies. You lay down willingly on your bed and you let that man cut your throat without a sound. Vahan Sarkissian was right in a way about your death. It was a kind of suicide. Silently İkmen started to cry.

'Your mother loved you very, very much,' Emina Ndrek said softly, wiping tears from her eyes.

Nodding his head in agreement, Ahmet added, 'You and Halil were what she used to call her jewels – her diamonds and emeralds. If it's any comfort, Çetin, what she did was done joyfully – thinking of all of you safe after she had gone.'

'But I missed her!' İkmen cried and gripped his

uncle's hand until his knuckles showed white. 'I still do!'

'Yes, I know, my boy. I know.'

'What am I going to tell my brother now? What am I going to tell Halil?'

Chapter 23

The drive from Karaköy to Ortaköy had not been easy on the icy roads. Not everybody deigned to drive with due regard to the conditions, with the result that several accidents, plus more than the usual number of near misses, had dogged Suleyman's journey. And there had been his own weariness to contend with too. Despite the horrendous events of the previous day, he had still been obliged to go to that meal with his father and brother – hours of listening to his father bemoaning his ruined finances, going on and on about having to sell a box of jewels nobody cared about any more. The old man had drunk almost half a bottle of lemon vodka – the family weakness. Murad, as Mehmet knew he would, had acceded to all of their father's unreasonable demands. There had been no rapprochement between them, not in any real sense. The old man had lied. Why it had to be like this, Suleyman didn't know. The fact that his father had taken him in so easily was galling in itself. At least the Cohens had been of some comfort to him over the events in the Aya Sofya. Berekiah had pointed out that had Ali Evren lived, he would probably have spent his life in an institution, which was a kind of death. Worse, if Balthazar was to be believed. But whether Zelfa would agree was another matter. It was therefore with some trepidation that he pressed the bell on the door of the Halmans' old wooden house and waited for someone to answer it. Luckily that person was his fiancée's father.

'You'll have to wait until she's off the telephone,' old Dr Halman said as he led Suleyman past Zelfa's office and into the family living room. 'Sit down, Mehmet.' He gestured towards one of the chairs placed around the log fire.

'It's an important call then?' Suleyman asked as he seated himself near the comforting warmth.

'She's talking to Dermot,' the old man replied as he too sat down, 'so yes, it's business.'

'Dermot?' Suleyman responded darkly. 'Who is Dermot?'

Babur Halman heard the jealousy in Suleyman's tone and smiled.

'Dermot is an Irishman,' he said gently. 'Zelfa met him when she was at university. He's a psychologist, or rather a parapsychologist, I should say. Dermot deals with ghosts and "manifestations" on a daily basis. I've often thought he should be one of Zelfa's patients.'

Still not really satisfied, Suleyman said, 'So why is she talking to this man now? I mean, do you know what it's all about?'

'No, I don't, but if you ask Zelfa, I'm sure she'll tell you.' And with that he got up to offer his chair to his daughter who had just appeared, still clutching her portable telephone. 'Mehmet's come to see you, Zelfa,' he said as he briefly touched his daughter's face on his way past. 'I'll go and make tea for us all.'

Suleyman, his manners impeccable as always, had stood up as soon as Zelfa entered the room and he waited for her to take a seat before resuming his own. She seemed distracted, to say the least, but he nevertheless determinedly pushed forward with his own agenda. After all, he was the man and that was what men did.

'I know you must still be tired,' he said with a smile, 'but we didn't really get a chance to talk yesterday.'

'No.' She leaned over towards him and kissed his lips lightly. 'I heard you're on leave. I'm sorry.'

Though the kiss was reassuring, he couldn't help noticing that her face seemed strained.

'Darling, are you quite well?' He took one of her cold hands in his. 'I mean, I know yesterday must have been awful for you and I was not very . . . I was upset and frightened, mortified . . .'

Zelfa smiled and squeezed his fingers. 'Ali Evren was far sicker than I thought,' she said gravely. 'I made a fatal error of judgement and I failed to consider possibilities that went beyond the derisory to explain his perceptions. I've just been speaking to an old friend about it.'

'Dermot?'

'Oh, Dad told you. Yes.' She sighed. 'Dermot's a parapsychologist. He works with people who claim to see ghosts, experience poltergeist activity and think they can predict the future – stuff like that. Some people think his work is very valuable and cutting edge while others feel he's just a nutter.' She shrugged. 'I don't know what he is myself, except that he's very knowledgeable. I contacted him about Felicity Evren.'

Suleyman took his cigarettes out of his pocket and offered the packet to Zelfa.

'Why did you ask him about her? I thought we were talking about Ali?' he said, puzzled.

Zelfa took a cigarette and waited for Suleyman to light both their smokes.

'Because of her claim that she cannot see herself in mirrors. On the face of it, it seems ridiculous, a delusion.'

'Yes.'

'To the average man and woman, yes. But Dermot isn't average and I knew that if anyone could shed some light on it, it would be him. After all, Felicity insisted she couldn't see herself in mirrors even though her life was in the balance, Mehmet.'

'Yes, but if Dermot is, by your own admission, just a little mad, I don't see—'

'It's called negative autoscopy, apparently,' she said, ignoring his objections. 'Unlike positive autoscopy, which involves the creation of images in the subject's field of vision, the negative variety involves the removal or blanking out of ordinary phenomena. Although there are many different explanations for this, basically images are created in line with a person's needs – wish fulfilment, sexual desire, grief. Positive autoscopy therefore equals ghosts. The negative variety may also emanate from desire or wish fulfilment, but this time the urge involves the need for the removal of something unwanted.'

'Yes, but—'

'Unprompted, Dermot cited the old vampire myth.

Modern thinking on the subject revolves around the idea that vampires were actually people suffering from a condition called porphyria. This disease involves victims becoming light sensitive, the skin becomes discoloured and there is considerable mental confusion. It isn't difficult to deduce from this that these so-called vampires didn't see themselves in mirrors because, being unaccountably disfigured, they didn't want to. In other words, negative autoscopy.'

Suleyman frowned. 'So . . . do you, or does Dermot, think that Felicity has porphyria?'

'Oh, no,' she said with a dismissive wave of her cigarette. 'At least, not as far as I know. No, Felicity has had gross physical defects from birth. No, what I'm saying is that the process is the same. She didn't want to be ugly – who does? When İkmen questioned her, she was quite genuine when she described herself as a beautiful woman, because that was what she wanted to be, that was what I understand her father told her she was and if she couldn't see herself she could be anything she damned well wanted to be!'

'Well, yes, but isn't this all a bit speculative?'

'To her brother, of course, it all made perfect sense. He'd read about vampires, seen films, and he knew they couldn't see themselves, so when Felicity said that she couldn't see herself either, he made what was to him a logical deduction. It also fell in with his desires. His mother's suicide bred in him a morbid fear of death and here was his sister, suddenly immortal. He wanted some of that. And so he emulated the morbid youth around him in the UK – goth kids with black hair, anorexic, obsessed with gravestones. His father was too busy with his businesses—'

The telephone at her side began to ring, interrupting her. She turned away to answer it. Suleyman was relieved that she had stopped talking to him for a while. He found it professionally and also personally disturbing to have her working so closely with people involved in 'his' crimes. Of course she had been involved before – Zelfa advised the police as part of her job. But this was the first time one of her patients had ever featured in a murder investigation. And, if nothing else, what she had just said threw into very sharp relief the fact that she and he had very different approaches to crime. For her, Felicity Evren and her now deceased family were a fascinating human source of speculative theory. For himself and for İkmen the main question revolved around whether Ali or his sister or their father had committed one or more of what was becoming quite a catalogue of murders. The boy had admitted that he had killed Rifat and even drunk his blood, and the woman appeared to be a possible for her father's death. Hard evidence was what was needed, of course, and hopefully they would find it in the days to come. Zelfa and İkmen, he knew, had agreed to meet after İkmen had interviewed Felicity.

He was suddenly distracted from his thoughts by the look on Zelfa's face. She had gone quite ashen. As she put down the telephone, Suleyman leaned forward and took hold of her shoulders.

'What is it, Zelfa? What's wrong?'

'That was Latife Aksu,' she said, 'my gynaecologist.

I had some tests done and, well, she wants to see me.'
She sighed. 'I know what she's going to say, of course,
about the menopause.'

'But Zelfa, you've been talking about that for a year
to my knowledge.'

'Yes, but I've never had it confirmed, have I, Mehmet!'
she cried. Abruptly she rose to her feet, raking her tan-
gled hair with her fingers. 'I know I've talked about it,
driven you mad with it, but . . . but to have it confirmed
– it's like the end of my being a real woman, and just
before my wedding . . .'

As her father entered the room carrying a copper tray
with tea glasses on it, Zelfa put her head in her hands
and burst into tears.

Both men moved quickly towards her.

Things were oddly quiet in the İkmens' kitchen that
morning. Çetin, who did at least usually have a hot
drink with the rest of the family, had risen from his bed
slightly later than normal. As a consequence, by the time
he appeared, only Fatma was left in the apartment. And
when he entered the kitchen, red-eyed and dishevelled,
she stopped her maniacal cleaning of the oven and
turned the heat up on the samovar. Ahmet had told her
what she now knew Çetin knew before she'd gone to her
sister's. She felt desperately sorry for him, something
she expressed by making him tea.

'What time did Uncle Ahmet leave in the end?' she
asked as she took a clean tulip glass off the draining
board and placed it on the table.

İkmen shrugged. 'I don't know. About midnight.'

'Did he go back with that Emina woman?'

'He took her home to Üsküdar and then he said he was going to go on to Samsun's place.' He smiled briefly. 'As I understand it, Abdurrahman appeared at the hospital yesterday, full of excuses and protestations of undying love.'

Resisting the temptation to make some acid comment about that, Fatma simply said, 'Oh.'

'The story is that his mother in Bursa was taken ill very suddenly. Quite why that would necessitate his switching his mobile telephone off and not even leaving Samsun a note, I don't know. Personally I think he's hiding something from her. But according to Ahmet, it seemed to satisfy Samsun – after, of course, she'd slapped Abdurrahman around for a bit. Such wild, excessive behaviour . . .'

Fatma poured strong dark tea from the pot on top of the samovar into the glass and placed it in front of her husband. Then she brought him a clean ashtray and sat down opposite him.

'So, what are you going to do about your brother, Çetin?' she said as she watched him light up a cigarette and then take a sip of tea.

'I've got to interview Felicity Evren this morning. Then I'm going to consult Zelfa Halman about her. After that I'll probably speak to Zelfa about Halil.'

'What about Arto?' Fatma asked. 'I mean, you started all this business with him, didn't you? You asked him to look at his father's records.'

'I'll speak to Zelfa first,' İkmen said. 'I mean, if I decide not to tell Halil the truth about Mother, it's probably best that Arto doesn't know either. You never know how people are going to react to things, do you? Arto and Krikor worshipped their father and if they knew that he was even unwittingly connected to what was a murder . . .'

'But Vahan Sarkissian was just as much a pawn in what seems to me some hellish Albanian game as you, your father and indeed the police who came to the scene.' Fatma was becoming agitated. 'I would kill them all if I could, you know, Çetin!'

'Fatma—'

'Depriving children of their mother! Bringing misery to my hearth with their murders and their infidel magic and . . . Vampires! Evil, blood-addicted . . .' Words failed her. She rose to her feet and took her disgust and anger out on the oven in a renewed onslaught of cleaning.

When she had recovered sufficiently to speak rationally, she raised her head from the oven door and asked, 'Who was that on the telephone this morning?'

'It was Mehmet. I asked him to call me. He was so upset yesterday, I wanted to know that he was all right.'

'And was he?'

'He's not too happy, but he talked more about the meal he had with his father and brother last night.' İkmen shook his head. 'Just between ourselves, Fatma, his father is in financial difficulty again. Mehmet's brother and his little girl are going to move back with his parents to help the old prince pay his bills.'

Fatma shrugged. 'I don't know why they didn't

go back when Murad's wife died,' she said a trifle sanctimoniously. 'Most of us have to start out with our parents anyway.'

'Yes. But for people like them it's different. The old man is having to sell yet more of his inheritance. His house went years ago, then many of their heirlooms. Now he's going to have to sell the jewellery that once belonged to his mother.'

'Well, at least he has jewellery to sell,' Fatma said and plunged her head back into the oven again.

'He wants Mehmet and his brother to choose a few pieces they might like to hold on to. His wife is furious.'

'Oh, is she?' Fatma responded acidly. 'If you ask me, Çetin, it's a judgement on that woman, all this trouble. Always thinking of herself and her own position! She should have given more attention to her children. Jewels!' she spat contemptuously. 'She should try having to worry about where the next meal is coming from like the rest of us!'

In a tone that was surprisingly mild for him, İkmen said, 'It's practical considerations like that that are at the bottom of all this actually, Fatma. With the economy in chaos, no one is safe. The lire just keeps on going down and down.'

'Well then, as I said before, Çetin, they are fortunate to have diamonds and emeralds to sell. As I'm sure even you have noticed, we haven't had meat in this house for over a month – and that's with the contributions from our older children.'

'Yes, I know.'

Troubled by what seemed to be an uncharacteristic mildness bordering on hopelessness in her husband's manner, Fatma wiped her hands on a cloth and walked over to him.

'Not that I blame you at all,' she said, placing her hands on his shoulders. 'You've always worked so hard. All that money from the sale of your father's house went to educate the children.'

'I just want to get them all through now,' he said. He took hold of one her hands and patted it. 'It's important. Like my father always said, education is the only light that exists in our human darkness, without it we are just animals.'

'Çetin . . .'

'I know you disagree,' he said. 'I know that you see religion as a guiding force for good too. But take the Albanians, and I include my mother in this, they live in absolute, illiterate ignorance. It's not their fault, their country has been ruined by corruption. But knowing no better, they continually turn to the past to make sense of their lives. And however we might like to romanticise it, the past was dirty and brutal and stupid. We must move on, we must educate and enlighten. If nothing else, we must teach our children not to hate.'

Fatma kissed the top of her husband's head before sitting down opposite him again. 'Well,' she said, 'since the, you know, the movement in the, er . . .'

'Earthquake?' he ventured, knowing how she nervously hedged around this subject.

'Yes, since that, this country and the Greeks have spoken together more than ever before.'

'Yes, it's good. The Greeks were there for us – their rescue teams didn't stop.'

'And we for them when they had their – their troubles too,' Fatma said, alluding to the smaller if no less devastating earthquake that had hit Athens just after the İstanbul conflagration.

'Yes.'

It had been a hard eighteen months for them but earthquakes and financial insecurity were ills that were common to everyone. The awful truth about İkmen's mother was another matter. That was personally wounding and, like the image of Ali Evren's head exploding in a cascade of blood, the pain of it would take a very long time to go, İkmen knew. And so, rather than sit and brood, he got his coat and made his way towards the police station. Felicity Evren would be there now.

Latife Aksu had been consulting and lecturing at the Cerrahpaşa Faculty of Medicine for most of her working life. And although she was aware that she didn't know everything there was to know about gynaecology, she was not accustomed to having her diagnoses questioned – particularly not when it concerned such a straightforward condition.

'Well, of course I'm sure, Zelfa!' she said as she looked across at what was now a very frightened-looking psychiatrist sitting opposite her.

'But I didn't know you were testing for—'

'I did it originally to rule it out!' Latife responded tartly. She was a blunt, middle-aged woman and Zelfa was trying her patience.

'But are you absolutely one hundred per cent sure?'

'Zelfa, you're pregnant,' she said baldly. 'You're also, and this is common as I know you know, mildly anaemic so I want you to take iron supplements.'

'But what am I going to do, Latife?' Zelfa said as she riffled in her handbag for her cigarettes.

'Well, you'll have to stop smoking for a start.'

Zelfa, chastised, put her bag down and twisted her hands nervously in her lap.

'As to what you'll do in general,' the gynaecologist continued, 'that's up to you. Abortion is of course an option, but if you do decide to go ahead I will have to book you in for a scan and you will have to have an amniocentesis. At your age there is a higher risk of Down's syndrome.'

'Oh, Christ!' Zelfa exclaimed in far more comfortable English.

Dr Aksu picked up her pen and pulled Zelfa's file closer. 'Any idea when you might have conceived?'

Zelfa didn't. But when she thought about it, the signs had been there for a while – the weight gain, the sickness sometimes accompanied by dizziness. More to the point, she hadn't had a period for two months. She told Latife this and the gynaecologist muttered as she wrote it down.

'But what about my practice?' Zelfa wailed as wave after wave of fears and difficulties broke across her mind. 'And my wedding! Oh, God!'

Latife Aksu put down her pen and looked at Zelfa sternly. 'You're pregnant, Zelfa, it's what women do! You're not ill! As far as I can judge, you'll be perfectly capable of listening to the psychotic ramblings of your patients for many months to come. As for your wedding,' she shrugged, 'I would say it's fortuitous that you already have it in prospect, wouldn't you?'

'But what will Mehmet think? I mean . . .'

'Mehmet, like so many of our menfolk, will have to accept the results of his lustful actions.'

Latife Aksu was known as a vociferous opponent of men and all their works. When she was a young woman she had always said that she would never marry a Turkish man because of their need, as she saw it, to dominate their women. But as the years had passed and Latife had seen more and more women of all nationalities pass through her surgery, not to mention the women's refuge in Harbiye where, once a week, she gave her time for free, she had extended this view to all men. Even the extremely handsome young lover of her now weeping patient left her cold.

But she managed a smile as she passed a box of tissues across to Zelfa. 'I would recommend that you tell him as soon as possible,' she said, not without kindness. 'Whatever you think his reaction may be.'

'Oh, I think he'll be pleased,' Zelfa said as she wiped mascara from her eyes. 'I mean, I think I'm more shocked than actually upset, to be honest. I didn't think I'd ever have a child. Not now.'

'You'll need some time to adjust, yes.'

'Yes.'

Exactly what she was going to say to Mehmet, Zelfa didn't know. She couldn't imagine his reaction either. She just hoped that the sneaking suspicion she had always had about him, that he actually wanted a child, was correct. After all, he adored his little niece. But then, her thoughts as ever racing ahead, her mind threw up the image of Mehmet's parents or, more precisely, the image she had gained of them from short glimpses and from Mehmet himself. On the way over to the Cerrahpaşa he had told her he'd informed his father about their impending marriage – news that the elderly man had apparently taken well. That 'Prince' Muhammed's volatile wife was probably at this very moment planning how she might bribe her prospective daughter-in-law to disappear was something that made Zelfa smile and yet feel bleak at the same time.

As she calmed down and returned to a rather more 'professional' version of herself, her mind took refuge in more immediate concerns. She was due to meet İkmen to discuss Felicity Evren. At this meeting he would, in light of his interview with the woman, ask her many questions. And even for a practitioner with over twenty years' experience, she suspected that some of his questions were not going to be easy to answer. So this was not a time to be distracted by other issues, such as worrying about Mehmet and his feelings. And when she expressed these thoughts to Latife, the gynaecologist agreed.

'Get your consultation over and then tell him afterwards,' she said as she saw Zelfa to the door.

'Right.'

'But don't delay after that time,' Latife added sternly. 'You've made a plan, so stick to it.'

Zelfa smiled before exchanging kisses with Latife and leaving her office.

Out in the waiting area, Mehmet Suleyman stood up and smiled as she approached.

'So?' he asked.

'It's nothing,' she said, forcing a smile. 'It's not what I thought and I'm fine.'

'Good.'

She slipped her arm through his and they made their way towards the exit.

Chapter 24

The police decided to conduct Felicity's interview in English. That way, it was felt, the possibility of misunderstandings would be greatly reduced. This meant İkmen had to recruit Çöktin to join him in the interview, as opposed to Tepe whose English was poor.

Although obviously medicated, Felicity Evren looked remarkably well given her recent horrific ordeal and when İkmen ushered her lawyer, Adnan Öz, into her presence, she even managed a smile.

The formalities complete, İkmen began.

'I'd like you to tell me, Miss Evren,' he said, 'about the night of Rifat Berisha's death.'

'I—'

'You do not have to answer anything you do not want to,' Adnan Öz reminded his client with a smile.

Felicity smiled back. 'That's all right,' she said. 'I'm OK with it.'

Öz shrugged.

'Well, Miss Evren?' İkmen asked.

'Rifat came to ask my father for some money. Someone had told him that the operation he'd had in London was illegal under British law. In fact, because no money changed hands, that wasn't so, but . . . Anyway, Rifat

391

and Father argued. David, my brother, and I were upstairs when we heard Father shouting.'

'So you went to see what was happening?'

'Yes. And as soon as I entered the room Rifat, smiling at me like he always did, handed me this little parcel. He said he'd come to bring a present for me and even though I knew that the present couldn't possibly be what he and Father were arguing about, I opened it.'

'And what did it contain?' Çöktin asked, though he thought he knew the answer.

Felicity sighed. 'One of those cheap coloured glass perfume bottles. They're made in Egypt. To be honest, if Father hadn't started raving on about why Rifat was really there I wouldn't have been bothered about the present. After all, I knew Rifat was very hard up.'

'Then what happened?' asked İkmen.

'I asked Rifat whether Father was telling the truth. I could tell by his face that he was. Then with Father going on and on about how Rifat was a gold-digger and how he only wanted me for my money, I lost my temper. It was so insulting. And I couldn't understand why Rifat was doing it – he should have been grateful to have someone like me. But I could see in his eyes that he wasn't. Father was right.' She swallowed hard. 'I smashed the bottle into his face and then I started crying. Rifat went wild, started swearing, saying all sorts of things, calling me disgusting, awful names.'

'What was your father's reaction to this?'

'He screamed at Rifat, who just laughed at him. Rifat pulled out a knife, which was very scary. Then after he'd told us how he really felt about us all, which seemed to go on for ever, he left. I cried, I wanted him to come back . . . Father and David followed him to the car. I didn't actually see what happened. My father came back into the living room about ten minutes later.'

'Why did he do that, Miss Evren?' Çöktin asked.

'To get something to mop up Rifat's blood.' It was said in a voice that was only a little above a whisper.

'So Rifat had been killed.'

'My father said that Rifat had tried to stab him,' she looked up, weary now, into İkmen's eyes, 'but David somehow got the knife from Rifat and then he cut his throat. Father said there was no struggle – it was too quick – one deep cut, then David sawing at his neck . . . Father was scared then . . .' She wet her dry lips with her tongue. 'I gave my father the curtains I'd bought earlier in the day – for the blood – and then I followed him out to Rifat's car. My brother had his . . . his mouth up to Rifat's throat.'

And then she started crying. They let her be, smoking a cigarette each until she had composed herself once again. Then, after a short consultation with her lawyer, Felicity resumed her story.

'Father wrapped Rifat's body up in the curtains on his own. He sent me back inside with David – told me to get him cleaned up. Father was furious. He said that David was an animal. He spent days afterwards screaming about all the money he'd spent on psychiatrists for David and it had all been a waste. David became very frightened. He told me he had been compelled to drink Rifat's blood. But Father didn't understand.'

'What about Rifat?' İkmen asked, his brow furrowing

into a frown. 'Didn't your father have any feelings about him?'

Felicity smiled now through her tears. 'My father was a bad man, Inspector İkmen. Killing was not unknown to him. The police back home must have been aware of his activities . . . My mother certainly was. She killed herself.' She cleared her throat. 'The only thing that worried my father was how we were going to dispose of Rifat's body. He reasoned that if he just flung it into a gutter somewhere near where Rifat lived, the police would assume that he had been slaughtered in one of those blood feuds Albanians have. I told him that Rifat lived in Eminönü, though I didn't know exactly where.'

'So did your father have some connections with Albanian people, Miss Evren?' Çöktin asked.

'My father would deal with anyone provided they were dishonest, Sergeant,' Felicity replied, 'and some of his contacts were Albanian, yes. False passports, stolen antiques, bodily organs, a little contract killing – my father was a man of many talents. He wore gloves to dispose of Rifat's body, I had to put plastic bags on the seats of the car. Then he destroyed all the clothes he was wearing that night. He was a clever, cautious man. Hardly surprising my brother became what he was, is it?'

'So he disposed of Rifat's body . . .'

'He left it some hours, until maybe three in the morning. Father reasoned there'd be little traffic on the roads by then. And anyway, a lot of people, those that remember the curfews, still don't wander about in the early hours, do they? It was foggy . . . He took Rifat to Eminönü and then dumped the car in Ortaköy. He was going to leave it in Eminönü, but he thought he saw people about and so he just drove on until he found a quiet place.'

'How did he get back from Ortaköy to Bebek?'

'I went and picked him up.'

İkmen scowled. 'I believe you told me you couldn't drive, Miss Evren.'

'I lied, Inspector,' she answered simply.

'I see. Did you also lie about what you felt for Rifat? I mean, you seem to have done all of this with remarkable ease. Did you just use him as an organ donor?'

'No!' Her face contorted with emotion. 'I loved him! I was distraught, it shouldn't have happened. David just reacted! He always protected me . . .'

İkmen looked down at the file in front of him and spent a few seconds perusing what was written there. When he spoke again, he was aware that she was watching him with interest.

'So what about all this business with vampires?' he asked. 'Tell me about that.'

'My brother was obsessed with them, wanted to be one.' She spoke with her face turned away from him. She obviously didn't want to talk about this.

All the more reason to make her do so.

'Why?' İkmen asked.

'What?'

'Why was your brother obsessed by the idea of the vampire?'

Felicity swallowed hard. 'It was a process,' she said, 'and it began with me.'

'What do you mean?'

'When I was a child, the way I look, whatever that may be, didn't worry me.' She leaned forward across the table, effectively cutting her lawyer out of the conversation. Mr Öz, in reaction, cleared his throat, but she ignored him. 'My mother and father were always – kind. Then two things happened. After years of no success, my mother became pregnant. Sadly she lost the baby and as a consequence her depression deepened. I stayed in more in order to care for her – Father was always out on business. And anyway I wanted to stay in by that time. I was eighteen and I'd grown tired of being pointed at, laughed at.' She took a deep breath. 'As you can imagine, I'd never liked looking at myself in mirrors, but as time passed that seemed to be getting more difficult anyway. My image was softer somehow, as if I was fading out, diluting. I know it sounds fantastic, but that is the way that it was. By the time David was born eighteen months later, I'd completely disappeared. All I could see when I looked into the glass was whatever was behind me. Not that I was unhappy about it. Had I continued to look every day at the face from hell, I don't think I would have been able to cope. I certainly wouldn't have had the gall to approach men like Rifat, to create a perfect face and body in my head . . . It gave me confidence. And my parents, without really understanding, played along.'

'I must admit that when you first came to see me, your confidence was – unusual,' İkmen observed.

She smiled. 'And you, like most people here, were very kind,' she said. 'But unfortunately my disability, or whatever you wish to call it, had a disastrous effect upon my brother. I am twenty years older than David and so, particularly when he was very little, I took care of him. The only time Father was in was when he had business associates over for dinner or when he wanted to hide either an illegal immigrant or a large bag of something I still don't want to think about in the garden. Mother was depressed and made twelve attempts on her life before she finally succeeded three years ago. David and I only had each other and we told each other everything. I think he must have been ten when I told him about this,' she said, pointing to her face.

'And what was David's reaction?'

'Oh, he understood completely,' she said, her eyes now drifting into a glassy stare. 'Mum, David and I had watched enough horror films together to know what it meant – Mum liked things like that. But it was our secret, David's and mine. Though nothing much happened until my mother died. Until then it was all just a joke between us – Felicity the vampire, can't see her face in mirrors, stays up all night – as of course people do who never go out, and I had kidney problems by then.'

'What changed when your mother died?'

'We had to go and see her – her body. David freaked.'

İkmen frowned. 'Pardon?'

'It frightened him, Inspector. Mum looked different, scary – dead bodies always do – things drop – I'm sure you know. He was terrified, couldn't sleep. He thought that if he did sleep he might stop breathing. He didn't want to die. He kept on and on saying how lucky I was that it wasn't going to happen to me. Not that I told him I was immortal, but then I didn't tell him I wasn't either. I said that he could be like me if he wanted. It seemed quite harmless, the vampire thing. Lots of kids in Britain are into it. They only wear black, don't eat very much, hang around graveyards. Usually they grow out of it.'

'But your brother didn't grow out of it, did he, Miss Evren?'

She looked down now, as if she was ashamed of what she had done, or perhaps in this case not done. 'No,' she said, 'he didn't. And then when my father wanted to get closer to his suppliers, to keep an eye on them, we moved here. Father said you lot were easier to bribe than the British police.' She laughed, bitterly.

'And was that so, Miss Evren?' Çöktin asked. 'Did your father bribe İstanbul policemen?'

She shrugged. 'I don't know. Certainly not you lot. Anyway, David, who Father now called Ali, his second name, stopped eating almost completely. The vampire thing still carried on, but here he was entirely alone, except for me. I humoured him, I admit, but he got worse – wouldn't eat at all. Father sent him to that psychiatrist. I think she just thought it was a phase, you know. But then suddenly he killed Rifat and there was that blood drinking . . .' She paused, mentally turning away from this image of such extreme disorder. 'You know at home we say that when people get what has been coming to them for a long while, their birds come home to roost. When David killed Rifat, that is what happened to me.'

'But in the Aya Sofya, Dr Halman asked you to tell your brother the truth about the mirror phenomenon and you said you really don't see yourself. People facing death rarely lie.'

'No. And I've explained about that, Inspector. I should never have told my brother. It caused all this and . . . He was going to kill me too, as you know.'

'When he found that the sight of crosses did not turn you to dust.' Ikmen smiled. 'I have seen the films too, I confess.'

'Yes,' she replied simply, 'although what I don't understand is why Dr Halman told David to take me to the museum. He tested me and, of course, I failed. I am mortal, of course I am. If I'd known that was what he wanted to do, I would never have gone with him. Dr Halman shouldn't have done that. He was so full of hate, up there in the gallery. I had to keep on and on talking just to stay alive.' She broke down again and this time Ikmen said they should all take a break. He sent Çöktin out to get tea.

While they waited for the Kurd to return, Ikmen observed Felicity Evren closely. Despite her tears, this interview had been very easy. She had described unspeakable events with great composure. True, the tranquillisers the doctor had given her would have helped. But, as Ikmen knew, they were not yet at the heart of the matter, from Felicity's point of view. The death of her father had not yet been addressed and also there was something else, something that Zelfa had intimated to him back at the museum, something he thought he may have observed himself . . .

He looked at the plump, satisfied face of her lawyer. Adnan Öz would, he knew, make much of Zelfa
Halman's seeming miscalculation of her patient's state
of mind. İkmen himself had, after all, heard Ali Evren
cite the doctor as a prime mover in his disordered
actions. Dr Halman had encouraged him to test his
hypothesis and, fearful that his father would soon have
him incarcerated, he had done just that. An attempt to
speed up his 'transformation', İkmen imagined. Not that
he was sure about any of this weird stuff. How a person
could fail to see their own reflection in a mirror was
beyond him anyway. It was fantasy, it had to be!
Deep down Felicity Evren did have a true perception
of herself, didn't she? She seemed to have when she
was talking just now. Or was the knowledge recent?
Had something happened to make her see herself as
she really was? He thought back to the room where
İlhan Evren had died and bit his bottom lip.

When Çöktin returned with the tea, they resumed.
İkmen went straight to the point.

'About your father, Miss Evren,' he said. 'In the
museum you appeared to know about his death. I would
like you to tell us about this.'

And for the first time, she turned to her lawyer. He
smiled at her and began to talk.

'Miss Evren discovered the dead body of her father
yesterday morning,' he said.

'Why didn't you report it to us?' İkmen asked,
addressing Felicity.

'Miss Evren was traumatised. It is not every day that
one finds the body of a close relative—'

'And yet you were not so traumatised that it prevented you from going out with your brother.'

This time Felicity answered. 'David was very agitated. Both he and I had argued with my father the previous evening.'

'What about?'

'Well, about what had happened with Rifat, of course!' she cried. 'My father was scared! You had been round and he wanted to find a way for us to get out of the situation we were in. He suggested to me that we use David's instability to our advantage.'

'Have him take the blame for the whole thing? Have him hospitalised?'

'Yes.'

'But you disagreed.'

'Yes!'

'Because you loved your brother?'

'Yes.'

İkmen leaned across the table towards her. 'And in what way exactly did you love young David, Miss Evren?'

'Inspector İkmen,' Adnan Öz interrupted. 'Just what—'

İkmen held up a hand to silence the lawyer. 'Yesterday, on the Aya Sofya gallery, you told your brother you had told your father about your part in your brother's condition and that he had not liked what he had heard.'

'I told him about the mirror, it was our secret, David's and mine . . .'

'Did you also tell your father that you had been sleeping with your brother? You were being pleasured by him when Rifat arrived, were you not?'

Adnan Öz rose from his seat. 'Inspector İkmen!'

'Well, were you, Miss Evren?' İkmen continued. 'Or did your brother's comments that Rifat had "taken what was his", that you had "cheated on him with the Albanian" refer to something else?'

Felicity's eyes told him the truth. Unmoving, they filled with a slow but intense hatred that Çöktin for one found he had to look away from.

Öz, still agitated, bent down towards his client and said, 'You do not have to answer this.'

'You see, Miss Evren,' İkmen said, resolutely facing her hatred, 'I have this theory that however complicated or deluded a person's reason for killing might appear to be, basically all murder stems from love or envy or fear. And although I accept that your brother was suffering from some type of complicated, deluded condition, I also believe that you and he shared a fantasy.'

'Who else would have loved me? I ached to be loved!' She began to cry. 'I wanted men like Rifat . . .'

'So you played little games. You were vampires. You were lovers. You were going to live for ever.' İkmen looked at her sadly. 'But he was growing up, Miss Evren, becoming a man. And like a man he did not want to share his lover.'

'But I never thought he would ever feel that way about me! I thought we could just carry on as always . . . I am hideous . . .'

'Yes,' İkmen said, 'you can see yourself in mirrors now, can't you? Perhaps you've always been able to.'

She looked up at him, her misshapen nose dribbling. 'I had to think for a while about why only one thing, apart from your father of course, was damaged in that office,' İkmen said. 'In the event both you, up on the gallery, and Dr Halman gave me my answer.'

'My father made me look at it! He held me down in a chair until it came,' Felicity Evren screamed. 'I told him and he laughed and then he made me look at it! "How," he said, "can you not see that? How could anyone love that?" And then I started to see . . .'

'So up in the gallery when Dr Halman asked you to tell the truth about what you saw in the mirror, you were lying again, weren't you? "I have no words to describe myself" – something like that was what you said,' İkmen frowned, 'but you were lying. You were, even in the face of death, perpetuating the game you just couldn't let go of. Because it was only the game, nothing else, that held you to your brother, your lover.'

'I . . .'

Adnan Öz cleared his throat. 'Inspector İkmen,' he said, 'I should like to have some time alone with my client.'

But İkmen was so nearly there. He continued to bear down on her.

'Your father wanted to put your brother in an institution and thereby remove sex from your life. You knew that no one else would love you. Rifat hadn't – didn't want to!'

Through her tears she cried, 'I wanted Father to take responsibility for Rifat's death! He disposed of him! He was finished with him! He never loved anybody he couldn't buy!'

'And so you killed him,' İkmen said. 'You smashed

your own image from that mirror and then you killed your father!'

'Inspector İkmen!'

'You knew he had enemies. You knew how to remove forensic evidence from a scene – you told me so.' He paused to take a large steadying breath and then said, 'And you knew you could create a story that just might convince me that your father had murdered Rifat. After all, dead people do not speak, do they, Miss Evren? But you made two miscalculations.'

Felicity looked up at him, all her energies focused on the hatred in her eyes.

'You didn't think I would piece together the true nature of your relationship with your brother – perhaps you felt that my sympathy for a person like you would allow me to overlook it. Wrong. And secondly, I don't think you had any idea just how insane your brother was.'

'He tried to kill me.' It was said with a calmness that seemed to suggest that even now she didn't really understand it.

'Yes, he did,' İkmen said, 'and now I am going to charge you, Miss Evren, for the murder of your father.'

Suddenly and without warning, everything closed down. Felicity Evren allowed the silence inside her to crash into the room. It still took the three men with her several minutes to work out just what had happened. And when it did become apparent, Adnan Öz was on his mobile to her doctor within seconds.

*   *   *

Mehmet and Mehti Vlora were allowed five minutes to see their mother before they were put into the transport designated to take them to Bayrampaşa prison.

'I thought the Turks burnt that place to the ground last year,' Angeliki said when her boys told her where they were going. 'Prisoners were making bombs and other weapons, so I remember hearing.'

'Well,' Mehmet said as he stole a quick, sly glance at the guard over by the door, 'I won't be doing that, Mother. Mehti and I will be doing better things than that.' He smiled. 'Maybe we'll keep pigeons.'

'Like "real" Turks,' his mother responded ironically. 'How proud I shall be!' Then turning to Mehti she said, 'If Allah and the Turks are merciful, at least you will not be there for long.'

Mehti bowed his head. 'No, Mother.'

'That they ever even entertained the idea that you were capable of murder is beyond me,' she added with a shrug, 'You're nothing, you always were.'

'I did it to try and get you and Mehmet out of here. I—'

'Oh, save your breath!' She put one thin arm round Mehmet's waist and squeezed him affectionately. 'You did it to try and impress us. You, on the other hand,' she said, looking up into Mehmet's face, 'you will serve a long sentence. Unless of course the one who was once your brother can be spoken to before your trial.'

He smiled. 'And will our *fis* do that for us, Mother?'

'I have no idea yet when I will be getting out of here,' she said. She saw the guard eyeing the three of them. 'But if I am released or I manage to get word out to other interested *fis*, you can be assured that it will be done, my son.'

'It will be a final solution, won't it, Mother?' Mehmet said as he bent down to kiss her cold, wrinkled cheeks.

'Oh, yes.' She looked over his shoulder at Mehti, who seemed close to tears. 'Not even Aryan is clever enough to evade the laws of Lek Dukagjini.'

There was a rattle of keys from outside the door. When it opened, the Vloras were greeted by the sight of a straightfaced Orhan Tepe surrounded by a squad of armed guards.

'Time to go now, boys,' he said as Mehti's tears began to flow.

The armed men moved into the cell and ushered the manacled Albanians towards the door.

Angeliki, crying herself now but in a wild, furious way, shouted, 'You treat my boys right, do you hear me! If you hurt them I'll kill every one of you with my own hands! Sons of donkeys!'

But no one, not even her own sons, responded to her words and when the cell had been cleared, Tepe shut the door and locked it without comment.

Alone now, Angeliki sank down to the floor, which she beat violently with her fists. By some sort of magic, probably instigated by that son of the Bajraktar witch, Ayşe, her Aryan had turned against the *fis* and was going to make sure that her Mehmet never walked in freedom again. Silently she cursed both the policeman and his *fis* – something she had never done before for fear that the arcane and powerful Bajraktar would come and pull both her life and her soul down into hell. But that didn't matter now. Angeliki knew that although she could send word via friends that Aryan should be dealt with in the traditional manner, she could not help her own situation. She had spoken the truth about Ayşe Bajraktar and now that woman's son was going to make her pay with her liberty.

Her actual offence, possession of cocaine, didn't even enter Angeliki's mind. As far as she was concerned, İkmen was incarcerating her as part of a personal statement of hatred. She cursed both him and his children at the very top of her voice.

They met, as arranged, in Zelfa's office, ostensibly because this was where she kept her records, though it was also accessible to everyone concerned, including policemen who were 'on leave'.

'Ali Evren was what we back home would call a goth, a morbid kid who finds death glamorous, or at least that was what I thought he was,' Zelfa said as she looked down at the pages of notes she had written about him. 'I was actually treating him for anorexia, which was not yet very serious, but it all revolved around issues he had with his mother's death and with mortality in general. Quite common in the bereaved. But,' she looked up at İkmen, 'in light of what you've just told me, obviously I didn't have the full picture, did I?'

'No, but then if he didn't want to tell you, how could you?' İkmen replied. 'According to his sister, Ali turned to the idea of being a vampire as a way of sidestepping, if you like, his own mortality. Felicity encouraged him – it was a way of taking the sting out of his mother's death. Apparently he was panting with anxiety about being around religious artefacts when he was in the museum, but I don't remember that myself.'

Zelfa shrugged. 'He must have been completely in the grip of the fantasy in order to do what he did.'

'Quite how the whole sex thing began or why Felicity persisted with this mirror business is less clear to me.'

'I'll come to that in a moment,' Zelfa said. 'So Ali Evren killed your Albanian.'

'According to Felicity, when she smashed the present Rifat had given her into his face, the sight of the blood excited her brother – or at least he said that it had after the event. Of course it was principally about sexual jealousy.'

'Exactly,' Suleyman put in as he offered Zelfa a cigarette which, strangely, she refused. 'I mean, Ali seems to have been quite selective about which parts of the vampire story he adhered to. As I understand it, vampires drink blood, cringe from religious symbols, avoid daylight, can't cross water or see themselves in mirrors. Ali did only some of these things.'

'Living out fantasies based on old legends or myths is obviously going to have its limitations,' Zelfa said. 'I mean people are not going to crumble to dust when they see a crucifix however much they may want that to happen. Somewhere along the line that person's concept of the fantasy must shift to accommodate reality. Fantasies have to be elastic to withstand everyday life. Ali Evren had to go out in the daytime, he had to go to school. He rationalised this by claiming that his transformation into a vampire wasn't yet complete. And anyway, if you read contemporary fiction on the subject you will see that a lot of the old notions about vampires have changed. We now have good vampires, child vampires, vampires who can hold on to crucifixes and laugh, and so on.'

'So Ali just took what he wanted from the available literature,' said Suleyman.

'Yes, and from the "evidence" provided by his sister. It may be that she even fed him a lot of pseudo-mythical stuff about the efficacy of sleeping with a vampire in order to get him to screw her. At any rate, when her vampiric status was called into question the night the Albanian died, his world was rocked. If she wasn't a vampire, where did that leave him? He needed proof, and unfortunately I had told him how to get it.'

'And yet,' İkmen said, 'at the end he was still convinced that he, if not his sister, would cheat death.'

'Yes and no.' She smiled. 'A psychiatrist's classic answer. I know. I feel he must have known the fantasy couldn't continue in its present form, and so the only way out of it was to throw himself from the museum and then either live as a fully formed vampire or face the hated spectre of death as a kind of punishment for not achieving his goal. I think he finally realised that whichever route he took was going to lead to hell.'

'So he was doomed,' Suleyman said.

'Yes. A familiar place for him,' she said as her fingers worked towards and then retreated from her cigarette packet. 'Your mother is a depressive and commits suicide, your father is mostly absent and thinks you're mad anyway, and your beloved ugly sister fucks you. You're hardly going to be comfortable in the world of nice people and positivism. With work, of course, he could have been.' She shrugged. 'But, true to his nature, he concealed too much from me, and his father just wanted him well, whatever that may mean.'

'His father wanted him in an institution,' İkmen said, 'after Rifat's murder.'

'Mmm.'

Both men knew Zelfa was still troubled by what she saw as her failure with Ali Evren. But neither of them alluded to this.

İkmen continued, 'Felicity argued with her father about this on the night of his death. She knew exactly why Ali had killed Rifat and the reasons for his drinking the Albanian's blood. She told her father this. She also told him that she didn't want Ali hospitalised. But İlhan Evren wasn't having it. We'd been to see him, he was already scared. He was also disgusted by the notion of his children having sex – unsurprisingly. And so to try, I presume, to bring his daughter back to reality and make her confront what she and her brother had done, he made her look at her face in a mirror. And she saw it, maybe as she says for the first time in years – I don't doubt that people can avoid their own image if they want to but whether she was actually invisible to herself is another matter.'

'And so she killed her father in a fit of rage, did she?' asked Suleyman.

'I've arrested her for his murder, yes,' İkmen replied. 'Felicity Evren does not seem to be as criminally adept as her late father was. İlhan could have screamed and shouted at us about Albanian blood feuds and with Mehti in custody we would probably have believed him. But he was too cautious for that. He knew that unless he had actually seen something like the green Fiat with his own eyes, he shouldn't allude to it. He had too much past to make mistakes. And so he let us draw our own conclusions, which we did for a while.'

'But İlhan did dispose of the body?'

İkmen lit a cigarette. 'Yes,' he said, 'he did, together with Felicity. And very professionally too. A pity for her that she didn't take quite so much care over the killing of her father. But then she isn't a gangster. She's just a deluded girl who had sex with her brother. It's hard to imagine what her state of mind must have been to enable her to kill her father like that. The rage she must have felt . . .'

'Her brother was more important,' Suleyman said.

'Yes. Ali gave her the sex she craved. And as I think I've said to you before, Mehmet, sex, envy and fear are the only three motives for murder. But then again, there was certainly a degree of cold calculation in her actions. She said she loved Rifat and yet she disposed of his body without a thought and then turned on the tears for his family. But she's not all that tough. We had to call the doctor down just before I left her. She sort of collapsed, though not physically. Became almost catatonic. Maybe she was thinking about what lies ahead for her. I don't know how long she'll get . . .' For just a moment İkmen slumped. His face, devoid of animation, was, Suleyman thought, really starting to look old.

İkmen sat up straighter. 'Still, that is for a judge to

decide and not us,' he said. 'She's really rather a pathetic figure whose brother . . .'

'I shot, yes,' Suleyman finished for him.

Zelfa reached out and took one of his hands in hers.

'Everybody's account of your actions includes the observation that you had no choice,' İkmen said. 'Only Yıldız doesn't proffer an opinion and that's because he wasn't there and couldn't see. You will probably have to prostrate yourself, metaphorically, before Ardiç with regard to your initial lack of procedure, but I don't think it'll go beyond that.'

'Ardiç is not happy about my involvement either,' Zelfa said. 'I underestimated the seriousness of Ali's mental state. I miscalculated badly.'

'Please don't say that in a public place, Zelfa,' İkmen said. But nobody laughed.

Suleyman, agitated now, got up and moved across to the window. The reflection of the thin winter light from the snowy street below made him blink.

'Anyway, when this is all over I'm going to stop working for anybody apart from myself,' Zelfa said as she watched her fiancé watch the street scene outside.

'Just private practice?' İkmen asked.

'Why should I put myself through the misery of admitting the wildly psychotic to medieval institutions or visiting wolf-men in prison when I can talk to bored housewives and under-achieving middle-aged men. Neuroses!' she cried, unconvincingly. 'That is the way forward.'

'But won't you get frustrated?' Suleyman asked as he turned back to the room and away from his own morbid thoughts. 'I don't want you to be bored just because our paths crossed over Ali Evren.'

'Oh, I was thinking I might take this step anyway,' she said as she, very consciously, placed one hand across her belly. 'If we're to be married, it's going to be awkward.'

Suleyman sighed. 'Yes.'

And then silence descended upon the group once again. İkmen knew that he was going to have to find an opportunity to ask Zelfa's advice about what he should do about Halil. But whatever his intentions had been earlier in the day, now did not seem to be the right time. Perhaps he would phone her later when she got home. Right now they were all preoccupied with the bizarre set of circumstances that had led to three people losing their lives in acts of what seemed to İkmen to be mad pointlessness. That the professional cloud that currently hung over poor Suleyman.

But there was still one thing he wanted Zelfa to explain to him, if she could.

'Zelfa,' he said, 'you mentioned earlier that you would return to the subject of this mirror business . . .'

'Ah yes,' she said. But although she was listening to İkmen she was looking at her lover as he leaned against the windowsill, staring up at nothing on the ceiling. He looked so tired and strained. All the more reason to get what she knew she had to tell him over with as soon as possible.

She rose from her seat and placed Ali Evren's file back in her cabinet. 'Yes,' she repeated, 'but I think I'll do that on the way home, if you don't mind, Çetin.'

'Oh, yes, er . . .'

'We'll take Çetin back first, Mehmet,' she said as she retrieved her coat from the back of her chair.

'Yes,' he said absently. 'Of course.'

None of them spoke until they reached Suleyman's car. Dusk and the still thickening snow had thrown a cloak of silence across the great city of Constantine and, until they got inside the car and Suleyman put the heater on, the three of them were struck dumb by its icy spell.

'Of course, theoretically, Ali Evren could have killed his father,' İkmen said from the back seat of the car. 'His prints are going to be all over that office. Adnan Öz will, I know, exploit that. But I suppose we'll just have to wait, as ever, for forensic.'

'Yes.' Zelfa turned round in her seat to look at him. 'But then why did he seem so shocked when his sister told him of his father's death?'

'Because he didn't do it,' İkmen replied, 'but Felicity Evren hasn't confessed to the murder of her father, nor do I believe she will. I know because of what she told us that I have a case but I would like some forensic evidence too.'

Suleyman switched on the front and rear windscreen wipers. The sound of mechanically moving snow swished dully.

'So where does all of this leave us with regard to Rifat Berisha then, Çetin?' he asked as he, to his fiancée's secret chagrin, lit up a cigarette. 'I know we all heard the boy admit to it and there is also the sister's testimony, but is that enough?'

'We have to check prints and samples against those taken from the Evren family. When it's done we'll know for sure. Or not.' He sighed. 'Useless Mehti Vlora! If only he'd stayed after he saw Rifat enter the Evren house. But he was too scared even to do that.'

'Well, I for one do think that Ali was telling us the truth,' Zelfa began.

'Oh yes,' İkmen nodded, 'I agree. But it's so much easier if you've got some concrete evidence too. But tell me something about Felicity and her mirrors, Zelfa.'

'Shall I take you straight home, Çetin?' Suleyman interjected as he slowly pulled out into the slush-filled road.

'Yes, that'd be good,' İkmen replied and then, turned back to Zelfa, idly noting that, unusually for her, she wasn't smoking. 'So, this theory, Zelfa.'

'The condition, or rather theoretical condition, is called negative autoscopy,' she began, and as the car travelled through the snow-bound city, İkmen was treated to an explanation that, even by his standards, was unusual. But he found that it made sense to him. Not seeing what one didn't want to see was understandable. In effect it was the reverse of what, some would say, happened during his encounters with his mother. He wanted to hear from her and so he did, at least that was what someone like Zelfa would say. Uncle Ahmet, like his other Albanian relatives, would describe this phenomenon as a ghost – which in a sense it was, whether one believed in the spirit or not. Something of a person remained – an intelligent energy of sorts. Felicity Evren, in contrast, had closed her mind to her own image and made herself a sort of blank slate on which she could impose whatever she wanted. And it occurred to İkmen that in some ways this was not so different from what Halil had done with what he had seen the day their mother had died. The mind did what it had to do to make life bearable.

How all this would go down at Felicity Evren's trial, İkmen really didn't know. Judges were notoriously conservative when it came to strange or paranormal crimes like this. Felicity Evren could very well be sent to an asylum. How very ironic that would be. But then, İkmen thought, so could he if he went too esoteric on them!

When they arrived back at his apartment building İkmen said goodbye to his colleagues and then spent a few moments alone in the snow looking at his reflection in the window of the jewellers beneath his home. And though he knew he was neither young nor attractive, he liked what he saw. His life was written in his face and, for all its hardships, he liked his life. To not have a reflection would be a denial of all that. İkmen scowled and then laughed at the image this created in the window. He lit a cigarette and went inside.

Chapter 25

A lot of people, including lawyers, consular officials and even one relative from England, came to visit Felicity Evren in the days that followed. Through thick snow and icy winds they came, anxious to provide comfort, encouragement and advice. But the woman herself just sat, silent since her interview with İkmen and, with the exception of occasional visits to the bucket in the corner of her cell, unmoving. And even when İkmen was finally called in to see whether he could rouse her from her torpor, she just carried on sitting, staring at the the walls that contained her. Whether, as some believed, she was play-acting or not, it was patently obvious that in this condition she was in no position to be brought before a judge. Dr Sezer was called in to spend some time with her. Hüseyin Sezer was, as Zelfa Halman told İkmen when he went to see her about Halil, an expert in the field of altered, especially catatonic, states.

'It is known that when long-held fantasies or delusions are brought to an end for whatever reason, the subject's mind can shut down,' she said. 'If Felicity did indeed experience negative autoscopy for many years, the combination of finally having to face the reality of her appearance, followed by her father's death plus her subsequent experiences, could well have primed the trigger.'

'I was actually making some progress with her,' İkmen said, 'but—'

'But you arrested her, Çetin, and so, like it or not, you provided the catalyst that pressed the trigger. You and I both know that nothing is truly decided until a person comes to trial, but to many lay people arrest equals guilt, which equals imprisonment. A whole host of negative concepts enter a person's mind when he or she is arrested – shame, guilt, imprisonment, ruin, death. And with somebody like Felicity whose world was already imploding . . .'

İkmen rose to his feet and stretched wearily. 'Mind you, Dr Sezer did say that when he went in she moved. "Inappropriate sexual gestures" was how he termed it.'

Zelfa raised an eyebrow. 'Really?'

'Çöktin, who accompanied the doctor, said that she made a couple of attempts at pulling Sezer's hand between her legs.'

'Which means,' Zelfa said with a shrug, 'that she may be play-acting but what is more plausible to me is that her underlying principal motivation is now coming through. I see a lot of this with my chronics. Years spent trying to repress some overriding fixation out in the world suddenly slip away when they're admitted to hospital. Although we place our patients in chemical straitjackets, we also accept far more from them when they are hospitalised. Mad people, Çetin,' she smiled, 'do stuff we would never countenance in the sane. But they're mad and so we make allowances.'

'You think Felicity may be some kind of nympho-maniac?'

Zelfa moved forward to help her visitor on with his coat. 'I think that had she been pretty or even ordinarily nondescript we wouldn't be seeing what we're seeing today. All part of the tyranny of youth and beauty,' she said bitterly. 'I feel sorry for her. All that woman ever really needed was a boyfriend who appreciated her as opposed to her money.'

'Which, given the sums involved,' İkmen said, 'makes you wonder why her father never put her forward for plastic surgery.'

'Well, I know they can do a lot these days,' the psychiatrist replied, 'but from what I've observed of Felicity there appears to be actual malformation of the bone structure, which is difficult to address. I don't know why she's like that, but what I do know is that if you start moving bone about you can get into real difficulty. Look at Michael Jackson.'

İkmen pulled a disgusted face. 'Indeed.'

They stood and looked at each other for a few moments. İkmen seemed reluctant to go.

'So you think that provided my brother has some support . . .' he began.

'Your brother has no history of psychological turmoil, Çetin,' Zelfa replied. 'It will be a shock, of course, but he is physically fit, you say. I know Arto is very worried about this but my own feelings are that if the truth is presented to Halil within the security of a loving Turkish family, you may find that the darkness that surrounds your mother's death is not as impenetrable as you thought. There are usually flashes of awareness even within the most intransigent cases of denial. I mean, if we accept that Felicity Evren has been suffering from negative autoscopy, even she had to have some notion of herself as she really was to behave as she did. Reflection or no reflection, she knew she was unappealing. Why else would she have turned to her own barely pubescent brother?'

'Well . . .'

'If you were to bring Halil along here to have me break the news about your mother, he would be insulted, wouldn't he?'

'I'd only be trying to protect him.'

'Yes,' she smiled, 'just like he tried to protect you when your mother died.'

Recalling his own feelings of resentment regarding this, İkmen nodded. 'Point taken,' he said. 'And anyway he is a man.'

'If you do need any help, you know where I am,' Zelfa said.

'Yes,' he smiled. She opened the door for him and he left. She did, İkmen thought as he walked away, look very well indeed for a woman in her forties who was pregnant with her first child. A little larger than usual, but . . . Not that either Zelfa or Mehmet had told him about their impending addition. All Mehmet had said was that they were going to marry sooner rather than later – news that İkmen had not commented upon. Unbeknown to his friend, İkmen had been in this situation himself long ago when Fatma had not been quite so staid as she was now. That and of course the fact that he was without doubt the son of the witch Ayşe Bajraktar. This meant that sometimes he didn't have to be told things in order to acquire knowledge. As he descended the stairs to the street, he smiled.

When he got back to his office, İkmen first went to see Commissioner Ardiç and then, alone, spent some time reviewing the forensic evidence they had so far. It wasn't good. No prints on the knife that killed İlhan Evren – but an immense amount of material pertaining to the Evren children, the chauffeur and the associate known as Dimitri Asanov, the man who had discovered Evren's body. Tracked down from paperwork in Evren's office, the police had found Asanov at his home, washing his blood-spattered clothes. İkmen had interviewed him. A nice enough man – a pimp – he'd been over in Polonezköy when Evren died. And no one had seen anyone either go into or come out of the Evren house during the night of the murder. Reserved rich Bebek folk.

And so it was possible that Felicity Evren could go free. There were no witnesses, no conclusive forensic evidence, no confession. But as he turned to the forensic reports pertaining to Rifat Berisha's car, İkmen allowed himself a little smile. İlhan had been very good, hadn't he? There was nothing of him in there. Ali and Felicity, yes, but İlhan? Received forensic wisdom stated that this had to be impossible. But as İkmen, if not the more technically minded Suleyman, knew, nothing is ever either foolproof or impossible. No wonder the British police had never been able to connect Evren to any acts of violence. They must have been so pleased to see the back of him when he came to Turkey. Clever old man!

But to return to Felicity. Who else could have killed her father? Apart from her brother, there was no one, and there didn't appear to be any forensic evidence that couldn't be accounted for, and no forced entry. Just a dead man and a broken mirror. According to Ardiç Felicity was going to be transferred to hospital. Dr Sezer was emphatic on the point. No date could be set for her hearing, nothing. Because that was just what they were getting from her – nothing. Where was she now in her mind? What strange landscapes was she viewing through the curtain of drugs they were already administering to her? The British newspapers were saying that she should be sent home and in a way İkmen felt they were right. After all, what progress could be made while she was surrounded by foreigners who did not speak her language? When people became ill like this it was common for them to regress to their first language. Yusuf Cohen was known to experience times when he could only communicate in Ladino, the language he had learned as an infant at his mother's knee. Grimly, İkmen considered the possibility of how such a breakdown would affect him. Would he suddenly start to speak the Albanian his mother had sung to him? Would the world of Lek Dukagjini suddenly make perfect sense?

In a way, he had to admit, it already did. If nothing else his experiences with the Albanians had taught him that change is only possible through understanding. The rules of the Kunan were very old and had been nurtured in spite of the repressive tactics employed by successive conquerers. They were something of their own, unique. First the Ottomans and then the communists had tried to ban the Kunan, suppress it or reason adherents out of it, but it continued to survive. Because, bloody though it was, it was theirs alone and they would continue to die for it, as his mother had.

Angeliki Vlora and her two sons were due to appear in court that Wednesday – on drugs charges. Mehmet would then appear later charged with the murder of Egrem Berisha. The 'boys' had already given statements that absolved their mother from actually dealing. They took full responsibility for that. Angeliki would go to prison, but not for as long as İkmen would have liked. And besides, the Vloras had enough friends on the outside to ensure that Aryan could never be truly safe. The only consolation being that they would almost certainly be able to keep Mehmet Vlora off the streets for good. That was something that would please almost everyone.

For the moment, however, there were practicalities to be addressed. Tepe was in the process of moving Aryan Vlora and Engelushjia Berisha to a safe house where they would be guarded night and day until after Mehmet's trial. After that, Aryan would be on his own. Hopefully, maybe together with Engelushjia Berisha, he would be able to disappear as totally as Aryan's brother Dhori – if the youngest Vlora had indeed disappeared. It made İkmen wonder again where, if anywhere, the missing Dhori might be. He was the only Vlora brother apart from the one who died in infancy that İkmen hadn't met.

*   *   *

There is an old saying about proximity to princes being
dangerous. Basically a prince is a fire that burns brightly
and with force, and anyone who gets too close is likely
to get burned. Some friends and colleagues applied this
to Ayşe Farsakoğlu. Ever since the end of her affair with
Mehmet Suleyman she had been edgy, something that
Orhan Tepe seemed helpless to remedy. It wasn't easy
being in Tepe's shoes because the edgier she got, the
more tactless she became – her comment to Engelushjia
Berisha being a comparatively mild case in point. 'I
hope that you and the old man,' she said, tipping her
head in the direction of Aryan Vlora, 'aren't committing
immoral acts.'

'No!' the girl retorted with, Tepe was pleased to
observe, some heat in her voice. 'Aryan is a friend.
He's looking after me now, like a father.'

'Sergeant Farsakoğlu?' Tepe said. 'Could I speak to
you for a moment please?'

As soon as they were out of sight of Engelushjia
and Aryan who was packing the last of his meagre
possessions into a box, Tepe gave vent to his anger.

'What do you mean by asking Engelushjia questions
like that about her friend?'

'Her friend!' she huffed contemptuously. 'Why should
a middle-aged man want to have a little kid like her
around unless he's fucking her?'

Tepe gripped her arm rather harder than she liked.

'Ow! Orhan, you're—'

'If you'd seen what her father did to her, you'd let her
live just about anywhere away from him! And besides,

these people will be giving evidence against someone we know is a killer – Mehmet Vlora. So whatever they're doing we need to keep them happy.'

'Yes, but didn't that sample from Egrem Berisha's shirt match the blood on the Vloras' floor?'

'Yes, it did, but that doesn't necessarily mean that Mehmet did it. Any good lawyer could argue that Aryan is lying to save his own neck. We must support him. Just keep focused on the job, Ayşe,' he said, relinquishing his hold on her arm, 'and stop taking out your own frustrations on others.'

Her eyes burned. 'What do you mean?' she said through gritted teeth.

'I mean that you should make up your mind to forget about Mehmet Suleyman, he's marrying Dr Halman now. Find yourself a husband before it's too late!'

'Oh, I thought I'd already done that!' she responded, venomously looking him up and down.

'I meant a husband of your own.'

Her face was a mask of pure fury. 'So do I take it you no longer want me to do all those little things that Aysel won't let you do to her?'

'Sergeant Tepe?'

They both turned at once, caught as it were in the spotlight of the innocent gaze of the young girl before them.

'We're ready to go now,' Engelushjia said.

'Right.'

Aryan Vlora joined them. 'I don't suppose I'll ever come here again,' he said simply, 'but then I'm not sorry for that. This has been a bad place – a place of death.'

Ayşe Farsakoğlu wordlessly walked towards the front door of the apartment while Tepe helped Aryan and Engelushjia with their belongings.

'Will we have a policeman with us at the house we're going to?' Engelushjia asked. 'To make sure that my father and Aryan's family don't harm us?'

Tepe smiled. 'Yes, of course,' he said, 'we won't let any harm come to either of you. I give you my word. You're very brave people.'

The girl, in her youthful enthusiasm, reached up and impulsively hugged his neck. 'Thank you.'

Ayşe Farsakoğlu opened the apartment door and then slammed it behind her.

It was dark by the time Çetin İkmen finally managed to get down to the cells to see Angeliki Vlora. It was bone-chillingly cold down there; the duty officer was not the sort who believed that prisoners should experience anything approaching comfort. But İkmen was of a different order and so he took a couple of blankets and an extra packet of cigarettes along with him.

'Come to gloat, witch's child?' the old woman said as she surveyed his figure in the doorway of her cell.

'No. I came to give you these actually.' İkmen threw the blankets onto her bed and placed the cigarettes in her hands. 'And to tell you that you were right.'

She looked at him questioningly.

'About my mother,' he continued. 'As you suggested, I spoke to my uncle and to Emina Ndrek also. And it seems my mother was murdered by her brother, but probably not in the way you imagine.'

'No?' She patted the small cot that served as her bed and motioned for him to sit down. 'Tell me.'

İkmen sat down. He lit a cigarette and then one for the old woman. 'My mother gave her life willingly to Salih Ndrek,' he said, 'in exchange for the lives of myself and my brother.'

'The witch was with child.'

'Yes, we think so,' İkmen responded calmly, 'although as I know you will appreciate, with my mother one could never be sure. She told such audacious lies.' He smiled at his memory of her. 'But then I've been thinking that if my mother's actions put an end to the blood between the Bajraktar and the Ndrek, as indeed they did, then perhaps her sacrifice was worthwhile.'

'The Bajraktar have other *fis* they are in blood with back home.'

'Yes, but not here, Angeliki, not in my city. Not in a place where that madness can harm my children.'

'*Gjakmaria* is a noble obligation.'

'*Gjakmaria*,' İkmen said, 'is an insult to humanity. One thing I have learnt in all this is that Ghegs are bright and tough and instinctively magical people. I respect you, Angeliki, I respect your resistance and your adherence to what is truly your own. But, like the rest of us, you can't just kill with impunity. No one will ever take you seriously or display any sympathy for you while you engage in this madness.'

Angeliki first spat on the floor and then said, 'You live in your world, Turk, and I'll live in mine. Ghegs don't need the Ottoman's permission to breathe any more.'

İkmen shrugged. 'No, you don't. But when you do

finally leave custody, I will be watching you, Angeliki.'

'In case I go after that coward that was my son?' She laughed. 'I expect you've put him somewhere safe now, İkmen.'

'Yes,' İkmen said with a smile, 'I have. He's a good man. He makes me believe that Albanians have a real future in the world. But Aryan is not the only reason why I will be watching you, Angeliki.'

'Oh.' It was said without apparent interest; the old woman seemed more interested in her cigarette.

'No. I will also be watching you because I cannot find it within myself to forgive you.'

Angeliki frowned. 'Forgive me? For what?'

'I don't suppose you have any idea how arduously I have had to prepare to tell my brother Halil how his mother died.'

She looked at him blankly.

'No, I thought not,' İkmen said with a sigh. 'I have searched my soul and, lain awake at night. He found Mother, covered in blood, dead. Not a thing you'd forget, is it? But my brother has. The psychiatrist who has helped me to prepare for this says that Halil is in what she calls denial. In other words, his mind was so damaged by what he saw that he has blanked it out in order to protect himself. He was happy enough like that. And if I had never met you,' he said, raising his voice slightly, 'he and I would have stayed happy. But now that I know, I can't keep the truth just to myself. Even taking into account the risk to my brother that telling him the truth involves, I can't keep it from him. That would be disrespectful to him and anyway, what if he should learn about it from another source – like some malicious old woman?'

'I did what I had to to protect my boys!'

'Oh yes, I know that,' İkmen said, 'and I have rationalised it to myself in just those terms, but I still can't forgive you.' He stubbed out his cigarette on the floor and rose to his feet. 'Must be the Albanian blood in my veins,' he added bitterly.

'Bastard!'

'So if you are ever free again behave yourself, won't you, Angeliki?' He bent down to whisper in her ear. 'Because the witch's child will be watching you and if you so much as steal a strawberry . . .' he clapped his hands hard right in front of her ear.

'Ah!'

'You will be back here as quickly as that.'

And then he knocked hard on the door to attract the guard's attention.

In the few seconds it took for the door to be unlocked, Angeliki Vlora said, 'So what was so special about the blood of the children of a Turk that Ayşe Bajraktar should give up her life?'

İkmen smiled. 'I think it's something called love, Angeliki,' he said as the door opened. 'It's something that doesn't depend upon blood or belong to any particular *fis*. Just love.'

Chapter 26

Mehmet Suleyman stood in front of Commissioner Ardiç's desk, his eyes trained upon the now rapidly melting snow on his superior's windowsill. Birds, mainly pigeons, were fighting over crumbs that only Ardiç could have put there, probably when he'd arrived that morning. Strange that so explosive a person could be sentimental about something as trivial as pigeons.

'İkmen tells me,' the older man said, closing what looked like an English newspaper, 'that the British press seem to have forgotten about us.' He shrugged. 'There is an election impending, I believe.'

'Yes, sir.'

'Mmm.' Ardiç inspected the tip of his cigar. 'Difficult times.'

Suleyman, his eyes still focused on the world outside, did not respond. British politics were as much a mystery to him as he suspected they were to Ardiç and besides, he just wanted to get whatever was going to happen over with and then get back to Zelfa – and his baby, of course. Unborn and unknown, the foetus was his baby and he already loved it – just thinking about it almost made him smile.

'And I am told,' Ardiç continued, 'that the British

431

Ambassador in Ankara is meeting the Minister of Justice about our silent prisoner.' He sighed. 'Our respective heads of state enjoy very good relations, I believe.'

Suleyman looked down at Ardiç. 'Sir?'

'Who knows what will happen,' Ardiç said. 'Only Allah, who in His mercy has seen fit to silence Miss Evren. That we, as mere servants of Allah, cannot see beyond the embarrassment both our nations are experiencing over this is a failing within us as humans.'

'Yes, sir.'

'If we accept that it was indeed written that Miss Evren should survive to bring us all this trouble, we must also conclude that her saviour must have a purpose too. After all, you were in a difficult situation, your weapon was only discharged the once . . . Anyway, the Turkish police force has a reputation for supporting its better officers.'

'Sir?'

'I'd like you to finish your holiday, Suleyman,' Ardiç said roughly, 'and return to duty tomorrow.'

Suleyman smiled.

'In future all hostage situations should be referred to me personally.' Ardiç held a match to the end of his cigar and puffed. 'There is no place in the Turkish police force for personalities.' Catching the incredulous look in Suleyman's eyes, he added, 'And don't even start to speak to me about İkmen!'

'But—'

'İkmen is a side issue, Suleyman! I don't want to talk about him. I like him,' he shrugged, 'but I don't want to talk about him.'

'No, sir.'

'Right, well, you'd better go now. Make the most of your last day on leave.'

'Yes, sir. Thank you, sir.' He was just about to salute and depart when Ardiç spoke again.

'Oh, and please extend my regards to ex-Constable Cohen. I take it you are still living with his family?'

'Yes, sir.' Suleyman was not a little surprised at this. Ardiç rarely, addressed that amorphous lump known as 'the men' by name. But then he suspected that Ardiç knew rather more about a lot of things than he admitted to.

'A pity his son has decided against a career in the police,' Ardiç went on.

'Berekiah, Mr Cohen's son, feels that his talents are more suited to the world of art.'

'Yes.' He gave Suleyman one of his infrequent smiles. 'One rarely dies or goes mad applying gold leaf or whatever to old pictures. And in view of the boy's brother . . .'

'Yes, sir.'

'Well, give them my regards anyway,' Ardiç concluded and then signalled with a wave of his hand that the interview was over.

Still smiling, Suleyman left Ardiç's office and ran towards his own. And when he opened the door, there was Zelfa waiting for him. After first placing a hand on her precious stomach he kissed her, then whispered his good news in her ear.

That evening, Halil İkmen made one of his rare visits

to his brother's riotous apartment in Sultan Ahmet. He and his cousin Samsun Bajraktar had been invited to a meal by Fatma, though Halil knew that Çetin must have been the prime mover behind this. After all, none of that business his brother had raked up about their mother had yet been resolved. As he prepared for his evening out, Halil found that he was more than a little nervous. Whatever Çetin had to tell him, if indeed he had anything, Halil wasn't entirely sure that he wanted to know. Not remembering an event, if that event is bad, is very comforting.

Nothing was said until after the meal was done. 'Imam Bayıldı', the aubergine dish cooked to Fatma's unique and slightly sweet recipe, was served with great ceremony to the İkmen males and five of Çetin's vast tribe of children. Small talk, mainly initiated by that gossipy old fruit Samsun, dominated the table and though trivial and sometimes even spiteful, the conversation was amusing and undemanding.

When the meal had finished, Halil followed Çetin and Samsun into the living room. Taking with them tea, brandy and cigarettes, the men effectively cut themselves off from the rest of the household, who either busied themselves in other rooms or went out for the rest of the evening. And so it was that over the next half-hour Çetin İkmen, the cat Marlboro asleep on his lap, smoked and drank his way through the series of events that had led to the death of Ayşe İkmen.

They all cried. Çetin as part of a continuing reaction to a tragedy he had now known about for some days, Samsun as much for her father as her aunt, and Halil with horror and also with a rushing sensation as the darkness that had engulfed his mind suddenly cleared.

'I must have always known it,' he said, the palms of his hands over his eyes. 'I must have seen . . .'

'Yes, you did,' his brother answered, catless now, crouching down beside Halil's chair, holding his shoulder tightly. 'But you put it away. You buried it.'

'I . . .'

'You protected me, Halil,' Çetin said. 'Your first instinct was to look after your little brother. I genuinely knew nothing. I've searched my mind and I know it. And you did that,' he squeezed Halil's arm, 'a very brave thing for a thirteen-year-old to do.'

And then the tears came again and Çetin's arm went round his brother's neck, rocking and comforting his pain.

'But what was my father thinking?' Samsun cried, her once clean skirt now covered with ash from her flailing cigarette. '*Gjakmaria*, yes, but for my father to actually . . .'

'Samsun, he did what he did because of who he is.'

'Yes, but he has killed a man, Çetin.' She was crying again too now, great deep manly sobs. 'He killed İsmail Ndrek. My father took part in *gjakmaria*. You should arrest him, you—'

'What for?' Çetin asked, his arms still circling his brother's neck. 'Emina Ndrek is not interested in pressing charges. However the blood between ourselves and the Ndreks started, it's over now. They made a deal, as I told you.'

'Yes, but as a policeman—'

'But as a member of the Bajraktar family, Samsun,' he said, 'I must move on. Emina Ndrek said that I should look upon what she told me not as a policeman but as a member of this family, our family. And as such, Uncle Ahmet walks free. It's that or stir up something that, once started, we may not be able to control.'

'What do you mean?'

'Well,' İkmen said, 'if younger members of our own and the Ndrek family hear this story, what do you think they will make of it? Those of a more volatile nature might take it into their heads to start it all up again.' He frowned. 'Things like this need to be left to die, Samsun.'

'Then why did you tell us?' Samsun indicated the still weeping Halil with her head. 'Look at him, he's destroyed!'

'No he isn't!' Çetin snapped back. 'My father bred tough children! Don't even say that, Samsun!'

'But—'

'I told you and I told Halil because you deserved to know the truth! We were all young children then – you lost your aunt and we our mother. The truth is important in a person's life. We know now that our mother sacrificed everything for us and we should thank and revere her for that.'

'But Father never knew, did he?' Halil said as he emerged from his brother's embrace, his face drawn and wet with tears.

'No, he didn't,' his brother answered with a sigh, 'but then that was how she wanted it to be, Halil.'

'Yes, I know.' He looked down at the floor and tried

to compose himself, but he couldn't. 'But she must have known that we would find her!'

'She made it look like suicide.'

'Oh, and is that supposed to make it any better! I walk into a room, the bed is flooded with blood . . .'

'Shhh! Shhh!' Çetin held his much larger brother and began rocking him again. 'Halil,' he said, 'I have lain awake for nights and nights thinking this through. She had no choice. It was either that or our own deaths.'

'You should ask her.' Samsun put out one cigarette and lit another. 'You talk, you—'

'Mother doesn't communicate with me in the way you imagine. Samsun,' Çetin said, 'when she does come its more like, well, ideas in my head.'

'Yes—'

'Mother is dead. She died in 1957.'

It was said so calmly that it took a moment for both of them to realise the words had come from Halil. Suddenly very calm, he cleared his throat before he spoke again.

'Whatever Çetin may experience of her now, that is a fact,' he said. 'I was there. She ended. For me.'

'Yes, but Halil,' Samsun began. 'Çetin—'

'Mother never communicates with me!' Halil roared. 'She never has, she never will! She is dead! It's the only way I can deal with this!' Halil looked at his brother whose eyes were fixed on his face with some concern. 'Now that I know the truth I want no more of it, no . . . Çetin, I don't want to know any more, nothing. To me she is dead, she—'

'All right, all right,' Çetin, soothed. 'It's OK, Halil. It's just that—'

'We're magical people,' Samsun, ever her own pub-
licist, interjected with a smile. 'We're different. You
aren't.' She shrugged. 'That's life, cousin!'

In spite of themselves the other two laughed.

And so life returned to normal, after a fashion, in the
stifling, smoggy confines of the İkmen living room. The
three of them smoking, drinking, arguing, crying. Life,
family life. Touched but now purged of a tragedy they
had dealt with all their lives in their different ways.
Çetin by building a huge wall of family around him,
both at home and at work. Halil by keeping everyone
out – of his mind and his heart.

They drank and smoked some more. Samsun Bajraktar
collapsed in a heap of inappropriate hysterics just before
dawn. Halil simply passed out. Which left only Çetin,
who just sat and smiled at the wall until Fatma came in
to prepare the apartment for yet another day. She said
the three of them, drunk and sleep-deprived, looked like
a nest of vampires . . .

Her cousin Julia was appalled by the conditions.

'You shouldn't be in a place like this!' she said,
looking around what Felicity imagined was a hospital
ward. 'We need to get you home.'

They obviously hadn't told Julia the whole truth about
what she'd done. Either that or she couldn't understand
their English. But then perhaps Julia did understand but
didn't care, after all, her mother's family had never liked
her father, the Turk. And in truth it had been Mary's
money that had kept them all for so long – the house
in Holland Park, her father's gangsterly lifestyle . . .

Not that she could tell Julia any of this. There was something in the way, something that lay between her and other things, other people. It wasn't a door or a screen or anything like that; it was something much more nebulous. And it was within her rather than outside her body. As if something had been switched off, something vital – stuck.

The sex still went on, however, which was good. She knew that David was dead, she'd seen his head explode all over her own head and shoulders. But somehow the feel of him remained, inside, that rush of orgasm every so often overwhelming everything around her. That was wonderful, and it was another reason why venturing 'out' had to be a bad idea. 'In' was safe now, because inside herself so much that was superfluous seemed to disappear. Here there was no conflict – couldn't be because there was no one else. She could neither hurt nor be hurt and physical appearance was irrelevant.

Here perhaps it had truly happened. Vampire. Not feasting upon others so much as feasting upon herself, slowly appreciating and absorbing her own mind. A digestion of one's totality until nothing remained.

She wondered vaguely whether her cousin Julia could see it, this contraction of her being. Next time she came perhaps Felicity, whatever that was, would have disappeared. Not just in the mirror now, but completely.

When İkmen, hungover and looking deathly, arrived at his office later that day, he found a message to call Samsun Bajraktar on his desk. What she could possibly want, apart from a hangover cure, he couldn't imagine, but he called her anyway.

'What is it?' he asked through a pall of comforting smoke. 'I thought you'd gone home to bed.'

'Well, I am at home, Çetin,' she said, 'and I am about to go to bed, but have you seen page three of *Bügün*?'

Horrified that any member of his family should even know the name of such a scandal rag, İkmen spluttered, 'Are you serious?'

'Can you get hold of a copy?'

'Some of the more inarticulate grunts down in the squad room may have a copy.'

'So go and ask them!' Samsun said. 'I'm not joking, Çetin. It's important.'

'It had better be,' he said ominously. 'I've got to walk downstairs and then, more importantly, back up again.'

'Call me back,' Samsun said, 'after you've looked at page three.'

'Right.' İkmen put the phone down and then, probably because he was still too fuzzy with alcohol and lack of sleep to think of anything else, he went and did as she had asked.

To say that the grunts in the squad room were surprised when İkmen asked them for their copy of *Bügün*, with its stories of alien abduction and breast enlargement, was an understatement. Roditi, for whom such reading matter was essential to a full and robust fantasy life, handed it over in a spirit of both disbelief and resentment. After all, if İkmen was reading *Bügün* then the world was indeed stranger than people thought.

When he returned to his office, İkmen spread the paper on his desk and opened it at page three. An impossibly large woman stared back. İkmen called Samsun.

'OK,' he said, 'I have page three.'

'Look at the photograph under the woman of silicone,' she said. 'The one of the boy and the old lady.'

'World's greatest age difference?' İkmen said, reading the title of the story.

'That's it,' Samsun said in a satisfied tone. 'He's twenty-nine and she's a ninety-year-old widow, originally from Kars. Her late husband was a cotton sultan, loaded, and now she's marrying—'

'Is this relevant to anything?' İkmen asked tetchily as he reached for yet another cigarette.

'Well, if you look at the caption to the picture, you'll know,' Samsun said.

İkmen did so and spluttered with shock.

Samsun laughed. 'Yes, Çetin,' she said, 'that is *the* Dhori Vlora, in case you were unsure. Hasn't he done well for himself?'

Now you can buy any of these other bestselling
Headline books from your bookshop or
direct from the publisher.

FREE P&P AND UK DELIVERY
(Overseas and Ireland £3.50 per book)

Seven Up	Janet Evanovich	£5.99
A Place of Safety	Caroline Graham	£6.99
Risking it All	Ann Granger	£5.99
Cold Flat Junction	Martha Grimes	£6.99
Tip Off	John Francome	£6.99
The Cat Who Smelled a Rat	Lilian Jackson Braun	£6.99
Autograph in the Rain	Quintin Jardine	£5.99
Arabesk	Barbara Nadel	£5.99
Oxford Double	Veronica Stallwood	£5.99
Bubbles Unbound	Sarah Strohmeyer	£5.99
Fleeced	Georgina Wroe	£6.99

TO ORDER SIMPLY CALL THIS NUMBER

01235 400 414

or e-mail <u>orders@bookpoint.co.uk</u>

Prices and availability subject to change without notice.